STONES

I hope you enjoy it!

RJG

D1521884

STONES

✳ STONES BOOK 1 ✳

RJG McManus

Copyright © 2020 RJG McManus

All rights reserved.

ISBN-13: 9798633756982 (paperback)

For Kevin –

You're my favorite.

✳ Table of Contents ✳

✳ Chapter 1 ✳

Fairies were real

Fairies were real. This much she knew.

When Amelia Davidson was eight years old, she came across her first fairy. Well, the first she really got a good look at, anyway.

She thought she'd seen them and other magical creatures her whole life, but whenever she mentioned it to her parents, they explained her experiences away as "an over-active imagination" or "a trick of the light." She eventually learned to keep quiet about them, knowing her parents wouldn't believe her. She did, however, suspect her younger sister, Emily, had seen them as well, and the two would spend hours playing make-believe together, pretending to be fairy queens or mermaid princesses.

She and Emily were staying with their grandparents for a few weeks that summer, when the reality of fairies was confirmed for her. She was alone outside at the time, playing in the field close to the house, picking wildflowers as the salty breeze of the nearby ocean kissed her cheeks, the distant sound of the waves crashing against the cliffs below. It was then that she heard a humming in her ear, similar to the buzzing of a bee, and felt something land on her shoulder.

Thinking it was an insect poised to sting her, she swatted at it, knocking it off, and then, as all little girls do when faced with a bug about to sting them, ran. Whatever it was, it was tenacious and undeterred, following her. She could still hear that buzz, and screeched as she bolted for her grandparents' house, a little beach cottage perched on the cliffs overlooking the sea.

Reaching the house, she opened the door, and quickly slammed it behind her—as it shut, she heard a tiny knock, as if whatever had been pursuing her had run into the door. Tentatively, Amelia slowly reopened the door to see what had happened—she gasped when she looked down, and on the doormat saw a tiny, lovely lady, no larger than Amelia's little hand. She had a shock of wild, fiery red hair and golden gossamer wings. She was clothed in a vibrant violet dress—it almost looked as though the petals of a flower had been sewn together to create her lovely little frock. The tiny woman looked thoroughly stunned, though miraculously, alive.

As she marveled at the colorful little creature, Amelia felt a hand on her shoulder. She whirled around, meeting the gaze of her grandfather, who smiled warmly. "I see you've met Lila."

"Grandpa!" she exclaimed. "Fairies are REAL?!"

"Yes, child. And this one looks like she's had a bit of shock to her system."

"I didn't mean to hurt her, Grandpa," she explained, tears welling in her eyes, thinking she was in trouble. "I thought she was a bee!"

"Don't worry, Amelia." He stooped, gently picking up the fairy. "Fairies are plucky little creatures and bounce back quickly. Lila just needs a bit of rest in a soft, warm place, and I'm sure she'll be right as rain in the morning."

"Are you sure, Grandpa?" The little girl followed him into the house.

"Oh, yes, Amelia, I'm sure," he replied as he walked into the kitchen. As he spoke, he cleared the fruit out of the fruit basket on the counter, and placed some fresh, clean hand towels inside as cushioning. Carefully, he placed the fairy on the makeshift bed. She looked up at him, a grateful expression on her face, and laid down. He covered her with a towel, and put the basket on the windowsill, which he left cracked open ever so slightly in the event she felt well enough to leave of her own accord. "Lila

2

likes to play tag, and this isn't the first time she's run into something and knocked herself silly while playing. She used to do it all the time when I was a boy."

Amelia's eyes widened. "Lila must be really old!"

Her grandfather chuckled. "Yes, she is. Much older than me—even older than my grandpa! He knew her when he was a boy too. And I'm sure someday, she'll try to play with your granddaughter."

"Grandpa, are there other fairies?"

"Oh, yes—there are many others. But Lila is the most playful."

Before Amelia could ask anything further—mainly, if fairies were real, why her parents had kept this fact from her—her grandmother entered the room to prepare dinner.

Elizabeth, known as Lizzie to her close friends and family, was a lovely woman, known for her big heart, her warmth, and her hospitality. The love of her husband's life, the two had been together since they were teenagers, and complemented each other perfectly. When Stuart went away to war as a young man, Lizzie faithfully waited for him. The two had been through everything together—from the sadness and frustration of PTSD after the war, to the difficulties that came with the life of a fisherman, to the joys of children and grandchildren and magic. Now, in their older age, they had finally settled into their own, and were enjoying what they called their prime years. Where Stuart was tall and imposing with salt and pepper hair, Emily was petite and graceful, her once fair hair now a steely gray.

Seeing the basket on the windowsill, and the fruit on the counter, Lizzie smiled knowingly. "I see Lila's here. Did she run into the window again?"

"No, Amelia accidentally slammed the door on her," her husband answered.

"That silly little creature. Have you fed her yet?"

3

"No, she's napping right now."

"Well, I'll leave out a bit of bread and honey for her, since I'm about to start dinner anyway."

"Grandma! You knew about the fairies too?" Amelia exclaimed, dumbfounded her grandparents had been keeping this secret from her.

"What fairies?" a small voice said behind them.

They turned to see Amelia's four-year-old sister, Emily, standing in the doorway, rubbing her eyes and yawning, having just woken from a nap. The two girls, though sisters, were like night and day. Where Amelia was excited and bubbly, Emily was careful and thoughtful. Even in looks, Amelia favored their mother: strawberry blonde, fair skinned, and eyes a similar shade of blue-gray as the ocean over which the cottage was perched. Emily resembled their father, with raven hair, olive skin, and brilliant green eyes.

"Emily, we have a fairy! A REAL FAIRY!" Amelia replied, giddy with excitement. "Come see!" She grabbed her sister's hand and led her to the basket on the windowsill. "Look!"

Emily peered inside, and gasped when she saw the tiny sleeping woman. "She's beautiful!"

"Be careful, girls," their grandfather said. "Let her rest." He led them into the dining room, away from the sleeping fairy.

As they sat at the table, the girls began their barrage of questions.

"Where did she come from?"

"Are there other fairies?"

"Where are the other fairies?"

"How come we weren't told about her before?"

Their grandfather chuckled, "One at a time, girls. She came from the forest, where she lives with other fairies. Yes, there are many more. As for why you didn't know about her…well, that's a long story. But you know about her now, and that's what's important."

"If fairies are real, does that mean mermaids are real?" Amelia imagined all the lovely magical things that could possibly exist in the world, now that the existence of fairies was confirmed—things she had always known in her heart to be true.

"And unicorns too?" Emily chimed in.

"Yes, yes they are," he replied. "So are Elves and dragons and nymphs and sprites and centaurs and all sorts of other magical creatures."

"Then why don't we always see them?" Amelia questioned.

"Well, Amelia, that's because they're protecting themselves."

"From who?"

"From anyone who would want to hurt them."

"But why would anyone want to hurt them?"

He smiled a knowing smile. "That, girls, is part of the story I will tell you later. For the moment though, you need to promise you will keep them a secret—do not talk about it to anyone except for us and each other."

"What about Mommy and Daddy?" Emily asked.

Amelia was glad Emily had asked the question. She was confused about why her parents would deny the existence—or at least, ignore the existence—of something so obviously real.

Their grandmother, hearing this, peered into the dining room from the kitchen. She and Stuart exchanged a glance, and she nodded at her husband, who, seeing this signal, turned to the girls. "You can talk to them about it. Just don't expect them to like it."

"Why wouldn't they like it?" Amelia asked, still confused.

"Because sometimes grown-ups have a hard time liking magical things, even if that thing is beautiful and right in front of them," her grandmother replied. "Now, go wash your hands, it's time for dinner."

As the two little girls skipped off to the bathroom to do so, giggling about the fairy in the kitchen, their grandmother turned to her husband. "You know you're going to have to tell them the whole story, Stuart."

He sighed, leaning back in his seat. "I know, Lizzie. Tomorrow. Tonight though, let them enjoy being little girls playing with fairies."

"Whatever you say, dear. It's your story. I just married into it."

"And I'm glad you did."

✻

The next morning, Emily and Amelia awoke, delighted by the prospect of spending their day playing with fairies. Bounding down the stairs, they were greeted by their grandparents putting breakfast on the table.

"Did Lila stay the night?" Amelia asked, bypassing the dining room table and heading straight to the windowsill to check on the fairy, with Emily close behind her.

"No, she went home after you girls went to bed," Stuart replied. "Now, sit down for your breakfast, and let me tell you a story."

And so, as the girls munched on blueberry muffins and eggs, Stuart began.

"Once, many years ago, there was a great, powerful sorcerer. He was the first of the magical creatures, the one who created all the others. We call him the Creator Sorcerer."

"Where did he come from?" Amelia asked.

"Well, we're not sure," her grandfather answered. "Some say he was a star who fell from the sky, and when the dust had cleared, there was a man standing there. Some say he rose out of the ocean with the lava from the volcanoes as they formed land. And some say he never had a beginning...he simply always was.

"Anyway, he created the magical creatures—fairies, unicorns, mermaids, and all the other good creatures you know about. They were able to live alongside humans and non-magical animals in harmony for many years."

"What was the first magical creature he made?" Amelia's eyes were wide as she listened to her grandfather's tale.

"Elves, Amelia," Stuart replied, patient with his granddaughter. "The Elves were the first.

"Anyway, some non-magical people were jealous they didn't have magic like the creatures, and they tried to hurt the magical creatures and take advantage of their powers—because as we know, not all people are good.

"The Creator Sorcerer realized he needed help with keeping his creatures safe from people who wanted to hurt them—he couldn't do it alone. So, from each corner of the earth, he found the bravest, most honest, most intelligent, and most compassionate human men and women, and gave them the ability to use magic. He called them Guardians.

"Their purpose was to protect the Creator Sorcerer's creatures from those who wished to harm them, to preserve the goodness of magic in the world, and to help those in need. You see, the world was a dark place at the time, full of war and sickness and fear, and the Creator Sorcerer hoped by allowing a few to wield magic, he could help the rest of the world's inhabitants and make their lives better.

"And for a time, all was well. Magic did make the world a better place. Guardians did their duty, faithfully. Years went by, and the next few generations of Guardians came into being, with powers they inherited from that first generation. Those who had the ability to use magic were increasing in numbers.

"However, some forgot their way and their original purpose. One of these Guardians became corrupt. Instead of using his power to help the creatures he was supposed to protect, he used it for his own gain, sucking the magic from these creatures to make himself more powerful, and he corrupted some of the other Guardians, convincing them to do the same."

"Which creatures did he take magic from?" Emily asked.

"Some of the purest," Stuart answered. "The unicorns. Unicorns have the powers of healing and immortality. He wanted to live forever and be even more powerful than the Creator Sorcerer. He killed many of them, trying to find the source of immortality in their blood in an attempt to take it for himself.

"When the Creator Sorcerer discovered what had happened, he gave the man and his followers the ultimate punishment: he stripped them of their powers, but left them with the immortality they had tried to steal. He scattered them to the ends of the earth, separated from each other and those they loved, doomed to wander forever without power, forced to watch the things and people they cared for wither and die, but stuck and unable to ever join them in the Beyond."

"The Beyond?" Amelia inquired. "Like Heaven?"

8

"Exactly, sweetheart. Like Heaven. After the incident with the unicorns, the Creator Sorcerer realized the world was no longer a safe place for magic, that it was too harsh. So, he cast a spell over all mankind, that they would forget it. With this, the magical creatures were also sent into hiding, so they couldn't be mistreated again.

"In addition, to prevent magic from being misused again, the Creator Sorcerer cast another spell, and from it he created seven stones, which were now the source of all magic in the world. The Creator Sorcerer took the stones and scattered them around the world, hidden and protected where no one could find them. The only way for magic to be fully back in the world is if all source stones are reunited."

"What happened next?" Emily said, entranced by the story.

"Well, Emily, as for the remaining Guardians, the ones who hadn't betrayed him—he left their memories intact, so they could still look after the creatures, and he left with them the ability to see them and call on them as needed. He did, however, let their magic die out through the generations, so now, no one can use magic. This was his way of preventing a rogue Guardian from ever misusing magic or harming any of his creatures ever again.

"This is how fairytales came into being—the Guardians told the stories as a way of passing down what once was, so when the time came, future generations would still know the old ways."

"What happened to the Creator Sorcerer after he hid the stones? Is he still alive?" Amelia questioned.

"No one is sure what happened to him," Stuart answered. "The story is he went into hiding as well, and I imagine he's still alive and well somewhere, watching over his magical creatures from a distance, doing what he can to keep the stones' locations secret and protecting his creations, waiting for the world to be ready for magic again. I have a feeling if he ever died, we'd know. You see, since he is the one that created the stones and the creatures, he is the ultimate source of magic. If he wasn't still around, I think the creatures would fade out."

"Grandpa, was our family once magical?" Amelia asked.

"Yes, child," he smiled. "That's how we know the stories—they've been passed down to us. That's why the fairies still come to us occasionally. They don't appear for people who aren't Guardians on purpose, and if someone who isn't a Guardian calls on them, they won't come. And, that's why even though we don't have magic anymore, we still do the best we can to protect the magical creatures and the land they share with us."

"What about Daddy? Is Daddy a Guardian?"

Stuart's smile flickered momentarily on his face. "Yes, Amelia, he is a Guardian."

"What about Mommy?"

"Your mommy didn't find out until she married your daddy. It was a little bit of a shock to her."

"Grandpa, if they know they're real, how come they always told me they weren't?"

Stuart clenched his teeth, unsure of how to answer this. Finally, after a momentary pause, he said, "Amelia, that is a question you will have to ask them. I can't answer that for you."

Amelia was unsatisfied by this response, but before she could protest, Emily asked, "Grandpa, do you know where any of the stones are?"

"No, Emily—and it's a good thing I don't," he responded quickly—if the girls were older, they might note it was almost too quickly. "If I did, someone could try to hurt me for that information, or hurt the people I love for it. That's one secret I'm fine with being kept from me forever."

10

Gravely, he continued, "Now that you know this story, you must promise you will never look for a source stone. The purpose of me telling you these stories is for your own knowledge and understanding—not to go on a treasure hunt. If you go looking for one, you will attract unwanted attention. Your purpose is to simply live in harmony with the magical creatures and to protect them as best you can. Do not try to find a stone, do not seek power for yourself. Nothing good will come of it. Promise me you will never go looking for one."

"We promise," the sisters said in unison, very seriously.

Upon this declaration, their grandfather looked decidedly relaxed, and smiled at them.

"That's my girls."

✳ Chapter 2 ✳

Summer's end

The rest of the time spent at their grandparents' place that summer was magical for the two little girls. During the day, Stuart spent his time running the local fish market and a small fleet of fishing boats in the sleepy, tight-knit New England town of Calvary, the outskirts of which he and Lizzie resided.

While he worked, Lizzie would take Emily and Amelia to the beach, where they spent their days building sandcastles and splashing in the waves. Some days, if it rained, Amelia and Emily would venture out to the old barn on their property and play make believe, spending hours pretending to be princesses or fairies or Elves, enacting their own versions of the magical tales their grandparents told them. Other days they might spend under the old willow tree bordering their land and the neighbors' land, reading books in the shade. In the evening, Stuart would return from work, and after having dinner, the family would venture outside. As the sun set over the hills behind them, fireflies would light the fields of wildflowers, joined by fairies. The little girls would chase the fairies, who sometimes allowed themselves to be caught and admired. Stuart taught the girls how to delicately handle the creatures so as not to hurt them, and told them stories about fairy queens and kings, magic spells, and happily ever after.

As all things must though, the summer eventually came to an end. The day came when the little girls' bags were packed, sitting by the front door. Amelia and Emily were with Lizzie at the beach, while Stuart remained at the house, waiting for his son, Brennan, to arrive for his daughters. The couple had planned it this way, as there was much for Stuart to discuss with Brennan that he did not want the girls around to hear. He and Brennan had a strained relationship occasionally, and he didn't want an argument to break out in front of the girls, especially as he was about to broach a sensitive subject with their father.

Brennan was set to arrive at 2:00. The plan was for Lizzie to return from the beach with the girls at 2:30, giving Stuart the time he needed with his son, and the time his son might need to cool down from their conversation. Stuart sat in one of the rocking chairs of the front porch, awaiting his arrival.

At 1:59, Brennan's white sedan pulled into the dusty driveway leading to the house. Stuart smiled wryly—how typical of his son, arriving at the last possible moment.

Brennan stepped out of the vehicle, a younger replica of Stuart. He was a tall man, handsome, with dark hair, broad shoulders, and striking emerald green eyes, which were currently covered by a pair of aviator sunglasses. A photographer by trade, he often traveled the world, his work often sought in some of the most prominent magazines and newspapers. He and his wife comprised of what his parents called the "perfect Bohemian power couple." Both free spirits, while he was a photographer, she was a writer, working to get her children's books published, occasionally being paid for a freelance piece here and there. Brennan's entrepreneurial spirit, as well as his raw talent, had paid off for his family in the last few years, and he was beginning to receive more jobs: his most recent being in Germany, which was why his daughters were staying with their grandparents in the first place. Rosalie, his wife, would often travel with him, acting as his assistant in between bouts of creativity with her writing.

Brennan approached his father, who stood to greet him. The two embraced, and Stuart said, "Why don't you come in for a second? The girls are with your mother. You and I need to talk."

Brennan raised an eyebrow, not saying anything in response, but following his father inside.

13

"Sit down, son." Stuart motioned towards the couch.

Brennan did as his father asked, only mildly curious about the conversation they were about to have. He had a feeling he knew what it was about. Stuart sat opposite him in the armchair.

"The girls met Lila," Stuart stated matter-of-factly, cutting straight to the point.

"I had a feeling they would," Brennan commented, his feeling confirmed.

"Listen, I know you don't want any part of it anymore. But it's important."

Brennan sighed, slightly annoyed. "I know, Dad. You've been telling me that for years. How much did you tell them?"

"I told them everything I told you when you were their age."

"So, they know all about the stones, and the Fallen Sorcerer, and the Creator Sorcerer."

"Yes."

"*Jesus*, Dad," Brennan exclaimed, frustrated with his father. "Even I knew I was too young to know that stuff when you told me! Do you have any idea how much of a responsibility you're putting on them?"

"Brennan, I didn't choose for them to find out this summer," Stuart snapped back. "And unlike *you*, I'm not going to lie to them when the truth is staring them in the face."

Brennan sighed. "We had our reasons."

"Your 'reasons' are ridiculous."

14

"Yes, well, it doesn't matter now, does it?" Brennan hissed. "We're their parents, and *we* were going to decide when it was time to tell them. But you couldn't be patient, you couldn't respect our wishes, even though we'd told you time and time again what our plan was."

Stuart stared at his son through slit lids. "You know how it goes, Brennan," he said firmly. "They find out in their own time, and I simply told them the truth about their background. Yes, maybe I was impatient with you, but enough was enough. It's time for you to step up and do what you need to do to raise those girls right. If it wasn't Lila here with us, it would have happened elsewhere—a mermaid on a boating trip with you, or a pixie at the park. They're ready to know the truth, so I told them. Just like I told you."

"Yes, and it got me into trouble, remember?" Brennan countered. "It almost cost me Rosalie."

"But it didn't. And you're fine. Besides, you knew what you were doing, and you shouldn't have been out there anyway. You were being foolish."

"I was just following in my old man's footsteps," Brennan said bitterly. He paused. "So, who saw Lila first? Amelia or Emily?"

"Amelia. Lila decided to come out and play with her when she was in the field."

"I always figured it'd be her first. I'm honestly surprised it didn't happen sooner." He sighed. "So, what do I need to do now?"

"They need to be taught the stories." Stuart paused, hesitant about what he was about to say next. "And the spells."

"Dad. *We can't use magic*," Brennan argued, clearly aggravated by this point. "We've never been able to use magic. I don't understand why you

15

feel the need to teach those spells if we can't even use them. Guardians were stripped of their powers, remember?"

"Yes, Brennan, I remember," Stuart said tersely. "But there will come a time when Guardians' powers will be restored. And personally, I'd like my granddaughters to be well-versed in the art of wielding magic if it happens in their lifetime."

"*If*," Brennan emphasized. "Even you don't know it will happen."

"No, I don't," Stuart agreed. "But I'd rather they be prepared *if* it happens. And Brennan, I'm telling you, that time is growing closer. Haven't you noticed the unusual activities happening with the magical creatures? Fairies are migrating sooner than they used to. Elves have been in hiding in the mountains and haven't come down to the valleys in years. Mermaids are being spotted in colder waters. Something is off."

"Global warming," Brennan replied sarcastically.

"Don't give me that attitude," Stuart snapped. "You know very well this isn't normal. It's like they're all bracing for something, like we're in the calm before the storm. And I don't know when that storm will hit—it could be years from now, but believe me, it will happen at some point. The prophecy will be fulfilled. And I want my granddaughters to be ready."

"Fine," Brennan said, resigned. "I'll teach them the stories. But I will not teach them the spells. It's too dangerous."

"And they'll be dangerously ill-equipped without it!" Stuart countered.

Though he hated to admit it, Brennan knew his father was right. He sighed heavily. "Then we'll compromise. You can teach them when they're here. For the time you get them each summer, do whatever you want when it comes to the spells. But the rest of the year, when they're with me and their mother, I won't have it under my roof. It already almost led to disaster. I won't let that happen again with them. And I expect them to be supervised at all times when they're learning."

"Of course," Stuart agreed, knowing this would be the best he could get from his son.

"But if anything happens to either of them, so help me God, you will live to regret the day," Brennan said darkly.

"I already have regrets. Believe me, I don't want more."

Brennan nodded stiffly. "Then it's settled. Now if you'll excuse me, I'd like to take my daughters home."

He rose, heading to the beach to go get them, but as he did so, Lizzie appeared in the doorway with Amelia and Emily in tow.

"DADDY!" the girls cried out in unison, running into his open arms.

"Hey, girls!" he said in return, just as happy to see them, holding them tightly. "I heard you two had a great vacation with Grandma and Grandpa!"

"We met fairies!" Amelia proclaimed.

"Yes, I heard that too." Brennan's tone was more subdued at this particular   comment.

"Lila is SO PRETTY, Daddy," Emily chimed in.

"She sure is," Brennan agreed quickly.

"What'd you bring us, Daddy?" Amelia asked, in typical eight-year-old fashion. Whenever Brennan traveled, he always brought back souvenirs for the girls. Her first memory of gifts from his travels was of a child's necklace with a teardrop-shaped amber pendant in it from Greece when she was three, before Emily was even born. The most recent trips

17

had gifted her with a little pink beret from France, and a pretty hand-embroidered skirt from Hungary.

"Well, you're just going to have to find out when you get home, aren't you?" Brennan grinned. "Now, say goodbye to your grandparents. It's time for us to go. Mommy's waiting for us, and she's making pizza for dinner!"

A few quick hugs and kisses later, the girls were in the car with their father, content with a happy, memorable summer, and looking forward to the prospect of hugs from their mother, gifts to open, and pizza for dinner.

As their son drove down the path away from the beach cottage with his daughters, Lizzie put her arm around Stuart. "How did it go?"

"Better than expected," Stuart said. "We'll have to fill in some gaps in their education when they come to visit…but it went better than expected overall."

"We can do that." Lizzie kissed him on the cheek. "Now come inside. Let's get dinner going."

✳

"So, girls, we need to talk," Brennan said as he drove. "Grandpa told me about Lila. And he and I agreed to teach you about magic. But you need to know something: whatever he teaches you at his house, you do not bring home, ever. And you do not do it out in public. Do you understand?"

"Yes, Daddy. But why?" Amelia asked.

"Because it would upset Mommy. And because I don't want you or anyone else accidentally getting caught or getting hurt. Does that make sense?"

"Yes, Daddy," the girls replied in unison.

18

"Good." Brennan breathed a sigh of relief.

"Daddy?" Amelia asked tentatively.

"Yes, Amelia?"

"Why didn't you tell us about Lila before, if you knew about her?"

Brennan sighed, having expected this. "It's complicated, sweetheart. And I'm sorry I didn't tell you. I had my grown-up reasons."

"What were your reasons?" she pressed.

"It doesn't much matter anymore, Amelia, does it, now that you know about Lila?"

"No, I suppose not," she said quietly, unsatisfied with her father's response.

"You know I love you, Amelia?" he said, sensing her dissatisfaction.

"I love you too, Daddy," she said monotonously.

"What about me?" Emily chimed in.

Brennan laughed as Emily brought that lighthearted touch so desperately needed in that moment. "Yes, Emily, I love you too!"

They drove the rest of the way home with Brennan silent, and the girls chattering away about their magical summer. As Brennan listened to his sweet daughters, his heart was heavy. He knew the responsibility that would be thrust on them when they were older, and he was sad for this. But for now, he enjoyed them as little girls, talking about fairies.

✳ Chapter 3 ✳

A flicker of light

"It looks like everything is in order, Stuart."

Jim McCarthy took off his reading glasses, looking up from the stack of papers on the desk in front of him. Though over twenty years younger than his client, physically, he was still no match, with a paunch belly, a receding hairline, and a bad case of asthma. Stuart Davidson, now seventy-five, still maintained some of the same vitality of his youth, with a full head of pure white hair, and sinewy arms that could still haul a good load of fish when needed. He'd slowed a bit over the years, of course— though more at the request of his wife than of his own volition. He currently sat opposite Jim in Jim's law office, his dog Cosmo by his side. Cosmo sat patiently next to his master, waiting for the two humans to finish their business. He was looking forward to a nice long walk in town.

Stuart sighed with relief, petting Cosmo. "Good."

"I can't believe you finally sold the market and fleet after all these years." Jim placed the papers in a manila folder, and stood to put said folder in the filing cabinet behind his desk.

"Manian's a good man. He'll take care of it."

"I'm sure he will. Still, your family owned it for generations. It's hard to believe it won't be in Davidson hands anymore."

"At least it will continue on. It's not like my son is alive to take over— not that he would've wanted to anyway, knowing Brennan."

"He always did march to the beat of his own drum, didn't he?" Brennan and Jim had attended school together, and Jim remembered his old schoolmate as a creative dreamer, with a mischievous streak.

"Yes—yes he did. But in some ways, not as much as you'd think."

"Hard to believe it's been ten years now. And they never caught the bastard that hit him?"

This truth stung Stuart sharply, even after all these years—ten long years since that terrible day; twenty since that carefree summer, when Amelia and Emily discovered the truth about magical creatures. Anxiously, he scratched behind Cosmo's ears, a reassuring habit he'd picked up since acquiring the dog. Cosmo didn't mind, enjoying the pets. "No. They didn't." Stuart paused, then changed the course of the conversation. "I won't be totally gone from the market anyway. Manian's keeping me on part-time until I decide it's time to leave completely."

Taking Stuart's cue, Jim asked, "When do you think that will be?"

"Not sure. Hadn't thought that far yet. Probably when things get more difficult with Lizzie."

"Well, the trust you created from the profits from the sale will be more than sufficient to take care of her."

"Good."

"And it was smart to update your will—though with the incredible shape you're in, I can't imagine it'll need to go into effect anytime soon. Still, it's always a good idea to keep these things up to date with major life events. Makes it easier for the people left behind if anything unexpected happens."

Stuart smiled wryly. "Lizzie always said, 'Prepare for the worst, hope for the best.'"

21

Jim sat back at his desk, facing Stuart. Crossing his hands, he looked at Stuart intently. "How is Lizzie, anyway?"

Stuart's smile faded. "She has her days. Some better than others."

"Mmm. She getting many visitors? Besides you and Rosalie, of course?"

"A few. Amelia and Emily come when they can, though it's been a few months."

"They're busy girls. Jude and Delia stopping in, I assume? You've all been best friends for years."

Stuart grunted in reply, not wanting to go into to the particulars of his current relationship with his neighbors.

"I heard they sold out to that company that's been coming around, Dunstan Enterprises," Jim commented, not picking up on this particular cue. "Got $1 million for their land, and they're picking up and moving to Hawaii to live with their son. I guess their place is going to be developed into a new subdivision or something."

"Yes. I heard that too," Stuart said shortly.

"What I still don't understand is how that whole thing passed—there was so much public opposition to them coming here and building, the fact they got permission to build at all is like a miracle or something."

"Or something," Stuart muttered.

"You gotten an offer yet?"

"Only every day," Stuart replied bitterly.

Jim sat back in his seat, analyzing the older man. "Stu, if you don't mind my asking...why don't you take them up on it? Sounds like a nice setup. You'll be taken care of. And that's more money to take care of Lizzie."

"There's more to life than money, Jim," Stuart said curtly.

"True. Not disagreeing with you there. But money certainly does help things along."

Stuart stood, deciding now was the time to make his exit. Cosmo followed his master's lead and also stood, his tail wagging, looking forward to the much-anticipated walk. Taking Cosmo's leash in one hand, Stuart extended the other to Jim, who tentatively took it, realizing he may have gone too far.

"Thanks for everything, Jim. It's been a pleasure."

Jim nodded. "Of course. And let me know if you need anything else."

"Will do."

Stuart stepped out of the law office into the brisk air of early March, Cosmo prancing along at his side. Putting his wool hat on his head and shoving his hands into his coat pockets, he walked down the sidewalk of the sleepy small town, heading towards the market. Today he was going to pull a four-hour shift, then make his daily journey twenty miles down the road to visit Lizzie in the nursing home.

Lizzie. His heart beat faster as he thought about his wife. He missed coming home to her every day: the cottage, though not a large place, seemed cavernous and empty without her, leaving a gaping void she had filled. He hadn't fully emotionally adjusted since she'd moved into the home. Still, he knew it was best for her to be there. Dementia was a horrible disease, he'd concluded. In that time in one's life when one would want to look back on all the lovely memories one had made over the course of a lifetime, dementia sneaks in and robs its victim of that opportunity. He couldn't think of anything worse.

Cosmo whined and pulled, though Stuart didn't pay him any mind. The dog probably saw a squirrel or something. Giving a quick, sharp, jerk on the leash, Stuart ordered, "No, boy. Keep walking."

He continued to walk, his mind wandering to Jim's comment about selling the land. The Dunstan Enterprises representative had visited yet again the day before—and he knew he would probably see him again before the day was done. The man was relentless. He'd been hounding Stuart for months, even before Lizzie was put into the nursing home— each time, increasing his offer, and sometimes throwing in other incentives. Still, Stuart refused. It wasn't about the money, and his blood boiled at the nerve of the man. He just wanted to be left in peace to live his life on his land—the land that had been passed down through generations of Davidsons. There had to be something he could do to get the calls and visits to stop. Perhaps he'd make a stop by the police station later that day, before visiting Lizzie, to see if there was something legally that could help him keep the man from trespassing and harassing him. It was a small town, after all, and not like the police had anything better to do.

His heart raced faster, frustration rising in him as he thought about the man. He was across the street from the market now, out of breath and lightheaded. Contrary to Jim's compliment, age, it seemed, was catching up with Stuart. He remembered a time when he could sprint from one end of the main street to the other, without even breaking a sweat. By this point, Cosmo was whining even more, pacing nervously as he noticed his master's agitation.

Stuart stood at the crosswalk, waiting for the light to indicate he could continue walking. His heart, however, was pounding even harder. The lightheadedness escalated to full-on vertigo, and he found himself clutching the light pole in a weak attempt to remain upright. The attempt was futile, and he crumpled to the ground, unable to keep his balance. He found himself on his back on the cold, hard sidewalk, and heard someone cry out, "Call 911!" In the distance, he heard Cosmo barking, pleading for someone to help his master.

Before his vision faded to darkness, Stuart caught sight one last time of a small, twinkling light, flickering against the backdrop of the vibrant blue sky. He took a deep breath, and released.

All was well.

✳

It had been twenty years since that summer when Lila first made her appearance. Amelia found herself longing for the simplicity of life from that time. Currently, she was working as a journalist for a prominent travel magazine just a few hours from the town her grandparents lived in—well, her grandfather, at least. Elizabeth had been diagnosed with dementia, and was currently living in a nursing home twenty miles from the home she once shared with her husband. Stuart, bless him, visited her every day, making the forty-mile round-trip trek to visit his wife. Some days were better than others, and she was more like the Lizzie everyone knew and loved…and other days, she was but a shell of the woman she had once been, a stranger trapped in a familiar body.

Fairies were not forgotten, but they were not the priority anymore. Adulthood had taken over, earlier than either of the sisters would have liked.

Ten years prior, when Amelia was eighteen and college-bound, and Emily fourteen and a freshman in high school, Brennan was killed in a hit and run. The driver had never been tracked down, though witnesses indicated whoever he was, he was most likely drunk—he had been swerving all over the road before striking Brennan as he was crossing the street. Unfortunately, no one was able to get a license plate, and the description of the car was too vague: just a black sedan.

After Brennan's death, Rosalie, their mother, fell into a deep depression for several months, leaving Amelia to delay college for a semester while she helped take care of Emily and get Rosalie through the worst of her grief. When it became all too much for the teenager, she would take her mother's car (sometimes with Emily, sometimes without) and escape to her grandparents' home on the weekends, where she would absorb the stories and lessons about magic. It became her refuge, one she would continue to return to even in adulthood as often as she could— though admittedly, in her current position, not as often as she would like.

Eventually, things got better. Rosalie channeled her grief into her writing, and wrote a series of children's books to help young ones cope with grief and losing a loved one. It was a success, and the books took off. She was now living comfortably in Calvary in a cute little townhouse, keeping a watchful eye on Stuart and Elizabeth, writing and living off the royalties from her work. Emily, upon her father's death, went through a sullen, depressed teenage stage that even as an adult, she couldn't seem to shake—though in spite of this, she worked hard at all she did, almost as though she was trying to prove herself. In both college and grad school, she graduated top of her class.

Amelia herself inherited her parents' nomadic spirit of their youth, first moving away to college, and after college, looking for jobs that would give her the chance to explore and live freely. After working a number of jobs that didn't fit, she decided to take her own path, building up her blog and a portfolio of her writing, taking freelance jobs where she could. The hard work paid off, her blog was noticed, she was picked up by the magazine of her dreams, and she found herself successful in her current venture as a travel journalist. Though lately, the travel required by her career choice had been taking up much of her time.

From her travels, she had acquired interesting items to add to her collection of souvenirs from around the world that her father had started, and her apartment was an eclectic, whimsical mixture of different pieces from different cultures. She still wore the teardrop shaped amber pendant he had given her as a child, though it now hung on a more adult delicate chain, as her neck was no longer child-sized. Each time she put it on she'd smile, a warm, comforting feeling coursing through her, a reminder of her father and his love. The embroidered skirt she had repurposed as lovely dining linens, used only for special occasions. The little pink beret she kept in case she ever had a daughter, and it was currently tucked away in a box in the back of her closet. She'd also added over the course of her own travels, among other things, a beautifully beaded bracelet from Peru, a delicate hand-painted bone china tea set from Japan, and a fertility doll from Ghana—though in her defense, she didn't realize it was a fertility doll until after the purchase; she simply thought it was an interesting, pretty hand-carved figurine. When asked about it by a previous boyfriend, so as not to scare him off, she lied and said it was supposed to bring wealth and fortune.

In spite of these wonderful travels, Amelia still found herself longing for those summer visits from her childhood, before her father died, when she and Emily would stay at the beach cottage for several weeks, staying out in the fields until late into the evening, playing with fairies. Life was carefree then. Once, when she was ten years old, Lila led the two girls to the beach, where Amelia swore she caught a glimpse of a mermaid before the lovely creature dove from the rock on which she'd been sitting and disappeared into the ocean. She never saw one again, and even her grandfather doubted it had been there (according to him, "Mermaids usually prefer warmer waters, like around Hawaii or the Caribbean."). But in her heart, she knew mermaids lived nearby, or at least migrated nearby, and it pleased her to know there were other magical creatures in the world, aside from her beloved fairies, who were out there somewhere thriving.

On this particular day, Amelia was looking at her schedule, trying to figure out a time when she could visit her grandparents. It had been several months, around Christmas, since her last visit, despite being a couple hours' drive from them. While the job at the magazine meant more money, it also meant more responsibility, and thus less time. But a concerning phone call from her mother the other day, indicating her grandmother's health was deteriorating, was giving her the push she needed to make the trip.

Her phone rang. She looked down at it, and saw it was Emily. Emily had finished her MBA a few months ago, which was promising, but she found herself currently unemployed and job-hunting in New York City, working odd jobs to make ends meet and living with four roommates, one of whom was an ex-boyfriend she couldn't seem to shake. For the past few months since the breakup (with Dan, the ex, leaving Emily for her best friend, Leslie, as drama would have it), Amelia had been encouraging her younger sister to leave the area and start over fresh elsewhere, far from the troubles that currently haunted her. Of course, she hinted her own city was full of a vibrant nightlife, slightly more affordable housing, and plentiful opportunities in a variety of career fields that would suit Emily nicely (and the fact she could keep a watchful eye on her younger sister went without saying, though Emily definitely picked up on this). Emily, of course, was stubborn, and saw leaving the city as defeat, instead of the healthy move her sister and mother had been trying to convince her it was. This caused a bit of animosity on Emily's part, and lately, she'd been cold and curt whenever she was in touch with her family.

Amelia braced herself as she picked up the phone, giving herself an internal pep talk to remain pleasant and optimistic, no matter what Emily threw her way. She knew Emily had received the same call about their grandmother from their mother, and was hoping to land on some common ground with that. She anticipated they'd both be visiting around the same time, as their mother indicated they should make it a priority to visit their grandmother "before it was too late."

"Hey!" Amelia said cheerily as she answered the phone, getting herself a glass of water while she spoke. Without even giving her sister a chance to return the greeting, she continued, "I already know about Grandma, Mom told me a couple days ago. I'm looking at my schedule right now, I've got a trip at the end of the month to Turkey, and next month I'll be heading to France, but I'm free to take off a few days next week to come down and visit. That work for you?"

"Grandpa died."

That was it. Whatever she was expecting from Emily, it certainly wasn't that. No hello, no greeting, nothing. Just two words on the other end of the line that changed Amelia's life forever.

Her stomach dropped, and leaning against the counter in her kitchen, she asked the only thing she could think to ask: "What happened?"

"Heart attack. He was walking to the market for work, and one of the guys saw him pass out across the street…by the time they got to him, he was already gone."

"When's the funeral?"

"Mom's planning for the wake next Thursday, funeral next Friday. I'll be coming in Wednesday to help her out with anything."

Amelia nodded—not that it mattered, her sister couldn't see this acknowledgement. Realizing what she was doing, she stopped herself, and said into the phone, "I'll plan the same." She paused. "What about Grandma?"

"We haven't gotten that far," Emily answered. "It's tough—most days, she doesn't know anyone anyway. But every once in a while, Grandpa said she knew exactly who she was and where she was. Mom's trying to figure out if it's worth upsetting her just for her to forget."

"She should know," Amelia said curtly. "It was her husband. It doesn't matter if she's going to forget it, she should know. And maybe it's a blessing that she'll forget it. But she should still be told."

"I agree," Emily replied. The first thing they'd agreed on in months, Amelia noted to herself. "But we're not the ones in charge here. Mom is."

"If Dad were still around, he'd agree with us," Amelia retorted.

"Don't mention Dad to Mom right now," Emily warned. "I already tried that, she flipped out. She's having enough trouble dealing with the death of her father-in-law and making all his arrangements, without her husband there to help with his own father."

Amelia sighed. "I miss Dad."

"I do too."

"I hate drunk drivers."

"I do too."

It had been ten years since their father's death, but this part of the conversation was always the same, even after all that time.

There was an awkward silence, which Amelia broke by asking about her grandfather's dog. "What about Cosmo?"

"Mom's got him with her for now."

"Good."

Another awkward silence.

"So…I'll see you next week," Amelia said, not sure how else to end the conversation.

"Yeah. I'll see you next week."

"I love you, Emily."

"I love you too, Amelia."

With this, the sisters hung up. Alone in each of their respective locations, but together in spirit for the first time in months, they each sat in a comfy chair, and cried.

Sometimes, adulthood was too much to handle.

✳ Chapter 4 ✳

Return to Calvary

A week later, Amelia found herself pulling up to that same, familiar dusty driveway, to the little beach cottage where she spent a portion of her childhood.

Parking and stepping out of her car, she took in her surroundings. The color on the house was a little worse for the wear, and the weeds were a bit overgrown, but that was nothing a good paint job and an afternoon doing yard work couldn't fix. Otherwise, the house looked as it always had. Further back though, beyond the house, Amelia noticed the old barn had seen better days and was falling into disrepair, its doors falling off the hinges, and the paint peeling off the siding from years of being exposed to the salty sea air. Beyond that, the whole piece of property seemed to be bleak and lifeless, fitting for her current mood: the grass in the field normally full of brightly colored wildflowers was dry and dead from the frigid winter that was only just now coming to an end, the branches on the willow tree were bare from the harsh cold, and even the sea and sky seemed to be the same shade of dreary gray.

She walked up the steps of the porch, and after rifling through her purse for a moment, procured a key, which she'd had since she was a little girl. When Amelia opened the door to the cottage, she was greeted by darkness. It was mid-afternoon, so she drew back the curtains to the windows, and as she did so, stirred up the dust that had settled on the fabric. It swirled in the sunbeams, now flooding the cottage with light, and as she looked around the tiny home, she was overwhelmed with a myriad of memories and emotions. The overstuffed red chair, now faded to a dusty pink, still sat in the corner between the bay window and the fireplace, unmoved since it had been placed there decades ago. The sight of it hearkened back to evenings where she sat on the floor at her grandfather's feet, feeling the warmth of the fire, and listening to stories about fairies, mermaids, unicorns, centaurs, and elves. Wandering into the kitchen, she saw her grandmother's tea kettle with the pink rose pattern sitting on the counter, perfectly preserved, as if Lizzie would be returning any moment to sit and have a conversation with her granddaughter over a cup of tea. Nautical nick knacks dotted the walls and shelves along with family photos, a nod toward Stuart's life as a fisherman.

She smiled over laughter shared, and even tears cried in this place. Of all the places to call a second home during her childhood, this had been the perfect one—and in many ways, she considered it more of a home than the one she shared with her parents. Here, she learned the truth about magic, free to explore and learn. Back home, though her parents didn't discourage it, there was always a stiffness about it, as if her curiosity was merely being tolerated, but never truly encouraged.

She glanced at the window, where a fruit basket still sat, and smiled, deep in the memory of Lila's first visit. She wondered if Lila would make an appearance during this visit, or if the fairy even knew what had happened to Stuart. She had a feeling the little creature did, and perhaps that was why she was not here now—she was in her own place, mourning the loss of Stuart in her own way. Amelia wondered what a fairy in mourning was like.

"So…I guess I'll take the kids' room?"

Twirling around, she saw her sister standing in the entrance, suitcase in hand. Without saying a word, Amelia rushed over to her, and embraced her tightly. Emily awkwardly gave her a one-armed hug in return, still clutching the suitcase in her other hand. "Hi?" she said hesitantly.

"Hi." Amelia was still holding her sister, and now failing to hold back tears. After a moment, she let go, furiously wiping the tears streaming from her face. "Sorry, this place—it just suddenly got the best of me."

Emily's eyes darted around to take everything in, setting down her bag. "Yeah, I know the feeling."

"And we'll both be in the kids' room...there's still two twin beds in there," Amelia answered, returning back to Emily's initial statement.

"Well, I mean, the master bedroom is free now, so..."

"I don't want it," Amelia responded, interrupting Emily's thought. "It's too early, and too weird for me. But if you want it..."

Emily shook her head. "No, no...I feel the same way."

"So, we'll share a room. Like old times."

"That sounds good to me."

The sisters stood there in silence for a moment, not sure what else to say to each other. It had been months since they last saw each other in person, and the tension in the room was palpable.

Amelia broke the silence. "I was thinking of visiting Grandma at the nursing home tomorrow."

"You're going to tell her about Grandpa?"

Amelia nodded. "She needs to know. Even if she *does* forget about it thirty seconds later."

"Did you talk to Mom about it?"

"Well...no."

"Don't you think she'll be pissed when she finds out?" Emily crossed her arms, eyebrow raised.

"Probably."

"I'll go with you."

"Really?" Amelia asked, perking up.

"Yeah. I will. I agree with you."

Amelia smiled. "There's something you haven't said in a long time."

"Don't get used to it."

✳

That evening, they called their mother, Rosalie, to assure her they had reached the cottage safely, and would meet with her the following afternoon for lunch and to help with last-minute funeral arrangements. The call was followed by take-out Armenian food for dinner (one of three places in the small town that delivered), and an early bedtime—not because they were tired, but because they were no longer sure what to say to each other after a certain point of time. Going to bed was easier than forced conversation.

After rising in the morning and eating breakfast in relative silence, Amelia and Emily found themselves twenty miles down the road, entering their grandmother's nursing home. It was a gloomy, soggy, early spring day, matching their mood perfectly. Winter hadn't quite left the region, a lingering chill in the air. A gust of wind practically blew them inside the building, each of the sisters clutching their hats to keep them from flying off their heads.

Inside, it was warm and tidy. The fireplace was lit in the main common area, a small crowd of the elderly tenants gathered around, being read to by a nurse. Some seemed actively engaged, eagerly listening to the story. Others were hunched over in their chairs, fast asleep. And several, Amelia noticed, were staring off into space, unaware of their surroundings. One man had a small dribble of drool running down the side of his mouth. When Amelia saw him, she quickly turned away, embarrassed at the prospect of being caught staring. Though Amelia hated to think of her grandmother in that condition, a small part of her hoped that was the way she would find her today—it would be easier to tell a shell the news she had to share, than to deal with the emotions of a lucid woman. Internally, she scolded herself. Dementia was a horrible thing.

They checked in with the nurse at the front desk, who guided them to their grandmother's room.

"She's having a good day," the nurse said cheerily as she walked Amelia and Emily down the hall. "She seems to know where she is and what's going on."

Though this would normally be good news, Amelia's stomach dropped. She would have to break the news of her grandfather's death to her grandmother, with the woman actually realizing what was happening.

"The one day we didn't want her to be aware of her surroundings—it *would* work out like this," Emily muttered, vocalizing their shared sentiments.

They entered the room. In a plush, pink chair in the corner sat Elizabeth, reading a book. Her reading glasses were perched on the tip of her nose, and her eyes sparkled with delight as she absorbed the words from the pages: a look the two sisters hadn't seen in a very long time. In that moment, sunbeams broke through the clouds outside and filled the room with a golden light as they shone through the windows. It was magical in its own way, lighting up Elizabeth's whole countenance, seemingly taking years off. This woman, who sat before them, was momentarily the grandmother they knew and remembered. They also knew at any moment, she could transform back into a stranger, a frail, shadowy thing.

Elizabeth looked up, hearing the door open. "Girls!" she exclaimed, setting down the book and standing to greet them. Slowly, Amelia noted, and with a cane, but still she stood.

"Hi, Grandma!" Amelia forced her own voice to be cheerful. "How are you?"

"Oh, I'm just so happy to see you!" Lizzie replied, giving each of them a hug and a kiss on the cheek. "How have you been?"

"We're okay," Emily said. She and Amelia exchanged a glance, to which Amelia nodded. She continued, "It's been a long few days."

"Well, I can understand that—you've traveled a long way! How is New York? Are you still with that boy—what was his name, Dick?"

"Dan," Emily corrected her.

"Close enough," Amelia snorted. Emily nudged her in the ribs.

"No, we broke up," Emily replied quickly, turning back to her grandmother.

Elizabeth breathed a visible sigh of relief. "Oh, good. I never liked him."

Emily rolled her eyes. "Thanks, Grandma."

Amelia decided it was time for her to take control of the conversation. Seriously, she said, "Grandma, listen, we need to tell you something."

Lizzie noticed the change in the tone of her granddaughter's voice. "Something happened, didn't it?"

"Yes," Amelia said softly, taking her grandmother's hand.

"Your grandfather hasn't been to visit in a few days, you know," Lizzie commented matter-of-factly, trying to hide a tremble in her voice. "I think he spends too many hours at that market."

"Well, he's always made time for you," Amelia said gently.

"Yes, he has," Lizzie agreed with a sad, knowing smile. "Me and magic. His two favorite things." A tear rolled down her face, which she hastily brushed away. Composing herself, she said, "Girls, do me a favor—whatever it is you came to tell me, don't tell me right now. Maybe after lunch, I'll be in a different mindset, and able to handle things better."

"Sure, Grandma. We can do that," Amelia said softly.

She and Emily exchanged a glance, understanding it was time to respect Lizzie's choice. Following their grandmother's lead, they walked with her to the dining hall. Lizzie would find out later about Stuart—though she wouldn't be there to remember it.

✳

The following two days were a blur of tears, forced conversation, and black clothes for the sisters and their mother as they attended the wake and funeral. Amelia and Emily at one point worked up the courage to tell Rosalie they told Lizzie about Stuart's death—though she was initially upset, she did understand their reasoning. The argument then came about if they should check her out for the funeral—Amelia and Emily were for it, but Rosalie asserted it would be too much for the elderly woman. In the end, their mother won, much to the girls' chagrin. To them, it didn't seem right that Lizzie was not allowed to say goodbye to her husband of over fifty years, but Rosalie insisted.

Their mother always did seem to prefer the easy way out.

The day of the funeral came. Stuart had truly been a loved member of the small community, and it seemed as though the whole town had come out to pay their respects and say their goodbyes to the kind, gentle man. This was all they could hope for: that he would be honored and loved and remembered.

After the funeral service, the girls and Rosalie found themselves in the cemetery next to the church. Stuart's casket was in the ground, dirt being shoveled on top. It was an oddly sunny day for such a gloomy event. The three watched in silence, having promised amongst each other they would not leave until the last pile of dirt had been thrown.

As they stood, they were approached by Jude and Delia Benedict. The couple was about the same age as Lizzie and Stuart had been, and had been the Davidsons' closest friends and neighbors for years, having grown up together in the small town and raised families together. Jude and Stuart had even served and gone to war together, looking out for each other. The two men had been convinced if not for the other, neither would have returned alive.

More than this though, each of the men were from Guardian lines. Jude was one of the few people Stuart could trust when it came to magic, and vice versa. Their father, Brennan, grew up best friends with the Benedicts' own son, Elliott, who had since moved to Hawaii for a job with the government. Emily and Amelia each had memories of Jude coming over to visit throughout their childhood, sometimes helping Stuart as he taught them what it meant to be a Guardian. The girls saw Jude and Delia as another set of grandparents, and loved them as such.

"We're so sorry for your loss," Jude said, giving each of the sisters and their mother a warm embrace.

"Is there anything we can do for you?" Delia asked, also hugging each of the three women.

Rosalie shook her head. "No, we're managing."

"Well, we're planning on stopping by the cottage later tonight with some food," Jude insisted. "It's the least we can do."

"Thank you."

"How is Lizzie?" Delia asked. "I notice she's not here."

"We didn't think it appropriate to put her through this in her current condition," Rosalie answered.

Amelia and Emily exchanged a glance between each other, biting their tongues.

"Makes sense," Jude said, noticing the sisters' look, and himself also not agreeing with this decision, but knowing now was neither the time nor the place to discuss it. "We feel so bad about how things are going for her. And I wish things had ended differently between us and Stu."

"What do you mean?" Amelia asked, confused.

Jude and Delia exchanged a look, to which Jude nodded.

"Jude's cancer is back. It's terminal," Delia said quietly.

"Oh, no…I'm so sorry to hear that," Rosalie said sympathetically.

Jude waved off her sympathies dismissively. "Please, don't feel bad for me. The thing is, I've been looking for a way to settle down and live the rest of my days in peace—living the life of an old fisherman isn't working for us anymore."

"That makes perfect sense."

"So anyway, as Delia and I were trying to figure things out, this man comes to our door, offering to buy our land. Says he's from Dunstan Enterprises, and he wants to develop it into some kind of new coastal community."

"He paid us $1 million for it," Delia whispered.

"WHAT?" Emily exclaimed. "$1 MILLION!"

"SHHHH!" Amelia hissed at her sister, giving her a little nudge.

39

"Yes," Jude continued. "$1 million. And the choice to either live in one of the homes they'd develop, or a new home anywhere of our choosing, fully paid for. We're moving to Hawaii to be with Elliott. I can live out my days in peace and quiet, and Delia will be taken care of after I'm gone."

This news hit Amelia like a sack full of bricks. Jude's land bordered their own, and though there may have been property lines in a legal survey, fairies don't know of any such boundaries—essentially, their habitat was now being parceled out. They were losing ground…and because a Guardian had given up.

"And you told Grandpa this," she said stiffly.

"I did. He didn't take it well."

"I can understand why." She imagined her grandfather felt incredibly betrayed by the very man who he had once trusted with his life. She herself was feeling the same way in that moment.

"You need to know, the same man approached your grandfather several times asking him to sell too—he didn't, but they hounded him," Jude said gravely. "I think it was the stress of it all that finally got to him—between running the market and the fleet, taking care of Lizzie, and trying to ward off this company…I think it all caught up with him."

"At least he died putting up a fight," Amelia said sharply.

Jude took her point, and winced, taking her point. "Yes. I wanted to tell you: whichever of you gets his land, know they will probably approach you too."

"We'll be ready."

Jude sighed, and turned to walk off with his wife, now feeling unwelcome. But before he left, he paused, and looking over his shoulder, said in a low voice, "I told Lila to tell her kind to stay away from my place—I told her to stay north of the big willow tree, at your place, that she'd be safe there."

Amelia nodded stiffly. "Thank you." She paused. "And by the way, we won't be needing that meal tonight. We can manage on our own."

Jude nodded, resigned. He and Delia turned and walked away, leaving Amelia, Emily, and Rosalie alone in the graveyard, reeling over the information they had just received.

It seemed the town was now running low on Guardians. And it was in this moment, Amelia realized the last of the Davidson men was gone. It was now up to the women to carry on.

✳

The next morning, Rosalie, Amelia, and Emily were sitting in the law office of Jones and McCarthy. Jim McCarthy was sitting in the same seat he'd been in when he met with Stuart just a week previous, with the same stack of papers in front of him. The women were each on the other side of the desk, waiting for Jim to finish sifting through his files.

"It's so strange," he commented as he went through them. "I was here with him just a week ago, literally the *day* he died, finalizing everything. I never thought we'd have to put all of this into effect so soon. I'm so, so sorry for your loss."

"Thank you, Jim," Rosalie said. Amelia and Emily sat on either side of their mother, silent.

"So, Stuart left a letter for me to read to the three of you," he explained, finally finding the piece of paper he had been searching for. "All these papers are the official documentation, but the letter is the basic gist of what he's left to you. Shall I begin?"

The three nodded, and Jim, taking a puff from his inhaler first, read:

"Girls,

"If Jim is reading this letter to you, it means my time with you is up. Please know I've cherished every second with you. I couldn't ask for a better family than you three.

"To my daughter-in-law, Rosalie: I leave you power of attorney over Lizzie. She is the love of my life, and I couldn't imagine entrusting her care to anyone but you. In addition, I want you to know the fish market and fleet has been sold to Charles Manian, my general manager: he is a good man, and will take care of it well. I have put the money from the sale into a trust for you to care for Lizzie. The remaining leftover, as well as the sum of our personal savings, is to be split three ways between you, Amelia, and Emily. I think you will find it more than adequate."

At this, the lawyer handed Rosalie a check. The girls looked over their mother's shoulder in an attempt to catch a glimpse of the amount.

Rosalie took it, and without even opening the envelope, placed it in her purse. "He was always so generous."

"Mom, aren't you going to see how much it is?" Emily inquired curiously, gaping at the idea of being left a small fortune.

Rosalie shrugged. "It doesn't matter much to me—I don't need it. I'll look later."

"Yeah, but we're a part of it too," Emily pointed out.

"And you will find out how much it is later," she said tersely. Looking at Jim, she nodded. "Please, continue."

He cleared his throat. "To my granddaughters, Emily and Amelia: I leave you our boat, *The Blue Mermaid*, our house and its contents, and all the surrounding land. I know how you love it. I hope you will make it your home, but even if you don't, I know you will take care of it, and do the right thing with it."

42

Amelia's eyes went wide. It was all she had ever wanted, that plot of land and little cottage—to live among the fairies and other creatures for the rest of her days. It was a dream come true. Emily, in turn, looked stunned, her jaw dropped in disbelief.

"Thank you," Amelia managed to get out. Emily was still silent.

Jim nodded, and finished the closing remarks of the letter, "Know I love each of you with all of my heart, and I am with you always. Love, Stuart."

He looked up and cleared his throat. "That's all he left. Again, please allow me to express my most sincere condolences to all of you. Stuart was a fine man."

"Thank you, Jim," Rosalie responded warmly, shaking his hand.

He nodded, and the women rose, exiting his office.

As the three walked out the door onto the sidewalk, Emily commented to her sister, "So…are we going to sell the place?"

"Of course not," Amelia snapped. "That's what killed Grandpa in the first place, trying to keep it from being sold."

"But we could get *so much* money out of it! That developer was offering them *millions*!"

"There's more to life than money, Emily."

Emily sighed, frustrated. "Well, what do *you* want to do with it?

"I think…well, I think I want to renovate the barn," Amelia replied thoughtfully. "It's the perfect location for a bed and breakfast, but the cottage isn't big enough for multiple guests. But I'd like to live in the cottage, and run the bed and breakfast out of the barn, once it's done. And

I can keep writing: I can do my job from anywhere, I just need access to a computer and an airport, and the airport isn't too far of a drive away."

"And the rest of the land?"

"Well, keep the garden, and cook meals for the guests out of the things we can grow…and as for the rest, just look after it."

"And let it grow free and wild?"

Amelia smiled. "Yes. And let it grow free and wild. It'll be a place of peace, where people can come to relax."

"We're going to need some serious seed money for that. Renovating a barn like that isn't cheap."

"There are such things as loans, Emily."

"Yeah? You think we can start earning enough right off the bat to start paying that loan off?"

"Forget the loan. I can help," Rosalie chimed in. She was holding the check, the envelope now open.

"Seriously, Mom?" Amelia asked, shocked. "Do we have enough?"

"We do now. And you can have my share. I told you both in there, I don't need this—I make enough to be comfortable off my books. I'd rather this be put to something good that honors him, and I think your idea does just that."

The sisters exchanged a glance. Rosalie's offers typically came with strings attached.

"Mom, that's sweet of you, but you don't have to do that. We can manage with our own share," Amelia said slowly.

"No, I insist. I want you to have mine."

"Mom—"

"Don't argue with me on this one."

"Mom—"

"I promise I'll let you run it your way. I won't get involved."

Amelie sincerely doubted this, but still, she acquiesced. "I…thank you."

Rosalie embraced her daughter, who grew stiff under her touch. "You're welcome, sweetheart."

"Okay, but what about me? What if this isn't what *I* want to do? I have an equal say in this too, you know, as co-owner of the property," Emily commented.

"Come on, Emily, let's do this," Amelia urged. "It's perfect. Besides, you're between jobs right now. It'll be good for you."

"So, what, you expect me to just drop everything and move here with you to live some weird rural dream?" Emily questioned, furious at her sister, and feeling pressured into doing something she wasn't sure she wanted to do. "My place is in New York!"

"Emily, you live in a crappy two-bedroom apartment in the Bronx with three other girls and your ex-boyfriend. You can't tell me you're happy there," Amelia commented. Emily shrugged, not dignifying that with a response, especially since her older sister was right. "You're twenty-four years old and you still have to rely on roommates. And that boyfriend you still live with, he just left you for your best friend, who you *also* live with. Your other friends are alcoholic idiots, and you're unemployed. Let's be real: life isn't really going your way right now."

45

Emily had to concede to this. "You don't have to be so brutally honest about it." The memory of Dan and Leslie was still fresh in her mind, and she had been trying to avoid reliving the entire experience as much as possible. Her sister bringing it up again was like pouring salt on wounds.

"Emily, now is the time for a fresh start for you," Amelia continued, putting her hands on her little sister's shoulders. "Leave it all behind, and live in the cottage with me."

"But what if that isn't what I want to do with my life?"

"Okay, well what do *you* want to do?" Amelia asked, aggravated by her sister's stubbornness.

"I don't know!" Emily snapped, agitated by this point. She turned to her mother, and helplessly, asked, "Mom, what do you think?"

Throughout this part of the conversation, Rosalie had remained silent, knowing it was something her daughters had to work out amongst themselves. But now, being asked for her opinion, she had to choose her words carefully. "Emily, all I want is for you to be happy in your life. And all I know is right now, you're not. I think some kind of change would be good for you."

Gently, Amelia said, "Listen, Emily, it's fine that you don't know what you want to do. But maybe do this with me in the meantime, until you figure it out. Besides, I think we need to be here. You heard Jude and Delia yesterday: they're bailing on us. That means the Davidsons are the only Guardians left in Calvary. We *need* to be here. This town is fighting giants right now. And we need to protect what's ours." She paused, then appealed to her sister's practical side. "Plus, it would look really good on your resume that you're the owner and operator of your own business."

"Now you're speaking my language, Davidson," Emily said with a wry smile. "Fine. I'll do it."

✳ Chapter 5 ✳

The offer

Jack Garridan stepped out of his car, removing his sunglasses as he examined his surroundings. He'd been at the Davidson residence several times before, but this was the first since Stuart Davidson's passing three weeks ago. He'd heard through the grapevine the property had been passed on to Stuart's granddaughters, and he sincerely hoped they would be easier to negotiate with than Stuart. Though if they were anything like their grandfather, he had his doubts.

He had to put in the effort, anyway—his boss was not pleased Jack had gone two months, "Without anything to show," he said. Jack reminded him he had managed to acquire the Benedict property, that Jude and Delia Benedict were all too eager to give up their land for the parley sum of $1 million (Dunstan Enterprises was willing to go as high as $3 million for the prime piece of real estate, but the Benedicts didn't need to know that). This, apparently, was not enough. According to Adrien Dunstan, founder and CEO of Dunstan Enterprises, acquiring the Davidson property was an absolute non-negotiable, a necessity for the development.

So, Jack found himself once again standing in the dusty driveway, mulling over his approach, hoping the granddaughters would be receptive. He was good at his job, self-made, starting in an entry-level position in the acquisitions department after receiving his degree, and quickly moving into a director position. That was why he was stumped by this particular case, and why he was on it in the first place: the specialist who'd initially been on the job failed after working it for several months, and had been fired. In the meantime, until they found a replacement, Jack was stepping into the role, leading by example. As soon as Jack took over, the Benedicts sold, and he was currently in negotiations with the Kowalskis and Ericksons, two other neighboring families. He knew how to get the job done, better than anyone else, and though he'd always been met with resistance whenever he went into the field, he also always succeeded in the end. But never before had it taken him this long to acquire a single piece of property.

He had to admit to himself, he wasn't entirely surprised at the holdout. The second Dunstan Enterprises entered the town, everyone was up in arms about the development. There was talk about "preserving a way of life," and things being "fine as they were." The general fear seemed to be the development would ruin the town, which seemed to already be doing well without Dunstan Enterprises butting in. They were a small town, yes, and perhaps a bit worn down in some areas that needed a bit of revitalization, but overall, they were a far cry from needing the entire makeover this development would bring. Hell, there had been *protests* against the development. The general public wanted to be left alone. Even Jack was surprised when the project was approved by the planning commission.

Jack had always been determined, exceeding everyone's expectations, though he never cared about what others expected, mostly because he never had anyone who expected anything from him but himself. A former foster child, he had bounced from home to home starting at the age of four, and upon being released from the system at age eighteen, joined the Navy for a few years to receive benefits he could use to pay for his college degree. An overachiever, he graduated with his bachelor's degree in three years instead of the anticipated four, and began working for Dunstan Enterprises the day after graduation. He'd been there for a few years now, and did a damn good job, if he said so himself. On the side, he enjoyed the freedom that came with running, and had completed a few marathons. He also participated in kick-boxing and other self-defense classes with his gym, because sometimes, there was nothing like punching something to get his frustrations out.

Jack sometimes toyed with the idea of seeking out his family to show off his success, to show them he didn't need them, that he'd been through the fire and back and had been just fine without them, but each time he had this thought, he pushed it from his mind. He wouldn't give them the satisfaction. It didn't much matter, anyway: he didn't even know where to begin when it came to searching for them. All he'd been told by his case worker as a child was he had been found wandering the street, and when brought to the police station, the only information he gave anyone was that his name was Jack Garridan. He didn't know his mother's name, or his father's. He couldn't even describe them. He didn't know where he lived. Notices were put out that a lost child had been found, but no one stepped forward to claim him. Searches for his family were met with dead ends. Hospital records, birth records, nothing could be found on him or his parents. He wasn't even sure if the birthday he had adopted for himself was really his birthday (May 12), or if he was actually four when he was found—that was a guesstimate made by the people who had found him. He could have been a year older, or a year younger. He had, it seemed, been completely abandoned, left to fend for himself, with only a name as a clue to his identity. His family, if he had any, clearly didn't want to be found.

Still, he sometimes wondered where he got some of his traits: if his blue eyes came from his mother, or if his sandy brown hair came from his father. Was his above average height a trait from his grandfather? Or his square jawline from a grandmother? Was his determination and work ethic a Garridan characteristic, or from his mother's side, whatever her maiden name might be (assuming she was married to his father and had changed her name...or was she a single mother, and *her* name was Garridan)? So many questions entered his mind on a regular basis.

In this moment though, he was pushing it all to the back, as he usually did. It was time to focus on the task at hand: acquiring the Davidson property. He'd been given permission to increase the offer yet again, and he hoped the Davidson granddaughters would bite.

In spite of the fact he was annoyed Stuart hadn't bitten at the opportunity when presented, Jack had to admit, he'd feel the same as Stuart if he were in his shoes. The land he had owned was lovely, almost magical in its own way. It was one of the few places in the world where

Jack truly felt at peace whenever he stepped foot on the property. There was something about this place that felt safe and warm, comforting in its own way.

Jack wouldn't tell anyone this, but he hadn't exactly been thrilled with his position for a few months now—not since the Calvary project had begun. He had seen a shift in Adrien Dunstan: his meticulousness had degraded to micromanagement, his persuasiveness to bullying, his suggestions to demands. He used to have more freedom within his job before this particular project, but now, he felt stifled. Jack would admit he had always doubted some of Adrien's business tactics—they seemed pushy and at times manipulative to him—but he was now behaving in ways that gave Jack pause, questioning if perhaps there was even something not completely legal going on behind the scenes. What it was about this particular project that caused the personality shift remained a mystery to Jack. It was a different arena, yes, building a subdivision instead of an urban development, but not that different, in the grand scheme of things. Jack sincerely hoped it was just a phase, and that Adrien's mood would shift back to what it had been before—bossy, snide, and even a bit entitled, but overall tolerable. Otherwise, if things didn't resume to what they had once been, Jack was contemplating a change in vocation. He'd grown weary of bothering people, of having doors slammed in his face every day. The only thing that kept him going was the thought he was helping to create something beautiful that more people could enjoy.

He approached the door of the small cottage, noticing as he walked up the steps of the porch that there seemed to be some renovations happening with the old barn on the property. From his vantage, he saw a small team of men was surveying the site, and in the midst of the group of men was a lively, petite, strawberry blonde woman, speaking with them and going over blueprints. He assumed this was one of Stuart Davidson's granddaughters, and thought it best to wait on the porch and not interrupt her. After all, at the moment, this was still her property, and it was best to be polite and civil.

What he wasn't counting on, however, was the front door swinging open behind him. He jumped and turned, finding himself face-to-face with a dark-haired, sullen looking young woman with emerald eyes, eyeing him suspiciously. She was clearly caught off guard at seeing him on her front porch just as much as he was by her.

"Who are you?" she demanded.

"Jack Garridan." He extended his hand. "I'm with Dunstan Enterprises."

She glanced at it in disgust, looking as though he had just offered her a dead fish. Without even introducing herself in return, she turned from him and shouted toward the blonde woman at the barn, "AMELIA! HE'S HERE! AND YOU OWE ME TWENTY BUCKS!"

This caught the other woman's attention, and she looked up from the blueprints. Seeing Jack standing next to her sister, she walked away from the crew towards the house.

As she stepped onto the porch, she said bluntly, "You must be the Dunstan Enterprises representative who's been trying to get everyone to sell out."

He had to admire her straightforwardness. "My name's Jack Garridan. And yes, I am with Dunstan Enterprises, but I'm not sure selling out is the right way to put it. I'm here with an opportunity for you and your family."

Amelia rolled her eyes. Reaching into her jean pocket, she procured a twenty-dollar bill, and handed it to Emily, who grinned. "If you need me, I'll be at the beach."

"What was that about?" Jack asked as Emily walked away, confused by this exchange.

"Just a bet between me and my sister." Amelia's eyes narrowed at him. "She bet you'd come knocking and asking for our land within a month of

51

our grandfather's death. I bet you'd have the decency to wait at least two months. I lost."

She was feisty, he had to admit. Though she might be over a foot shorter than him, she certainly had a large presence.

"Shall we get this over with?" She sat in one of the chairs on the front porch, and indicated for him to do the same. He did, placing his briefcase on the patio table between the two of them.

"You seem like a straightforward woman, so I'll get to the point and not waste either of our time. Miss Davidson—it is Miss Davidson, correct?"

Amelia nodded stiffly, eyebrow raised. "Amelia Davidson. Yes."

"Miss Davidson, Dunstan Enterprises is willing to offer you a sum of $2 million for your land. All you have to do is sign." With this, Jack pulled out a small stack of papers from his briefcase and pushed it across the table to her.

Amelia eyed this warily. "No, thank you," she replied curtly, pushing the documents back towards him.

"Miss Davidson, if I were you, I'd take it. You'll never get this good of an offer again."

"Good. I hope not."

"Pardon?"

"I hope you and your company will find somewhere else to build and leave me and my neighbors *alone*. This is our land, our home, and you have *no* right to scoop it up and develop it into some kind of suburban nightmare."

"That 'suburban nightmare' will become home to dozens of families! You could even be part of that, if you wanted to. We'd pay for the house for you, in addition to the $2 million. All you need to do is sign."

"Thanks, but no thanks. My sister and I have plans for this land, and we intend to follow through on it."

"What *are* you planning?"

"We're opening a bed and breakfast. Not that it's your business. But we're going to help revitalize this town. We're taking care of our little corner of the world. And we don't need *you* to do it."

"Miss Davidson, if I may be blunt: that plan is entirely impractical. One small business isn't going to make a difference here. Calvary needs a total overhaul. Dunstan Enterprises can help."

"You may think it impractical, but all it takes is one person to make a difference and inspire others," Amelia retorted. "And let's be real, your company has *no* intention of 'helping' us. Tell me, are you going to bail out the businesses you destroy when you bring in chain franchises? Or are you going to let them die out, and buy up their space for another box store, destroying the livelihoods of the families who built them from scratch? Are the fishermen going to be welcome here anymore, or are they going to have to uproot their lives and move down the coast because you're going to turn this into some kind of beachy tourist trap? Are you going to respect our privacy and our coastline, or are we going to be overrun with rude seasonal tourists and their trash? Tell me, Mr. Garridan, what *are* your plans to 'help' Calvary?"

Jack was taken aback, not sure how to respond to this line of questioning. Amelia was proving herself to be a more formidable foe than even Stuart—and the old man had been incredibly difficult to deal with.

"You have my answer. *No*," Amelia continued. "You cannot have my land. And you have no legal right to it. You're not a government entity, so you can't enforce eminent domain. All you can do is bother me and

53

keep asking, and I'll tell you this, sir, I'm much more stubborn than you are. So, bother away."

Jack, at this, regained his voice. "No, not at the moment, we don't have the right to it. But you need to know, if you don't agree, we will work to obtain the necessary permissions." He was bluffing of course, but she didn't know that. Money wasn't working with her, nor was reasoning. Trying to plant a bit of fear was his next tactic. "It's only a matter of time before we're able to claim the land—*without* asking you. I suggest you make the right decision before that time."

"Why do you want *this* land so badly anyway?" Amelia snapped. "There's plenty of land—open land—just a few miles inland, without a single house on it. You wouldn't have to ask people to leave their homes. Why *this* land?"

"Our CEO is looking to create a new coastal community—a utopia, of sorts. Something to help revive the infrastructure of this area."

She glared at him. "Tell him it already *is* a utopia, *without* him."

"Miss Davidson, we know you and your neighbors are struggling. Your properties have been assessed at a higher tax rate than what you can afford *because* of their prime location," he explained, trying to reason with her. "Do you really think a start-up bed and breakfast will pay the taxes and bills? If you're lucky—and this is a very big *if*—you'll be just breaking even in around five years. Until then, it's going to be a struggle. We can help you. We can take that burden off of you."

"First of all, you have no idea what I'm able to afford, so do *not* throw me into some demographic when you know nothing about me," Amelia snapped. "Second, our town fine just the way it is, and those assessments came from *your* company. I know a fear tactic when I see it, so don't even try to use that on me. Nobody wants you here. We're fine without you."

Frustrated, he retaliated, "You're just as bad as your grandfather."

With this, the blood rushed to Amelia's face, and she turned red with fury. "Your harassment is what *killed* my grandfather. *Now get off my property.*"

Jack stood, snapping his briefcase shut, knowing the point was moot for the time being. "You know I'll be back."

"And I'll be ready. Now *leave.*"

✳

While Amelia was talking to Jack on the porch, Emily took this opportunity to walk to the beach. She and Amelia had agreed ahead of time Amelia would handle the initial discussion with the Dunstan Enterprises representative, mostly due to the fact Emily's temper would probably cause more problems than they wanted to bring on themselves. Emily smirked at the thought of someday hitting the man in the face, though she had to admit, she didn't really want assault charges brought against her. So, she took this time to retreat to the water, while Amelia, the more cool-headed of the two sisters, would stay behind to handle the tough stuff.

Years ago, her grandfather had built his own dock on their land for his fishing boat, rather than harboring it with the boats of the other fishermen in town. Though he was an extrovert with many friends, in that particular area of his life, he preferred solitude. Emily could relate.

She smiled as she approached the boat, nostalgia washing over her. *The Blue Mermaid* was a small vessel, and true to its name, painted a bright, aquamarine blue, with red trim, and a navy-blue mermaid painted on the hull. It was quirky and comfortable, with a personality of its own, and decades of stories to be told—much like her grandfather.

She stepped aboard and inside the cabin, walking over to the helm, her fingers gently caressing it. She remembered the day Stuart had let her steer for the first time: she was thirteen years old, and he was still fishing with the other men a couple times a week, though just starting to cut back on his time at sea to spend more time on land, managing the market—mostly due to Lizzie, who insisted the stress of doing both full-time at the same time would kill him, and the sea was a dangerous place for an old man to be on. He conceded a bit, though refused to leave it completely at that point. He told her that's where his heart was.

Emily understood that feeling, and had begged him to take her on the boat. He did, on a clear, calm day, while Amelia was busy with her grandmother at the cottage. It was freeing, feeling the ocean breeze and salty spray on her face, not a care in the world as land disappeared from sight behind them, with nothing but shades of blue before them. That day, they didn't talk about magic or spells or source stones. She was just a granddaughter, and he was just a grandfather. In that moment, neither were Guardians: they were simply inhabitants of this great planet, specks of dust in the vast expanse. From that moment on, the ocean had her heart.

"I thought I'd find you here."

Emily turned around to her sister's smiling face. "Done with the idiot?"

"Yeah. For now."

"How much did he offer?"

"Doesn't matter."

"*Amelia.*"

"$2 million."

Emily's jaw dropped. "Jesus."

"I know."

"You know we could do a lot with that kind of cash, right?"

"Yes, I know. But *you* know what we're doing is more important, right?"

Emily sighed. "Yes. I know."

Deciding it was time to change the subject, Amelia said, "So I wanted to get your opinion on paint color for the exterior of the barn, once it's done. I was thinking red?"

Emily shook her head, touching the railing of the blue vessel they were currently standing on. "No. Blue. Red is overdone."

"I like it. Blue Barn Bed and Breakfast. It's catchy."

"And it'll be super photogenic for the magazine, if you decide to write about it." Emily paused. "I miss him."

Amelia knew she meant Stuart. "I do too."

"It's just not the same here without him, you know?"

"Yeah. I know."

Both sisters had officially left their places in their respective cities and moved into the cottage within the past couple weeks, and were each having trouble settling in. Part of it stemmed from the fact they were trying to incorporate their own belongings and tastes into what was already in the cottage, and having trouble figuring out what should stay and what needed to go: this resulted in a mish-mash of items, multiple unpacked boxes, cramped quarters, and a newly-rented storage unit until they figured things out.

The main cause of their unease though was the fact their grandparents were no longer residing in the cottage, and they felt almost like intruders: the place they had once considered a second home was now their primary home, but wasn't the same without Lizzie and Stuart there. Every little change they made, every wall they painted, every piece of furniture they brought in felt invasive, like they were desecrating sacred grounds. They had to remind themselves and each other Lizzie and Stuart would be *pleased* with what they were trying to accomplish, happy they were staying on to protect the creatures so dear to their hearts and continuing with the family traditions, but in the moment, it just didn't feel right.

Amelia broke the silence that had fallen between them. "I'm going to head out to Mom's to pick up Cosmo now. Do you want to come with?"

Emily shook her head. "No, you go. I'll get dinner ready and have it waiting for when you get back."

✳ Chapter 6 ✳

Not today

After a short drive up the road from the cottage, Amelia walked up the front steps to her mother's townhouse. It was a lovely little place, perfect for a single, middle-aged woman living on her own. The small brick path leading up to the red door was lined on either side with an abundance of colorful flowers. The townhouses that flanked hers were the same, making for a visually appealing line of painted brick homes. It was all very quaint.

"Hi, buddy!" Amelia exclaimed as Cosmo bounded toward her when she entered her mother's home.

Cosmo was a good medium-sized dog, about fifty pounds, and at around five years old, he still retained some puppy-like energy. They weren't sure what kind of dog he was, but suspected he was a cross between a boxer and German shepherd, given his size, coloring (brown, with hints of black here and there and a white chest), head shape, pointed ears, and temperament. He was also an incredibly intelligent dog, sometimes too smart for his own good, and was often mischievous.

Four years earlier, Stuart had found him abandoned on the side of the road on his evening walk. About a half-mile in, Cosmo had pranced right up alongside Stuart and followed him. Stuart, having seen a couple of stray dogs in the area before, at first didn't think anything of it, and figured the gaunt little thing would veer off at some point. But he didn't: he followed Stuart for the entire three-mile walk, and Stuart, not having the heart to turn away a dog in need, brought him inside, where he and Lizzie cleaned him up and fed him that night. They took him to the veterinarian the next town over the next day, where he was declared to be in perfect health, aside from being underweight at only twenty-nine pounds and "just in need of a little fattening up." Without a chip or a collar, Stuart and Lizzie put word around Calvary and the surrounding towns a dog had been found. After about two weeks of no one coming forward to claim him, they decided to take him in as their own, and named him Cosmo, because as Stuart declared, "All the cosmos aligned that night to bring him into our family."

Since Lizzie had been placed in the nursing home several months prior, Cosmo had become Stuart's constant companion, keeping the elderly man company as he mourned the void in his life left by his wife no longer living there. The two had been inseparable, and the poor pup, though he loved Rosalie and she him, had been confused the past few weeks by living with her, not understanding why he wasn't home, and why he wasn't with Stuart. Rosalie would often tell her daughters Cosmo would sit by the door, whining, as if he was waiting for Stuart to pick him up and take him home. After some discussion, Amelia and Emily agreed since they would be moving to the cottage, Cosmo needed to be there with them. He might not understand why Stuart wasn't there, but at least he'd be home, in familiar territory. Rosalie also agreed. Though she loved having him around, with the amount of energy Cosmo had, she felt he needed to go back to wide open spaces, not be cooped up in her little townhouse with her tiny yard.

As Amelia was bent down petting the dog, who was so excited to see her his whole body seemed to be wagging, not just his tail, Rosalie came from around the corner, carrying a large bag.

"Hi, Mom." Amelia stood to hug her.

Cosmo also jumped up, trying to get between the two, as if to say, "I'm not done getting *my* pets in yet!"

Amelia and Rosalie laughed, and Rosalie stepped in to hug her daughter, saying, "Hi, sweetheart."

"That all his stuff?" Amelia asked, indicating the bag.

"Mostly—his toys, bowls, treats, and meds are in here. His food's in the garage, bed's still in the living room."

Amelia opened the bag to inspect its contents. Pulling out one of the bags of treats and reading the label, she commented, "Organic, free-range, grain-free treats? Turning him into a posh puppy, are we?"

"That wasn't me. That was your grandfather," Rosalie remarked. "He spoiled this dog rotten. I tried to get him to eat some cheaper treats I got from the pet store, but he was having none of it."

Amelia laughed, putting the treats back in the bag. "Sounds about right."

"How's progress on the barn coming?" Rosalie inquired, changing the subject.

"We're getting there." Amelia paused. "That Dunstan Enterprises guy showed up. Offered to buy the land off us."

"The nerve," Rosalie said through gritted teeth. "Your grandfather hasn't even been in the ground for a month and he's already come creeping around?"

"Yeah."

"If I *ever* meet him face-to-face, I'll have a few words for him, let me tell you!"

"I know, Mom."

"I assume you gave him a piece of your mind?"

"I did."

"Good girl."

Amelia smiled. Even though she was nearly thirty years old, it still felt good to be praised by her mother.

"So, what are you going to do about him?" Rosalie asked casually.

"What do you mean?"

"I mean, how are you going to get him to stop bothering you? Because I'm sure he'll be pretty persistent. He was harassing your grandfather. I'm sure he'll just start over with you and Emily."

"I don't know, Mom, my plan is to pretty much just keep saying 'no' until he eventually gives up and leaves us alone. Maybe take legal action if it gets too be too much, but we'll cross that bridge if we get there."

"You're not going to use anything to your advantage?"

Amelia raised any eyebrow. "Like what?"

"Like…you know."

Amelia did know, all too well. Her mother still had some difficulty saying the word "magic," even after all these years. Rosalie hadn't been born into a line of Guardians, and didn't understand everything being one meant. She had fought Amelia's father when the girls were young about teaching them the old traditions, to a point where she and Emily were only allowed to practice anything at their grandparents' house—but at her parents' home, she could only read, and even then, she was made to feel like what she was trying to learn was wrong.

"Seriously, Mom?" Amelia was irked. The warm, fuzzy feeling she'd had a moment prior when basking in her mother's praise was now gone. "You spent all that time not wanting me to learn about magic or about the creatures, and now you want me to use that against someone?"

"I'm not saying I like it. I'm just saying you have it in your tool bag. If you have an upper hand on something, you should use it to your advantage."

"And what exactly should I do? You know I can't actually *use* magic. Any spell I know, any potion I can produce is useless without it coursing through my veins. What do you expect me to do, sick some fairies on him and drive him off the land?"

"Well…yes. Something like that."

"It doesn't work that way, Mom." Amelia clenched her teeth. "I can't just call them to do my bidding. I can ask them for help when I summon them, but I can't force them into anything that goes against what they're designed to do. And even if I could, doing so would be wrong and taking advantage of them. That goes against what it means to be a Guardian. And if you'd bothered to pay any attention to any of this when we were kids, you'd know that."

Rosalie wouldn't meet her daughter's gaze. "I was trying to protect you and your sister."

"From what? You've been saying that for years, but you still never told us from what! Jesus, Mom, you made me feel stupid as a kid when I came to you telling you I saw fairies, and you said it was a trick of the light—I had to go and find out the truth from Grandpa! How do you think that felt, knowing you'd lied to me, and had *knowingly* made me doubt myself? And you never gave me a reason why. So why, Mom? Why?"

Rosalie shook her head. "I had my reasons. That's all you need to know."

Amelia sighed. She'd heard that response before. "Fine, Mom. We'll keep playing that game. Let me know when you want to have a real conversation about it."

She proceeded to gather Cosmo's bed from the living room and his food from the garage, and loaded her car with his items without saying another word to her mother about the subject. When she re-entered the home to retrieve Cosmo, her mother was sitting at the dining room table, a weary look on her face. Amelia attached a leash to Cosmo's collar, and Cosmo, knowing this meant he was going somewhere, pulled towards the door.

"I'm going now, Mom."

Rosalie didn't respond.

Amelia sighed, and turned back to the front door. Her hand on the knob, she was about to turn it to leave when Rosalie said, "You know all I've ever done is because I love you girls."

Amelia looked over her shoulder. "I know, Mom. But you know someday, you're going to have to explain a few things.

"I know."

Amelia looked her mother up and down. "Today's not that day, is it?"

Rosalie shook her head. "No. Today's not that day."

Amelia sighed again, and turned her attention back to Cosmo, who had gotten himself tangled in the leash while waiting for Amelia to walk him outside. She untangled him and opened the door, walking out with Cosmo prancing along happily at her side.

Inside, Rosalie sat at her table, wiping away the tears forming in the corners of her eyes. Her daughters might be physically closer to her now, but she still felt so far from them.

She was alone once again.

✳ Chapter 7 ✳

A shift

"Hi, Cosmo!" Emily exclaimed as Amelia walked in with the dog, bending to greet him.

Cosmo quickly gave her a lick on the face and allowed a few scratches behind his ears, then turned to the more important task of sniffing out the changes in the cottage. He was home, he knew that much, though it didn't look the same as it had before.

Emily smiled as Cosmo went about his investigation, then turned to Amelia, asking, "How'd it go getting him?"

Amelia shrugged, walking into the dining room, where Emily had dinner ready. She sat on one of the chairs and helped herself to a serving of the food in front of her. "Okay, I guess. Mom and I got into it."

"About what?"

"Same old same old."

Emily knew exactly what Amelia was referring to. While Amelia had the luxury of going off to college and leaving home after their father's death, Emily still had to live in her mother's emotional cage for the next few years—this included her condemnation of all things magical, and insistence upon normality. Emily's only reprieve for those formative teenage years were when she was able to spend her summers with her grandparents along with Amelia.

"Typical." Emily took a bite of her food, rolling her eyes.

"Yeah. I know she means well and loves us, but I just wish she'd give us her reasoning," Amelia sighed. "It's so frustrating."

"Try living with it alone," Emily retorted, a bit disgruntled as a series of teenage memories flashed through her mind.

"I don't know how you did it."

"Mostly just didn't talk about magic. That's all. It was easiest."

"But see, that's the *issue*!" Amelia insisted. "You shouldn't have had to do that!"

"I did what I had to do to keep peace. It was just us alone, except when you came home every once in a while. If I didn't, it would've been pretty terrible. That at least made things tolerable until I was able to get out."

"I'm sorry, Em. Really, I am," Amelia said, genuinely sympathetic.

"It's in the past," Emily replied, brushing off her sister's sympathy. "Now, how long do you think it will take Cosmo to find the new toys we bought him?"

In that very moment, they heard a clatter, followed by a quick short, excited yelp. Peering out the dining room into the hallway, they saw a blur of fur whizz by, happily chasing a squeaky, glowing ball.

✳

That evening, after dinner, Emily headed outside to the garden to gather some items for the next day's meals, Cosmo prancing behind her, while Amelia cleaned in the kitchen. She'd left the window open, letting the lovely aromas of ocean air and perfumed flowers waft in. It was a beautiful evening, the sky bursting with orange, red, pink, and gold hues as the sun set.

66

She washed the dishes, every once in a while looking out the window to enjoy the glorious view. It was in one of these moments she saw Lila perched on the windowsill, smiling at her.

"I was wondering when I'd see you again." Amelia smiled. "Where have you been?"

The fairy made a few frantic gestures, which Amelia translated to mean "all over."

"We've missed you."

Lila indicated she'd missed Amelia as well.

"Did you hear about Grandpa?"

Lila made a few more gestures.

"You were there? You saw it happen?"

Lila nodded sadly.

"Lila…did he suffer?"

Lila shook her head, and made a few more gestures. *No, child. He went peacefully.*

Amelia sighed with relief, glad for this.

"I'm glad you were there with him."

Lila smiled, and motioned she was glad she had been there with him as well. Though Lila would never tell this to Amelia, of all the humans she had known, even in centuries of the Davidson family line, Stuart had been her favorite, the one she considered to be her person. Though she loved Amelia and Emily, without Stuart, things simply were not the same.

67

"What have you been doing since then?" Amelia asked. "His funeral was weeks ago. I thought you'd make an appearance earlier than this."

More gesturing, and this time, Lila pointed out the window. Amelia approached it, and expecting to look out into the growing darkness of the evening, was surprised to see thousands of tiny glimmering lights spread out over the fields: fairies. Specifically, displaced fairies from the neighboring land that had been purchased by Dunstan Enterprises.

Amelia furrowed her brow, disturbed by the sight, her heart aching for the now homeless creatures. There were too many fairies in one place at one time. "Where will you all go?"

Lila pointed north.

"Will you be okay up there?"

The fairy shrugged. Amelia took this particular gesture to mean, "We do what we need to do."

"What about inland?"

The fairy shook her head, and made a motion that meant, "Too crowded by humans."

Amelia sighed. "I understand. You know you're all welcome to stay as long as you need. But so many at once…it's so risky. Eventually you could be noticed, even with the protection spells on you."

Lila indicated she understood this predicament, but appreciated the place to stay for the time being.

"When will you leave?"

The fairy gestured they would be leaving in waves, to scout out and establish a settlement before bringing everyone in—the first wave would be at the end of spring. The second would be at the end of summer, and the final at the end of fall, before the bitter cold winter months, when they would go into hibernation.

"Will you go with them? Or will you stay?"

Lila motioned she would go with her people.

"I thought as much." Amelia smiled sadly. "Still, I had to ask. You've all been here longer than we can remember. It's hard to imagine this land without fairies on it."

Lila nodded her agreement.

"Will you go with the first wave?"

Lila shook her head no—she would go with the third, to stay with the majority of her people until they were given the all clear.

"I suppose we should've seen this coming," Amelia commented, referring to the development happening on the Benedict land.

Yes, but it's more than that, Lila indicated. *We've been feeling something for decades now—magic has shifted. And it's time for us to leave for somewhere safer.*

"It's like something is off," Amelia murmured, echoing her grandfather's sentiments from decades prior.

At this moment, Emily burst into the house with her basket of vegetables, eyes wide. "AMELIA. There are thousands of fairies in the field!" Behind her, Cosmo was running amok through the field of tiny glowing people, chasing after every single fairy in his eyeline. Some had taken to teasing the dog, and were purposely causing him to run in circles—a few were even riding on the dog's back, giggling as he ran about, like it was a great game.

69

"Yes, I know, Lila was just explaining to me they're all migrating north." Amelia motioned towards the fairy on the windowsill.

"Migrating north? Why?" Emily set the basket down.

"They're establishing a new fairy colony. It's getting too crowded here, their land is being disturbed," Amelia explained.

"It's that damn Dunstan Enterprises, isn't it?"

"Yes," Amelia confirmed.

"We need to stop them," Emily said, enraged. "Amelia, we need to figure out how to get them to stop buying up land, and we *can't* let them have ours."

"I know. That's what I've been saying this whole time."

"So, what do we do?"

"I don't know," Amelia replied, uncertainty creeping into her voice. "I just don't know."

✳ Chapter 8 ✳

Settling

The next few weeks went by in the blink of an eye. Amelia and Emily were settling into the cottage, refurnishing and repainting it, making it their own, though at the same time, still struggling to keep the integrity of what their grandparents had done. Progress was being made on the barn renovation every day, and was almost completed. The sisters had been working on marketing, and had already filled a few spots for their opening day. In the meantime, Amelia was still traveling for her job as a journalist, while Emily manned the home front—including managing the constant flow of offers from Jack Garridan on behalf of Dunstan Enterprises. He had become something of a regular visitor on the Davidson property, much to the sisters' chagrin.

On this particular day, Amelia had returned home from her aforementioned trip to France. As she stepped out of her car onto the dusty driveway, she was greeted by a frenzy of activity—the painters were painting the exterior an aquamarine blue, and the sign people were installing a sign at the front of the property with the words "Blue Barn Bed and Breakfast." Emily was sitting on the porch, watching everything unfold, occasionally shouting instructions at passing workers, like, "You missed a spot!" or "No, a little more to the right!" Cosmo, meanwhile, was trailing after the workers, barking at them, as if he too was giving instructions. Amelia smiled, pleased with the initiative her younger sister was taking. This suited her.

Cosmo was the first to see Amelia arriving home, and came running down the driveway, barking merrily. His commotion caused Emily to turn, and when she saw her older sister walking up the driveway, she smiled and waved. Amelia returned the greeting.

"How's the barn coming?" Amelia asked, bag slung over her shoulder as she approached Emily, Cosmo trotting alongside her, demanding to be pet. Amelia complied, dropping her bag and scratching behind the dog's ears while she conversed with her sister. After he decided she had fulfilled his pet and scratch quota, he bounded away to go back to barking at the crew.

"Good," Emily replied, observing the construction site. "We're on track to be done by the end of June. The landscaping and painting are the last pieces. Everything on the inside is done, all the furnishings are in. We should be open before July 4th, just in time for the holiday tourists. How was France?"

"French. I brought back some cheese and wine for you."

"The perks of having a sister who's a travel journalist." Emily smiled. "What's the next adventure?"

"Here," Amelia said. "Right now, I kind of want to stay put for a bit."

"Says the one with the glamorous lifestyle." Emily rolled her eyes.

"Right. Because taking the red-eye from France while sitting next to a man who is clearly in denial about his sleep apnea is glamorous."

"You were in France. I don't want to hear it."

"Fair enough. I'm going to head in, clean up, unpack, and take a nap for a few hours, if you're okay with that. Do you need anything from me before I knock out for a bit?"

"No, you're good. I'm planning on chicken and some vegetables for dinner, it'll be ready by the time you're up."

"You are the perfect little bed and breakfast hostess," Amelia said with a grin.

"Yeah, yeah." Emily again rolled her eyes, but this time with a small smile on her face. "By the way, Mom came by a few times—she has opinions about the paint color."

Amelia sighed. "I knew this would happen."

"But you took her money anyway."

"Hey, so did you."

"Yeah, yeah." Emily waved her hand dismissively. "Also, our friendly neighborhood Dunstan Enterprises representative came by to visit while you were gone."

"Oh yeah?" Amelia raised an eyebrow, her smile disappearing.

"Yeah. Seven times."

"*Seven times?!*" Amelia exclaimed, aghast. This was escalating to the harassment level.

"Yeah. I'm starting to think Grandpa dropped dead on purpose just to get away from him."

Amelia shook her head in disbelief, saying, "What the *hell* is wrong with him? Did he *not* see the construction we were doing? You'd think that'd be a tip-off we're not interested in selling."

"You'd think. But no. He offered to cover the full cost of the construction, on top of the $2 million and rehousing deal he already offered. I'm not going to lie, his offer is becoming tempting...more to get rid of him than anything else."

"That was probably everyone else's reason," Amelia commented wryly. "I appreciate you not giving into the temptation."

"Of course. The next few times he comes around though, it's *your* turn to deal with him."

"Got it."

✳

Around the same time Amelia was returning home and conversing with Emily, Jack found himself having his own conversation about the Davidson property with his boss, Adrien Dunstan. That day, Jack had been called into Adrien's office in reference to the property acquisition in Calvary. Though Jack was pleased with much of the progress that had been made, he somehow had a feeling Adrien would not feel as such.

Adrien Dunstan was not what one might call an imposing man physically. Probably around forty years old, he was gaunt and pale, and slightly below average height. He had a pointed nose, and chin to match. The only features striking about him were his jet-black hair and his ice-blue eyes, which seemed to be able to pierce the souls of those who he encountered with a simple glance. He frequently wore expensive tailored suits that were almost as dark as his hair. In terms of physical stature, he was far from Jack's equal. Jack imagined he was the kind who was picked on for his diminutive frame in school as a young man, and who compensated for that in adulthood with his wealth and cutting, almost heartless business strategies. Jack had to admit, it worked. The man was a millionaire several times over, having appeared seemingly out of nowhere to within the past two decades, rising in ranks and becoming one of the most well-known property developers and investors in the Northeast.

Adrien's office, which Jack currently found himself standing in, reflected his wealth: it was minimalist and uncluttered, with large, floor-to-ceiling windows looking out over the city of Boston. The few objects in the office were extravagant: an oversized, custom-made mahogany desk, a large, leather chair, with two smaller, leather seats in front of it.

74

On the wall without windows, an exact replica of Rene Magritte's Son of Man hung—Adrien would often say he was in the process of acquiring the original, currently in negotiations with the owner. In the meantime, he'd collected an original Picasso, which hung next to the Magritte replica, and in the corner of the room, he had a to-scale prototype statue of The Republic by Daniel Chester French, which French had worked off over a century prior to design the final statue for the World's Columbian Exposition in Chicago.

"Any update on the Davidson property, Jack?" Adrien took a seat behind his desk, and motioned for Jack to sit as well.

"None yet—but the Benedicts officially moved out a few weeks ago, and development on their plot is underway," Jack answered. "The Ericksons have given verbal agreement to sell, we're in the beginning stages of drawing up their contract, but I anticipate that will go smoothly. And we're working on some revised paperwork for the Kowalski property—Ruth Kowalski wants a few adjustments on the contract before she signs. So, we're making some excellent progress."

"I didn't ask about the Benedicts or Kowalskis or Ericksons," Adrien commented simply with a heavy sigh. "I asked about the Davidson property."

Jack sat silently for a moment to collect his thoughts, baffled by his boss's obsession with this particular piece of land and irritated at his indifference with the progress made with the other families.

"Well, no. The Davidsons still refuse to sell. But I'm working on it. And we have enough to at least begin working on the development."

"Yes, Jack, but what's the point in beginning something if you can't finish it?" Adrien asked coolly.

"Sir, I understand your frustration, but with all due respect, we've acquired fifty acres of land from the Benedicts alone. Once the Kowalski and Erickson properties go through, we'll have over a hundred acres. We have plenty to work with for the time being. The Davidson property won't even have much being built on it if acquired."

"*If* acquired? What are you saying, Jack?" Adrien leaned forward in his seat and looked at his employee intently. "Are you saying you're giving up? Not pushing as hard as you should?"

"Not at all, sir—but what I am saying is the Davidson sisters are stubborn," Jack said defensively. "They're not going to give up their land without a fight. They've blown off every offer I've made."

"Jack, you're the best. That's why I sent you in. I have to say, I'm awfully disappointed right now. I thought you'd be able to handle a couple of girls, but I guess I was wrong."

Jack was seething at this point. "Sir, I'm telling you, even with my expertise, they're tough. These two are a force to be reckoned with."

"And you're saying Dunstan Enterprises isn't?"

"I'm saying they'll take longer than usual."

"We've already been working that property for several months, Jack. How much longer can you possibly need?"

"With all due respect, I wasn't even *on* the case for the first few months. Gallagher was," Jack pointed out, referring to the man that had been on the case previously. "And when Stuart Davidson died, I had to start from scratch with his granddaughters. They're younger, they're building on the property, and they have plans. They're not going to be as easy to sway."

"You never should have let them get as far as building!" Adrien snapped. "Do you have any idea how much more difficult it will be to get it out from under them now?"

"I'm aware, sir," Jack said curtly. "I don't like it any more than you do."

76

"I don't think you fully understand just how *much* I dislike this," Adrien retorted. "I fired one employee for not getting the job done, what makes you think I won't get rid of another?"

Jack was stunned speechless. It took all his strength to keep from hitting Adrien in the face. But he didn't let his emotions show. He knew better.

Calmly, he said, "Sir, I'm sorry you're disappointed. Give me six more months to work them. If, in six months, the Davidsons haven't signed over their property to us, fire me. But I need *time*. I need to earn their trust. I need to sway them to see our side. They're smart women. They don't give up easily. This one is going to take a bit more finesse than our usual tactics."

Adrien slumped back in his seat, his arms crossed in front of his chest. "Fine. Six months. It'll take about that long to find and train someone to replace you anyway."

Jack winced at this comment, but kept his mouth shut.

"And you have permission to go as high has $5 million if needed," Adrien continued. "But if we don't have the Davidson property under contract six months from today, you are *gone*, Garridan. And you'll be lucky if you can ever find work again."

Jack nodded stiffly. "I understand. Thank you, sir. I appreciate the opportunity."

He rose to leave the office, but stopped when Adrien said, "I mean it, Jack. Six months. Or that's it for you."

Jack nodded once more, then walked out of the office, closing the door behind him. He needed to go home and pack an overnight bag—he'd be returning to Calvary the next day. His job depended on it.

✳

The next morning, Amelia woke up incredibly early, jet lagged. After tossing and turning for about an hour, she gave up on trying to go back to sleep, and instead wandered to the living room, where she went about sorting through some of her grandparents' boxes, something she'd been procrastinating on since she and Emily had moved into the house. Cosmo, who was sleeping in the living room on the couch, groggily opened his eyes for a moment to glare at her as she turned on the light, displeased with having his sleep interrupted. He gave a small *ruff*, then buried his head under a pillow.

"Sorry, buddy," Amelia whispered.

It didn't matter though. Within a few minutes, she heard snoring coming from under the pillow. Amelia went about her task of sorting.

After about an hour, and one large *thump!* as she accidentally dropped a stack of books, she looked up to see a groggy Emily standing in the entryway of the living room, glaring at her.

"It's five in the morning."

"Sorry, did I wake you?" Amelia asked, still going about her business of sorting.

"*What* are you doing at five in the morning that can't wait until a more reasonable hour?"

"Going through these boxes we've been putting off going through. I couldn't sleep. My body's still on France time."

Emily grunted, wandering into the kitchen to brew coffee. She returned a few minutes later with two cups in hand, one of which she placed on the end table next to where Amelia was working. Cosmo, by this point, had woken back up, and annoyed with his masters, had wandered into the study where it was quieter and darker to continue sleeping.

78

"Thanks." Amelia took a sip and continued with her sorting.

Emily sat in the overstuffed chair and deeply inhaled the aroma from her own cup, watching her sister work.

"Find anything interesting?" she asked after a few minutes of silence and a few swigs of coffee.

"Mostly nick knacks and random stuff. A few books that might look interesting, but that's about it so far. I've put everything in two piles: keep and giveaway. Take a look at the giveaway pile, let me know if you're good with it, or if there's anything you think should go in the keep pile."

"I trust you." Emily took another sip of her coffee. She paused, then hesitantly, said, "So, since you're here, I've been meaning to talk to you about something."

"Shoot," Amelia said, still rifling through the boxes.

"What are you going to do about the magazine? Because I'm going to be honest, I can't be left to take care of the Blue Barn by myself while you wander around the world. That wasn't the deal."

Amelia stopped and looked up from her work. She knew this conversation would be coming sooner or later.

"I know it wasn't. And I understand. That's not fair to you."

"So, what are you going to do?"

"Well, I've been doing some thinking about it, and I've talked to my bosses about it. Instead of doing monthly trips like they've been having me do, they've agreed to let me do every other month. I'll be able to spend the majority of my time here. And when I'm in town, I'll be submitting columns about travel tips and tricks, and writing about things to do in the area—kind of talking up our little part of the world."

"Really?" Emily was dumbfounded. She hadn't expected her sister to already have a solution.

"Well, *yeah*," Amelia said with a smile. "Anyway, my contract lasts through the end of the year. After that, we'll reassess. If the Blue Barn is doing well and we're seeing an income, I'm going to drop the magazine and stay on here full-time. If it's not, well, I might have to up the traveling again next year to bring in some money for us. But we'll cross that bridge if we get there."

Emily nodded, relieved. "Okay. Sounds good."

"What about you? Any side hustles in the works to help bring in some cash until the bed and breakfast starts making a profit?"

"Yeah, actually," Emily said slowly. "I was thinking we could rent out Grandpa's boat for charter fishing. I mean, we might not have many people at first, but as we get the word out, I'm sure there will be a few city people who will want to get away to the coast on some kind of weekend warrior sea voyage thing."

"I like it! Do it!" Amelia exclaimed.

"You think so?"

"Absolutely! I think that's a great idea. We've got the boat, may as well use it."

"Oh, good...I was hoping you'd like it. I've already started getting the permits and licenses together for it. We should be up and running within the next few weeks, around the same time the Blue Barn opens."

"Well, look at you go! Aren't you the perfect little entrepreneur?"

Emily grinned. "I try."

"You succeed. You're doing a great job, Emily. I'm proud of you. And I really do appreciate all you do. I couldn't do this without you."

"Thanks," Emily replied, her grin widening.

✳ Chapter 9 ✳

Bad falafel

That afternoon, while Emily was in town working on the necessary paperwork to get the boat properly licensed for charter fishing, Amelia was outside doing some pruning and gardening, picking a few items for her and Emily to cook with their dinner that night. Cosmo was in the garden with her, nibbling on the petals of some of the flowers. As she went about trimming back a few of the bushes, she heard the distinct sound of a car pulling up the driveway. Cosmo stopped nibbling and started barking, racing around to the front yard. Amelia sighed and set down the shears and pulled off her gloves and hat, knowing full well who was coming around.

As she walked toward the front of the house, her suspicions were confirmed. Jack Garridan was stepping out of his car, that same briefcase in hand containing paperwork he wanted her to sign. Cosmo was jumping at him, barking like a madman. She noted Jack had given up on looking impressive, dressed in just jeans and a polo instead of a suit and tie this time. She smiled to herself—the casual attire indicated to her he was feeling defeated. She and Emily were winning.

"The answer's still no, Mr. Garridan," she said as he approached her, cutting straight to the point. "Cosmo, sit!"

In an instant, the dog sat still, ceasing his jumping, though still eyeing the intruder warily.

"Thank you," Jack breathed, relieved the dog had ceased for the moment. Regaining his composure, he commented, "I thought you were in France."

"And I thought you got the hint after Emily turned you down *seven times*. Seriously, what the hell is wrong with you? Who even does that?"

"Just doing my job, Miss Davidson," Jack said. "And what's wrong with *you*? Who turns down two million dollars, a new house, and the cost of whatever you're spending on construction?"

Amelia crossed her arms. "What I do with my life is none of your business, Mr. Garridan. You and I both know I'm not going to give in, and I know you don't have a leg to stand on. You're not getting any 'necessary permissions' to claim my house, I already looked into that a few weeks ago after that little threat you made."

"How did you—"

"I'm a journalist, Mr. Garridan," Amelia interrupted him. "I research. It's what I do. Your company can't do anything but just keep bothering me, and frankly, you've taken it to such a level that if you *ever* stop by again, we *will* be filing a restraining order against you. Enough is enough. I'm not signing anything. Nor is my sister. The only way you will get this land is over our cold, dead bodies. Now, if you'll excuse me, I have some gardening to do. *Goodbye.*"

"We're willing to up the offer," he persisted.

"And I'm willing to turn it down."

"Three million."

"No."

"Three and a half?"

"Go away."

With this, she turned on her heel and went back around the house to continue working in the garden, Cosmo trailing behind her. Jack, momentarily dazed, whispered a few obscenities about the Davidson family to himself, then headed down the driveway to his car to regroup.

He climbed in, slamming the door behind him. "That obnoxious woman," he murmured. But at the same time, he felt somewhat guilty; after all, he was trying to convince a woman to leave a home that had been in her family for generations. He'd have to try a gentler approach, especially if he wanted to keep his job. The six-month deal he'd made with Adrien was weighing on him.

He sighed, and turned the ignition to drive off.

Nothing.

He toggled the key a bit.

Still nothing.

"Damn it."

He popped his hood and got out of his car to see what was going on. As he peered into the machine, checking the oil and fluids, it started smoking. He jumped back, coughing.

Waving at the smoke pouring from his car, he regretted not yet investing in a roadside assistance plan. He'd have to look up the nearest tow truck and mechanic shop in the area, and would probably have to spend an arm and a leg to have it taken care of—this was beyond his capabilities, and didn't make sense to him.

He pulled his cell phone out of his back pocket to do a quick search for a truck and a mechanic. Except as he did this, there was one minor issue:

when he went to dial, the screen went blank—his battery was dead, and he'd left his charger at home.

"You have *got* to be kidding me," he muttered to himself.

At this point, he looked up at the cottage he had just stormed away from, and groaned, knowing what he had to do. Reluctantly, he walked up the path leading to the garden behind the house, where Amelia was working. Seeing Jack approach, she commented coldly, "I told you to leave."

"I'm trying. My car is dead."

"So call a tow truck."

"My phone's dead too. Can I use yours?"

She looked him up and down, and grudgingly agreed, "Fine."

She opened the back door to the cottage, and without saying another word to him, pointed toward the landline on the wall in the kitchen.

"Thank you. Do you know the number of the closest mechanic?"

She sighed, and pulled out a phone book from one of the cabinets, slamming it on the counter in front of him.

He winced. "Really? A phone book? You couldn't just look it up on your own cell phone?"

"Doing that would imply I actually give a crap about you. Which I don't. So, no. Figure it out yourself, then get out of my house." With this, she stormed out the back door to continue with the gardening he had interrupted.

He rolled his eyes, and turned his attention toward the phone book. The listing for mechanics and tow trucks in Calvary was slim—only two. He dialed the first one, only to get a message stating that number had been disconnected. Dialing the second, he crossed his fingers as it rang. A moment later, a gruff voice answered, "Yeah?"

"I—yes, is this Dave's Auto?"

"Yeah," the voice responded suspiciously.

"Yes, my car broke down at 1307 Calvary Road. I need a tow truck."

"We're closed."

"But—but you just answered your phone," Jack argued.

"Doesn't mean we're open. I'm heading out on another job right now that's going to take all night."

"Well, when *do* you open?"

"Tomorrow morning at eight. You said 1307 Calvary?"

"Yes."

"You a friend of Amelia's or something?"

"Or something," Jack muttered.

"Well, your car will be safe with her until I can get to you in the morning. Think you can hold out until then?"

"Well, I guess I'm going to have to. Where am I supposed to stay in the meantime?"

The voice on the other end laughed. "You know you're stranded at a bed and breakfast, right? I'm sure you'll figure it out." With this, a *click* as he hung up.

Jack cringed, knowing the conversation he was about to have with Amelia would be an unpleasant one. He was already unwelcome in her home, but it appeared he was out of options for the moment and about to be an overnight guest. He made a mental note to himself to *definitely* invest in roadside assistance when this was all said and done.

Slowly, he shuffled out to the garden, hands stuffed into his pockets as he approached her. She was on the ground, clipping herbs to use for dinner that night, Cosmo sunning himself beside her. She was wearing a large, floppy gardening hat to protect her fair skin, and at first did not even notice him approach her because of this. It was when Cosmo gave a low *woof* and she saw Jack's shadow in the corner of her eye that she jumped.

"What?" she demanded, standing to look him in the eye. "What do you want *now*?"

"They can't tow my car to the shop until tomorrow morning."

"Not my problem." She picked up her basket of herbs and tomatoes and walked back towards the house.

"I need a place to stay for the night," he explained, following her.

"So, get a cab and stay at one of the other inns in town."

"I don't want to leave my car behind and inconvenience you with having to watch it."

She whirled around to face him. "You don't want to *inconvenience* me? Are you *kidding* me right now? And you staying here is less of an inconvenience?"

"Listen, I can pay you for the night. I know you have a business to run."

She glared at him, processing this for a moment. "Fine. It's $250 for the night."

"Your website says your prices start at $150," he argued, having done his research on the bed and breakfast since they launched their website a few weeks prior.

"Call it an inconvenience fee for a last-minute booking," she retorted. "Besides, *you're* the one who said I wouldn't be breaking even for at least five years. I clearly need to work on making up that difference."

"Fine, $250 for the night," he sighed, pulling out his wallet to examine its contents. "I'm low on cash. Do you take credit cards?"

"It's a $20 processing fee."

"*Fine.*"

He followed her into the mostly-painted renovated barn, where she went to her computer in the foyer to check him in and process his card, Cosmo trailing behind the pair to keep an eye on them. "Breakfast is obviously included in the cost, but will you be wanting dinner tonight?"

"I mean—yeah, I have no way of getting to any other restaurant in town right now."

"That'll be an additional $75."

"...I'll have a pizza delivered."

"We don't have a pizza delivery in town."

"Chinese?"

She shook her head.

"Okay, what *does* deliver around here?"

"There's an Armenian falafel place down the road from here."

He blinked. "Seriously? You have an Armenian falafel delivery place around here, but *not* a pizza delivery or Chinese delivery?"

"That's right."

"Then I guess I'm eating Armenian tonight," he resigned. "Are they any good?"

"Eh."

"Eh?" he asked, eyebrow raised. "What does 'eh' mean?"

"I mean, it depends on who's cooking tonight. If the owner, Saul, is cooking, you're good. If it's his son, Derek, you might have an issue."

"I'll risk it."

"Suit yourself."

She collected the rest of his information, and once done, showed him to his room. He had to admit, the sisters had done well on the place. Everything was bright and airy, and meticulously painted with a simple, beachy palate of white, light gray, seafoam, and sand colors. The decorations were also simple, with coastal photographs and paintings throughout, bronze fixtures, and minimalist furniture with clean lines. It was warm and welcoming in a bright, modern sort of way.

As they walked down the hall, he caught a glimpse of one of the guest rooms—it was large and spacious and bright, with a big, beautiful bay window looking out over the cliffs to the ocean, and a king-sized bed that seemed to be beckoning him.

"That's not your room," Amelia commented, noticing his pause at that particular door. "*This* is your room."

Opening the door to the room she indicated, Jack looked around—it was tastefully decorated in the same beach cottage sort of style, but it was tight, clearly built for someone much smaller than him. Instead of a king bed, there was a twin—and not even an extra-long twin, so his feet would be hanging over the edge as he attempted to sleep that night. In place of the large bay window, there was a small portal window which barely let in any light and overlooked the front yard, not the ocean. He glanced into the bathroom—a small, pocket shower (which he had some serious concerns about being able to turn around in), pedestal sink, and toilet. All tastefully done, and he imagined perhaps comfortable for someone of shorter stature, but all small for a man of 6'4.

"Why can't I have that other room?" he asked, nodding in its direction.

"You can, if you'd like to upgrade for an additional $200," she responded with a smile. "This is our most economic room, created specifically for the solo, short-stay traveler—the clientele booked for this room when we open consists mostly of single women on soul-searching trips."

"I can see that." He picked up a doily from the nightstand, examined it, then set it down. "This will be fine."

"The Wi-Fi password, TV channel guide, and list of local restaurants and menus are all in the binder next to the TV. Fresh towels are in the bathroom. Can I get you anything else?"

"No, I'm fine."

"Then I'll leave you to it. Have a good evening." With this, she turned and slammed the door behind her, Cosmo trotting beside her, heading back toward the beach cottage to cook dinner for herself and for Emily, who would be arriving home from town shortly.

Yes, Jack would *definitely* be getting roadside assistance for his car when he returned home the next day. This was ridiculous.

✳

About an hour later, Jack found himself face to face with a pudgy, hairy man delivering a bag of slightly suspicious smelling food. As Jack accepted the bag and sifted through his wallet for a few dollar bills, he asked the delivery man, "Who was cooking tonight?"

The man raised an eyebrow. "I was."

Jack glanced briefly at the delivery man's badge to read the name *Derek* printed across it. Internally, he groaned, remembering Amelia's warning.

"And I'm sure it will be delicious." Jack forced a friendly smile as he handed Derek the cash. Derek looked Jack up and down suspiciously, swiped the money from Jack's hand, grunted, then turned back to his car.

Jack retreated to his room, where he opened the bag of food. The smell, it seemed, grew even worse when he opened the container. Jack normally enjoyed falafel, but this just looked unappetizing. He worked up the courage to take a bite, and regretted this decision immediately, gagging and spitting the food out into a napkin.

He glanced out the window, where he could see the cottage. Inside, he saw a light on in the kitchen, and Amelia and Emily each working on cooking their respective dishes. He could see the sisters engaged in conversation as they worked, Emily doing most of the talking. Whatever was being cooked in their house, it *had* to be better than what he had just wasted his money on.

✳

As Emily and Amelia sat down to dinner, they heard a knock on their door. Cosmo, upon hearing the knock, ran to the door, barking like crazy. The sisters looked up from their meal, and glanced at each other briefly.

"I'll get it," Emily volunteered.

Pulling Cosmo away from the entrance, she opened the door to find Jack standing there, a sheepish look on his face. "Can I help you?" she asked, crossing her arms.

"Derek was cooking," he stated simply.

Inquisitively, Emily turned around to look at Amelia, who nodded. "Let him in."

"Thank you." He stepped inside and took off his jacket. Emily closed the door behind him, bewildered.

"There's some fish, mashed potatoes, and salad on the kitchen counter," Amelia instructed. "Plates are in the cabinet to the right of the microwave. We have tap water, or there's some wine in the fridge."

"Wine sounds good. How much extra?"

"No charge."

He paused, and turned to meet her gaze. "Really?"

"Not for the wine. Dinner's still $75. I'll put it on your tab when you check out." She grinned, taking a bite of her own meal. "Wine glasses are in the cabinet next to the plates."

"Thank you," he grunted, heading toward the kitchen to prepare his plate. Cosmo followed, keeping a watchful eye on the strange man.

When he had disappeared from sight, Emily turned to Amelia and hissed, "What is going on?!"

"We have our first guest at the bed and breakfast," Amelia said nonchalantly.

"Yeah, I can see that, but *him*? Why didn't you tell me sooner?"

"I was going to, but you were so busy telling me all about the different things we needed to do to get the charter boat up and running, I didn't want to interrupt you and lose your train of thought. His car broke down. Dave can't come out until morning."

"Damn it, Dave," Emily muttered. "He couldn't get a room at one of the other places in town?"

"He was pretty insistent he stay here. He didn't want to 'inconvenience' us with watching after his car until morning."

"You're kidding, right?"

"Nope."

"You know he's probably spying on us or something? Trying to figure out our weaknesses to use against us?"

"Of *course* I know that."

"Then why let him stay here?"

"Keep your friends close, and your enemies closer."

Emily sat back in her chair, bewildered. "I don't get you."

"You don't have to."

"Do you really think his car broke down? Or do you think it's some kind of ploy?"

"It really broke down. I saw the thing smoking myself. What I can't figure out is *how*. It looks like a newer car. Doesn't make much sense to me."

"Me neither," Jack's voice came from behind the sisters. They jumped, startled. He was standing there with a plate of food and glass of wine in hand. Cosmo stood beside him, tail wagging: Jack had clearly fed him some human food in the kitchen, and Cosmo decided they were now best friends because of this. "If it means anything—and I'm sure it doesn't to you—but I promise, I didn't hijack my own car. I paid good money for that thing. And I'm not here to spy on you—that's above my pay grade."

"Why do you keep harassing us?" Emily demanded.

Jack sat, and took a sip of wine, relaxing after the day's ordeal. Cosmo sat beside him, putting his head in his lap, silently begging for more food. Jack, however, ignored the dog for the moment. "Believe it or not, I'm trying to help you."

"Help us? By taking our family home from us?"

"Listen, I don't make the call on that—it's not my job to figure out where these communities will be built. It's my job to inform the current residents they *will* be built. I'm just the messenger. I'm trying to help you by offering to buy the land. If you agree, you won't have to work for the rest of your life. You'll be set up. You'll have a place to live, and cash to burn. *That* is how I'm trying to help you."

"We've already made our decision," Amelia retorted. "*No.*"

"What is this place to you anyway?" he asked as he cut into the fish. "Besides the obvious sentimental value, the fact your family has been here for generations, all that."

"Isn't that enough?" Emily asked.

"No. Because generally, when faced with the opportunity for millions of dollars and a home completely paid for, people tend to go for it. I see it all the time. What I don't understand is why you're fighting so hard against it."

"Because it's worth fighting for," Amelia insisted. "It's a way of life. It's a promise we made to protect the land and all the creatures that inhabit it."

Jack raised an eyebrow as he took a bite of mashed potatoes. "Pretty sure the bunnies and butterflies will find a new place to live."

In this moment, as soon as he said this, Jack saw something out the window—just a flash of a tiny light, but before he could get a good look at it, it was gone.

"Are you okay?" Amelia asked, noticing Jack notice the light. She knew what it was, but she was surprised to see him see it. She turned to Emily, who had also seen it, and saw Jack see it—her eyes were wide with disbelief.

"Yeah, I just—I saw something out the window." Jack shook his head. "Must've been a firefly or something. Sorry, what was I saying?"

"Bunnies and butterflies," Emily reminded him, looking at him uncertainly.

"Right, anyway, like I said, I'm pretty sure they'll find a new place to live, if that's what you're worried about."

"No, that's not what we're worried about." Amelia hesitated and turned to Emily. The sisters exchanged a knowing glance. Having seen the light out the window, and having seen Jack see the light, they knew it was time to broach the topic with him.

Jack saw this, and looking back and forth between the two women, asked, "What? What is it you're worried about?"

Emily took a sip of her own glass of wine, and to her older sister, commented, "Go ahead. He's not going to believe you anyway."

"Believe *what*?" Jack asked.

95

"In magic."

This caught Jack off guard. "I'm sorry, what?"

"Do you believe in magic?"

He raised an eyebrow. "What do you mean by magic?"

"Like…regular magic. Fairies. Mermaids. Unicorns. Sorcerers, magic spells, that sort of thing."

He looked at the glass of wine in his hands, and slowly put it down and pushed it and the plate of food away, as if each contained some kind of hallucinogenic drug that might poison his mind. "I…I should head back to my room." He stood, grabbing his jacket from the back of the chair.

"You didn't say no."

He paused and met Amelia's gaze. "I'm sorry?"

"You didn't say no, you don't believe in magic."

With resolve, he said coolly, "No, I don't believe in magic."

A small, wry smile crossed her face, and she took a sip of her own wine. "Liar."

"Thank you very much for the dinner—it was delicious," he said quickly. "I'll expect the bill in the morning."

As he hurried out the door, slamming it behind him, Emily turned and smiled at her sister. "Told you he wouldn't believe you."

"They never do," Amelia replied absently, looking at Cosmo, who was whining sadly at the door, distressed his newfound friend hadn't fed him more human food.

But still, they saw him see that fairy light. And that had to mean something.

All of a sudden, the sisters were filled with hope.

✳ Chapter 10 ✳

Something in the wine

Jack had trouble sleeping that night, a combination of the bed being too small for him to lie comfortably, and the fact he was convinced his hostesses were either crazy, or playing some kind of prank on him. Either way, for whatever reason, the mention of magic stirred something in him he found to be rather uncomfortable.

After tossing and turning for a few hours, he decided a walk would help settle his mind. Throwing on his jacket, he wandered outside. The evening air was crisp and cool, and the full moon hung low in the sky, lighting his way. Looking up, the sky was so clear he could see the Milky Way galaxy with all its clouds of stars. All at once, he felt so incredibly small in the midst of something so vast—yet at the same time, he felt at peace, as though he belonged, as if he was in complete harmony with the universe around him. He took a deep breath, catching a whiff of the salty ocean breeze. He walked in the direction of the cliffs to catch sight of the moon reflecting off the inky blue waters. He stood in the midst of the tall grass under the willow tree on the property's edge, pulling his jacket a little tighter around him as a gust of cool air hit him.

He stared out over the sea, not sure where the water ended and the sky began—it was all hues of deep navy, and twinkling lights from the sky reflecting onto the sea. He caught a glimpse of a shooting star, and smiled—as a child, one of the foster parents he'd lived with taught him to make a wish whenever he saw one. His wish tonight was the same as it always was: for clarity, peace of mind, and magic. For as long as he could remember, something always felt off, as though he wasn't living the life he was meant to live. The problem was, he didn't know what the life he was supposed to live looked like. The best way he could describe it was magic—he needed magic in his life. That word, *magic*, was the word that always sprung to mind when he examined himself and what he wanted. He assumed it was magic in the symbolic sense—the magic of love, or of a charmed life. Never in the literal sense.

But when Amelia spoke of actual, literal magic, of fairies and other magical creatures, it made sense—and that was what troubled him. Why was it something so ludicrous as fairies seemed commonplace to him? That was why he walked away from the conversation. Intellectually, he knew they couldn't exist—which meant the sisters were either messing with his head, meaning he shouldn't trust them...or they were insane, meaning if he agreed with them, he was insane as well, or feeding their insanity.

He watched another shooting star fall from the sky. Except there was something different about this one. It didn't disappear, or continue on in a straight line, but instead, seemed to fly *towards* him. As the light came closer, he faltered back a step, tripping over the root of the willow tree.

In that same moment, something pummeled into him, knocking him off his feet. He laid on his back in the dirt, groaning and holding his head.

"What on Earth....?"

He looked up, seeing the night sky full of its twinkling lights, the branches of the willow...and one glowing, person-shaped light in the foreground, perched on the tip of his nose. As his eyes focused, he could make out the shape of a tiny woman with golden wings, vibrant red hair, and a dress that appeared to be made out of purple flower petals. He blinked, and she stepped off his nose and hovered above him, looking him over. A smile crossed her tiny face.

Suddenly, he heard a voice behind him say, "I see you've met Lila."

He sat up and turned around. Amelia was standing there, wrapped in a robe. "I couldn't sleep either," she explained. "I like to go for walks out here too."

Lila fluttered over to Amelia and sat on her shoulder, still smiling that mischievous fairy smile.

"Am I hallucinating?" Jack asked. "I am, aren't I? There was something in that wine."

"Nothing in the wine," Amelia replied calmly. "You're not hallucinating."

"Dreaming, then. I'm asleep right now."

With this, Lila left Amelia's shoulder, picked up a small pebble from the ground, flew over to Jack, and dropped it on his head.

"OW!" he yelped as Lila took her place back on Amelia's shoulder. He glared at the little fairy, who stuck her tongue out at him.

Amelia laughed. "No, you're not dreaming either."

"But there's a fairy on your shoulder."

"Yes, there is."

"*Why is there a fairy on your shoulder?*"

"That's a long story. Come inside. I'll make you tea and tell you all about it."

She turned back towards the house and walked. Jack, at a loss for words and not knowing what else to do, followed her.

When they entered the home, Amelia went straight into the kitchen to prepare the promised cup of tea. Lila took her place on a small pillow next to one of the windows in the living room, one of which was cracked slightly. Jack, in a daze, sat in the armchair opposite the fairy, where he continued to stare at her in disbelief. Cosmo, who had been fast asleep on his bed in the corner, looked up momentarily at the two, then sleepily rolled over, snoring again within seconds.

"How do you like your tea?" Amelia called out from the kitchen.

"What?" He shook his head, snapping out of his thoughts momentarily.

"How do you like your tea?"

"Just a teaspoon of honey," Jack responded, his gaze remaining fixed on the fairy.

A few minutes later, Amelia emerged with a tray, which contained two teacups and saucers, and one thimble. She handed one of the teacups to Jack, and the thimble to Lila, who smiled, nodded appreciatively, and began sipping on it right away. Jack, mesmerized, simply sat, unmoving.

"You know your tea will go cold if you don't drink it," Amelia commented with a small smile, sipping on her own.

Robotically, Jack lifted the cup to his lips, his stare still not breaking from the fairy opposite him. Finally, after a few moments of silence, the three of them sipping their tea, Jack stated, "There's a fairy by the window."

"Yes, there is," Amelia agreed nonchalantly, as if she was simply agreeing to the fact the sky is blue or grass is green.

"Why is there a fairy by the window?"

"Because she's a friend. She likes to visit us sometimes."

"No, but, I mean, *why is there a fairy here*? How is this possible? Where did she come from?"

"Well, that's a bit of a longer story," Amelia answered, setting her cup and saucer on the end table next to her. "Jack, is this definitely your first time ever seeing a magical creature?"

"Umm, *yes*."

"Are you *sure*?"

"Yeah, pretty sure I'd remember a fairy hitting me upside the head before now."

"It's just…well, it's unusual, you see," Amelia tried to explain. "We usually see them our whole lives, starting in infancy. I've never heard of someone seeing one for the first time as an adult."

"We? Who's 'we?' What are you talking about?"

"Guardians. That's what we are."

"What the hell is a Guardian?"

"We're protectors of magical creatures. Long story short, there used to be magic in the world. Magical creatures were created by a being we call the Creator Sorcerer. He gave a few humans magic to help protect his creatures from those who might wish them harm. One of the humans used his magic for evil to try and gain immortality. In turn, he was punished, and all other Guardians were stripped of their magic to prevent it from happening again. But we can still see the creatures and interact with them, and try to protect them as best we can. As for magic itself, it was hidden so it couldn't be abused again."

Jack's eyes darting back and forth between Amelia and Lila as he tried to comprehend all this. "So, what, you're a witch?"

"Witch, sorceress, whatever. We've been called a lot over the years," Amelia replied with a shrug. "And not really, I can't use magic. So just Guardian for now."

"So…fairy tales are real."

"Yes and no. The creatures are real. Some of the stories are probably real. Some are exaggerations of the truth, but do have some basis in fact. For instance, the Little Mermaid isn't true. Mermaids tend to keep to themselves, and aren't attracted to human men at all. They think humans are more of a novelty, and occasionally a tasty dinner if they're desperate, but they'd never fall in love with one."

Jack blinked. "A tasty dinner?"

"Yes. So that's clearly not true," Amelia remarked, continuing her story unfazed. "Beauty and the Beast, on the other hand, based on a true story. Some poor aristocratic schmuck in France really did piss off a Guardian a few centuries ago. Apparently, he'd built his castle on the same forest land where some fairies she'd been protecting lived. So, she turned him into a beast as punishment."

"And he really did fall in love with a girl who loved him back and broke the spell?"

"Well…that part is a bit romanticized. That was the curse he was placed under. And he really did try to find a girl to fall in love with, who would love him back. But then his animal instincts got the best of him and…well, yeah, it didn't end well." She paused. "Magic can be messy sometimes."

"Clearly," Jack rasped, taking a gulp of his tea. "So how did fairies end up here?"

"They were here before we were," Amelia explained. "My family came here as Guardians centuries ago. Some of the neighboring families were also Guardians, but most of the people who knew the stories and their purpose died out or moved away. As far as we know, we're the only ones left in the area." She paused, looking him dead in the eye. "So, you see why I can't give you my land. I don't have magic. But I will still do whatever it takes to protect these creatures. It's up to us to save what we can. This is their home. I don't know how many fairies are left in the world, but you can't have mine."

Jack glanced over at Lila, who was still sipping tea from her thimble, then back at Amelia. "I understand."

"So, will you please leave us alone? Go back to your boss, tell him to stop hounding us."

He sighed. "I can't make a promise like that."

Amelia sat back in her chair. "Jack, you need to understand—what impacts magical creatures also impacts non-magical creatures. We're tied together. I need you do to more than *try*."

"Amelia, I can't give you more than that. You don't know my boss. I will *try*. But I can't make any promises."

She sighed. "Then I guess trying will have to do. But you need to know I won't go down without a fight."

He smiled wryly. "I wouldn't expect anything less."

✳

Jack awoke the next morning, disoriented by the previous night's events and conversation. He laid in bed, trying desperately to wrap his mind around everything that had happened. It didn't seem real.

And in that moment, he realized it *couldn't* be real. It was too ridiculous, fairies and magic. It simply didn't make *sense*.

He wracked his brain, trying to remember everything, when it hit him—he'd had wine at dinner that night. He didn't think he'd had that much, but perhaps he had? Or, perhaps they'd put something *in* the wine? Would the sisters have done that?

They might have. Was that their way of trying to get back at him for everything, for harassing them? If it was, it was low, but the confusion it caused in his mind seemed to be doing the job.

He hastily showered and changed, throwing his toiletries into his overnight bag. It was almost eight, Dave would be here shortly to get him and his car, and he'd be on his way. He decided he'd give the Davidson sisters exactly what they wanted: to be left alone. After everything that had happened, he didn't want to ever step foot on that property again. Things were too strange. He'd have to figure out how to tell Adrien, and he had no idea how he'd do that, but he was sure he'd manage something.

Jack stepped into the dining room of the Blue Barn, hoping no one else would be there. After the events—or hallucinations? —of last night, he desired nothing more than to quickly eat and get out of there, and was not in the mood to talk to anyone. If he could make it through his morning without running into either of the Davidson sisters, he would be happy.

He had no such luck, however. The moment he crossed the threshold into the dining room, he saw Amelia at the dining table, setting out a basket of warm, fresh buttermilk biscuits, a tray of bacon and eggs, and a bowl of fruit. Not noticing him at first, she proceeded to prepare the coffee, filling the room with the pleasant, nutty aroma.

Jack figured there was no avoiding it, so he stepped in, and silently picked up a plate at the opposite end of the table to serve himself, trying his best to not make eye contact with her.

"Oh, good! You're awake!" she said cheerily, hearing the clank of plates as he picked one up.

He grunted, trying his best to remain non-conversational.

Amelia chalked this up to him not having coffee in his system yet. She could be the same way at times. Trying to be helpful, she poured him a cup.

"How do you take your coffee?"

"Black," he replied pointedly, taking a seat and shoveling food into his mouth. The look on his face indicated irritation, but also, a hint of fear. She'd seen it before.

Now she was worried.

"Did you sleep well?" She set the mug in front of him, not allowing her voice to betray her concerns.

Again, mouth full of food, he just grunted.

She sat next to him, silent for a moment, wondering how to broach the topic of the events of the previous evening. Jack was clearly in shock over everything that had happened, everything he had learned. She had to admit, if she had found all of this out at an older age, rather than being raised in it like she was, she'd be feeling the same. She tried to figure out how to ease into it, but decided with Jack, it was probably best to just go straight to the point.

"Jack, are you okay? I know last night was a bit surreal."

That's putting it mildly.

He took a gulp of his coffee, still not making eye contact.

"Listen, I'd be shocked too, if I were you," she continued. "It's totally normal. But you need to know it's all going to be okay."

"What did you put in my drink last night?" he said, finally breaking his silence.

106

She blinked, taken aback. "I'm sorry, what?"

"What did you put it my drink last night?" he asked again, this time slower.

"Nothing." Her eyes growing wide in sudden realization, she asked, "Wait, do you think I drugged you?"

"I don't know what to think. I just know last night doesn't make any sense at all. And the only thing I can think of is it was all some kind of drug-induced hallucination."

"Jack, be reasonable—why would I drug you? I have a brand-new business I'm trying to run. That's not the kind of reputation I need."

"I don't know, Miss Davidson," he snapped, reverting back to formalities by refusing to use her first name. "I've been after your property for months, I suddenly trip out and start seeing fairies after eating food and drinking wine you served to me, and all I can think is maybe you're trying to get back at me for everything, trying to mess with my head! I'm just trying to do my job!"

"I know you are," she responded tersely. "And I'm trying to do mine— as a Guardian!"

"You're insane!" he declared.

"Yeah, well, you're the one still eating my food and drinking my coffee while claiming I drugged you," she countered with a smirk on her face. "Who's the insane one now?"

Upon this realization, Jack pushed away the plate of food with disgust and stood, wiping his mouth with a cloth napkin. It couldn't come at a better time—out the window, Jack saw a tow truck pull into the driveway, with the words "Dave's Autobody Shop" printed along the side.

"That's my ride," Jack said. "If you'll excuse me, Miss Davidson, I have to take care of my car and get out of this godforsaken place. You have my card on file. Charge whatever you need to, I don't care. Just e-mail me the itemized receipt and leave me alone. And I'll leave you alone from now on."

With this, Jack took his leave, leaving a bewildered, hurt, angry, and confused Amelia sitting alone in the dining room.

So much for finding another Guardian.

"You okay?"

Standing in the doorframe between the kitchen and the guest dining room was Emily, who, unbeknownst to Jack, had been helping Amelia prepare breakfast that morning, and had overheard the entire ordeal through the door.

Amelia sighed sadly. "Yeah, I'll be okay."

"At least he said he'd leave us alone," Emily said brightly, trying to get Amelia to look on the positive side of things—rarely-treaded ground for her, as it was usually Amelia who was trying to get Emily to be optimistic.

"Yeah, I suppose so," Amelia said vacantly.

"It's for the best, you know. We didn't know if we could trust him. And this just proves it."

"I don't know, Em…I really thought it'd be different after last night."

"Yeah, well, you're also Miss Polly Positive. Things aren't always rainbows and butterflies."

"I guess."

Clearly the conversation with Jack had taken a toll on Amelia. She stood. "I'm going to go check him out in the system."

"Okay. Hey, by the way, when you do, don't charge him for that wine he drank last night. We don't have the liquor license yet and could get in trouble."

"Yeah, I know. I was never going to charge him…he'd had a rough day, I was just trying to be friendly and give the man a drink."

So much for that idea.

Emily watched her sister sullenly head towards the check-in desk, then turned to the window, where she saw Jack getting into the tow truck with Dave to head back to the shop, his car now hooked up to Dave's huge truck. She sighed, frustrated at her sister for being so naïve, and frustrated with Jack for being so rude and pig-headed.

Still, in spite of everything that happened that morning, and in spite of the fact she selfishly hoped they'd never see Jack Garridan on their property ever again, she had the distinct feeling this wasn't over.

✳ Chapter 11 ✳

A way out

"So, what's wrong with it?"

Jack currently found himself standing in the garage of Dave's Auto, praying there was nothing seriously wrong with his car. He was itching to get out of Calvary, but the lack of vehicle was prohibiting him from doing so.

"How long did you say you'd had this car?" Dave asked as he peered under the hood.

"About a year. What's wrong with it?"

Dave shook his head, wiping the oil and grease from his hands with a towel, his brow furrowed. "Strangest thing. You've got a blown cylinder head gasket. Never seen that in a car this new."

Jack didn't know what that meant, but didn't really care. His priority was to get out of town.

"Can you fix it?"

"Sure can."

"How much?"

"A grand."

Jack's jaw dropped. "*A grand*?"

"Best deal you'll get for fifty miles."

Jack sighed. "Fine. How long will it take?" He crossed his fingers Dave would say it would be done before the end of the day.

Luck, however, was not with him.

"A few days."

"*A few days?!*" Jack exclaimed. "I don't *have* a few days! I need to get back to Boston!"

"Well, I don't have the part you need. I have to order it. And I'd rather take my time on this sort of thing if you want the job done *right*."

Jack ran his hands through his hair, aggravated. "Fine. But how am I supposed to get home? Is there a rental car place or something so I can get around until the job is done?"

"Son, does this seem like the sort of town that has a rental car place in it?" Dave almost laughed. "You're going to have to stay put here for a few days. Or call a friend to come get you."

"That's *not* acceptable," Jack retorted, wracking his brain to think of any friends he might have who could help him, dismayed when he realized he was coming up short in that department. "What about a cab service or something?"

"Again, does this seem like the sort of town that has a cab service?"

"No," Jack grimaced.

"Well, then I don't know what else to tell you. Either call a friend or go back to the Blue Barn for a few days."

"I can't do that," Jack said through gritted teeth.

"Did I hear you were looking to go to Boston?" a voice said from behind Dave and Jack, interrupting their conversation.

The two men turned around. Before them stood a small, middle-aged man with a stocky build, dark hair, and blue eyes. His skin was tan and weathered from spending time outdoors, and he wore a large, friendly grin on his face, exposing his coffee-stained teeth. He was dressed in a pair of worn jeans and a button-up shirt, with the name *Charles* embroidered across the breast pocket.

"I am," Jack replied, looking the stranger up and down.

"I happen to be taking a shipment into Boston tonight," Charles replied. "Got some lobster going to one of the fancy restaurants down there. I can give you a lift—provided the truck's ready like you said it would be, Dave."

He turned to the mechanic, who nodded, indicating it was. "Sure is. Just like new."

"I appreciate that." He turned back to Jack. "So what do you say?"

Jack weighed his options: he could either go home by way of this complete stranger, who seemed friendly enough, but who he knew absolutely nothing about. Or he could call Adrien and tell him he wouldn't be back in town for a few days, be chewed out about it, and stay in town and risk running into Amelia or Emily and all the strangeness that came with the two of them.

He'd take his chances with the stranger.

"I say yes. Thank you." Jack extended his hand.

Charles smiled that toothy grin, and heartily shook Jack's hand. "Charles. Charles Manian."

"Jack Garridan."

"Yeah, I all know about you, son."

Jack let go of Charles' hand, sheepish. His reputation for "driving people off their land" seemed to be alive and well.

Charles saw Jack's reaction. "Don't worry about it, Jack. A man's gotta do what a man's gotta do. Your business is your own. Anyway, I've gotta get things tied up here, then get the truck all loaded up. Meet you around three, and we'll head out?"

"Sure, that'll work. Where?"

"You know where the fish market is?"

Jack's heart sank: the fish market, otherwise known as the place the Davidson family owned.

Again, Charles saw the look on Jack's face. "I wouldn't worry about running into the Davidson sisters there. They don't come around as much as they used to since Stuart sold the place to me and they started focusing on their bed and breakfast venture."

Jack nodded, relieved. "I didn't realize he'd sold it. That's good to know."

"Three good for you?"

"Yeah, sure. Any suggestions for what I should do around town in the meantime?"

Charles smiled. "Oh, go for a walk on the boardwalk. Grab some pie at May's Diner, but avoid any of the melts, especially the tuna one. Maybe work on that contract for the Kowalski land."

Jack blushed. "Word goes around pretty quickly around here, doesn't it?"

"It does indeed. No judgment. Personally, I think this little town could do with some change. Not sure your kind of change is the kind I was thinking, but it might not be so bad."

"Not so bad—well, that's encouraging," Jack said wryly.

Charles shrugged. "It's a small town with small people who are set in their ways. They're going to fight you. It's just their nature."

"And what do you think?"

"Me? I don't really care either way, to be honest. I'm always up for a good adventure."

"Charles, you're a breath of fresh air, you know that?" Jack was looking forward to the couple of hours he'd be in a truck conversing with Charles.

"You're not so bad yourself, Jack. I'll see you at three."

"See you then."

✳

A few hours later, after taking Charles' suggestion to go for a long walk on the boardwalk, Jack also took his other suggestion, and was eating lunch in May's Diner. He was heeding Charles' advice and avoiding any of the melts on the menu, opting instead for a bowl of soup and a slice of apple pie. The soup, some kind of seafood bisque, wasn't anything to write home about, but it was tolerable. The pie, however, was spectacular, and he was about to order a second slice when he saw a crew of construction workers walk into the diner. Instantly, he recognized them as the Dunstan Enterprises construction team for the development. The work on the Benedict property was underway, and he had noticed this morning when

114

driving with Dave back to his shop that the frames of a few of the new homes had been erected already. Some were even as far along as having the interiors started.

Happy to finally see a few friendly faces, he waved the team over to his table. The project manager, Max, noticed Jack first, and approached him. Max Goshay was a portly man, with a red face and dark, thinning hair.

"How's it going out there?" Jack asked as the crew gathered at the table.

"About as good as it can be." Max sat opposite Jack, a clearly aggravated look on his face. The other men with him were oblivious, caught up in studying the menus or ordering food.

Jack cocked his head, surprised by Max's reply. From his point of view, it had seemed like everything was going well, given the progress being made on the site. "What's that mean?"

Max sighed, obviously distraught and frustrated. "Jack, can I ask you a favor?"

"Sure, what's up?"

Max leaned in so as not to catch the attention of the rest of his crew. "Can you talk to Mr. Dunstan about the conditions we're dealing with here? We can't work like this."

Jack raised an eyebrow, confused by this statement. "Max, I don't know what you're talking about. What kind of conditions?"

"Well, it's about some of the materials we've received."

"What about them?"

"They're not exactly the best quality. Hell, the drywall we've got was recalled—asbestos or something in it. Yet we've got it here on the construction site. I won't let any of my guys touch it, it's a health hazard. I've tried to call to get it out and get it replaced, but I'm not getting any answers from anybody over at Dunstan Enterprises."

"Yeah, sure, Max, I'll check on that for you." Jack was baffled by the information he was receiving. "They might not have realized it was recalled when they ordered it and are trying to figure that out on their end before they get back to you."

"I hope so. I can't justify building these homes with those materials. It's not right, you know."

"I know, I agree, it isn't. I'm heading back into the city this evening, I'll talk to Adrien about it first thing in the morning."

"I appreciate that. You're a good man, Jack. Thanks for the help."

"Anytime."

Max turned his attention to the menu. "I swear, the only edible thing in this place is the pie," he muttered, having clearly tried the food before.

"The soup isn't so bad." Jack took another sip of the mediocre concoction from his spoon.

Max looked over at Jack's bowl, wrinkling his nose slightly. "I'd hope not. You'd think in a fishing village, the main diner here would know how to do fish right."

"Well, I wouldn't say it's done *right*, but it's not done terribly."

"Good enough." Max closed the menu. "Thanks again."

"Anytime," Jack said. "Get the pie too. You won't regret it."

Max laughed, patting his stomach. "Buddy, I'm beyond regrets."

Jack smiled, trying to keep up pleasant pretenses, but suddenly a bit anxious. He sincerely hoped *he* wouldn't regret fulfilling Max's request by talking to Adrien about the issues the crew was experiencing when he next saw him. Something about the situation made him uneasy.

✳

A few hours later, after another long walk up the boardwalk and a stint in the tiny library, where he read some antiquated, battered books from the facility's limited selection, Jack eventually made his way to the fish market. Charles Manian was already in the front, loading the last bit of merchandise into the back of his truck. Seeing Jack, he smiled.

"Almost ready, Jack! Just give me a few more minutes."

"Can I give you a hand?" Jack offered.

Charles grinned. "Sure! The faster we get this loaded, the faster we get on the road."

Jack didn't hesitate. He had spent enough time in this town, and desperately wanted to get home and onto familiar territory. Without another word, he picked up the crate closest to him and placed it on the truck.

After a few minutes of this work, Jack and Charles were buckled in, settled in for the long drive. Jack found he rather liked Charles. He was friendly, personable, outgoing, and down to earth. Jack imagined under different circumstances, and if Jack lived in town, the two might actually become friends.

As they drove, they talked about anything and everything. Jack talked about his stint in the Navy, and was delighted to learn Charles had also spent time in it as well. They exchanged stories and laughed about similar experiences. Charles shared about his time after the Navy as well, and his family. Jack, in turn, talked about what he'd done since he got out—which led, of course, to talking about his position with Dunstan Enterprises.

"So, you just go around asking people for their land and offering them your company's money?" Charles asked.

"It's a bit more complicated than that, but essentially, yes."

"Damn. If I'd known that was a thing, I would've gotten into the development business myself."

Jack laughed. "It's not too late for a career change."

Charles shook his head. "Nah. Life is good. I've got a good job, a beautiful wife, a couple of daughters, and a roof over my head. I'm fine, thanks."

"Sounds like you've got it made."

"I really do. Life has been good to me. Took a while to get that way, but it got there eventually."

"You're a lucky man, Charles."

"It's not luck, kid. It's effort." He paused, then took on a serious tone. "So, I've got to ask the inevitable, Jack. You've been going around trying to get all these properties from people, and word travels quickly in small towns."

"Yeah, I know." Jack knew what was coming. "Just ask it, Charles."

"Why you so interested in the Davidson property anyway? Those girls keep turning you down, why don't you just let them be?"

"Personally, I'm *not* interested. My boss is."

"Okay, so why is your boss interested?"

"Honestly, at this point, I'm not sure. We've got plenty of land already under contract for the development, and the Davidson property would only have a few buildings on it—the bulk is being built on the other properties. It's really not all that necessary to what we're doing. But he's kind of one of those guys who's obsessive and never backs down until he gets what he wants. Once he's got his mind set on something, he won't stop until it's done his way."

Charles nodded, eyes on the road in front of him. "Mmm. I know that kind. I've met a few people like that in my life. I'll tell you this, things don't typically end well for a man like that. Usually they ruin their own life in the process of ruining everyone else's. I've seen it before. There's a fine line between ambition and mania, and it sounds like your boss is straddling it."

"You just described Adrien Dunstan to a tee."

"That's his name? Adrien Dunstan?"

"Yeah. You know him?"

"Heard of him. He was in one of those 'fifty under fifty' articles I read in a magazine a few months back. Didn't realize that's who we were dealing with."

Jack remembered reading that same article when it came out, and grimaced. He knew Adrien had probably paid someone off to be included in it, because there was no way he would've made it otherwise: yes, he was successful, yes, he was a millionaire, but he didn't have the same character as the others included in there. Adrien could be conniving and manipulative, not exactly the philanthropic type he knew that magazine usually went for. "Yeah, that's him."

"So, here's my question for you: why are you working for a man like that?"

119

Jack blinked. He hadn't thought about it before. "Well—the pay's decent. Benefits are great. It's not a desk job, which is a perk. And I'm good at what I do."

"There are plenty of jobs out there that meet those requirements. Why *this* job? Why *this* boss?"

Jack sat silently for a moment, pondering this. "I guess…well, I guess it's the whole thought of being a part of something new and exciting. It's getting to see places developed into something beautiful. And even if he is a jerk sometimes, and obsessive, he's trying to build something bigger than himself where future generations can enjoy and find peace. I respect that."

"So, you don't think the Davidson property is beautiful and peaceful as it is?"

"I didn't say that."

"So, you *do* think it's beautiful and peaceful?"

"Honestly? It's probably one of the most beautiful and peaceful places I've ever been."

"I agree. There's something almost magical about it, when you think about it."

Jack winced a bit at the word "magical," but didn't say anything. He was trying hard to forget his experience on the Davidson land.

"And it's not just the landscape, though that's part of it. It's how you *feel* there, you know?" Charles continued. "All warm and comforting. The Davidsons did a good job making it welcoming."

"They did," Jack admitted.

"Stuart was a great man. I think you would've liked him if you'd taken the time to get to know him, and had met him under different circumstances. Lizzie was a pip—she was spunky and lively and friendly. Real sad what's happened to her now."

"What's happened to her?" Jack had noticed he didn't see her around after a time during the process of trying to acquire the land from Stuart, but he'd assumed she had decided to either keep her distance from him and not be in the same room whenever he came calling, or worse, she had died.

"Alzheimer's. Her mind is going. She's in a nursing home about twenty miles from Calvary. Stuart, bless him, went to visit her every day before he died, making that forty-mile round trip journey. He loved her more than anything."

Jack now felt terrible. He didn't realize Stuart had been dealing with all of this before his death. He was sure his own persistence at trying to acquire his property didn't help with his stress levels at all. He felt sick thinking he could've been a contributing factor in the old man's demise.

"Still, it's nice what Amelia and Emily are trying to do, trying to revive our little corner of the world while keeping the integrity of the town," Charles continued. "It's nice to see young people return to their roots instead of leaving it for something bigger and shinier like most do."

"I guess it is."

"And those sisters, they're feisty. Emily especially, she's got an attitude on her."

"I think Amelia can give her a run for her money," Jack replied coolly, looking out the window.

Charles laughed heartily. "Yeah, I'm sure she can, you're probably right about that. She's gentler than Emily, but she can hold her own. She's no pushover, that's for sure. That girl's got a big heart in her. She's filled with passion. Funny, she's not the type to give up either—going back to that ambition/mania line, but she's a different type. I like to think of her as chaotic good."

"Chaotic good?"

"She does what she wants, when she wants, how she wants. She's impulsive. But what she does is *good*, and to try and make things better for the people around her. She's a fighter and a lover all wrapped up in one."

"That's probably the best description you can come up with for Amelia," Jack said, speaking from his own experience with her.

"And her sister…she's similar, but she's got a little of that sullen streak in her. She could almost go either way. Right now she's good, but it wouldn't surprise me if she ever took a turn. The two of them balance each other out nicely."

Jack nodded, also agreeing with this assessment.

"What they're building—well, it's beautiful, when it comes down to it. A real monument to their family and all they stood for, just trying to build a better place where people can find peace."

"I guess it is," Jack agreed.

"So, can Adrien Dunstan make it even better?"

Jack didn't have a response to this, mostly because he knew what the answer was, and didn't want to admit it out loud.

Charles, ever keen at reading people, smiled at Jack's lack of response. "I'll take your silence as a 'no.' You've got some things to think about, son."

They spent the rest of the trip in silence, Charles concentrating on driving, and Jack pondering the conversation and his life's purpose.

✳ Chapter 12 ✳

An order

The next morning, Jack once again found himself in Adrien's office in Boston, thanks to Charles' generosity. The men had arrived earlier than expected, and though one might think that would mean Jack would get a decent night's sleep, this wasn't the case. He had spent much of the night restless, thinking over his conversations with both Max and Charles, and dreading having to face Adrien, who he knew would be pushy, and who he had determined he needed to talk out of pursuing the Davidson land.

That morning, fueled by coffee and arriving to the office via bus, Jack was summoned into Adrien's office within moments of his arrival by Stephanie, Adrien's secretary. Jack grudgingly obliged, not looking forward to the conversation he was about to have, but knowing it needed to happen.

"Jesus, Jack, you look like hell," Adrien commented when Jack walked into his office, looking up from his computer and closing a few documents he had open.

Jack knew he did, and didn't argue. When he'd last looked in the mirror that morning before leaving his apartment, he had dark circles under his eyes, and he knew his overall appearance was disheveled, as he'd woken up later than expected and was rushing to try to catch the bus into work, which he'd initially forgotten he needed to do, not used to not having access to his car.

"Didn't sleep great," Jack replied simply, sitting in the chair in front of the desk.

"I'm sorry to hear that."

"Sir, if I may ask, where do we stand with finding Gallagher's replacement?" Jack asked, referring to the employee who had previously been on the Davidson case, but who was removed, and the reason Jack was on it now. "I haven't heard anything from human resources about where we are in the hiring process."

"What, are you not enjoying Calvary, Jack?" Adrien sneered.

"Well, I've been at it for a few months now, and as director, it's time I get back to my actual job as a supervisor, rather than working the field," Jack explained. He knew this was a transparent tactic to get out of working the Davidsons, but at this point, he didn't care anymore. He didn't want to go back.

Adrien sat back in his chair, his arms crossed over his chest.

"No."

Jack blinked. "No?"

"No, Jack, I don't think so. As director, *you* need to be the one to tie up this project. You didn't exactly do a great job 'supervising' Gallagher to successfully acquire the land. So now you need to be the one to clean up the mess he left behind."

"But sir, my other duties—"

"You'll still be expected to complete those as well. You're former military, I'm sure you'll have no trouble multitasking and going above the call of duty."

"Sir, this is unreasonable," Jack argued.

125

Adrien pursed his lips and leaned forward in his seat. "No, Jack, unreasonable is my employees not doing the jobs they're being paid to do. I'm holding you accountable. We made an agreement the other day. Six months, remember? *You* have six months. Not someone else. We'll talk about replacing Gallagher after *you* have successfully acquired the Davidson land."

Jack sighed. He knew it'd been a long shot to bring up a replacement, but he had to try. "I understand."

"Good." Adrien sat back, his posture now more warm and friendly. "So how is everything going in Calvary, Jack?"

Jack knew he was alluding to progress on acquiring the Davidson property, but Jack also knew Adrien already knew the answer to that. So, he decided not to talk about that particular project, but rather, about his encounter with Max, as he had promised he would.

"Fine," Jack replied. "I ran into Max yesterday."

"And how is Max doing?" Adrien inquired casually.

"Well, he has some concerns about the progress on the construction site."

"What sort of concerns?"

"Something about some low-quality materials they've been given to work with—he specifically mentioned recalled drywall."

"Really?" Adrien leaned back in his chair, looking a bit surprised. "Sounds serious. Why hasn't he been in touch with us?"

"Well, that's the thing, I guess he's been trying to call the office about them, but no one's been getting back to him."

"Is that so?" Adrien raised an eyebrow and pressed a button on his intercom. "Stephanie?"

"Yes, Mr. Dunstan?" Stephanie's voice reverberated through the room.

"Has Max Goshay called the office at all?"

"No, Mr. Dunstan."

"Thank you, Stephanie."

Adrien looked back at Jack, crossing his hands in his lap. "Interesting, that Max would say he's been trying to reach us, but Stephanie says she hasn't heard anything from him. Our lines are always open for him."

Jack also thought this odd. "Maybe Stephanie missed his messages."

"Perhaps," Adrien said with a thin smile. "But I appreciate you bringing it to my attention. I'll look into it and see what we need to do to rectify the situation."

"Of course."

"Now, why don't we move onto the real purpose for this meeting? The Davidson property."

Jack knew the topic couldn't be avoided. "We're in the same place as when we last spoke."

"Really? No forward progress whatsoever?"

Aside from the hallucinations caused by Amelia's wine, no.

"I'm afraid not," Jack said aloud. "But I do need to talk to you about them—I know I asked you to give me six months, but I think we need to give up on that property."

"Give up?" Adrien looked astonished at this suggestion. "Why on *earth* do you think we need to give up?"

"Sir, they're determined. They're threatening legal action if we continue with what they're calling 'harassment.'"

"Let them."

"I just think we need to move on," Jack pressed. "I don't want to see us tied up in litigation."

"I don't *care* about litigation, Jack," Adrien insisted. "Don't you understand? I'd hoped our conversation the other day would motivate you. I'm disappointed. Be a man of your word and get that property. Rome wasn't built in a day, after all."

"I'm working on it," Jack said, resigned and irritated. This conversation was futile. If he wanted to keep his job, he needed to keep on keeping on…even if it meant dealing with the strangeness of the Davidson sisters. He grimaced at the thought of having to encounter them again, especially after everything that had happened over the past couple of days.

"Yes, yes, of course you are." Adrien waved his hand. "My apologies, I know the Davidson sisters are challenging, even for a man of your caliber."

Jack clenched his teeth. "Is there any other business you'd like to discuss?"

Adrien smiled. "No, Jack, that will be all. You may go back to your business now. But I do hope you don't intend to use the *entire* six months."

Jack stood and turned to leave Adrien's office, downcast.

"Oh, and Jack?"

"Yes?" Jack turned to meet Adrien's gaze.

"You worry about yourself. Don't worry about Max and his part. That's not your job. You stick to what you know best, let him stick to what he knows best."

Jack thought this a strange comment to make, but nodded, and silently headed out the door.

When Jack was well outside of earshot, Adrien called Stephanie over the intercom.

"Stephanie?"

"Yes, Mr. Dunstan?"

"Take Max Goshay off the Calvary project. And the rest of his crew too."

"Yes, Mr. Dunstan."

Adrien sighed and sat back in his chair. He needed this project to move forward, and quickly. At this point, he didn't care how he got there. Not that time was much of an issue, but he didn't like waiting to reap his rewards. The conversation with Jack had been slightly concerning. He hoped Jack would pull through in the end, but right now, he couldn't be sure. Only time would tell.

✳ Chapter 13 ✳

Brownies and fairies, nuts and berries

That evening, Jack returned to his apartment, thoroughly worn out from the past few days.

Absently, he poured himself a bowl of cereal and sat on the couch munching on it as he watched television in an attempt to unwind. No such luck, however, as his mind reeled with a million thoughts. He still wasn't entirely sure what to make of the events of the other night on the Davidson property, but he knew he didn't want to go back. He also knew he didn't have a choice *but* to go back after the conversation with Adrien, if he wanted to keep his job. But after his conversation with Charles, he wasn't sure he even *wanted* to keep his job anymore. He'd been feeling out of place at Dunstan Enterprises for a few months now. Perhaps this was the time for a fresh start? And there was that conversation with Max…something wasn't right, but he couldn't put his finger on it.

He shook his head, turning off the television. He wasn't paying attention to the program anyway. He considered taking out his frustrations on the punching bag in the corner of the room, but he wasn't sure that would do any good.

What he needed more than anything was a stiff drink and a good night's sleep. Perhaps things would become clearer in the morning.

Wandering into the kitchen, Jack set the empty cereal bowl in the sink, some milk still left in the bottom. Rummaging through his liquor cabinet, he procured a bottle of scotch. Pouring himself a glass and sipping as he stood alone in his kitchen, he mused over everything from the past few days, trying to make some sense of it all. After finishing the drink, he set the glass in the sink alongside the cereal bowl, telling himself he'd clean it in the morning.

Right now, he needed rest, and a chance to give his brain a break from everything.

✳

Clank.

"Wha…?" Jack rolled over in bed, awoken by the noise. He glanced at his alarm clock, which read 3:07 a.m.

Clank.

He started, and sat up in bed, bewildered. Someone was in the apartment. Throwing off his blankets, he quietly tiptoed to the other side of the room, where a baseball bat was leaning against the wall. Slowly, he opened his bedroom door, careful not to let it creak. He did not want to make his intruder aware of his presence.

Treading lightly, he crept down the hall towards the noise, bat poised over his shoulder, ready to swing. The clamor was clearly coming from the kitchen, where he noticed there was a light on—he distinctly remembered turning all the lights off before heading to bed.

Peering around the corner into the kitchen, his eyes fell on the strangest sight he'd ever seen. A tiny man in tattered clothes was standing on top of the kitchen counter, scrubbing the dishes in the sink. He was portly in nature, with a worn, wizened face, leathery brown skin, and tufts of unkempt hair protruding from his head. His bright, amber eyes were focused on the task at hand, so he hadn't noticed Jack yet. Jack guessed if the two of them stood side by side, this strange little creature wouldn't even reach his kneecap, and with his small, pointed ears, he vaguely reminded Jack of a Christmas elf—though perhaps one down on his luck.

131

The little man was picking up the glass from the sink to scrub, when he saw Jack standing in the doorframe, gripping his bat. He gave a little yelp and dropped the glass, smashing it.

"Oh, Mr. Jack! Please, pardon me! I didn't mean to break your glass!" he squeaked.

"Who the *hell* are you? *What* the hell are you?" Jack demanded, his knuckles white as he clenched the bat.

"I'm your brownie, sir! You left out milk for me, so I came to clean!"

Jack tried to wrap his mind around this statement, which made no sense to him at all. "What?"

"Mr. Jack leaves out milk. I come clean," the brownie said, slower, as if this would help Jack understand. "Mr. Jack hasn't left out milk in a very long time. So, I haven't cleaned in a very long time." He looked around the state of the kitchen and the apartment, wrinkling his nose. "Mr. Jack should leave out milk more often."

"What the hell are you talking about?" And it dawned on him—he had eaten cereal that evening, and left the bowl of leftover milk in the sink, telling himself he'd clean it up in the morning. "Are you a magical creature?"

"Yes, sir."

"And you're summoned by *milk*?"

"Yes, Mr. Jack!" the brownie nodded enthusiastically.

"That is the weirdest thing I've ever heard."

"I don't make the rules, Mr. Jack."

Jack looked the creature up and down, still in disbelief. At this point, he had come to the conclusion he had to be dreaming. The whole situation was too surreal.

"I must be dreaming."

"Not dreaming, Mr. Jack."

"Then I've cracked."

"Cracked, Mr. Jack?"

"Lost it. Completely." Jack was pacing now, still holding the bat. "It's the stress. Yup. That's it. Work has been crazy. My boss is ridiculous. And don't even get me started on the Davidson sisters…yup. Cracked." Moving closer, he poked the little man in the stomach. "Didn't think it would happen this way, but I guess you never really do know what your mind will do under pressure. And apparently my mind is capable of some weird, ugly things."

The tiny creature furrowed his brow and clenched his little fist, clearly insulted. "I'm not in your mind, Mr. Jack! And it's not nice to call someone weird and ugly!"

With this, he hopped up, popping Jack in the nose.

"OW!" Jack stepped back, reflexively putting his hand to his nose, which was now bleeding. He glanced at his reflection in the toaster, and noticed a bruise already forming where he'd been hit.

"It serves Mr. Jack right!" the brownie screeched. "See if I ever come back, milk or not!"

And with a loud *POP,* the creature disappeared into thin air, leaving a bewildered, bloodied, and bruised Jack alone in the kitchen, clutching his bat.

Jack, unable to fully process what had just happened, wandered through his living room and the rest of the rooms, searching for the little man, who had disappeared just as quickly as he seemed to have appeared. Without finding any trace of him anywhere, Jack sat on the foot of his bed, bat in hand, utterly confused. Eventually, exhaustion took over, and before long, Jack was once again asleep, a little worse for the wear.

✴

Jack awoke a few hours later to the blaring of his alarm block, the early morning events faded from his mind. He concluded it must have been a dream—a very strange, realistic dream.

He was having a lot of those lately.

As he laid in bed, pondering, he couldn't help but notice his nose was throbbing slightly. He rolled out of bed, turned off the alarm, and made his way to the bathroom to check himself in the mirror. Sure enough, a large bruise had formed on the bridge of his nose.

"What...?" he muttered, gingerly putting pressure on the swollen area with his fingertips.

He stepped out of the bathroom and made his way down the hall to further investigate his apartment. It had to have been a dream. It just *had* to.

He entered the kitchen, where he observed the dishes he had left out the night before were cleaned and put away—though one of the cabinets was not closed. Shattered on the floor was one of his glasses. Slowly, he approached the open cabinet. With the way the kitchen was laid out, this was one that was not hanging over the kitchen counter, but rather over the built-in pantry, and when left ajar, left open the possibility of him knocking his head into it—specifically, the edge of the cabinet door hung just at nose level.

Closing the cabinet, he concluded he must have been sleepwalking—or rather, sleep *cleaning*—the previous night, and at some point, had accidently knocked into the open cabinet. He had been known to do so in the past on a few other occasions, having been caught in some precarious situations when he was a child in foster care. Though he hadn't done it in years, it appeared the stress of the past few days had caused this childhood habit to once again rear its ugly head.

Satisfied with and relieved by this conclusion he had created for himself, Jack cleaned up the broken glass, and made his way back to his bedroom, where he changed into his gym shorts, a t-shirt, and running shoes. He needed to clear his head.

After taking a few minutes to take some of his frustrations out on the punching bag hanging in the corner of his living room, he made his way downstairs, taking in a breath of fresh air as he emerged from the apartment complex. He loved to run early in the morning in the late spring and summer, before the sun rose fully and the temperature rose unbearably. His neighborhood was lovely, filled with old, brick buildings, the streets lined with equally old, shady trees. Some of the apartments and houses kept flowers in their window boxes, giving the dusty red brick buildings a splash of color. It was peaceful at dawn, the neighborhood just waking up, the sun barely peeking over the horizon.

He ran along his usual route on autopilot. He knew to his left, an elderly woman would be stepping out with her yappy little dog to go for their early morning walk. Across the street to his right, a middle-aged man would be getting into his cherry-red convertible, carrying the same black briefcase he always carried, starting his morning commute into downtown. Ahead, the stop walk would turn red just as he arrived at it, and he would have to jog in place for a few moments before it turned green again. It was the same as it always was.

What he didn't know was that day, when he turned left after the stop walk, he would run full-force into a cloud of fairies.

There were probably twenty of them, all massed together, hovering like a small, glowing haze, vaguely reminiscent of a cloud of gnats—they even gave off a similar sound as they flapped their little wings. They whizzed about his head, catching him so off guard he tripped, barely catching himself on the bars of a fence as he went down. Righting himself, he turned to the fairies, his eyes wide in utter disbelief. One landed on his shoulder, another on the top of his head—the others continued to whirl about him as if taunting him, a blur of light and brightly-colored petals.

"What the hell?!" he exclaimed, brushing off the fairies that had landed on him.

The one he had brushed off his head made her way to a tree, where she plucked a piece of fruit. Making her way back to him, she dropped the fruit on his head with a soft *thunk.*

"OW!" he shouted, rubbing his head where the fruit had landed. Hearing a little giggle right above him, he looked up, where he saw Lila hovering.

"*You.*" He glared at her, recognizing her in an instant.

Mimicking surprise, she made a *"Who, me?"* gesture.

"Yes, *you,*" Jack responded, his face red and his eyes slits. "What's going on? Is this real?"

Lila's response was a mischievous smirk. Raising her arm, she snapped it down into a tomahawk chop. Immediately on cue, the other fairies, who Jack hadn't noticed had gathered above his head, dropped their own nuts and fruits and berries on top of him, bombarding him in a blitz attack. Berries splattered on his shirt, juices ran down his face.

"Ow, ow, OW! Okay! I got it! You're real!" he cried as the fruit fell. He looked at Lila, and wryly, asked, "What do you want?"

Lila crossed her little arms, and simply stared at him, a serious expression on her face.

"You want me to apologize to Amelia and Emily?" he asked, taking her meaning.

She nodded.

"I can do that." He brushed off the fruit and berry bits from his shirt and hair. "Anything else?"

Flitting to him, she gave him a little kick in the side of the head.

"Hey!" he snapped, rubbing his head. "What the hell does *that* mean?"

Her response was to simply stick out her tongue at him. Motioning to the other fairies, the group of them flew off into the branches of the trees, out of sight.

The sun was higher by this point, indicating to Jack it was time for him to head home before the day heated up too much. Shaking his head, remnants of nuts and fruit and leaves dropping to the ground around him, he made eye contact with the old lady with the yappy dog, out for their morning walk. The woman was staring at him, eyebrow raised as he passed by. He must have been a sight to see, covered in bits of fruit, his nose black and blue and swollen. Awkwardly, he waved at her. She responded in kind, and the little dog yapped and tried to nip at his ankles as he jogged by.

It was going to be a long day. He had a distinct feeling life wouldn't be normal from here on out.

✳ Chapter 14 ✳

Groveling

A few hours and an expensive cab ride later, Jack was once again in Calvary, procrastinating on visiting the Davidson property. He had his car back, having received a call from Dave shortly after his run-in with the fairies that it was ready to be picked up. It was almost as if the fairies *knew* he'd have a reason to come back to town, and had planned their visit around that. He wondered if they had anything to do with his car being in the shop in the first place. But how exactly does a fairy sabotage a cylinder head gasket?

As he pondered this over coffee and pie in May's Diner, he saw a familiar face walk in. Charles Manian saw Jack and grinned, approaching the younger man.

Taking a seat at the booth opposite Jack, Charles asked, "Back so soon, Jack?"

"Car was ready to be picked up."

"How the hell'd you get back in town to get it?" He waved over the waitress for a cup of coffee, who complied.

"Cab."

"Jesus. That must've been a hell of a fare."

Jack snorted. "You can say that again."

"Next time that happens, seriously, just give me a call. I'm in Boston enough with deliveries that I probably could've gotten you."

"I appreciate it, Charles. But I didn't want to bother you."

"It's no bother at all. Really."

"Thanks."

"So, how's work going since we last spoke?" Charles smiled a knowing smile, taking a sip from his cup.

"Oh, you know—same old same old."

"That bad, huh?"

Jack laughed. "Sure."

"You doing any work while you're in town today?"

"Sure, something like that."

"Hitting the Davidson place?"

Jack nodded.

"Prepared to be turned down again?"

Jack laughed at Charles' blunt honesty. "You know it."

"And still not giving up?"

Jack didn't reply, instead taking a sip of his own coffee. Charles raised an eyebrow at this.

Before Charles could pry any further, a team of construction workers walked into the diner, settling in for their lunch break. Jack started, noticing they were all wearing Dunstan Enterprises shirts and hardhats—but he didn't recognize a single one of them as the construction crew from a couple of days previous, when he'd run into Max at this same diner.

"Jack?" Charles also turned to glance over at the men.

"Do you know any of those guys?" Jack said under his breath.

Charles furrowed his brow. "Don't you?"

Jack shook his head. "No, I don't. That's just it. They look like an entirely different team."

"Well, it *is* construction," Charles pointed out. "There's a lot of moving parts. I'm sure you don't know *everyone* who was hired."

"No, I don't, but I knew at least one: Max Goshay, the project manager. He's not here."

"Maybe he got lunch elsewhere?" Charles suggested.

"What, for Armenian falafel? Or the three seafood restaurants that don't open until five?"

"Fair point. Maybe he brought his lunch and is eating it elsewhere."

"Maybe." Jack bit his lip as he contemplated this possibility. "It's just…"

"What?"

"Listen, I was here a couple days ago, and the construction team walked in. Max came over to me and said he was having some issues with the build…something about the materials not being up to standard. He asked me to talk to Adrien Dunstan about it, since he'd been having trouble reaching corporate, so I did. So, I have this conversation with

Adrien…and suddenly, here we are today, no Max, and no familiar faces in that group at all."

Charles leaned back in his chair. "What are you suggesting, Jack?"

"I think—well, I don't know what to think."

"Well, there's only one way to find out what's going on."

"What's that?"

"Ask," Charles said simply, taking another sip of his coffee.

Jack stood, approaching the man who seemed to be the best-dressed of the bunch. He was tall and lanky, with a stubbly beard and dark hair—and young, Jack noted, even younger than himself. What distinctly separated him from the rest was he was wearing a red Dunstan Enterprises polo and a pair of khakis, whereas the other men were donned in dirty t-shirts and jeans, indicating he was in some kind of supervisory role.

"Excuse me?" Jack tapped the man on the shoulder.

The man turned. "Yeah?"

"Hi, Jack Garridan—I'm with Dunstan Enterprises as well, I'm the acquisitions director. I saw you guys walk in and I wanted to introduce myself."

The man smiled and shook Jack's hand. "So, you're the man who gets the land so we can work. Nice to see a friendly face in this place. Jeff Black."

"Nice to meet you, Jeff. What's your role?"

"Project manager."

Alarm bells went off in Jack's mind.

141

"Really?" Jack inquired. "I thought Max Goshay was the project manager?"

Jeff shrugged. "Don't know what happened there. I heard it was a 'difference of opinions' or something like that. Didn't get more than that. All I know is I got a call, and here I am."

Jack forced a smile, trying not to show he was disconcerted. "Well, we're happy to have you and your team, Jeff. If you need anything, just let me know."

"That's awfully nice of you. Thanks, Jack. Hope to see you around more."

"Hope to see you around more too." Jack sincerely meant it. He didn't know what to make of this sudden turnover, and didn't know how he'd react if there was more down the line. Something didn't sit well with him about all of this.

Jack turned and sat back in the booth, where Charles was still sitting, eagerly awaiting an update.

"Well?"

"Something's wrong," Jack commented, shaking his head. "Something's definitely wrong."

"What are you going to do about it?"

"I don't know."

But in that instant, Jack did know at least *something*: he couldn't procrastinate on visiting the Davidson sisters anymore. From his point of view, it appeared Adrien didn't care about anything but getting his project done, and would do what he needed to do to those who stood in his way.

And right now, Amelia and Emily Davidson were in his way, that much was clear.

For the first time in a long time, he didn't want to just do his job. He wanted *more*. Knowing the little bit he knew about magical creatures and Guardians, and finally acknowledging everything that had happened as *definitely not* a dream or a hallucination, he knew he was a part of something much bigger. And he knew he had to be a part of protecting that magic.

It was time to learn how to be a Guardian.

✳

A few minutes later, Jack walked back up that familiar driveway leading towards the Davidson cottage. He hesitated for a moment when he reached the front door, suddenly questioning himself. He knew if he knocked, his life would change forever. Was he ready for that?

Fate, it seemed, didn't care if he was ready or not. Before he could even knock, Cosmo, in all his playful glory, had heard Jack walk up the front steps with his extraordinary dog hearing, and was barking like a maniac on the other side of the door.

Inside, Jack heard Amelia's voice yell, "Cosmo! What on *earth* are you making a ruckus over?"

Jack froze, waiting for her. A few seconds later, he saw her push back the curtains and peer out the window next to the door, clearly surprised at him standing on her porch. They gazed at each other for a moment, and he called out to her, "Can we talk?"

She raised an eyebrow, then disappeared from view. A moment later, she cracked open the door ever so slightly, looking him up and down, Cosmo slipping past her, jumping to greet Jack.

"What do you want?" Amelia demanded, not even bothering to help Jack as he struggled to get Cosmo to settle.

"I want—okay, can you help me with him?" Jack pleaded, trying to push down the dog.

"Cosmo, SIT."

Cosmo did, panting and wagging his tail excitedly, waiting for the command that would allow him to play again.

Amelia turned back to Jack, and asked again, "What do you want?" She saw the bruise on his nose, and briefly wondered what had happened, but figured however it got there, he deserved it.

"I wanted to apologize."

She crossed her arms. "That's a good start."

"And I want you to teach me. Everything you know, I want to know it too. Magic, fairies, all the history, how it all works, I want to know it all."

Amelia stood in the doorframe in silence, stunned. This was not what she was expecting.

"You called me crazy the other day."

"I did. And I'm sorry."

"You said Lila was just a dream."

"Well, she proved me wrong on that. Again, I'm sorry."

"You literally ran from here."

"I was an idiot. I'm sorry."

She furrowed her brow and squinted, examining him skeptically. "How do I know this isn't a ploy to get on my good side so I'll sign over my land to you?"

"You don't. But it's not. And that might not mean much to you, but the thing is, I've been looking for something bigger my whole life. Something's been missing. And this is it."

She stared at him, not sure how to respond.

"*Please*," he pleaded. "Teach me."

"No," she said after a moment of consideration.

Jack blinked. "What?"

"No. You must be used to me saying that word by now."

"But I apologized."

"So?"

"But…" he leaned in and said in a low whisper, "But I can see fairies!"

"So can I. And so can Emily. Doesn't mean I'm going to help you. You've been a thorn in my side since day one. I gave you a chance the other day, you blew it. So now I'm done."

"But—"

But before he could utter another word, she'd slammed the door behind her, leaving him alone on her porch, bewildered.

✳ Chapter 15 ✳

Dog on the run

Jack drove back into town, deciding to go for a walk down Calvary's Main Street to clear his head, contemplating what his next steps should be. Amelia had turned him away—not that he was surprised, after the way he'd acted the last time he saw her, and given her track record of turning him down. But in a way, he did feel a bit rejected—he'd genuinely thought after Lila's appearance that morning, it was a sign he would be immediately forgiven and given a chance.

Clearly though, Amelia didn't see it that way. Not that he blamed her. First, he'd hounded her grandfather, then her, then he insulted her...

He shook his head at himself. What was it about the Davidson family that drove him so crazy?

Probably the magic.

He looked up, just now noticing where he stood: in front of a weathered gray building, beneath its' giant navy-blue wooden sign, with large, blocky white lettering that read *Davidson's Fish Market*. He scoffed. He couldn't seem to get away from them.

He wondered if Charles was inside. He could use a friendly face after the beating he'd just taken.

He entered the building, the bell at the entrance tinkling as he did so, announcing his arrival. He looked around, in awe of the assortment of ocean treasures before him. He'd never entered Stuart's place of business before, and he had to admit, he was impressed. Before him were glass refrigerators full of the best cuts of Atlantic cod, halibut, mackerel, salmon, bass, and more; sitting on ice, bushels of mussels, clams, scallops, and crabs; and of course, tanks full of some of the largest live lobsters he'd ever seen. The smell of fresh seafood filled the air, though he noted it wasn't the repugnant stench of rotting fish as some seafood shops were: everything here was clean—immaculately so—and stored properly, the merchandise kept as fresh as it could possibly be. Clearly, Stuart had taken pride in this place, and Charles was following suit.

Having heard the entrance bell ring, a worker stepped from the back room to the register, greeting Jack with a hearty, "How ya doin' today?"

"Fine, thanks."

"Can I help you with anything?"

Jack shook his head. "No, just looking. I've never been here before. Just wanted to see what it was all about."

The worker smiled. "We're about fish, if it helps."

Jack snorted, a small smile crossing his face as well. "Clearly. Thanks."

As he meandered the rows of tanks and refrigerators, Charles appeared from the back room, looking for his employee to help unload one of the boats that just came in. Seeing Jack, he grinned and approached him.

"Jack! Amelia turned you away again?" he teased.

"She did," Jack said shortly.

"So, you came here to sulk?"

Jack smiled at Charles' bluntness. "Something like that, I suppose. I was walking down the street trying to figure out what to do next, and found

147

myself in front of the building…I've never been inside here before, thought I'd stop in and see what it was about."

"We're about fish."

"So I hear."

"Is there anything I can actually help you with? Or are you just browsing?"

"Just browsing."

"Well, if you need anything, just holler. One of the boats just came in, I'll be around back unloading it."

"Can I help?" Jack asked. The question surprised even himself.

Charles raised an eyebrow. "I mean—you're not an employee, I can't pay you."

"I'm not asking to be paid. I just need something to do, to get my mind off…things. Besides, you let me help you load the truck the other night."

"True enough," Charles remembered. He waved for Jack to come behind the counter. "Well, come on. An extra set of hands will make it go quicker."

Jack followed Charles to the back of the building, adjacent to a set of docks. One of the fishing boats was moored, and men were already unloading trays of lobsters, setting them on scales to be weighed, then placed onto flatbeds to be put into a few buyers' trucks waiting nearby.

"Where are they going?" Jack asked, curious about this process.

"Not far—today I'm just supplying to a few of the local restaurants, and keeping a few for myself here for the market for the locals to buy," Charles answered.

"So, you run the shop and have a fleet of boats?"

"Sure do. I have ten boats in my little fleet."

"Sounds like a lot to manage."

"It is. But that's the Davidson family—they're all overachievers, right down the line. Stu got that trait from his grandfather, who got it from his father, and so on."

Jack thought on this a moment. "From his grandfather? Not his father?"

"Stu never knew his father," Charles said solemnly. "He died in action in World War II. Stu was just a baby when it happened. His grandparents helped his mother raise him after that."

"I see." Jack suddenly felt like he and Stuart would've had a lot in common had they known each other under different circumstances. He didn't know his father either. "So how long did this belong to the Davidsons before they sold to you?

"Over a century."

"Damn."

"You can say that again. Stuart's great-grandfather started the whole thing with just the shop, but he got annoyed being dependent on the fishermen for his supply. So, he got himself a boat and took to fishing himself, stocking his own shop. He was a typical Davidson. They don't like depending on anyone else."

Jack smirked. He was all too familiar with that particular Davidson trait.

Charles continued, "Over time, business grew, and more boats were added. We've got a nice little business going here, and our buyers cover a

149

good chunk of New England. Most of them will meet us at the docks and pick up themselves, but I'll drive down and make deliveries to a few of our customers." He grinned at Jack. "You got lucky a couple days ago. I wasn't originally supposed to go to Boston, but that particular customer's truck broke down, and mine just happened to be getting out of the shop that same day. Funny how things work out like that."

Jack smiled in return as he unloaded the trays. "Sure is."

They went about the business of unloading the lobsters. Jack wouldn't say it was mindless work by any means, but it had a rhythm to it, allowing him to refocus. He surprised himself when he realized he sort of enjoyed it—it was good, hard work that made him break out in a sweat, made him feel like he was doing something worthwhile. The lobsters he was unloading would feed somebody, and that in and of itself was a notion that made for a decent, honest living. He couldn't remember the last time he felt that way about Dunstan Enterprises. He knew once, long ago, he'd been excited about the prospect of taking part in the creation of something people could call home. But that excitement and satisfaction had faded over these past few months, leaving him feeling instead like he was trudging through each day with no real purpose.

As he worked, he looked up, noticing some seals sunbathing on the rocks in the harbor. He smiled, thinking how nice it must be to be a seal, to not have any real cares in the world but feeding and breeding, to be able to bask in the sun on a rock without worrying about an eccentric boss, paying rent, or any of those other human anomalies.

As he watched the seals, he noticed they had turned their attention and seemed to be watching *him*—he was sure he was imagining things, but he was almost convinced one of them made eye contact and held it with him for just a moment before laying back down and continuing to soak up the sun.

As he considered the ludicrousness of this notion, that a wild seal should actually notice and pay any attention to him, he was pulled from his thoughts by a familiar voice calling out Charles' name. Looking up from the boat, he saw Amelia approaching the dock with Cosmo on a leash at her heel, looking for Charles. She, however, hadn't noticed him. He kept his back turned to her, crouching low behind some of the lobster cages on the boat, hoping to avoid a confrontation.

"What can I do for you, Amelia?" he heard Charles ask.

"Well, first, I'd love a couple of those lobsters for dinner tonight." Amelia pointed at one of the trays. "Second, I wanted to talk about getting a vendor contract going with you."

"A vendor contract, huh?" Charles asked, a hint of amusement in his voice.

"Well, *yeah*. It only makes sense I get the seafood for the Blue Barn from the place my grandfather used to own. That way we're still sort of keeping it in the family."

"Nothing would make me happier," Charles responded. "I've got my hands full the rest of the day, but why don't you come by when we open in the morning and we'll work something out?"

"Sounds good to me. Thanks, Charles!"

When she'd turned the corner and disappeared from view, Cosmo trotting along at her side, Charles turned to Jack, who was still hidden behind the lobster cages.

"You really that afraid of that little girl?" Charles asked, bemused.

Jack slowly stood up straight, but not before looking over the cages to see if he was in the clear.

"She's gone, son," Charles confirmed "What the hell did she do to you to scare you so badly?"

"She didn't scare me. Just not in the mood to see her again today."

151

"Mmm hmm."

It was in that moment they heard Amelia's voice clearly ring out from the street in front of the market, "COSMO, NO! COSMO! STOP! NO! COME!"

The two men exchanged a glance, and instinctively, went running off the dock towards the sound of her shout. When they reached the front of the building, they saw her standing in the middle of the sidewalk, a panic-stricken look on her face, no Cosmo in sight. They ran towards her.

"We heard you shout, what happened?" Charles asked.

"Cosmo—he saw a squirrel and he just...he pulled so hard, and my hand slipped, and he just took off!" Amelia's face was red with worry.

"Which way did he go?" Jack asked.

Amelia stood there, staring at him, dumbfounded to be face-to-face with him again, bewildered by him being there with Charles.

"AMELIA. Which way did he go?" Jack repeated, refocusing her.

"That way." She pointed down the road. "I tried to run after him, but he's so fast, and he just ran across the road and disappeared..."

Jack simply nodded, and took off running as fast as he could in the direction she pointed, calling Cosmo's name and dodging cars, who stopped suddenly as he crossed, honking at him.

He, however, didn't even notice this: he was on a mission. Throughout the pursuit, he would occasionally catch glimpse of the dog and call his name, but the dog, in return, would simply wag his tail, let him get close, then bolt again, like it was some great game of chase.

After about ten minutes of this, Jack noticed the buildings were spread farther and farther apart, and before long, he was at the edge of town, beyond him, fields of flowers spotted with groves of pine trees. He stopped, panting. He wasn't even sure he was on the dog's trail anymore.

It was in that moment he heard a soft whimpering sound. He whirled his head about to see where it came from. There, behind a nearby tree, he heard it again. He approached the tree slowly, cautiously, not wanting Cosmo to run again.

But Cosmo wasn't going anywhere. When Jack looked behind the tree, he saw the dog curled up on the ground, licking his paw.

"Hey, buddy," Jack said softly. "Whatcha doin' there?"

He crouched down—Cosmo had snagged his paw nail on something during the chase, splitting it. Blood was pouring from the wound, and he was crying.

"Oh, buddy…we need to get you to a vet." Jack scooped up the dog like a baby. Surprisingly, Cosmo didn't fight Jack, but let him carry him back down the road into town to where Charles was standing with Amelia, comforting her.

When they saw Jack approach, Amelia ran over. Seeing Cosmo's wound, she asked, "What happened?"

"He snagged his paw on something." Jack continued to walk quickly towards his car. "We need to get him to a vet."

Not even asking for Amelia's permission, Jack gently placed the dog in the backseat of his car, and got into the driver's seat. Amelia, without hesitation, jumped into the passenger seat.

"I'll direct, you drive," Amelia instructed, glancing back to look at Cosmo, who was still whining and licking his paw. As Jack pealed out of

153

the parking spot, she scratched the dog's ears, saying gently, "You're going to be okay, buddy."

✳

A couple hours, three hundred dollars, and one emergency vet visit later, Jack and Amelia found themselves standing in the living room of the cottage. Cosmo was resting on his bed, sedated with a bandaged paw and a cone around his neck.

The vet had trimmed the nail back as short as she could, cleaned the area, wrapped it, and sent Amelia home with a plethora of different pills for Cosmo to take while he healed for the rest of the week—but not before snidely commenting to Amelia this never would've happened had she trimmed Cosmo's nails the proper length. Amelia, in turn, chewed the vet out, defending her grooming of Cosmo, and Jack had to step in and almost forcibly remove the feisty woman from the clinic before she caused a bigger scene, trying to carry a heavily sedated Cosmo as he did so.

"Jack…thank you." Amelia was crouched next to Cosmo, gently stroking his face.

Jack smiled. "You're welcome. Happy to help, and happy it wasn't worse."

Amelia nodded her agreement. "Vet said he'll be able to get out of the cone and back to his normal routine in a week."

"That's good. Though how you'll keep him chill for a week is beyond me," Jack laughed.

"That's what the sedation pills are for," she smiled. She paused. "Maybe…maybe you could come by in a week, when the cone's off. I'm sure he'd love to see you."

"I'd love to see him. But Amelia…you don't owe me anything."

"I know. But I feel like I do."

"I'm not pressuring you."

"I know. But I think—well, you're a Guardian. What you did today…well, you're a good person, Jack. And I was being stubborn. So, I'll teach you."

"Really?"

"Yes. But I have two conditions."

"Name them."

"When it comes to studying magic, you do everything I say."

"Of course."

"And you stop trying to buy my property."

He hesitated. That would be a more difficult agreement, given Adrien's persistence.

Amelia noticed the hesitation. "This is your last shot, Jack. I'd take it, if I were you."

He sighed. "Okay. I give. I'll stop trying to buy your property."

"Good," she said, satisfied. "What happened to change your mind anyway?" She sat in one of the chairs in the living room, motioning for him to do the same.

"Lila attacked me, and a weird little brown elf dude punched me in the nose." He winced at the memory, noticing his nose throbbing again.

"Sounds about right." That explained the bruise on his face. "And they're called brownies."

155

"So, what exactly is it you do?" Jack sat in the same chair he had sat in the other night, where Amelia had first told him about Guardians and magic. "I mean, can you do magic?"

Amelia laughed and shook her head. "No, like I said the other night, I can't. And like I told you the other night, we're Guardians. We record and pass down the stories of magic—both the stories from before us, and our own that we live. We help look after the creatures that remain, and we keep their secrets."

"But if we can't use magic, how do we actually protect them and look after them?"

"It was easier when we could use magic," Amelia explained. "But now we basically just keep track of the land magical creatures live on and make sure it's protected—sometimes using legal action to protect it, sometimes buying it up and passing it down through the generations, sometimes having it turned into parks."

"What kind of parks are we talking about? Just regular parks? Or like state parks or national parks?"

Amelia smiled coyly. "Yes. To all of the above."

"There are Guardians in the *National Park Service*?"

"Well, yeah. The National Park Service was founded by a Guardian."

Jack was flabbergasted. "Teddy Roosevelt—*President* Teddy Roosevelt—was a *Guardian*?"

"Rumor has it he enjoyed tracking Bigfoot," Amelia stated nonchalantly. "He didn't ever kill one, of course, because that would be against the Guardian code of conduct. But he liked the sport. It was kind of a game between them and him—like a really elaborate version of hide and seek. Apparently, the Bigfoot are pretty playful creatures once you get to know them."

"Teddy Roosevelt played hide and seek with Bigfoot," Jack repeated in utter disbelief.

"Supposedly."

"And the National Park Service is a front for protecting magical creatures."

"Started that way."

"Wait, what magical power does Bigfoot have?" Jack inquired, backtracking.

Amelia smiled. "Invisibility."

Of course.

"So are all national parks home to magical creatures?" Jack continued, still in disbelief.

"For the most part, yes. Though I'm kind of surprised you're hung up on the whole National Park thing and not on the part that we used to be able to do magic," Amelia commented, eyebrow raised.

"Listen, you're telling me there's this whole secret magical protection conspiracy thing happening behind the scenes at our National Parks. I can only process one thing at a time," Jack retorted. "But yeah, that whole part about you used to do magic? Why can't you anymore?"

"I personally couldn't ever do magic," Amelia explained. "Guardians in general could. But after the Fallen Sorcerer betrayed his duties, the Creator Sorcerer stripped all Guardians of their magic, so they could never manipulate the magical creatures again. He did, however, leave us with the ability to call on the creatures we were meant to protect."

"What does that mean?"

"If you're not from a line of Guardians, magical creatures won't be drawn to you. They'll avoid you. You might accidentally catch a glimpse of one, but you'll forget it quickly after, and they won't purposely reveal themselves to you. And if you call for one and you're not a Guardian, they won't come. That's part of the protection spells the Creator Sorcerer placed on his creatures. But if you're a Guardian, they will come when you call. It's almost like you're a homing beacon for them. It makes it easier for us to keep track of them, and to help them as we can."

"So, here's what I don't understand—you said the other night you've been able to see magical creatures since you were a kid. I'm only just now seeing them. Why?"

Amelia shook her head. "I don't know the answer to that. It's weird to me too."

Jack sat, ruminating on this, wondering if his family being Guardians had anything to do with him being abandoned as a small child. But that was a question for a later time, and not something he wanted to burden Amelia with right now.

"So, we have this homing beacon thing going, we can see magical creatures, and we used to be able to use magic and we can't anymore," Jack summarized, more for his sake than Amelia's. "And somehow, without magic, we're supposed to protect the creatures."

"Yes. Legend also has it there will come a day when we will be able to use magic again, when that little dormant glimmer of magic inside of us will come alive."

"When is that supposed to happen?"

"Supposedly when the world is on the brink of destruction."

"Typical," Jack snorted. "Any idea when that will be, or how that will turn out?"

"It's sort of unclear."

"Try me."

"You'll have to read it for yourself." With this she stood, plucking old journals and books from the shelves, handing them to him. "We've got a good chunk of stuff recorded. There was a point in time when Guardian families used to keep in touch and share information with each other…but that doesn't happen much nowadays."

"Why not?"

"Well, for one, we've become more secretive. It's not exactly something you go around publicizing in this day and age. So, we don't really know *who* other Guardians are unless explicitly told."

"That makes sense."

As Amelia handed Jack the books, Emily walked in the front door after having been out in town running errands. Seeing Jack sitting in the living room, her jaw dropped and her eyes went wide.

"What are *you* doing here?" she demanded. Seeing Cosmo curled up in the corner with the cone on his head and the bandaged paw, she cried out as she ran over to him, "What happened to Cosmo?"

"He's fine," Amelia reassured her. "Just broke a nail. Vet said he'll be good in about a week."

"And what does *he* have to do with it?" Emily demanded, jerking her head in Jack's direction, crouched down and petting the injured dog.

159

"He helped. Cosmo got loose in town, he chased him down and helped take him to the vet," Amelia responded. She paused. "He's also asked us to teach him."

Emily's lip curled into almost a snarl. Turning to Jack, she said, "Just because you helped our dog doesn't mean we owe you."

"I know it doesn't," Jack said curtly. "I didn't say it did."

"I offered," Amelia stepped in.

"What changed your mind anyway?" Emily scoffed, eyes still on Jack.

"Lila and a brownie attacked me," Jack replied.

Emily glanced briefly at the bruise across his nose. "*Good*. Serves you right."

"So…what do you say? Will you help me?"

Emily snorted. "Why should I trust you?"

"Honestly, you don't have any reason to," Jack answered. "But I need to make a change in my life, and I think this is it."

"Well, I'm not interested, not after the way you acted."

"*Emily*," Amelia scolded, appalled by her sister's reaction.

"No, she's right." Jack stood. "I've been putting you both through hell the past few months. I want to start over. But if you're not comfortable with me around, I understand. I'll go now."

"Good. *Go*," Emily snapped.

Amelia, however, handed Jack the stack of books she had pulled for him as he headed out the door, and pointedly said for Emily to overhear, "Read these. Come back this time next week and we'll discuss, okay?"

Jack nodded, relieved at least one of the sisters was receptive to him. "Okay."

She smiled at him, and he turned and headed out the door, eager and excited to absorb the information she had just given him.

Emily, meanwhile, was filled with irritation as she watched this scene unfold.

"I don't trust him." Emily stared skeptically at the door Jack had just exited. "And I don't understand why you *do*."

"I know you don't," Amelia sighed, heading to the kitchen. "I don't either completely."

"So why the *hell* are you agreeing to teach him about everything?" Emily demanded, standing now. "All he's done is harass us, and when he stopped harassing us, he insulted us! How do you know this isn't some kind of scheme to get us to trust him, and he'll use it against us?"

"I *don't* know that," Amelia snapped. "Don't you think the same thing crossed my mind?"

"So *why* are you going along with it?"

"Because my gut is telling me it's the right thing to do."

"Your damn gut also said we should start a bed and breakfast, and we're not exactly profiting from that," Emily retorted.

"Okay, first of all, we're not even *open* yet."

"We're also not booked to capacity yet for our opening!"

161

"We've got a month yet until that happens. Building a business takes *time,*" Amelia said crossly. "You knew what you were getting into and you went along with it anyway."

"You *forced* me into it, let's make that clear."

"Well, that's plain untrue. I wanted you a part of it, but there was no forcing. Second, I'm just trying to help him figure out who he is. He's *clearly* from a Guardian line."

"Don't you think it's a little strange he's just now figuring out he's a Guardian as an adult? How do you know he's not messing with us?"

"Emily, I *saw* him see Lila for the first time. *You* saw him see her. I don't know why he's figuring out so late, but I know he saw what he says he saw. He's not making that part up."

"That's all well and good, but that doesn't mean we're responsible for what happens to him."

"Listen, Grandpa always said we should give people second chances. He taught us we need to forgive people. He also said Guardians need to help each other. And how many other people our age have you met who are Guardians? Because I haven't met any, and honestly, it's kind of nice finding another one who isn't directly related to us or isn't from around here."

"Grandpa was too trusting and said a lot of crazy stuff. And I'm pretty sure he wouldn't want us to help the man who basically drove him to the grave."

"I think that's where you're wrong."

"Think what you want. I'm just *sick* of you telling me what we're doing with *my* life. You did this when we were kids, telling me what was best for me. You did this with the bed and breakfast and made me uproot my life and move to some podunk town with *nothing* to do! I had a life, you know! And friends! And now you're doing it again by making us help this guy who doesn't deserve our time!"

"Take some ownership for your actions, Emily," Amelia snapped at her younger sister. "*You* followed me when we were kids. You didn't have to listen to me, but you did. Regarding the bed and breakfast, you didn't have to move. *You* could've stuck to your guns. *You* could've sold out your share of the land—you were so hung up on the money, after all. But you didn't. *You* made the choice to team up with me. And let's be real, I didn't drag you away from anything worthwhile. You didn't have much going for you, and you know it. You were unemployed, and in a ridiculous living situation. And if you don't want to be involved in this, *fine*. You don't have to. I'm not forcing you. But *I* will teach him. And *I* will own any consequences that come from it. Because I'm an adult, and at least I take responsibility for my actions and don't blame everyone else around me for what's going on in *my* life."

The sisters stared at each other in silence, Amelia immediately regretting the harsh words she had just spoken, Emily mulling over the truth in them. Without another word, Emily exited the room to garden, slamming the door behind her. Amelia sat on the floor next to Cosmo and sighed, petting him.

Emily's words rang in her ears. Amelia determined she'd have to go slow with Jack, start small, make him earn her trust—*their* trust.

She sincerely hoped she was doing the right thing.

163

✳ Chapter 16 ✳

Questions

A week later, Jack and Amelia were sitting in the dining room at the cottage, drinking coffee and eating breakfast. Emily had made herself scarce that day, still peeved about the fact Jack would be spending time in their home, learning about magic.

Jack had spent the week pouring over the books and journals Amelia had supplied him, and after several phone calls to her with questions, Amelia finally said, "JACK. Write them down, bring them when we meet. I can't keep taking your calls—I'm trying to get a bed and breakfast up and running *and* write articles for the magazine, and I can't do that when you're calling me every half hour. I have a job too, you know."

And so he did: every time he had a question, he'd write it down, anxious for that meeting.

"Hi, Cosmo!" Jack greeted the dog when he walked in. Cosmo had noticeably improved, the cone off and bandage removed. One of his nails on his right paw was shorter than the others, but it would grow back— aside from that, he was back to his usual, spunky self.

Sitting at the table where Amelia was setting out coffee mugs, he procured his list of questions from his pocket and opened one of the journals she had loaned him. Diving straight in, he asked, "So, who exactly is the Fallen Sorcerer? Where did he go?"

"Hi, nice to see you too," Amelia said, eyebrow raised.

Jack stopped, realizing he hadn't so much as greeted Amelia, just the dog. "Sorry. That was rude. How are you?"

"I'm fine." Amelia smiled and poured coffee for the two of them. "How are you? Aside from anxious to get started?"

"I'm fine." He looked around the house, noticing Amelia was the only one there. "Where's Emily?"

"She's spending the morning with my mom," Amelia said curtly.

"Doesn't want to be here when I'm here?"

"Well…can you blame her? I mean, I'll admit even I'm having my doubts."

"No, I guess I can't." He paused. "I appreciate you meeting with me and doing this. Really."

Amelia nodded and sat. "You're welcome. Anyway, the Fallen Sorcerer?"

"Yeah." Jack took a sip of the coffee in front of him. "Where is he now?"

"We're not sure," Amelia answered. "He was sent into exile, and cursed to roam the earth as a powerless immortal. Guardians throughout history claim they've encountered him, but none of the stories were confirmed. He looks like an ordinary man. He doesn't have his magic, so the worst he could inflict on anyone is the same thing any other human could—which, yes, can be bad. For a little while in the 1930s and 40s, Guardians at the time thought it might be Hitler. When Hitler died though, that theory was written off."

"So, he can't be killed?"

"That's part of his curse. He can't die. He's doomed to wander without magic forever. It's said he remembers all—every loss he ever suffered, every loved one who ever died, every defeat he ever faced. With mortals, that pain fades over time, and we tend to get over most things, even forget. He doesn't. He's forced to face everything every day, for eternity. It's meant to be torturous, like what he did to the unicorns."

"A man like that deserves death." Cosmo, who was at Jack's feet, gave a small *woof*, almost as though he was agreeing with the human.

"I don't necessarily disagree," Amelia said slowly. "But the Creator Sorcerer decided he deserved a fate worse than death."

"The problem with that logic is now you have this psychopath wandering the earth, probably looking for ways to regain his power." Jack looked at his list. "What happens if he finds all the stones? He'd be able to steal their magic again."

"It could go one of two ways, I think. Either his power is restored, and we're in trouble...or the power destroys him. No one is sure, if we're being honest. We do think eventually magic will come back in the world, but we don't know how it will play out."

Jack sat, trying to absorb all this information. "So...when is this going to happen?"

"My grandfather thought it was already beginning. He was constantly talking about the shifts he was seeing with magical creatures, that they were acting differently, changing some of their habits and patterns, as if they were preparing themselves. He said he started noticing it when he was young, that things just started changing with them out of nowhere. Like they're in the calm before the storm."

"And what do you think?"

"I think there's something to his theory. But I don't know what it means, what's happening, or what to do about it. All I know is to do what

I've always done: protect the creatures, create the potions, and study the spells. Because someday, the stones will be reunited, magic will come back into this world, and there's going to be a struggle because of it. And if it happens in my lifetime, I intend to be ready."

Jack looked at his list once again. "Okay, another question: where did the Creator Sorcerer go? Why doesn't he just appear and make things right? And why didn't he fix things from the start?"

Amelia smirked. "That's more than one question."

"Just answer, please."

"We have a theory about that. The thought is the world needs to *choose* him, to choose magic. That's part of his love for his creation—he lets us decide our own fate. That's not to say there won't be consequences in our choices. But he doesn't desire to control us. To appear now and say a magic spell and POOF! make everything all better, and have us bend to his will…that's not love. That's control and manipulation, exactly what the Fallen Sorcerer was doing.

"We choose love. Every time we choose to love, and to do right, and to protect, it keeps that little bit of magic alive. And the Creator Sorcerer is in that little bit of magic We hope someday he'll come back. We don't know when that will be, or even *if* it will be, if I'm being honest, but we hope."

"Sounds like a religion."

"Not so much a religion as a lifestyle."

Jack looked at his list again, scanning it for a question that hadn't been answered yet. "So, what happens when the stones are reunited?"

"Nobody knows."

Jack raised his eyebrow skeptically. "So theoretically, *nothing* could happen."

"Theoretically, yes. There are a few schools of thought. One is magic will be restored to the world as it once was, but that also means dark magic will come back, which opens up the potential for it to be abused and for magical creatures to be harmed again."

"Not great."

"Right. Another theory is whoever reunites the stones will absorb the magic that's released, and become some sort of demi-god capable of destroying the universe."

"That's somewhat terrifying."

"Agreed. But there are others who theorize the reunification will call forward the Creator Sorcerer, who will return and bring a new era of peace and magic to the world."

"Best case scenario."

"Yes."

"What do you think would happen?"

Amelia hesitated. "I don't know. What I *do* know is whatever happens, I wouldn't want the stones to fall into the wrong hands. Magic is malleable, and if used by someone with evil intentions, can cause terrible damage."

"So, it's a good thing they're hidden."

"Yes. And that's why we were taught to not go looking for them— because we don't know what the consequences will be. We're called to protect magic and its creatures. If the stones are reunited, it could literally destroy the world."

168

"It could also make the world better," Jack retorted, playing devil's advocate. "Seems like magic could make life a lot easier and it'd be pretty awesome."

"It's complicated. We *do* want magic back in the world. The problem is, because of the Fallen Sorcerer, the world was corrupted with dark magic prior to the Creator Sorcerer creating the stones and freezing all magic."

"Why didn't he just remove dark magic?"

"It doesn't work that way. Dark magic is intertwined with good magic, but used improperly. The things the Fallen Sorcerer and his followers created were the result of that improper use. They created things that were never supposed to be. Guardians were never supposed to *create* life, just protect it. But they tried to play God, and dark, twisted creatures were the end result."

"Like what?"

"Like vampires. Or werewolves. Or goblins. Or kelpies. Chupacabra."

"Kelpies and chupacabra?"

"Kelpies are aquatic horses that lure people into bodies of water and drown them and eat them. Chupacabra are horned creatures that feed on livestock and blood."

"That's somewhat disturbing."

"Yes. And those are just the least powerful ones, supposedly. I have a journal about the dark creatures we know about, I'll let you borrow it."

"Again, why didn't he get rid of them?"

169

"Because once the Fallen Sorcerer created them, they became living beings. That's not how the Creator Sorcerer operates. He doesn't take life…even life that was never supposed to be."

"He sounds like a magical immortal hippie."

Amelia chuckled. "That's probably the best way to describe him." She paused, and more seriously, said, "All those dark creatures the Fallen Sorcerer created were put into hibernation, so they couldn't inflict any further damage and harm humans or the Creator Sorcerer's creatures. The thing is, if magic seeps back into the world, they will wake up again. That's partially why Guardians don't try to find and reunite the stones. If they're put back together, the general thought is the Fallen Sorcerer, whoever he is, wherever he is, will regain his power, and he'll have all his minions at his disposal. Essentially, there will be a war for the world."

"That sounds terrible," Jack said, his eyes wide.

"It will be."

"How can it be prevented?"

"It can't, except to keep the stones separated—which we know won't be forever—or unless the Fallen Sorcerer changes his ways and decides to use his magic for good."

"And the odds of that happening?"

"Slim to none."

"Got it. So…we're not just Guardians."

"No. We're not. Someday, when our magic returns, we'll be warriors."

"How will it end?"

"I don't know. But I do know Guardians won't go down without a fight."

"So, our job is to leave things be, protect the creatures, and fight when it's time."

"Yes. And if I'm being honest—and maybe this is my own fear and doubt, but take it as it is—I'd rather play it safe and keep things as they are by not looking for the stones, knowing the world will still be intact tomorrow, than take my chances and risk blowing it up. Kind of a basic rule I live by."

"Don't blow up the world?"

"Exactly."

"Good rule."

"I like to think so."

"Okay, so another question." Jack perused his list as he flipped through a different journal. "I kept reading about this place called the Beyond in this stuff you gave me. What is that?"

"We think it's where the Creator Sorcerer first came from."

"So, like an alternate dimension?"

"Something like that."

"What's there?"

"Peace. Joy. Love. Magic. Basically, the things that were supposed to be here in their purest forms on Earth before humans went and screwed it up."

171

Jack, remembering lessons from his childhood, particularly when he spent time with a church-going family, commented, "That sounds like Heaven."

"We think it might be that too."

"So an afterlife?"

"Why do you look confused about that?"

"I just never really thought about it."

"You mean you never really believed in it," Amelia corrected him, a knowing smile on her face.

"Well…yeah."

"Why is that so difficult to believe? You didn't believe in fairies until last week, but now you do. Why is the thought of an afterlife so out of reach? Just because we can't always see something, doesn't mean it's not real."

"Fair point. So, on that topic, how does magic align with all the other religions of the world? Which one is right? Which ones are wrong? Which one do you believe in?"

Amelia smiled. "There's an existential crisis waiting to happen if I ever saw one."

"You're not answering the question."

"You really want my answer?"

"Yes."

"I believe in love. I believe our souls aren't of this world, and they'll continue to live on when our bodies die. I believe what we do in life, what

172

we believe in life, will impact our afterlife. I believe in magic, and I believe in miracles. I believe there are things beyond human explanation—and even beyond magic's explanation. I believe there's a master plan, and we each have a purpose here in this world. I believe in second chances, and that we're given one. I believe the universe and the surrounding dimensions are too big and too complicated for us to ever fully comprehend, so I believe we all need to have faith in something bigger than ourselves. I believe there's a Creator, and I believe he has the capacity to take whatever shape he needs to take to work in our lives, and I believe he loves us."

"So…Christianity?"

Amelia simply smiled.

"Oh, come on, you're really not going to give me a straightforward answer?" Jack pressed.

"Jack, what do *you* believe?" Amelia asked, turning the tables on him.

"I don't know," he answered, taken aback. "I guess…well, I believe *you*."

"That's sweet. But I'm not a savior or a creator. I don't deserve that."

"But I can see you. And I believe you."

"And I believe in things that can't always be seen. I'm also flawed. You shouldn't put your faith in me, or in any human for that matter."

"So, show me what I should believe."

Amelia smiled and took a sip of her coffee. "We're working on it right now. Any other questions?"

Jack shook his head. "About a million."

"How about we walk and talk?" Amelia suggested. "I find walks help me organize my thoughts."

"Sure, that sounds good."

They exited the cottage, where they saw Lila, fluttering about in the sunshine. Seeing Amelia, she grinned and perched on her shoulder. Amelia smiled in return, and continued on with the conversation as normal.

"So just ask whatever comes into your mind," Amelia said, carrying on. "Nothing is too ridiculous."

Jack, however, still wasn't used to the sight of magical creatures, even though he'd experienced a few at this point, and found the fairy a bit distracting. He was stumbling over his words when he almost stumbled over Cosmo, who was napping on the porch in the mid-morning sun. The dog barely moved, lazily opening one eye to look at Jack briefly before closing it again.

"What about other animals? Are they aware of magical creatures?" Jack asked, Cosmo reminding him of another question he had in mind.

Amelia looked at Lila and nodded. Lila, in turn, fluttered over to Cosmo. Daintily, she landed on Cosmo's snout and tickled his nose. Cosmo, without even opening his eyes, sneezed. Lila, perturbed by being ignored by the dog, gave him a little tap on the head. His eyes popped open, and seeing the fairy before him, he gently swiped at her with his paw, as if to say, "Leave me alone!" Lila, however, was undeterred, and flew about the dog's head, trailing fairy dust behind her as she whizzed about. As she did so, Cosmo was overcome with a sneezing fit. Annoyed with the little woman by this point, he got up, chasing Lila through the field, with Lila giggling as she flew just beyond the dog's reach.

Amelia and Jack watched this series of events unfold, laughing at the antics of the dog and the fairy.

174

"Does that answer your question?"

"It does," Jack answered. "So, when dogs or cats sort of freak out for no reason, it's probably some kind of magical creature they're seeing?"

"Sometimes," Amelia agreed. "Not always. Sometimes animals are just plain weird."

With this, they turned back to watch Cosmo, who had decided he was done chasing Lila, and instead determined his own tail was much more interesting than the sparkly winged woman. After a few moments of him circling, he caught his tail in his mouth, and proud of himself, attempted to walk sideways to present it to Amelia and Jack. However, after a few awkward steps, he flopped over, where he proceeded to roll about in the grass.

"I love dogs," Amelia said with a smile, watching Cosmo. "Of all the creatures, both magical and non-magical, they're by far my favorite."

Hearing this, Lila, bee-lined over to Amelia, and furiously, gave her as hard of a kick in the head as she could muster.

"OW! HEY!" Amelia protested. Rubbing her head, she tried to redeem herself by saying, "But fairies are my favorite *magical* creatures!"

Lila, however, ignored her, and flew off in rage.

"She'll be back," Amelia said, still rubbing her head. "She always comes back."

"You think so? She seemed pretty upset," Jack said hesitantly.

"Fairies are only capable of feeling one emotion at a time. They're very intelligent, but also very simple little creatures," Amelia explained. "So yeah, once another emotion overcomes her, she'll come back. Believe me, she's done it a thousand times since I've known her."

"What's your least favorite magical creature?" Jack asked, looking after the fairy as she zoomed into the distance and out of sight.

"I don't know that I have a least favorite." She paused for a beat, thinking on this. "But Elves are kind of pretentious."

"Has anyone ever tried to use animals to find magical creatures?" Jack looked back at Cosmo, who was now prancing through the field, chasing a butterfly.

"Probably. But that means they'd have to believe the creatures existed in the first place. They'd also probably have a hard time with it. Even though animals can see magical creatures, magical creatures still keep themselves pretty well hidden. Lila's just a bit of the exception."

"Clearly. But what I don't understand is why hide them from humans, but not from animals, if they can potentially be used to hunt them?"

"Couldn't tell you that. Probably has to do with them sharing the same habitat and needing to be aware of each other. But really, think about it: what kind of animal would tell you where to find a fairy anyway?"

"Parrots," Jack replied gravely. "Parrots are creepy. And they can talk. They'd do it."

"Okay, weirdo." Amelia rolled her eyes. "Next time I read a fairy tale where a magical creature gets hurt, I'll blame it on the parrot." Turning back to Cosmo, she called, "COSMO! COME!"

The dog looked up from the flower he was sniffing, and bounded back to Amelia, his tail wagging and a big, happy puppy smile on his face.

"Good boy!" she praised, scratching behind his ears. "Good Cosmo!" Bending to kiss the top of his head, she continued, "Thanks for not eating Lila earlier. That was such a good boy, I'm so proud of you! You're such a good, smart, handsome boy!"

176

Cosmo may not have known exactly what his master was saying, but based on the cheerful, pleasant tone of her voice, he didn't care. After receiving what he considered to be a suitable amount of pets from Amelia, he trotted back to the cottage, wagging his tail the entire way. While the humans continued on with their walk, he remained on the porch. Curling up once again in that same spot of sunshine, he continued with the nap the fairy had interrupted.

✳

Around the same time Amelia and Jack were discussing magic and the meaning of life, Emily was having breakfast with Rosalie.

Emily's relationship with her mother, though complicated in her youth, had blossomed into something resembling mutual respect, though still with a twinge of bitterness from those teenage years. Emily knew what to say and not say after having lived alone with her for those years—and Rosalie knew any kind of chastising or criticizing would end in frustration for the two of them; therefore, both would try to keep the conversation light and shallow in an attempt to keep things as pleasant as possible, though this usually resulted in misinterpreted comments and walking on eggshells. In this way, they were much like each other. Topics of conversation they tried to avoid included magic, magical creatures, Brennan's death, and lately, Emily's ex-boyfriend, Dan, who had left Emily for her best friend.

"How are things going with the Blue Barn?" Rosalie asked as the waitress served her a plate of eggs, bacon, and toast, settling on what she thought was a safe topic to discuss. The two had met at May's Diner that morning.

"Good," Emily replied shortly, taking a bite of the pancakes from her own plate.

Rosalie examined her daughter for a moment. "Just good?"

"I mean, yeah, I guess. Renovations on the barn itself are done. Just a little more landscaping and we'll be ready to open. We're not fully booked yet for opening day though."

"But you have *some* bookings?"

"Yeah."

"Then that's a great start. You're not totally empty, and that's what matters."

"We only have four guest rooms, Mom. Two of which *are* still empty. It's not remarkable."

"It's better than nothing," Rosalie encouraged her. "And you've got a few weeks yet, I'm sure they'll fill for you. Building a business takes time. Believe me, your father and I were living off ramen for a couple of years there before he was able to build up his reputation enough to where he was getting work regularly. And you've got his determination and entrepreneurship. He was successful, I have no doubt you will be as well."

Emily smiled, needing to hear that. "Thanks, Mom."

"Of course. Not to mention, you've already got a leg up on him: you got the money from Grandpa's will." Rosalie took another sip of coffee. "You're not using any of your own. So, you should be making a profit from the start if you've used it wisely and didn't just sink it all."

Emily rolled her eyes. There was always some kind of backhanded comment with her mother. "We're still working hard, Mom."

"Of course you are, dear," Rosalie said casually. "I didn't mean to imply you weren't. I'm just saying, you're not desperate, so you shouldn't worry so much."

"Thanks. I guess."

Rosalie took this as her cue to change the subject. "How's your sister? I haven't seen her in a few weeks, not since she came to pick up Cosmo."

Not the best topic to change to.

"She's okay, I guess," Emily said distantly.

"Just okay? Are you two working together all right?"

"I mean, on the bed and breakfast, yeah, we're fine. We're on the same page about everything."

"Then what's the issue?"

Emily hesitated, knowing she was about to broach her mother's least favorite topic. "We met another Guardian, Mom."

Rosalie stopped mid-bite of her toast, caught off-guard by her daughter's statement.

Emily saw her mother's reaction. "Mom? You okay?"

Rosalie slowly set her toast down. "I'm fine." She paused. "How did you meet this...person?"

Emily leaned in. "You know that guy who's been coming around trying to get us to sell the land?"

Rosalie felt her face draining of all color.

"Him. He's a Guardian."

"But—how—I don't understand," Rosalie stammered, her eyes wide.

Emily shook her head, speaking in a hushed voice so the people at the tables surrounding them couldn't overhear. "Me neither. But he saw

179

fairies at our property last week. His car broke down and he had to stay the night until Dave could get it taken care of."

"Damn it, Dave," Rosalie muttered.

"Tell me about it. So Amelia stayed up that night talking to him about everything. And the next day he freaked out and called her crazy, that she had drugged him and made things up. But something must've happened, because he came back a couple of days later, apologizing and asking her to teach him about magic and all that. The weird thing is, Mom, apparently that was his first time seeing anything magical. He'd never seen a creature before then. It doesn't make sense. Amelia and I could see them our whole lives, but he's an *adult* seeing for the first time. Something's wrong."

Rosalie was stunned. "So, what, your sister's just teaching him?"

"That's the deal they worked out. She teaches him, he stops trying to buy our land."

Rosalie sighed. "I love that your sister thinks the best of people. But it's also one of her biggest weaknesses: she's too naïve and trusting."

"That's what I said," Emily said bitterly. "We got into it last week when it all went down. But you know her: once she's got an idea in her head, she won't stop until she sees it though."

"That's your father in her," Rosalie remarked, motioning for the waitress to come over and pour her another cup of coffee. Once the waitress had done so and left the table, Rosalie turned back to her daughter. "Keep an eye on them. Something about this doesn't feel right to me, like he might be using her. You're more pragmatic than she is. You get that from me. Look out for her."

"She's my *older* sister. And an adult. She doesn't need me to look out for her."

"I think she might, in this case. Don't let all you're working so hard for go out the window because your sister's head is in the clouds. I know it's tempting to let your guard down, especially meeting someone else like the two of you, but stay grounded. Try to keep *her* grounded. You've got so much ahead of you, don't let this man ruin it all."

Emily took another sip of her coffee. Finally, something she and her mother could agree on.

✳ Chapter 17 ✳

Fighting a giant

Jack hadn't slept well that night, having been up reading the book on dark creatures Amelia had loaned him, as promised. He was disturbed by the gruesome depictions of the creatures, but more than that, disturbed by the fact these creatures were all still *alive* somewhere, just in hibernation.

He sincerely hoped they wouldn't wake up in his lifetime.

When he entered the office the next morning, eyes bloodshot from lack of sleep, before he could even settle in at his desk, Stephanie, Adrien's secretary, approached him. She was a bit older than Jack, attractive and curvy, with brunette hair she frequently kept pulled back in a French twist. She was married to a prominent neurosurgeon in the city—the giant ring on her finger and expensive car she drove to the office indicated she didn't need to work, but still, she apparently enjoyed her job, as she kept coming back day after day. She was considered to be Adrien's "right hand man," as she was the only one in the company privy to his schedule or the details of his life.

"Mr. Dunstan would like to see you, Jack." She paused. "You look like hell. Maybe get some coffee before you see him."

Jack snorted. "Thanks, Steph. What's he want?"

"Same thing he always wants."

Jack sighed heavily. Adrien Dunstan's persistence becoming a bit obnoxious—obsessive, really. Annoyed, but keeping a poker face, he entered Adrien's office, where he found Adrien standing at one of the full-length windows, looking out over the city. When he heard Jack enter, he turned, and smiled.

"Good morning, Jack."

"Good morning."

"Beautiful day, isn't it? I love the view of the city in the morning."

"Lovely," Jack said shortly, irked by the pleasantries and waiting for Adrien to get to the point.

"So, Jack, I heard you were in Calvary again yesterday. Working the field?"

"Yes, sir."

"And where do we stand with acquiring the Davidson property?" Adrien asked, taking a seat behind his desk.

There it was.

Jack remained standing. "The Davidson sisters still refuse to sell."

"You've given them our incredibly generous offer?"

"I've gone as high as three and a half million so far, yes," Jack answered truthfully. "I'm working my way up to the five."

"I see. You offered them a house in the new development, totally paid for?"

"Yes."

"You offered to cover the cost of the construction they're currently undergoing?"

"Yes."

Adrien sat back in his seat. "Interesting. Did they give a reason for their stubbornness?"

Jack hesitated. To tell Adrien Dunstan about fairies would be ludicrous. He would think Jack insane.

"They just said it's their family's property for them to preserve for future generations, and they wouldn't give it up," he answered, telling half the truth. No need to go into the fact they were preserving it as a haven for magical creatures.

"Sentimental value, then," Adrien deduced.

"Yes."

"Amazing how people hang onto silly things like houses and land, even when given the opportunity to improve their quality of life."

"With all due respect, Mr. Dunstan, the land is beautiful, and the bed and breakfast they're about to open is charming. I can see why they would want to leave it as is."

"A charming house on beautiful land in a failing town will ultimately fail. It's not enough to bring people in, to earn a profit and make a living."

"See, that's the thing, Mr. Dunstan, that I don't understand—I've been there several times, and the town doesn't seem like it's failing. Small, yes. A bit sleepy, yes. But they're not poor. People aren't leaving town. They're not losing businesses. They're actually trying to build new businesses. And a lot of people were opposed to the build, saying it *would* drive their businesses out. So what makes you say they're failing?"

Adrien smiled coolly. "Things aren't always as they appear, Jack. And that's not your department anyway, to answer that question. You just focus on your part and get the land."

"But why do we need their property anyway? It's on the outskirts of the rest of the development. When I looked at the plans, their land was only going to be comprised of four houses, and the rest would be a large park. There's no real money in that. The other properties we've already acquired have plans for neighborhoods full of houses, and apartments…things that will bring in a profit."

"Not everyone wants to live in an apartment, Jack."

"I understand, but four houses? They own something like sixty acres, and only four houses are going on it? It doesn't make sense, and doesn't seem like their land is all that important to the rest of the community."

"On the contrary, Jack, their land is incredibly important. Yes, there are only four houses planned for the moment…but if this development is successful, we will need the room to grow." He paused. "It almost sounds like you're trying to talk me out of acquiring their property."

"Not at all," Jack responded hastily. "I was just trying to understand the reasoning behind it, to see if it was worth all the effort before we take it to the next level."

"I see. And do you think it's worth the effort?"

"Of course. But they will fight. You need to know that."

"Let them," Adrien replied coldly. "They will lose. They don't have the money or the resources. But let them try anyway."

Jack momentarily imagined a cloud of fairies wreaking havoc on the construction workers that would try to step foot on the land—he had seen what Lila alone could do. A whole army of fairies would cause absolute chaos. The Davidson sisters certainly had all the resources they needed, though maybe not the kind Adrien Dunstan was thinking of. He smiled at this thought, not realizing he was doing so.

"What's so funny, Jack?" Adrien asked, seeing Jack's smile.

"Nothing, sir," Jack answered quickly. "Just agreeing with you."

"Good. Go back and try again. Up the offer again. Everyone has their breaking point. Let's find theirs. And if they still refuse, that's fine. We'll do it the hard way."

Jack raised an eyebrow. "The hard way?"

Adrien smiled. "That part won't concern you. We're done here, Jack."

Jack left Adrien's office, unsettled.

✳

Jack went home that night, discouraged. He had a job to do. Adrien made that much clear. He wasn't the type to shirk his duties—he'd never been. But he also had another duty, one that suddenly seemed so much more important than the one Adrien had assigned. He needed to protect that land, and the creatures who lived on it. It was too late for the Benedict land, it was already under construction, but he could maybe delay on contracts for the Kowalski and Erickson land. It was worth a shot, at least. And it was the least he could do, considering he'd already helped destroyed acres of magical creature habitat.

As for the Davidson land—it was clear he wouldn't be acquiring it. He *couldn't* now, knowing what he knew, and especially after making that promise to Amelia. He wouldn't. But he'd been given a timeline. He'd been told if he didn't acquire it, he'd be let go, no questions asked.

He walked into the bathroom and turned on the sink, splashing his face with water.

186

Looking into the mirror, he said out loud to himself, "I'm going to be fired."

That was all there was to it. He knew he wouldn't have anything to show at the end of the six months. He'd have to bluff the entire time, let Adrien think he was working Amelia and Emily. But he wouldn't be trying to acquire their property. He'd be learning from them—well, Amelia more than Emily. And he'd be fired at the end of it when he came up empty-handed.

In some ways, it was a relief, coming to this conclusion. He knew ahead of time what the result would be, and what he had to do. He'd be able to job hunt, and have something lined up to fall back on for when it all went down. He'd been unhappy at Dunstan Enterprises for a few months now anyway—though he liked the job in general, and loved the pay, and got along fairly well with most of his coworkers and employees, he hated working under Adrien. The man was demanding and intolerable, and had grown increasingly so since the start of the Calvary project.

Since it had begun, Jack had been growing suspicious of some of Adrien's business practices, and had questioned his own decision to remain with the company. Some of the Adrien's tactics had seemed unethical, almost manic, and his own conscience had become troubled in recent months—especially since the disappearance of Max from the project, and Max's concerns prior to his disappearance.

He didn't have exact proof of questionable practices, but his gut was telling him there was something off—and his gut was usually right. He'd have to look into it. The remaining months gave him time to compile evidence and build a case, if there was a case to be built. If there *was* something there, if the things Max had mentioned were legitimate, he could go to the authorities with evidence at the end of those six months, helping to ensure Dunstan Enterprises would leave the Davidson sisters and the remaining neighbors who hadn't sold out yet alone. But he had to remain the six months—he couldn't leave sooner, he couldn't let Adrien catch on. He had to protect Amelia and Emily for at least six months, he owed them that.

187

But what if it doesn't work? What if there was nothing there?

There was that nagging doubt. What if there was nothing there, and he lost his job over a wild goose chase? Or, what if there *was* something, but he didn't have enough evidence, the authorities dismissed his allegations, he was fired in six months anyway, and Dunstan Enterprises hired someone else and the harassment started for the sisters all over again? What if he wasn't able to find another job, his reputation was ruined, and he couldn't provide any kind of protection? What if the sisters eventually grew so sick of the harassment that they, like the Benedicts, caved? What if Dunstan Enterprises continued to acquire more land, eventually driving out other creatures in other areas of the country, ruining their habitats and leaving them helpless? What would happen to them then?

He splashed his face again, shaking his head. No. He couldn't think that way. There was something there. He knew it. He just had to figure out what. And those six months also gave him time to learn as much as he could from the Davidson sisters about what it meant to be a Guardian, and what his role was—because if he ended up in another job (or worse, imprisoned, if Adrien was able to twist it), he might not have the luxury anymore to visit them. And he needed to know who he was. He was grasping for straws, trying to find something, *anything*, that could tie him to the family he never knew. He was a Guardian, so one of his parents must have been one, and their parents, and so on. He didn't know what it meant to be a Garridan, but with this, he had something to go off. It wasn't much, but it was *something*.

He looked at himself in the mirror, jaw set, determined.

He was going to fight a giant.

✳

The next few weeks went by in a flurry of activity. Jack kept his regular weekday meetings with Amelia to make it appear to Adrien as though he was still pursuing the Davidson property—in addition, he and Amelia agreed to also meet on the weekends. He'd become their first regular guest at the bed and breakfast before it even officially opened. When he was not in Calvary, he spent his time at the office in Boston, doing his actual job to keep up appearances, while simultaneously covertly trying to find a lead on any sort of malpractice on the side of Adrien Dunstan. So far, nothing—just his hunch and several dead ends.

As for the Blue Barn, it was up and running, and much to Amelia and Emily's delight, was booking up. Despite Emily's doubts, they were fully booked for their opening day. With the influx of bookings, Jack was kicked out of his "regular" room, relegated to sleeping on the couch in the cottage during his visits, "To make room for *actual* guests," as Emily so tactfully put it.

Emily was also pleased some people were taking an interest in the charter fishing option. It was summer, and that meant people flocked to the coast for their beach vacations. With the addition of their bed and breakfast to the town businesses, along with the promise of an ocean excursion, the small town of Calvary was becoming an alluring option for city-dwellers who wanted to get away, but who were tired of the over-crowded hubbub of the regular coastal vacation spots. Calvary was starting to get on the map, thanks in part to the sisters' wise investment in marketing their business, as well as Amelia's ability to write about the area in the magazine she worked for.

Their hard work was paying off, and they were already planning for the fall. Though still a few months away, the sisters planned promotions in order to keep a steady flow of business during the off-season, coming up with "Autumn Harvest" promotions for September and October, a "Thanksgiving Feast" special at the end of November, and a "Winter Wonderland" retreat for the holiday season starting just before Christmas and lasting through the New Year.

As for Emily's relationship with Jack, grudgingly at first, she made an attempt to be friendly with him after her conversation with her mother. It was simply the easiest way to keep an eye out for him and on Amelia. She'd keep reminding herself of the saying, "Keep your friends close, and your enemies closer." Though she had her doubts about him, she did find herself eventually warming up to him, even hoping she was wrong about him. She had to admit, it *would* be nice knowing another Guardian who she could trust. It would make life a little easier.

Even Rosalie would stop by the bed and breakfast occasionally, checking on her daughters, and noting Jack's increased presence on the premises, but biting her tongue—Emily had told her she would handle it, and she trusted her daughter to do so, but as the girls' mother, she found it difficult to step out of the fray completely. She simply didn't trust Jack, something Jack picked up on. He sighed with relief every time she left, more at peace without her hovering. Though he was never completely at ease, as even though Emily was making an attempt to be friendly (though rather weak, in his opinion), he could sense much of her disdain stemmed from her mother's opinion of him.

While all this was happening, the first wave of fairies made their exodus north. It happened on a warm night in late spring, in the middle of the night when no one else was awake to see it, just days before the bed and breakfast opened. Lila had let Amelia know it was time, and the three stayed up to bid the fairies farewell. Jack stood in awe on the porch as he watched, dazzled by the sight of thousands of tiny fairy lights emerging from the grasses and trees and shrubs of the surrounding land, and all migrating upward, then away. He couldn't help laughing as Cosmo stood in the field in the midst of all this, confused by the activity of the little people and barking into the night, prancing about as fairies swirled around him. Jack likened it to fireflies who would emerge from the woods and light up the darkness, or perhaps to thousands of twinkling falling stars, except instead of coming down to the earth, they all floated up, gently blown by the breeze. It was a sight he'd never seen before.

Amelia and Emily, on the other hand, were more sober that night, not as dazzled by the sight or even amused by Cosmo's antics, saddened by what the fairy migration represented. Two more waves remained, and once gone, it meant the end of an era. Their hearts were broken that night, and they left the scene more determined than ever to make sure their business succeeded, to not give Dunstan Enterprises any reason to pull the rug from under them. Jack swore up and down he would abide by his promise to not try to buy their land out, and he was becoming frantic in his effort to find a legitimate way to keep his company away from the sisters and their home. He'd come to a standstill for the time being, hoping and praying something in his lessons with Amelia might inspire him to look at things from a different angle. In the meantime, however, he still had to keep up his front with Adrien that he was a loyal employee, not an easy task.

It was early July, and he was getting a bit antsy with his lessons, as even they seemed to be becoming stale. Up until that point, Amelia had just been having him read and review old journals and books about magical creatures, spells, and potions. While he would read, she would sometimes sit on her laptop and type, working on some article for her job. He had to admit, he wondered if his plan to leave Dunstan Enterprises and get them off the Davidson sisters' backs would be worth it. He was growing weary of pouring over old, yellowed pages and asking questions. Each time they met, he had to mentally prepare himself for another day of reading books, drinking tea, and overall, being bored out of his mind— not something he'd expected to be when he first learned about magic. He felt much like a high schooler again, disinterested with class, not feeling challenged. He wanted to know more, to do more. He knew he needed to talk to Amelia about it and express his concerns.

That day, when he arrived at the Davidson cottage, he sat, wrinkling his nose slightly as he saw Amelia walk into the dining room with a pot of tea. It was going to be another day of reading.

Amelia dove right in, handing him a journal about magical creatures and reading off their descriptions. Jack sat in a stupor, not able to concentrate.

"Amelia, when are we going to do more than this?" he asked, interrupting her monologue about the life cycle of mermaids.

Amelia looked up at him. "Do more than what?"

"*This*." He motioned to the piles of books and papers in front of them. "Just…talking. When am I going to apply things practically?"

Amelia set down the journal from which she had been reading. "Jack, I've told you this a hundred times: we can't use magic."

"Okay, but there must be more than *this*," Jack argued. "You said your grandfather taught you every summer for *years*. You can't tell me he just read old journals to you."

"No, he didn't," Amelia admitted.

"So, what else is there? I've memorized everything you've given me. I've read all the books. I've asked all the questions. What's next?"

Amelia hesitated. "There is more we can do."

Jack sat up straight, his interest piqued. "Well? What is it?"

"I just…Jack, what does your boss think you're doing when you're out here with us?"

"What does that have to do with anything?"

"Just answer the question."

"Working your weaknesses to talk you into selling," Jack answered bluntly, taking a sip of the tea in front of him.

Amelia fell silent, stunned by his answer.

"I'm not, you know," Jack commented, noticing the look on her face.

"I know."

"Do you really?"

Amelia didn't reply. She knew Jack wouldn't like her answer.

"Amelia, what do you need me to do to prove I'm not trying to trick you?" Jack set the teacup in front of him, picking up on her hesitation.

"Maybe stop going after my neighbors too."

"That wasn't part of the agreement," he argued, shaking his head. "I said I'd stop trying to buy from *you*."

"Well, I'm sorry, but I'm having some trouble completely trusting someone who's still taking land from my community."

"Amelia—"

"No, you need to listen to me," she interrupted. "You and I know very well once this development pops up, there will be no place left for the people who were already here. We won't be able to afford to live here anymore."

It was Jack's turn to fall silent, mulling over Amelia's argument.

"You know I'm right," Amelia said.

"Is that why you won't do more with me? You don't trust me, you're afraid to show me more, so you're just having me read a bunch of old books hoping it will satisfy me?"

Amelia remained silent, not meeting his gaze.

"Amelia."

She nodded. "Yes."

He sat back in his chair, frustrated. "That's not fair, Amelia. I've been keeping up my end. You're purposely trying to hold me back."

"I know…I know." Amelia felt incredibly guilty in that moment. "But you have to admit, this is a pretty weird situation. We went from basically hating each other to…*this*, whatever this is." She motioned towards the books and papers in front of them. "And it doesn't help Emily is still pretty unsettled about it all, and brings it up regularly. We fought about it when I first agreed to teach you. I still think about that fight, and it still bothers me."

"What do you want me to do about it?"

"I already told you. *Stop*. I know our agreement was only about my land, but Jack, I can't fully trust you unless you stop altogether. And if I don't trust you, our lessons won't go anywhere."

"I can't."

"Why not?"

"Amelia, I need to do my job." He paused. Now was the time to tell her about his agreement with Adrien, and his plan to get out. "Adrien is going to fire me in a few months when he finds out I'm not getting your land."

"What?"

Jack sat back in his chair and sighed. "Yeah. That was our deal. Before I knew about the fairies and everything, he wasn't happy I hadn't acquired your land yet. He threatened to fire me on the spot. I talked him into giving me six more months to work you. But he said if I didn't have your land by the end of that time, I was gone." He looked at her, and very seriously, said, "Amelia, I'm going to lose my job for you. I've been bluffing for weeks now. In the end, he's going to know I didn't get your land, and he's going to let me go. I've already accepted it. I've even started job hunting so I have something to fall back on when it all goes down. But in the meantime, I need to keep doing my job, for two reasons: one, to pack as much money into savings as I can so I have something to tie me over if I'm between jobs; and two, to keep having a reason to come out here and learn from you—because once the next job rolls around, I don't know if

I'll have that luxury. If that doesn't earn your trust, I don't know what will."

"I don't understand though…if you know you're going to be fired anyway, and you're already job searching, why don't you just quit now?"

"Because I'm trying to protect you. Don't you see that? Once I'm out of a job there, Adrien will put somebody else in my place, and they'll come after you again. And I guarantee, with as impatient as he's been with *me*, he'll be ruthless about it when he puts someone else in, because by that point, he will be completely out of patience. I'm trying to hold that off as long as possible. If I leave now, it will just happen sooner."

"So, what am I supposed to do then?" Amelia asked frantically. "If you're going to be gone in a few months, what's the plan? How do we get them to leave us alone when they come after us?"

"You won't need to worry about that, I hope. I'm working on something to take care of it. I've got a gut feeling about a few things, and I think I know what I need to do in order to get them to leave Calvary alone. I'm going to help you. But I need to keep doing my job in order to do so. Do you trust me?"

Amelia nodded slowly. "Yes."

"Good," Jack said, satisfied. Going back to the book between them, he changed the topic. "Now, you were telling me about the different stages of a mermaid's lifecycle?"

✳ Chapter 18 ✳

Energy

The night before they were supposed to meet again, Amelia texted Jack with instructions to dress comfortably. She didn't give any other information. He arrived at the Davidson house that day, wondering what they were going to do, wearing running shorts and shoes and a t-shirt, hoping they'd be outside doing something active.

Amelia was there to greet him at the door, a smile on her face. She was dressed in a comfortable tank top, a pair of yoga pants, and flip flops. Her strawberry hair was pulled into a ponytail, though Jack noticed a small strand that kept falling into her face. Jack was a bit startled to see her this way—he'd grown used to seeing her dressed in flowy tops, skirts, and dresses, usually hiding her figure. This outfit, however, was more form fitting. He'd never noticed until now how shapely she was, or how toned.

She hugged him a greeting, which he returned, a bit surprised by the friendliness.

"Listen, I did some thinking after last week, and you're right, Jack. I've been holding out on you. And I'm sorry. So, I've decided today's the day."

"The day for what?" Jack asked, shifting his weight.

"It's time for you to see magic, not just read about it."

Jack's heart leapt at these words, excitement filling his chest. *Finally*, at long last, he was going to do something besides having his nose in a book!

As they walked down to the willow tree, where it seemed to Jack they were going to be having their lesson, Amelia continued, "So you've been doing a good job at reading and understanding everything. You know the basics of how a spell should work, if were we able to use magic."

"Except for the summoning creatures thing. Which is the only bit of magic we currently have in us," Jack reiterated from his readings.

"Correct."

"Are you going to show me how to summon something today?" Jack wracked his mind for the different summoning spells he'd been reading about.

"No, we'll get to that. Right now, you need to actually come face to face with magic."

"But…wait, what?"

Amelia smiled. "The way Grandpa once described it to me is it's like having a phantom limb. You know how amputees say they can feel the limb that's been removed, and even the movements they make with that limb? Magic is kind of like that for Guardians. We can still feel it. And it is, in fact, still there—we just can't quite reach it to use it completely. So we still need to exercise our minds for the day when we might eventually be able to use it again."

"So how do we do that? Memorizing incantations or something?"

Amelia shook her head. "No. That's a myth. I mean, yes, we use incantations for summoning creatures, but for pure, raw magic—to do something beyond that—it's a visualization and control process."

Jack blinked. "You're kidding, right? All I have to do is *visualize* myself doing magic, and I can do magic?"

"I mean, yeah—no, but yeah. Remember, you *can't* do it. But that's how Guardians in the past used to do it. And magic can be tricky, so it's important to do this visualization. Each magical energy has a different feel to it, and needs to be handled differently, and it's learning those energies. It's weird, but the energy sort of tells you how to handle it when you conjure it up."

"So, potions," Jack said, remembering his readings. "What's the point in potions, if we can just conjure up magic?"

"Potions are physical manifestations of that particular spell you want to cast. Their energy requires a combination of physical elements in order to be put into being. Some magical energies can't just be conjured out of thin air—they need to go through certain processes and require certain elements to be used. Sometimes, magic needs to go through something else to be altered the way you want it."

"How do you know if it can be conjured, or if it needs to be put into a potion? And how do you know what needs to be in a potion?"

"You'll know. Like I said, the magic sort of tells you how it needs to be handled. Practicing handling it will make you more comfortable with it."

By this point, the pair had reached the willow tree on the edge of the property and sat in its shade, gazing out over the cliff towards the ocean beyond.

"So, what are you having me do today then?"

"Just sit here and feel for magic."

His heart fell. He thought he'd be doing something more than that.

"Really?"

"Really. Your goal is to sit quietly and feel for the magic around you, and once you've felt it, to get to know it and try and manipulate it."

"How will I know if I'm manipulating it if I can't even use it?"

Amelia smiled. "You'll know. You'll feel it taking form."

"So, you're making me meditate all day."

"Not all day. Just until you get it."

"So, all day," Jack repeated, knowing himself.

Amelia chuckled. "Yes." She paused. "Jack, this is going to be a pretty big test for you. If you're able to reach out to magic, we'll know for sure you're from a Guardian line."

Jack blinked. "Wait, are you telling me you've been doubting if I'm a Guardian this whole time?"

Amelia hesitated. "I haven't. I mean, yeah, I had some trust issues with you, but I didn't doubt you were from a Guardian line. But Emily has."

Jack snorted. "Typical."

"Listen, she's not totally wrong," Amelia commented, defending her younger sister. "It *is* sort of weird you weren't able to see magical creatures until you were an adult. Guardians are the only ones who are supposed to see them right now, so that's why I trust you're one. But we're also able to see them as soon as we're born, which is why it's a little strange. You're kind of an anomaly."

Jack nodded, unsure if he'd be able to concentrate, now knowing the kind of pressure that was on him. "How do I start?"

"Just find a soothing, comfortable place and clear your mind. That's why I brought you here, and why I told you to dress comfortably. Focus your attention on your breath. Acknowledge any thoughts that wander through your mind, but let them pass."

"So…do we need any props or anything? Like a wand?"

Amelia laughed. "No. We're not characters out of a fantasy novel. We don't need wands. Just ourselves."

The two sat in the grass, legs crossed, facing each other. The salty ocean breeze gently blew offshore, and sunshine penetrated through the clouds and the spaces between the tree's leaves, warming their skin where it touched. Jack shifted his weight to settle in, as the glint of sunlight from Amelia's necklace shone in his eyes. Jack made note of the sound of the gentle rolling of waves crashing against the shore. They hadn't even begun, and Jack already felt very serene.

"Okay, so close your eyes," Amelia instructed. Jack obeyed. "Are you comfortable?"

"Yes."

"Focus on your breathing."

Jack did, and the two sat in silence for a few minutes.

During the silence, Jack found his mind wandering, anxious to get to what he considered the "good stuff."

How will I know what it feels like? When will I feel it? Will I even be able to feel anything? Or will I be sitting here all day? Oh, God, what if I'm not a Guardian? What then? What does that mean? How can I see the creatures if I'm not a Guardian? My leg is cramping. I should probably adjust that.

He shifted his weight.

Better. Okay, where were we? Breathing. Just…breathing. A lot of breathing. Okay, Amelia, I think I know how to breathe now. Been doing it my whole life. This isn't new. How much breathing do I need to do?

"Don't focus on your thoughts, but acknowledge them as they come, then let them pass," he heard Amelia say softly into the silence.

Let them pass. Okay. Am I learning magic or am I taking a yoga class? No. Focus. Relax, let it pass.

Before he knew it, he found his thoughts drifting in front of him, as if they were merely leaves blowing in the wind—he saw them, he acknowledged them, but he didn't stay fixated on any of them. Thoughts of work, thoughts of his past, all filling the recesses of his mind, then quietly slipping away.

Then suddenly, nothing. Emptiness. But no, not empty—a blank canvas, a dark space, but hints of light in the distance, swirling in the black mist. It was almost as if he was physically in a vast void. He looked at the light.

"Where am I?" He looked into the nothingness, fixated on the light.

"Where magic dwells," he heard Amelia say, her voice distant, echoing.

And then, there she was in the darkness, beside him, smiling. As he examined her, it was almost as if a bright white light was emanating from her body. He looked at his own arms, and saw he too was radiating that same light.

"What is this place?" he asked, bewildered.

"It's where magic is kept hidden and safe."

"Is it a real, physical place? Or is it just in our minds?"

STONES ✳ RJG McManus

"Yes."

"That's not helpful."

"Focus, Jack."

And so he did. He turned towards the light in the distance. "What is that?"

"You know what it is. Walk with me."

Every step towards the light seemed like an eternity, and it didn't seem like they were moving any closer.

Until suddenly, it was upon them in an instant. Brilliant hues of light and energy swirled around them in the midst of the darkness and emptiness. Jack likened it to what it must be like inside of a rainbow, if one were able to do so. Colors he'd never even seen in real life whirled about him in wisps of delicate smoke, caressing his skin. He could actually feel them. Each one had a different energy, a different sensation, needed to be handled a different way.

"Hold one," Amelia instructed.

Hesitantly, Jack touched a warm, orange eddy that blew past him. It stopped short in his reach, still wriggling and spinning. He noticed as soon as he had it in his grasp, his own skin glowed with the same orangish light from the energy in his hands, as if he were a conduit for it.

"What is it?" Amelia asked, urging Jack on.

"Movement." Jack smiled. "It's movement. I can move things with it."

"How?" Amelia pressed.

"It just needs aim—it's like a quick release," Jack said, demonstrating. The light, however, disintegrated in front of him as if it hit an invisible wall, just as he was about to finish the motion. He turned to look at Amelia, confused.

"Where'd it go?"

"You can't use it, remember. Just before you complete the action, it stops."

Jack was frustrated with this, but Amelia said, "Try another."

He reached for a red one—it was soft, hotter than the orange one, but it had a slow, low glow to it, almost like an ember.

"What's that?" Amelia asked.

"It's…love?" he replied, a bit confused by the feel of it. He found he had to be gentle so it wouldn't break, but found it was also strong, solid, sturdy if held correctly.

"Yes."

"I can't use it without…without a lot. It needs time. And even then, it won't become real unless it's in both the maker of the potion, and the receiver."

"Yes." Amelia grinned. "Good. Try one last one."

Jack reached for a soft, blue glowing orb, further into the fray of magical energies spinning about. It was slightly cold to the touch. He found it was one that couldn't be held for long, that it needed to be let go of almost immediately. He pulled his hand back, watching it hover in front of him.

"Name that one," Amelia said. "What does it do?"

"It forgets," Jack replied, surprised at his quick response.

"Close."

"It…it makes you forget," Jack corrected himself. "If it's used, it makes the person on the receiving end forget. That's why it can't be held long by the person using the spell—otherwise they'll forget as well."

"Good. What else?"

"It needs something else." Jack touched it again, watched it spin and twirl. "Not a potion…not an incantation…" He looked up at her. "It needs an intention, a reason. It can't be used unless the user has a good enough reason to use it."

"Yes," Amelia said, grinning now. "Well done."

Jack smiled, pleased with himself. There was now no doubt in his or Amelia's mind: he came from a magical line. The fact he was in this space, could feel the magical energies, touch them and manipulate them, cast out all doubt.

"I think we've had enough for today," Amelia said.

"Can't I stay longer?" Jack was mesmerized by the swirling colors of light and smoke in this vast expanse.

"Yes, you can stay if you like, but I have guests I need to get back to."

He sighed. Though she'd told him he could stay, he wasn't comfortable being here alone yet.

"No….no, I'll come with you. How do we get out of here?"

"Open your eyes."

He cocked his head, squinting at her. "My eyes are open."

Amelia smiled. "No, they're not."

And in the blink of an eye, she was gone. Jack panicked, looking about the void wildly. "Amelia! AMELIA!" he called out.

"Jack, just open your eyes," she called gently, her voice echoing through the chamber.

He focused his attention. He could feel his body in the waking world...and his eyes were indeed shut. In this dark expanse, he closed his eyes...

...and when he opened them, he was back under the willow tree, sitting in the grass, face-to-face with Amelia. The sun was still shining on them. She smiled.

"What'd you think?"

"That was...trippy." Jack wasn't sure how else to describe what he had just experienced.

She laughed. "That's how I felt the first time Grandpa showed Emily and I how to reach out to it."

"What exactly happened? I thought magic was in the stones?"

"It is."

"So, were we able to tap into a stone or something?"

"No, we're able to tap into the magic within us. The stones' existence in the world act almost like blocks to the use of magic—like keys to lock or unlock it."

"And putting all the stones together would unlock magic...and that place."

"Yes." She paused. "You did well today, Jack. Really well. You got there quicker than I thought you would."

He smiled. "Yeah, well, I had a good guide."

She blushed as the two of them stood, heading back towards the cottage. "Well…thanks."

"So, I guess this proves Emily wrong?"

Amelia grinned. "I guess it does. You're still an anomaly, Jack. But you're definitely a Guardian. You couldn't have gotten there if you weren't."

"So, should I go do my victory dance in front of her, or…?"

Amelia laughed and playfully punched him in the shoulder.

"So, what now?" he asked. "Now that we know I have magic in me, what's next?"

"For now, just keep practicing getting there on your own," Amelia answered. "The more you practice, the quicker you'll get there."

Jack nodded, though he wasn't sure how getting to know magic that couldn't even be used would help him with the problem of Adrien Dunstan.

✳ Chapter 19 ✳

Potions

It was a hot day in August when things started to make traction. Jack was once again at the Davidson property, and upon entering the cottage, found himself in the midst of a flurry of activity, as Amelia and Emily were buzzing about the kitchen and dining room, gathering items for what appeared to be a day of cooking and canning. Even Lila was there. Cosmo, meanwhile, was sitting perfectly poised in the kitchen, waiting for someone to drop something he could gobble up.

"Oh, good, you're here!" Amelia said as Jack entered.

"Yeah…what's going on? Are we cooking today?" He glanced about the kitchen and all the ingredients and supplies strewn about.

"Something like that. For today's lesson, I wanted to go over the basics of potion-making with you. You've read the pages I gave you about potions, right?"

"Yes," Jack answered, leaning in the doorframe of the kitchen, as Amelia proceeded to rummage through her cabinets for supplies. Lila whizzed about, picking up smaller items and helping Amelia assemble them on the counter. Emily, meanwhile, was also there, bringing a large copper pot full of water to a boil.

"Good." Amelia pulled a ceramic bowl from one of the cabinets. "Guardians should always have a few basic potions on hand, and it's a good idea to refresh them when they're expired. My healing potion went bad a couple days ago, and that's a pretty basic one, so I thought we could work on that today and see what you've picked up from the reading."

"But we're not able to actually *use* the potions, right?" Jack asked, surprised, especially after his recent stint in the void with the magical energies. He'd been practicing with Amelia each time he came over, still not comfortable going to that place without a guide. And from all the energies he'd been encountering, he knew potions were a conduit for certain magical energies—but the potion without magic, or magic without the potion, would be essentially useless.

"Well, a few of them are useful even without magic. The healing potion works kind of like an antibiotic ointment without magic in it."

"And with magic?"

"It's supposed to be able to heal just about anything when applied. If you've been shot or stabbed, this thing would be your best friend."

"What if your head is cut off?" Jack asked with an amused smirk.

"Then you're dead. Even magic has its limitations." Jack opened his mouth to comment, but before he could say anything, Amelia cut him off by sharply stating, "And don't ask if there's a potion to raise people from the dead or regrow heads. I don't go there."

"So, there *is* a potion to regrow heads?" he pushed, a mischievous grin crossing his face.

"*I don't go there.*"

"Got it. We don't like dead or decapitated people," he said, backing down. "I don't get it though—you have Lila right here. Why can't she just zap it and make it work?"

"It doesn't work like that," Amelia explained. "Fairy magic is different from the magic needed to make potions and spells work."

"How?"

"Think of it like the difference between fresh water and salt water. One you can drink. One you can't. But each has its own purpose. One brings life to all land-dwelling plants and animals. The other brings life to sea-dwelling creatures. But you wouldn't throw a saltwater fish in fresh water, or a freshwater fish in salt water, and expect either to survive. That's kind of how it is."

"So, fairies have salty magic, and Guardians had fresh magic." At this point, Lila, with a frown on her face, flew over to him and kicked her little foot at his ear. "OW! Hey, I like your salty magic!"

Amelia laughed. "Yes, that's the basic gist of it."

"What would actually happen if you put fairy magic into one of the potions though?" He rubbed his ear as he glared at the fairy, who was now perched opposite him on the windowsill, sticking her tongue out at him. He stuck his tongue out at her in return.

Amelia pulled a half-used potion from her cabinet and uncorked it. Inside was a dark liquid, the color of dirty motor oil. She motioned to Lila, who grinned and approached the potion.

"I'd stand back if I were you," Amelia said to Jack, who complied. She also looked at Cosmo, and gave the command, "Cosmo, *leave*." The dog hesitantly obeyed, not wanting to miss out on an opportunity for any falling food, but also knowing he'd get a swat on the butt if he didn't do as he was told. After a moment of looking between Amelia and the door, he plodded out into the living room, where he proceeded to lay in his favorite ray of sunshine.

As soon as Cosmo left, the tiny winged woman rubbed her hands together, sprinkling a bit of fairy dust into the bottle. Jack watched with amazement as the contents within the bottle glowed, its contents turned from black to purple. For a moment, he thought the potion might be viable.

That is, until the contents of the bottle bubbled over, and in an instant, exploded out, leaving splotches of black liquid overhead, dripping from the ceiling. The bottle itself shot across the room, leaving a slight indentation in the wall opposite them. Jack immediately understood why Cosmo had been sent away—the explosion would have most definitely scared, and possibly injured the dog if he had been standing in the wrong place.

Jack's mouth dropped. "What potion was that?"

"That's one to help with upset stomachs," Amelia said with a smile, as she and Emily stood on the kitchen counters to wipe up the mess above them.

"Not exactly something you want in your body if the wrong kind of magic is in it," Emily chimed in.

"Got it. Fairy magic causes chaos," Jack said. "But seriously, what's the point of learning to make potions if you can't even use them the way they were meant to be used?"

"Like I said, some of them are still useful even without magic, just not *as* powerful," Amelia replied. "And it's always better to have some homemade, natural things around the house than the mass-produced, toxic stuff these big companies try to sell."

"Right. Hippie," Jack snorted.

"And proud of it," she retorted. "But more importantly, someday, we might be able to use them the way they're supposed to be used. So, it's a good idea to practice making them and to know what you're doing and have a few batches ready, then to be starting from scratch." She paused, examining the contents of the cupboard she was currently rifling through, looking for the healing potion's ingredients. "Emily, we're out of lavender in here. Can you get some from the garden, please? And hang some to dry for our stock?"

"Yeah, sure," Emily answered. As she walked to the door, passing Jack, she whispered, "I think it's dumb too."

"So why go along with it?" he whispered back.

"Curiosity, mostly. If she's right, it'd be pretty cool to see these potions in full effect someday."

"And if she's wrong?"

"At least they make the house smell good. And that healing potion works pretty well on paper cuts."

Jack smiled wryly, and Emily continued out the door to the garden.

Amelia, meanwhile, turned back to Jack. "Let's get started, shall we?"

✳

About a half hour later, Jack stood over a boiling pot, stirring its contents slowly with a large wooden spoon as he examined the mixture. The aromas of lavender, frankincense, rosemary, and other lovely scents filled the air, throwing his nose into sensory overdrive. Amelia was sitting at the countertop nearby, typing a column for the travel magazine, all the while keeping a close eye on him as he muddled through the instructions in the journal in front of him.

"Okay, that looks good, but you're going to want to reduce that heat a bit now," Amelia instructed, glancing over at the pot.

"But the instructions say to bring to a rolling boil for five minutes," Jack argued, pointing at the notes in the journal. "It's boiling now. So, shouldn't I leave it where it is for five more minutes?"

Amelia raised an eyebrow, closing her laptop. "You don't cook much, do you?"

In this moment, they heard a large *pop!* They jumped and turned back to the pot, which had splattered a portion of the potion onto the wall behind the stove, as well as onto Jack's shirt, leaving behind a gooey, purplish stain. Cosmo, who had been standing underfoot, was also coated in the purple goo, but rather than looking dismayed about it, was licking at his nose and paws with his long tongue in an attempt to consume the delightful-smelling potion.

As Jack stood motionless, aghast at what had just happened, Amelia turned one of the knobs on the stove, reducing the heat. She smirked. "Okay, so maybe we should've started with basic cooking techniques before diving into potions."

"I *can* cook," Jack insisted, wiping the potion off his shirt with a towel.

"Clearly." Amelia rolled her eyes. "I bet you're one of those guys who throws the pasta in *with* the water as it boils, not *after* it's already started boiling."

"What's wrong with that?"

Amelia sighed. "Just follow my instructions and don't argue. This is an exact science. I've been doing this a lot longer than you. I kind of know what I'm doing by now."

"Fine." Jack paused. "But seriously, what's wrong with boiling pasta with the water?"

"Emily!" Amelia called out.

Emily, who had been reading in the living room, entered the kitchen upon her sister's call. "Yes?" Seeing the splattered wall and stain on Jack's shirt, she smirked. "So, how's it going?"

"It's *fine*," Jack said through gritted teeth, unamused by the younger of the Davidson sisters.

Amelia, meanwhile, plucked the spoon from Jack's hand and handed it over to Emily. "Can you finish this potion for us, please? I just found out I have a different lesson to teach."

"Yeah, sure." Emily grabbed an apron from the hook on the wall and stepped into position in front of the stove.

Amelia proceeded pulled a box of macaroni from the pantry and a different pot from the cabinet, which she handed to Jack.

"Okay, so step one: fill the pot with water."

✳

That afternoon, after a basic cooking lesson and being allowed to try the potion again (with mixed results), Jack sat at the dining room table, a plan formulating in his mind.

He'd reached a point of desperation in trying to figure out what was going on within Dunstan Enterprises, and knew he needed to access the computer of Adrien's secretary, Stephanie. She was his most-trusted employee, had tabs on all the projects happening in that moment, and if anyone had anything in their possession that led to wrongdoing within the company, it was her. But getting into her computer was going to be difficult—she was always at it, and whenever she took a break, she always locked it so it wasn't accessible. The trick was to get her away from it, and to make sure she was so frazzled she forgot to lock it. It was that little potion explosion with Lila that led to an idea—a stupid, simple idea, but desperate times called for desperate measures.

"I think I need to practice these potions at home," Jack commented as Amelia handed him a cup of coffee. Lila, meanwhile, was sitting on the table, sipping from her thimble.

She laughed, sitting across from him. "You think so?"

213

"Can I get some ingredients for that upset stomach one Lila blew up earlier? I think that'd be useful to have around. And I want to try to replenish what you lost."

"Sure, no problem. Do you want some fairy dust as well?" she quipped.

He smiled and laughed, then looked at his watch. "Listen, I need to head out if I'm going to get home at a decent time. I have to be in the office tomorrow. Do you mind getting the stuff together for me now?"

"Yeah, sure," Amelia said, standing again.

"Thanks, I appreciate it."

As soon as she had stepped out of earshot, Jack turned to Lila and in a low hush, said, "Lila, I need your help. I have an idea. And it's probably a stupid one."

Lila's ears perked, and a mischievous smile crossed her face. She was all about stupid ideas.

✳ Chapter 20 ✳

A stupid idea

The next morning, Jack stood in the parking garage of the Dunstan Enterprises building, looking for Stephanie's car, Lila perched on his shoulder. He had spent the entire evening after leaving Amelia and Emily's house attempting to brew the stomachache potion under the watchful eye of Lila. After a few attempts, he'd managed to recreate it, setting some aside for Amelia so his story would corroborate, and putting the remainder into a rather substantially sized vial for himself.

When he came across Stephanie's car, he felt relief—her car was parked in an area that was in a blind spot from the garage cameras. If it hadn't been, he'd have to reassess and delay the plan until another day, when she was parked elsewhere. He felt a small twinge of guilt for what he was about to do, but not too much—if this worked, only a small dent would be made, and hopefully, it would cause enough of a distraction to pull Stephanie away from her desk.

"It's that one," he whispered to Lila. "The red one there."

Lila fluttered over to the car. Jack pulled the vial containing the stomach potion from his pocket, setting it next to her. "Remember, when you hear the church bells ring nine times, zap the potion," he hissed. "And make sure the bottle's pointed at the car. Otherwise none of this matters."

Lila gave a little salute, understanding her orders. Jack smiled, and proceeded to step into the garage elevator to head up to his office.

215

"Morning, Stephanie," he said as he stepped off the elevator, passing her desk.

Stephanie looked up from her computer, glancing him up and down.

"Morning, Jack. How was Calvary yesterday?"

"Oh, you know—small, quaint, the usual."

Stephanie raised an eyebrow. "You know what I mean, Jack. What's the report?"

"Really, Steph? *You're* asking me now?" Jack asked, annoyed. His annoyance, however, disappeared, as he heard the church bells ringing. He knew in that moment, Lila was setting things into action in the parking garage a few floors below them.

Stephanie shrugged. "Just doing my job."

"Where's Adrien? Why isn't *he* grilling me today?"

"He's out of town. On vacation," Stephanie answered curtly.

"Well, when will he be back? So I can talk to him directly instead of you playing messenger for him."

Stephanie rolled her eyes, but before she could respond, her direct line rang. "Dunstan Enterprises, this is Stephanie."

Whatever was said to her must have been upsetting, as a concerned look crossed her face. "Yes, I'll be right down." She quickly hung up.

"Everything okay?" Jack asked.

"I just—I'll be right back," Stephanie stammered, stepping out from behind the desk. She quickly crossed the hall to the elevators leading to the garage, her kitten heels clicking as she kept a brisk pace. Jack smiled—

in her frantic exit, she'd forgotten to lock her computer, just like he'd hoped she would. He had to act quickly.

As soon as Stephanie was behind the closed elevator doors, Jack sat, finding the file on her computer labeled "Calvary Project." Inside, he was found other folders filled with invoices and payroll statements from vendors and workers. Sure enough, Max had been removed from payroll for the Calvary project the day after he had spoken with Adrien, and it appeared he was moved onto a different project here in the city—but why? Was it because of Adrien and Jack's conversation? But why would that cause upset? Why wouldn't Dunstan Enterprises just go ahead with getting the right materials?

He flipped through the files and statements, not really reading them, but taking a few quick pictures of the screen with his phone to review later, hoping they would turn out all right, and making a mental note to himself that he needed to keep a flash drive on him if he was going to do this type of thing again. Once done snapping the photos, he quickly exited the folders back to Stephanie's main desktop and sat in the chair in front of her desk.

Just in time, too—a few seconds later, he heard the unmistakable clicking of her heels as she walked back down the hall. She appeared in view, a confused, frazzled look on her face as she sat back in her desk.

"Everything all right?" Jack asked.

"I think so." Stephanie furrowed her brow. "Security said my car alarm was going off, like someone had tried to break in, but there was nobody there."

"That's a bit disconcerting." Jack felt a bit guilty in the moment.

"Yeah, well, whoever it was, the bastard left a dent in my car," she said, fuming. "And there was this stuff all over the side of the door—it looked like motor oil or something. Seriously, who does that?"

"I'm so sorry, Stephanie." Only he knew though he was apologizing as the culprit, not as a sympathetic coworker. "Is there anything I can do?"

"No…no, insurance will cover the damage," she sighed. "I wish these garages had more cameras, you know? It's creepy in there sometimes."

"Talk to Adrien. He likes you, and I'm sure after this, he'll make sure they're installed. In the meantime, let me walk you out after work tonight, yeah?"

"Yeah…thanks, Jack, I appreciate it. Anyway, you were asking when he'd be back in the office?" Stephanie asked, attempting to resume her work but looking clearly distracted.

"Yes, that's right." Jack felt even more guilty. She was visibly shaken up.

Stephanie clicked through the calendar on her computer. "He's out all week, but he'll get back next Thursday."

"Well, I guess I'll see him then." Jack stood. "Also, by the way, I got that e-mail about the anniversary party. You're the one taking RSVPs for that, right?"

Jack was referring to the annual anniversary party Adrien put on for the entire company, celebrating the founding of Dunstan Enterprises. Each year, Adrien opened his home to all the employees, throwing a lavish celebration—it was the event of the year, especially since his home was situated on his own private island off the coast. Guests would be ferried from the mainland, where they would eat and drink and be entertained all night. Jack had attended each year since starting with the corporation, and hadn't missed a party yet—he knew now more than ever he needed to be there, if for no other reason but to keep up appearances.

Stephanie raised an eyebrow. "I am. What would you like me to put you down for?"

"I'm planning to attend."

"You sure that's a good idea? Showing up to his party with the way he feels about you right now?"

"And how exactly *does* he feel about me?"

"You already know the answer to that, Jack—he's not happy with you right now. You haven't done great on the Calvary project, which is a little surprising, given your track record. We know you can do better than this."

Jack shrugged. "Everyone meets a challenge in their career at some point in time. This is mine, apparently. Besides, he invited me. Why shouldn't I go?"

"He invited the whole company. It's the anniversary party. Of course he's going to invite you. But you do know you're more of a courtesy invite, right?"

"And I'll be a courteous guest. Put me down in the yes column."

Stephanie sighed, opening her RSVP spreadsheet. "I think it's a bad idea, but it's your funeral. Marking you as a yes. Do you have a plus one?"

Jack surprised himself when Amelia crossed his mind—but no, that was ridiculous, he couldn't bring her. For one, she would be out of town on an assignment in Ireland for the magazine she worked for when the party was scheduled to happen. But even if she wasn't, the thought of bringing her in the presence of Adrien was an overall bad idea.

"Jack? Do you have a plus one?" Stephanie repeated.

Jack snapped out of his thoughts. "No, just me."

Stephanie looked him up and down. "You know, I've got a younger sister who you might get along with—why don't you let me introduce the two of you sometime? Maybe you can finally stop going to these things alone."

Jack laughed. "I appreciate the offer, but I'm good. Really. I can find my own date. Besides, it's a couple months from now. Anything can happen between now and then. But thanks."

"Suit yourself. But if you ever get tired of going back and forth between the office and that podunk town and want to do something else, let me know, and I'll set it up."

"I will. Thanks, Steph."

✳

Jack sat on his couch at home that evening, flipping through the photos he had taken with his cell phone, crossing his fingers he would come across something that would lead him down the right path. Max's sudden disappearance from the project was concerning, and the talk about shoddy materials still echoed in his mind. At the moment, though, all the documents he reviewed didn't look out of the ordinary. It was frustrating. Had he dented Stephanie's car for nothing?

He kept flipping, when he came across an account statement. Carefully, he zoomed in to analyze the photo further, looking for any indication something was off. So far, nothing. Typical transactions for materials, contractor payments, etc.

But wait—what was that?

Jack zoomed in even more, looking closely. There was a sizeable payment made out to a William Foster. Why did he know that name?

Quickly, he hopped on his laptop, typing in the search term "William Foster."

About a thousand results came up, and he furrowed his brow. He tried to narrow it down, searching, "William Foster Dunstan Enterprises."

And there it was. An article about Dunstan Enterprises' intent to build in Calvary from several months back—with a statement in it from William Foster, the town's planning director, about how "pleased the town of Calvary is to have been chosen for this project," and how it would "improve the lives of all the people in town."

William Foster was the planning director for the town of Calvary—the man in charge of the town's planning commission, responsible for making recommendations when it came to approving or denying requests for land development. And here it was, in black and white—William Foster was on Dunstan Enterprises' payroll.

Jack sat back in his seat, reeling. Foster was paid off. If he hadn't been paid off, surely, the development never would have been approved. Jack himself noted there was an unusual amount of resistance to the project by the public, a strong disapproval of what they were doing, and he had wondered why the project had been approved in the first place, given general public opinion. But here it was: William Foster was bought out by Adrien Dunstan, and in exchange, Dunstan Enterprises got the go-ahead to build, essentially bypassing all other considerations.

This was big. Even the shoddy building materials didn't compare to this—if this one thing hadn't happened, the rest wouldn't have followed.

But doubt hit. What if this was a different William Foster on the payroll? What if it was a coincidence there was a William Foster in Calvary? Couldn't there also be a different William Foster within Dunstan Enterprises? That was a common name, after all. He didn't know the names of everyone involved in the project, all the contractors, subcontractors, vendors, etc.—hell, he didn't know the names of everyone in just his office. This could be a legitimate business transaction.

221

So, what now? Approach William Foster, the planning director, and see what he could find out? Or just roll with what he had, and pray he was right in his conclusion?

He'd have to chat with Foster, he concluded. If he was guilty, he'd have to get him to slip up, say something that would incriminate him. Foster would probably be receptive to him, after all, knowing he was a Dunstan Enterprises representative. He'd trust him. A man like that—if he indeed *was* a man like that—would always be after more money.

✳ Chapter 21 ✳

Pieces of the past

While Jack was at home trying to put together the pieces of the mystery of William Foster, Amelia and Emily were making their own discovery.

That evening, after dinner with their most current batch of guests at the Blue Barn, the sisters were back in the cottage, finally down to the last few boxes of their grandparents' things. Amelia was currently sorting through a box of books from the study, carefully examining them to decipher their worth; Emily was going through a box of kitchen supplies.

After throwing about ten books in the "toss" pile and five in the "keep," she came across a journal. It was worn and leather bound, its reddish cover containing yellowed pages, delicate to the touch. When Amelia opened it, she was delighted to find her grandfather's scrawl on its pages. Yes, this would go in the keep pile.

"What's that?" Emily looked up from her own work, noticing her sister had stopped sorting for the moment.

"It's an old journal from Grandpa," Amelia replied, not taking her gaze off the pages.

"Really?" Emily moved next to her sister to also take a look. "What's it say?"

"It's a travel journal."

There was no doubt that's what it was—there was a pocket in the back with a few vintage maps and brochures, and each entry was labeled with not just the date, but the location where the entry was written—many of them far, far from Calvary.

"Look at this." Amelia pointed to the top of the weathered page, where, in her grandfather's handwriting, the words *August 2, 1962 – Auckland, New Zealand* were scrawled.

"What was he doing in Auckland?" Emily asked. "Just taking a vacation or something?"

"I don't know, I haven't read the entries yet, I know about as much as you do. It looks like he was backpacking or something. But look, a few pages later, *June 17, 1960 – Geneva, Switzerland*." She flipped the pages again. "And here, *August 16, 1963 – Honolulu, Hawaii*. It goes on like this…every year, basically since he turned eighteen, he traveled somewhere far from home. Look, he went to Jerusalem, he went to Greece, he went to Scotland…" Amelia kept flipping the pages, her eyes growing wide with amazement as she ventured into her grandfather's secret travels. "Looks like he hit just about every continent."

"Where did he even get the money to travel like that?" Emily asked, bewildered. "I mean, I know the family wasn't poor, but they also weren't exactly rolling in so much money that an eighteen-year-old could just leave the country on vacation."

"I remember him mentioning something about the family receiving compensation after his dad was killed in World War II…maybe it was leftovers from that?"

"Maybe. That's so strange he wouldn't mention any of this while he was alive. When does it end?"

Amelia flipped to the last page, and read the entry aloud.

December 1, 1969 – Halifax, Nova Scotia

Lizzie called today—I've been drafted.

I'm heading home tomorrow. My trip to Japan will have to wait, it seems…at least I'll be in that general vicinity of the world. Maybe something will turn up while I'm there.

Probably not. But I can hope, at least.

I didn't find anything here—I didn't have the time. Four are safe. The other three, wherever they are, must be as well. Maybe if I'd had those few extra days I was supposed to be here.

Damn this war.

I don't know what happen to me. All I can think of is my dad—I never knew him because of his own damn war. Will Brennan remember me if anything happens? He's so little.

I don't feel old enough to go to war. I'm too young to die.

Jesus. I need to stop thinking this way. I need to go home and put on a brave face for them—tell them I love them, tell them it'll be all right.

Damn this war.

"Jesus…Grandpa's draft date. That's rough," Emily commented softly.

Amelia nodded her agreement. "He made it out though."

"That part about 'the other three'…the other three what? What was he looking for?"

Amelia flipped through the pages, looking for context. "He never says."

225

"Let me see." Emily outstretched her hand. Amelia handed her the journal for her to examine.

Carefully, Emily turned the pages, trying to understand the meaning behind her grandfather's travels, the things he was looking for. But nothing. She sighed, handing it back to Amelia.

"You're right, he doesn't say." Emily felt defeated. She proceeded to go back to her own box to continue her sorting.

While Emily sorted, Amelia opened the journal back up, when she noticed something she hadn't before—two pages at the front of the journal were stuck together. She squinted, and saw there appeared to be writing in between. Gently, she slid her finger into the crease, freeing the pages from each other. Reading the words that had been hidden, her heart raced.

"Em, you've gotta read this."

Emily looked up from her work. "What?"

"This...this poem. There was a hidden poem at the front, two pages were stuck together."

"Well, what's it say?"

And so, Amelia read:

"One buried in ice, high up above
The first of all, made with love

One in the thick, close to the coast
Give up that which you love the most

One in a mountain, under the ground
Engulfed in flame, water surrounds

One in the deep, where no light can reach

226

Waiting where the giants breach

One at the start, where life took root
Bitter is the sweetest fruit

One with man, the last of their kind
Who keeps the old ways locked in their mind

The last with the One, Creator of All
As he shall rise, so shall he fall."

Emily's eyes went wide when Amelia finished reading. "What the hell does that mean?"

But her question was rhetorical. She already knew perfectly well what it meant. They both did.

Amelia's mind was racing. *Four are safe. The other three, wherever they are, must be as well.*

"Grandpa found four of the seven stones," she whispered.

Emily nodded, feeling her own heart racing.

"But I don't understand," Amelia wondered aloud. "Why was he looking for them? And where the hell did this poem come from?"

Emily shook her head. "I have no idea."

In that moment, Amelia's phone rang. She looked down, seeing the words "Benedict Home" pop up on the screen of her cell. She furrowed her brow, rejecting it.

Emily raised an eyebrow. "Who was that?"

"Jude Benedict," Amelia answered shortly, stuffing the phone back into her pocket.

227

"Why didn't you answer?"

"Because I don't want to talk to him."

The phone buzzed again, and she sighed exasperatedly, pulling it out to see a voicemail notification in the left corner of the screen. Without even listening to it, she deleted the message. She was in no mood to hear what he might have to say.

"You know you're going to have to get over that eventually," Emily commented, observing her sister's action.

"Yeah, and you're going to have to get over Dan eventually," Amelia snapped, referring to her sister's ex-boyfriend. "But you've told me you'll do it in your time, so let me do this in *my* time."

And thus, the wonder of finding the journal went away for the time being, as each of the sisters went back to sorting, consumed by their own thoughts and frustrations.

✳

Jack was at the Davidson household the next day for another lesson with Amelia, having trouble focusing. He hadn't been able to reach that place where he could feel magic—his thoughts were elsewhere, and no matter how hard he tried, he couldn't push William Foster from his mind. He needed to make the call, to meet the man, to see what he could find out, to see if he had anything to do with the Calvary project going through.

Amelia noticed he was distracted, and she too was having trouble, her mind constantly turning to her grandfather's journal, and the possibility of him hunting for stones. She was also still worked up about the missed call from Jude Benedict, and though she didn't want to associate with him, she was curious about what he could possibly want since he'd moved to Hawaii.

228

Since neither of them seemed to be in the right mindset, she'd let the lesson digress into a casual meeting, chatting over coffee on the porch. It was strange, how easily conversation came with Jack when they weren't talking about the development or magic, how it was almost as if they were becoming friends. She found she rather enjoyed their time together.

"So, what drew you to writing?" Jack asked, taking a sip from his coffee as he looked out past the fields of wildflowers to the ocean beyond.

Amelia smiled, twirling the pendant on the necklace around her neck with her fingers as she spoke. "It was an excuse to travel, mostly. I don't really care about writing, but apparently, I'm good at it, so I used it to my advantage. I figured if I wrote about beautiful places in the world, somebody eventually would hire me to go to more beautiful places and write about them."

"And it worked?"

"I work for a travel magazine, don't I?" She grinned, taking a sip from her own cup. "What about you? What drew you to acquisitions?"

Jack sighed. "Truth? The pay and benefits. The stability. Things weren't super stable for me growing up, and even being in the Navy, having to bounce around between stations…I just wanted to settle for a while."

"Except you're not settled right now," Amelia pointed out, acknowledging his current mental state and tentative career future.

"Fair point." He paused. "I will be again someday. I hope."

"If you could do anything else in the world, what would you do?"

Jack contemplated this for a moment. "I was always fascinated with architecture. Even took a couple classes in college, but it never went anywhere."

"Why not?"

"It wasn't practical. The economy was crap, and again, I was looking for stability. So, I settled on studying business. But it's something I've always thought about."

"What do you like about it?"

"The ability to create." He paused. "I've been doing some thinking, by the way. You've been teaching me about magic, but I haven't been doing anything in return."

"I don't need any money, Jack."

"No, not money—I think I can teach you self-defense. You're traveling so much, it'd be good for you to know it."

"I appreciate it, but I'm fine, thanks."

"Okay, so what happens if you're in a foreign country and someone attacks you?"

"I have pepper spray."

"They got a hold of your pepper spray."

Amelia didn't have a reply. Jack smiled. "Yeah. I'm teaching you self-defense."

"I haven't needed it up until this point."

"That's because you didn't know it. If you'd known it, you probably could've gotten rid of me a lot quicker," Jack chided.

Amelia laughed. At this point, they saw Emily coming from the beach, having finished a charter fishing session with some guests.

"How'd it go?" Amelia asked as her sister approached.

"Not bad," Emily said, sitting. "They caught some stuff, so they were happy."

"That's good. Any more trips lined up?"

"I have one next weekend. And another three weeks from now." Emily knew Amelia wouldn't exactly like that, and she was already incredibly frustrated and disappointed in herself, not seeing the business she'd like to see. In fact, she'd felt on-edge for weeks now, not seeing much coming from her half of the business. She hated that Amelia's idea for the bed and breakfast was a hit, but her idea for the charter fishing seemed to be a bust.

Amelia simply nodded when Emily told her the schedule, not saying anything else about it. She knew Emily was trying her best, but at the moment, business seemed slow. She hoped this was just start-up growing pains, but she knew they couldn't operate at this pace forever. Luckily, the Blue Barn itself was doing well, making up the difference. She knew eventually, they'd have to have a talk about it, but now was not the time.

"So, I have a question for you two," Jack said, noticing the tension that had arisen since Emily entered the conversation. "Do you know any other Guardians? It's something I've been wondering, how many of them are around."

"We did," Amelia replied shortly.

"We *do*," Emily corrected her.

"Who?" Jack asked.

"The Benedicts." Emily shot him a dark look. "You know, the guy with cancer and his wife who you took advantage of and convinced to leave, driving off the fairies who lived on their property."

"Emily, stop," Amelia hissed, the memory of the missed phone call still fresh in her mind. "They made that choice themselves. They could've stayed. Jack didn't know they were Guardians."

"And if I *had* known—if I'd known any of this beforehand—believe me, I would've left them alone. I would've left all of you alone," he interjected. "Hell, I wouldn't have gotten into this line of business. I'd be doing something else with my life."

"Okay, but you *do* know now, so why are you still working for Dunstan Enterprises?" Emily demanded.

"It's not that simple," Jack said, shaking his head.

"No, but it *is* that simple. Either you're with us, or you're with them, and I don't trust the fact that you're with both."

"He's trying to protect us," Amelia jumped in, coming to Jack's defense. "He's working on building a case against them so eventually, they'll leave us alone. But he has to keep acting like he's doing his job so they don't catch on in the meantime. He's doing what he's supposed to do—he's being a Guardian."

"And you believe that?"

"I do."

"Well, I *don't*."

"Yeah, well, that's pretty typical of you," Amelia said with a weary sigh.

Emily was fuming. "Maybe it's typical of me to not trust him, but it's pretty typical of *you* to trust too much. You don't live in the real world, Amelia. You bounce around like some kind of fricking Pollyanna with your head in the clouds. You're naïve, and you're stupid to think you can trust him."

232

"*Hey,*" Jack interjected.

"You stay out of this!" Emily snapped. Jack shut his mouth.

"Don't talk to him that way," Amelia said shortly. "And I'd rather be naïve and trusting than cynical and mean."

"Mean, huh?" Emily felt her face turning red.

"Yes. *Mean.* And frankly, I'm *sick* of it. You're *constantly* judging everyone around you, you're unfair and unkind, and honestly, you're *exhausting.*"

Emily, at a loss for words, simply stormed off the porch and into the house, slamming the door behind her. Jack sat there awkwardly, not sure if he should say anything to Amelia.

Amelia rolled her eyes as Emily disappeared inside. "She's such a pain. I don't get why she's so negative all the time."

"You're lucky to have her."

Amelia sighed. "I know. I love her to death. I just don't get her. Do you have any siblings?"

"I...don't know." Jack was surprised at himself. Normally he lied and said "no" and didn't give any details. But for some reason, with Amelia, he couldn't bring himself to do that.

"What does that mean?"

He wasn't expecting to have this conversation today, but here he was.

"It means I was abandoned as a kid and I have no idea who my family is. I grew up in foster care. Went into the Navy as soon as I aged out of the system. Got my degree after that, and now here we are."

"I had no idea," Amelia said apologetically.

Jack shrugged, brushing off her sympathy. "Most people don't. I like to keep it that way. Usually when people find out, they treat you differently, you know? I don't want that. I want them to just see me."

Amelia nodded, understanding this sentiment. "I get that. I do. Whenever anyone finds out my dad died when I was a teenager, it's like a switch in them flips, and suddenly instead of seeing me and my abilities, I'm the girl with the dead dad, as if that explains everything. And it does explain some things. But it's not *all* of me."

"I didn't know your dad died. I'm sorry." He paused. "If you don't mind my asking—and you don't have to answer if you don't want to—but—"

"How did it happen?" Amelia interrupted, anticipating the end of his question, one she'd heard hundreds of times. "It was a hit and run. He was crossing the street, and this car came out of nowhere and ran him down. They think it was a drunk driver, but they never caught the guy—he was driving too fast for anyone to even get a license plate." She paused. "They say Dad died instantly, that he was gone when the witnesses ran up to help him. I'm glad for that, because it means he wasn't suffering in his last moments. Mom didn't do well for a while after that, and neither did Emily…I'm not sure Emily ever really got over it, to be honest."

"And you? Did you get over it?"

Amelia was silent for a moment, not expecting this question. "No—no, I'm not sure I ever did. It heals with time, and it gets easier to manage, but there's always a void that will never be filled. He was my dad. He *is* my dad. He'll always be my dad. That will never change. And no one else can ever fill that hole."

Jack nodded, understanding what she was saying. For him, it was a hole that had always been there, that he didn't even know how to fill, or if it would ever be filled.

"We're a pair, aren't we?" she said, trying to make light of the situation.

"Yeah, we are," Jack said, bemused.

There was an awkward silence between them for a moment, where neither knew how to continue the conversation. Amelia, an idea running through her head, decided to be the one to speak again.

"Jack…have you ever tried to find your family?"

He shook his head, looking at his coffee mug to avoid making eye contact with her. "No. They already tried when I was a kid, nothing came up. They couldn't even find my birth record. I don't actually know how old I am—I could be a year or two older than what they said, or a little younger. Whoever my family is, they did a good job hiding themselves, and they clearly don't want to be found. I wouldn't even know where to look."

"Do you remember them at all?"

He shook his head. "No. I know, it's weird, you'd think I'd remember something…but there's nothing. I guess I was so young and it was so traumatic I just forgot them."

"Do you *want* to find them?"

"Sometimes I do. It'd be nice to know where I came from. But sometimes not. If they didn't want me, why should I want them? But like I said, I wouldn't know where to start."

"If you had a chance, if you had *anything* you could go off of, would you pursue it?"

Jack contemplated this. "I suppose I would. But I don't have anything, so it doesn't matter."

That was the answer Amelia had been looking for.

"That's where you're wrong. I think you do."

Jack looked up from the mug, startled. "What do you mean?"

"Jack, you said a brownie punched you in the nose when we first started all of this."

Jack winced at the memory. He hadn't purchased milk the past several weeks for fear of accidentally leaving it out again. He'd read in one of the journals Amelia had given him that brownies were in fact summoned by milk being left as a gift for them, which he still thought was strange. In fact, he'd cut most dairy products from his grocery lists, just to be safe. He was really starting to miss cheese on his pizza.

"Yeah, so?"

"Well…brownies typically attach to families. I mean, there's the occasional one-off that attaches to an individual, but nine times out of ten, the brownie attaches to a family and stays with them for generations."

"So?"

"So…that brownie might be attached to *yours*."

Jack sat silently, this information crashing down on him. The brownie might know who his family was—*is*. He might know the whole Garridan family history. He might know where to find them, if they were still alive.

He might know why Jack wasn't with the rest of them.

"Jack? Are you okay?" Amelia now wondered if she'd made a mistake in telling him this particular characteristic about brownies.

236

He shook his head, dazed. "Yeah…I'm fine. I just—I think I need to go home."

"I understand."

Jack stood, grabbing his coat off the back of his chair and walking briskly towards his car.

"Hey, Jack?" Amelia said before he walked away.

He turned around to face her. "Yeah?"

"Don't forget—milk in a bowl. That's how you summon a brownie."

"Milk in a bowl, got it."

"And Jack?"

"Yeah?"

"Be patient with it. They're sweet little creatures, but they're slow sometimes and get easily confused, so just be patient."

"Patience, got it."

"Also don't insult it this time. And don't be surprised if it doesn't come around tonight because you insulted it last time."

Jack nodded, his hopes receding, now slightly unsure of himself. He had messed up last time. He hoped his was a particularly forgiving brownie and it would reappear for him.

"And Jack?"

"*What?*" he asked exasperatedly, becoming irritated at the holdup.

237

"Good luck."

✳ Chapter 22 ✳

Talking it out

W hen Jack returned to his apartment that evening, he found himself dwelling on what Amelia had told him. The notion that there was a creature who had possibly been attached to his family for centuries both intrigued and frightened him. First of all, he was a bit disconcerted by the thought that he was never really alone—or maybe he was sometimes? He wasn't sure, and didn't really understand where the brownie went when it wasn't there, or how that worked. Second, despite finding the brownie's attachment a bit unnerving and invasive of his privacy, he was intrigued by the idea that this brownie might know his family. He could find out about his mother and father, his grandparents, even siblings, if there were any. For all he knew, the brownie could also still be attached to *them*, if they were alive, and where they were—and more importantly, it might know why Jack was separated from them.

But do I really want to know who they are and where they are?

He was torn. He'd been abandoned at a young age. There must have been a reason for that. And as far as he knew, no one had ever come looking for *him*. No distant relatives had shown up on his doorstep, no long-lost cousin had ever called him and declared, "We're family, come home!" Nothing. No one wanted him. So why should he want to find *them*?

Because they were family, he conceded. Because there was blood shared between them. Because he wanted to know where he got his eyes, his nose, his hair color. Because he wanted to know if his father had the same laugh he did, or if his mother had the same sense of humor. Because

239

he wanted to know if his grandfather was a war veteran, and if he was high school sweethearts with his grandmother, or if they'd met later on in life.

He was terrified though. What if they were awful people? What if they were rude, unkind, abusive? What if they were lazy slobs, self-centered narcissists? What if they were the exact opposite of him, and he'd miraculously dodged a bullet in his youth by being abandoned, and reuniting with them would do nothing but bring him misery?

Was that a risk he was willing to take?

Yes. It was. Then he would know what they were—and he'd know he rose above anything he could have ever accomplished by being with them. His curiosity would be satiated, and he'd move forward—possibly wiser and sadder, but he could accept that. He'd done it before, he could do it again. At best, he would finally have a family, people to claim as *his* people; at worst, he'd at least be able to find out some medical history and continue to carry on through life without them.

Or, what if they were dead, all of them? What if this whole thing was futile, and he wouldn't find anything ever?

Then he'd have to move on, and do what he'd always done: live his life the way *he* wanted.

Jack opened his fridge, rummaging through to the back, where he found the same carton of milk from a few weeks ago—the one he had dared not touch for fear of summoning the brownie again. He opened it, gagging as the sour stench of spoiled milk wafted from the container. Holding his breath, he poured a bit into a bowl, and set it next to the kitchen sink. He proceeded to dump the remainder of the carton down the drain, and the carton itself into the trash can.

He wasn't sure if the brownie would be summoned by spoiled milk, or if it would come at all since Jack had unintentionally insulted it the last time, but it was worth a shot. He'd never summoned anything intentionally before, now that he thought about it. Amelia hadn't gotten to that part in the lessons with him.

He hoped this would work. Now all he had to do was wait.

✳

A few hours later, Jack awoke with a start to the sound of clattering in the kitchen. He looked around the room, momentarily disoriented. He had fallen asleep on the couch waiting for the brownie to appear. The room was dark, the only source of light in it being the glow of the television.

CLANK!

Jack sat upright, and saw a light on in the kitchen. He turned off the TV and stood, quietly walking towards the noise.

Sure enough, when he reached the doorframe of the kitchen, he saw the same strange little brown man hard at work, cleaning dishes. This time though, he was muttering to himself. Jack stood silently so as not to startle the creature, listening to its monologue, biding his time until the moment was right to approach him.

"He insulted me last time, and leaves me *spoiled* milk this time. *Bleh.* Mr. Jack doesn't appreciate all I do for him. Next time I see him, I'll give him a piece of my mind. Maybe I'll dump this spoiled milk on his head. That would teach him. Stupid Mr. Jack. I could leave him anytime I want. I *choose* to stay with him. It's my choice. Doesn't appreciate me at all…next time I see him, I'll tell him I *choose* to leave him. That would show him. He'd be lost without me."

Jack decided now was the moment to interject.

"I wish you wouldn't leave."

The brownie, surprised by someone else being in the room with him, gave a little yelp and whirled around to face Jack. Fortunately, he didn't have any dishes in his hand this time around, so nothing broke.

"Mr. Jack! I'm so sorry, Mr. Jack! I didn't mean what I said!" he stammered, his cheeks turning a shade of crimson in his embarrassment.

"It's okay," Jack said, moving forward slowly. "I'm not mad. You have every right to be upset with me. I was rude last time, and I'm sorry."

The brownie blinked, clearly taken aback. "You're sorry?"

"Yes, I am." He paused. "And I'll make sure to put out fresh milk next time. I just didn't have any, and I needed to talk to you. I'm glad you came. I thought you'd left forever."

"I would never really leave you, Mr. Jack. You're my person. And I'm sorry for hurting your nose last time."

"It's okay. What's your name, anyway?"

"Donn, sir," the brownie answered.

"Donn," Jack repeated, holding out his hand. "It's nice to meet you."

Donn looked at Jack's hand suspiciously. "Do you want me to give you something, Mr. Jack?"

"No, Donn, I just want to shake your hand."

"Shake my hand?"

"Yes."

Tentatively, Donn extended his hand. It was a quarter of the size of Jack's own hand, about the size of a small child's. Slowly, Jack shook the brownie's hand up and down. The brownie, confused at first, came around and vigorously shook his hand in return, laughing with glee as he did so.

"Does this mean we're friends, Mr. Jack?"

Jack smiled. "Yes, Donn, this means we're friends."

"I haven't had a friend in a long time, Mr. Jack."

"You know what, Donn? I haven't either."

It was true. Amelia was the closest he came to having a friend nowadays, and even then, she was still sometimes cautious and tentative about him. Emily made it clear she didn't like him. Charles was maybe a friendly acquaintance, but not yet an actual friend. Adrien wasn't a friend by any means, and all his coworkers were merely his employees or colleagues. Donn, however, seemed more than happy to fulfill the role of "friend."

Letting go of each other's hands, Donn said, "You said you needed to talk to me, Mr. Jack."

"I did, Donn. I've been working with a lady to learn about magic."

"Yes, I know. I like Miss Amelia. She's very nice."

"You know her?"

"I've seen her when you're with her sometimes. She's a friend too, isn't she, Mr. Jack?"

"Yes, I suppose she is." Jack was a bit put off by the fact the brownie seemed to know these details about his life.

Sensing his unease, Donn explained, "You left out milk a couple times at her place. I saw you talking to her."

Jack wracked his brain, and remembered one time he'd had cereal while he was at the Blue Barn—he thought he'd dumped the remaining milk down the drain before setting the bowl in the sink, but there must've been a few drops left. He also remembered he'd had ice cream at another point—same sort of thing. He'd have to get better about cleaning up after himself. He liked this strange little creature, but he didn't need him to know every detail about his life.

"Well, Amelia was telling me about magical creatures—she told me about brownies."

"What did she tell you?" Donn asked with childlike curiosity.

"She told me is brownies typically attach to families."

"That's right, Mr. Jack!" Donn said enthusiastically.

"So, I have a question for you, Donn…how long have you been with me?"

"Since the beginning, Mr. Jack."

This was what Jack wanted to hear. The brownie knew Jack as an infant, which meant he must've been attached to his family, and would know who Jack's parents were.

"Donn…did you know my parents?"

"No, Mr. Jack."

Jack was confused. "But you said you've been with me since the beginning."

"That's right, Mr. Jack."

"So, you didn't attach to my family?"

"No, Mr. Jack. I attached to *you*."

Jack was a bit perturbed. He *would* get the one rogue brownie that decided to attach to him as an individual, rather than a family like other normal brownies.

"But even then, you must've seen them at some point around me when I was a child," Jack insisted.

"Not unless you left out milk when they were around."

"Donn—this is very important, Donn—when was the first time I left out milk for you?"

The brownie furrowed his brow, his face resembling a wrinkly leather bag as he thought hard.

"A long time ago, Mr. Jack," Donn finally responded after a moment of silence.

"Was I a little boy?"

"I don't remember, Mr. Jack. It was a long time ago."

"Yes, but how long, Donn?"

"I don't know, Mr. Jack!" Donn cried out, agitated by the line of questioning.

Jack realized in this moment he had crossed a line with the little creature. Amelia had said brownies sometimes got confused easily and were a little slow, and this was apparently one of those times. He needed to back off. This was a futile effort anyway. He wouldn't find his family through the brownie, that much was evident. And maybe it was better that way. Even if he *did* find them, even if Donn *did* know something about them, he had no idea how they'd react to, "Hey, I found you through a weird little magical brown man!" Then again, if they knew they came from a Guardian line, they might not think anything of it, and it might be normal to them. Still, he was disappointed he wouldn't find out about his past tonight.

"It's okay, Donn," Jack said softly. "Don't worry about it. Thanks for answering my questions."

"I'm sorry I couldn't answer them better, Mr. Jack," Donn said despondently. "My memory's not so good from so long ago."

"It's okay, Donn," Jack said gently. "I just appreciate you tried."

"Are we still friends, Mr. Jack?"

"Yes, Donn. We're still friends."

✳

While Jack was questioning the brownie and working on building that relationship, Amelia knew she too needed to repair her own relationship with her sister. Emily hadn't spoken with her since the blowup earlier that day except as it related to their current guests.

It was the middle of the night, and she couldn't sleep—thoughts of her grandfather's journal still drifted in and out of her head, along with a replay of the fight. She could hear Emily moving about in her own room, also unable to sleep.

Quietly, she got out of bed and tiptoed next door. Emily's door was shut, but she could see the light through the crack and hear typing. Softly, she knocked. The typing stopped abruptly.

"Hey, Em? Can I come in?"

She heard Emily shut her laptop, then footsteps walking across the room towards the door. Emily opened it, looking red in the face and exhausted.

"What do you want?" she asked.

"I wanted to talk to you about earlier."

"What about it?"

"Can I come in?"

Emily sighed exasperatedly and stepped aside, allowing Amelia to enter the room. Amelia saw the laptop sitting on Emily's bed, but didn't say anything about it. She instead sat, and said, "Listen, I know you're still not totally comfortable with Jack."

Emily snorted. "*That's* an understatement."

Amelia ignored Emily's snarky comment. "You need to know I appreciate you and the things you do around here, and I appreciate that you let him hang around. It's important."

"I don't get *why* it's so important."

"Because we don't know many Guardians anymore. We're on our own now."

"We don't have to be on our own. *You're* the one who won't call Delia or Jude."

"I don't see you calling them either."

Emily shut her mouth. Her sister was right about that.

"The point is, right now, we're all we've got. And I came in here because I wanted to say I'm sorry for my part of the fight earlier—I'm sorry for calling you mean and all those other things. It wasn't right. You're doing your best, and you're trying to protect us, and I appreciate that."

247

Emily sighed. "And I'm sorry for calling you a Pollyanna."

Amelia smiled. "I *am* a little bit of a Pollyanna sometimes. And you balance me out. You keep me grounded, Em. I can't do this thing without you."

"I know."

Amelia chuckled. "Listen…I just need you to have a little faith in what I'm trying to do, okay? Just trust me, please."

"I trust you. I just don't trust *him*."

At this point, Amelia instinctively started playing with the necklace hanging around her neck. "I know, I know. It's just…I don't know, Em, there's something about him."

Emily raised an eyebrow. "Are you falling for him?"

Amelia shook her head vigorously. "No! It's just—he's different. And he's refreshing."

Emily rolled her eyes. "Yeah, okay."

"He really is trying, you know. He's trying to learn, he's trying to keep us safe, he's trying to help us and the creatures."

"Sure, fine."

"*Really*, Em. Just…at least try being a little nicer to him."

"Yeah, sure, okay."

"Pretend he's someone you like."

"I don't like much of anyone, you know that."

"You like Cosmo, right?"

"Yeah…"

"Then pretend he's Cosmo."

Emily had to laugh, Amelia joining in. For the night, it seemed, the sisters were back on good terms.

✳ Chapter 23 ✳

Double or nothing

Jack sat outside Foster's office a few days later, nervous and having second thoughts. He'd made the appointment shortly after his discovery on the statement, but now that he was here, actually enacting his plan—if it could indeed be called a plan, it seemed so feeble and thrown together now—he wasn't sure if this was the best course of action. What if he was putting himself on a wild goose chase, and there was nothing here?

But he had to know. If William Foster was involved with Adrien somehow, the development project could come to a standstill if it was made public—and the Davidson sisters, and their neighbors, could live in peace.

He was angry he'd been made a part of this process. He wondered how many other projects he'd worked on that shouldn't have happened, that wouldn't have been approved had it not been for someone paying someone else off. He thought about the countless people who he'd talked out of their homes, their memories—who, in a moment of weakness, succumbed to the prospect of more money.

And the people who had purchased the properties…what was happening with them right now? Were they living in the luxury, high-quality homes they were promised, that they *paid for*? Or were they too victims to low-quality materials and workmanship, living in what was essentially a ticking time bomb?

His thoughts were interrupted by the secretary saying, "Mr. Foster will see you now, Mr. Garridan."

Jack stood and entered the office. It was exactly what he expected of the planning director for a small town like Calvary—small and cluttered, lit with harsh fluorescent lighting. Paperwork was piled on Foster's desk, and he couldn't figure out the organizational system. Behind the desk, a shelf full of binders, which he assumed contained details of different projects over the years.

Behind the desk sat William Foster, a lean man who Jack placed in his late fifties, early sixties. He wore his gray hair slicked back, though he had a youthful face. Despite his surroundings, he wore a well-tailored, charcoal gray suit with a blue tie, indicating he clearly valued his personal appearance over his office's. Jack raised an eyebrow over this, as the man seemed a bit out of place—the expense of the suit didn't quite match what the man himself was probably making.

"Jack Garridan, pleasure to meet you!" Foster stood when Jack entered the office. He extended his hand, which Jack shook. The man had a warm smile to match the warm handshake, and all of a sudden, Jack doubted himself again—his first impression was that of a genuinely nice guy.

"Thank you for seeing me, Mr. Foster," Jack replied, as Foster motioned for him to sit.

"Please, call me Will."

"Okay, Will."

"So, what brings you here today, Jack? Can I call you Jack?"

"Of course. And I need your help."

At this point, Jack pressed the record button on the device in his pocket, and said a quick prayer it would pick up their conversation.

"What can I do for you?"

251

"Well, I'm in a bit of a bind right now. You know the project has been going smoothly—we've already started building on the Benedict property, and the Kowalski and Erickson properties are next in line."

"Yes, yes, I know." Foster waved his hand to indicate Jack needed to get to the point.

"Well, I'm having some difficulty acquiring the Davidson land. You see, Amelia and Emily Davidson refuse to sell."

Foster chuckled. "Doesn't surprise me. That whole damn family is stubborn."

"Yes, well, I'm wondering if you might be able to offer any…assistance."

Foster raised an eyebrow. "Assistance? How so?"

"Well, Will, you're respected and trusted in the community," Jack said, buttering Foster up. "A good word from you, or a push in the right direction might help steer things along."

"I don't think so, Jack." Foster leaned back in his chair. "That's not exactly my area."

Jack knew he had to play his trump card now. This could go terribly wrong, but he needed to risk it. "That's not my understanding."

Suddenly, William Foster's entire countenance changed. The smile disappeared, and he leaned in, his gaze now steely cold. "Excuse me?"

Jack's heart dropped. He'd made a mistake. This was a mistake. He needed a way out, but he couldn't think of how to get out.

He had to continue. He had no other choice.

"My understanding is this *is* your area."

Foster sat in silence for a moment, looking Jack up and down. Jack maintained his composure, though every part of his body screamed for him to flee the scene and drop this whole thing.

Finally, after an excruciatingly long pause, Foster said slowly, "I told your boss that I'd make sure your company got the permissions and zoning to move forward with the project, but it's up to *you* to acquire the land. That was the deal. Do you have any idea how hard it was, trying to get the whole damn commission to agree to it? Nobody wanted your project to happen. *Nobody*. But *I* made it happen."

"And that's why we need you again, Will." Jack tried to contain his excitement as the conversation progressed. "You make things happen. We'd sincerely appreciate further help."

"If you want more help from me, it's going to cost you more," Foster countered. "I've already done my fair share, above and beyond. I'm not doing anything else unless I see more."

Bingo.

"How much more?" Jack asked, trying to keep from shaking at this point.

Foster sat silent for a moment, thinking about it. "Double."

Jack's mind reeled. He'd see the account statement with the first payment. Double that amount was exorbitant. "Double?"

"Double or nothing."

"That's quite a bit of money, Will."

"Yes, well, I'll have to do quite a bit of work to make it happen for you, Jack."

Jack stood. "I understand. I'll talk to Mr. Dunstan and let him know your terms."

Foster nodded and also stood. "You do that."

"Thank you, Will, this conversation has been helpful."

Foster extended his hand, which Jack took to shake again. This time, however, it seemed as though all the warmth had drained from it. He felt slimy.

"Anytime, Jack. You let me know when you're ready to talk again. I'll be here."

"I will."

Jack hurried out of the office and raced to his car so he could listen to the recording. Climbing in, he pressed the *play* button, crossing his fingers.

After a moment of static, clear as a bell, he heard William Foster's voice utter the words, "*What can I do for you?*"

The recording continued to the end. Every word, every syllable, it was all there.

He had it. He had proof William Foster had been paid off by Adrien Dunstan.

Now he just needed to use it.

✳

"How'd it go?" Amelia asked as soon as Jack stepped foot inside the Blue Barn a few minutes later. She was sitting at the check-in desk with her laptop, typing away at another article for her magazine.

254

Jack started, staring at her. He hadn't told Amelia he would be stopping by William Foster's office before meeting at her place. How did she know?

"What?"

"The brownie—you were going to summon him last night. How'd it go?"

He grunted. Amelia knew Jack's grunts well enough by now to know this one meant "not well." Part of her was relieved, and she felt bad for feeling as such—but it meant he wouldn't be going on some kind of crazy quest for his family that would take him away from her. Another part of her felt sorry for him, as she knew he'd wanted to find an answer, something that would tell him who he was and where he came from. This was the sentiment she chose to express.

"I'm sorry to hear that. I know you were hoping you'd find something," she said as she closed her laptop. She reached for a cup sitting at the desk. Knowing he would be arriving soon, she'd already prepared a cup of coffee for him and pushed it his way.

He accepted, gulping down the hot liquid. "We can't always get what we want," he said with a shrug.

But sometimes we can, he thought, his mind wandering to the recording of the conversation with Foster.

Now was Amelia's cue to change the subject, before he became too wound up in his own head.

"Why don't we go to the front room and do some meditation?" she asked. "You're getting better at getting to that place, and it seems like you might need to go there again today. And then after, you can teach me some self-defense stuff. I got a punching bag."

"Did you really?" Jack asked, bemused.

Amelia nodded, proud of her acquisition. "I've been practicing."

Before either of them could move though, the phone at the front desk rang. Amelia looked at it and sighed when she saw the light blinking, indicating the call was coming from one of the guest rooms.

"That's Mrs. Patterson," she said, disdain dripping from her voice.

"Tough customer?"

"Like you wouldn't believe. Apparently, she's allergic to down, lavender, rose, pine, wheat, shellfish, and chocolate. And she's demanded we make sure she doesn't have contact with any of it."

"Jesus. I'd be in a bad mood too if I had that many allergies."

"Yeah, well, here's the thing—she walked in yesterday wearing a down jacket, eating a bar of chocolate. She ordered lobster for dinner tonight. And when I went to clean her room this morning, I found lavender body wash, rose perfume, and a half-eaten box of Wheat Thins. Also, she's signed up for the nature walk tomorrow, which takes place in the forest, which consists of mostly pine trees."

Jack blinked. "So, she's insane."

"That or very needy for attention. I even explained to her about lobster being a shellfish, but she insisted she's not allergic to lobster 'if it's cooked right.'"

"How does it need to be cooked for the allergy to disappear?" Jack asked in amazement.

"Beats me. But I'm sure I'll find out tonight."

"And the nature walk? What'd she say when you explained the pine forest?"

"She said she'll take a little allergy medicine and make do—and hold her breath every time she walks by a pine tree."

"So, she's going to be passing out within the first five minutes."

"Basically."

"Lovely."

The phone rang again, its tone jarring, much like Mrs. Patterson's voice, Amelia noted to herself.

"I should probably get that before she has a conniption," Amelia remarked. Picking up the phone, she switched to the most pleasant tone of voice she could muster. "Hello, Mrs. Patterson, how are you doing? No, the towels are not wool. Yes, I'm sure. Of course, I'd be happy to switch them out for you anyway. Right now? Of course, I'll be right up with some fresh ones." She rolled her eyes and hung up. "I'll be back in a minute. Go ahead and start without me."

Jack walked into the front room after Amelia left, sitting on the floor in the space and observing his surroundings before diving in. He noticed the blue and white overstuffed armchair in the corner, and briefly wondered if he should be sitting there to be comfortable, rather than on the floor. But no, something felt right about him sitting where he was. He took notice of the potted succulent, dead center on the end table next to the armchair, basking in the sunlight coming from the window. He observed the way the curtains blew gently in the breeze from the opened windows. He felt calm, comfortable, and at peace with where he was. Taking a deep breath, he closed his eyes once again. He became aware of his breath, of his thoughts, and released those that did not serve him.

He was in that big empty space again—the Between, he called it, though Amelia hadn't told him that was its name. It seemed appropriate to him, as it was a holding place for magical energies—a place between realms, as it was. Not quite able to be used in the world, but not quite gone either. A purgatory of sorts.

He'd been able to reach it much quicker this time. Amelia was right, with more practice, the easier it was becoming. He gathered if magic became viable again, he wouldn't have to meditate anymore, he'd be able to simply reach out to this place and pull from it.

Alone, he walked towards the light, and in an instant, the darkness disappeared, and he was once again surrounded by those vibrant colors, those pieces of magic, swirling about in the midst of the black void.

He smiled, seeing that familiar orange movement piece from the first time he'd ventured in with Amelia. Had he been able to use it, with the flick of a finger, or even a mere thought, he could move something telepathically without even needing to actually touch it. How useful that would be—to be able to move a bookcase, a boulder, a car, without moving a muscle. But without it being able to be pulled into the world, he couldn't even move the plant he saw sitting on the end table in the bed and breakfast's lounge.

He thought about the plant, and wondered if maybe, just *maybe*, he could move it. With this piece of magic in his hand, he felt confident, certain he could use it. It was tangible, it was real. As he thought about this, almost as if he'd conjured it out of thin air, the plant on the table sat before him, as if under a spotlight. All he had to do was aim and flick the orange light at the plant, and it would grab hold, and like a magnetic force, he could direct the plant where he wanted it to go.

But no sooner had he flicked than the same thing that had happened last time happened again: the spell inevitably hit an invisible wall, disintegrating into a million shards of light before him. He sighed, knowing the plant in the waking world was untouched. The plant disappeared, and he was once again standing in a void of swirling colors.

He looked around at the lights beyond his reach—the ones above him, the ones far from him. One, he saw, was far above his head, a dark, billowing black smudge, shimmering with bits of violet, hovering over all the other energies, its tendrils swirling, grasping at all the others. Jack knew eventually, they would all succumb to this one. He didn't even need to touch it—he knew what it was: death, just out of his reach.

Curiously, he stretched out his hand, wanting to know what it felt like. The cloud grumbled, and slowly, very slowly, inched his way. It was *heavy*, like dragging a boulder with a chain, its weight tied with the weight of all the other energies with which it was intertwined. He was breaking into a physical sweat as he urged it towards him. After what felt like a lifetime of coaxing it, pulling it, willing it to him, it stopped in front of him. It was larger than it had looked from a distance, looming, terrifying, yet at the same time, serene in its own way. As he focused in on it, he felt its sadness, its sorrows, its fears. It was colder than anything he'd ever touched. Surprisingly, if needed, he could feel it wouldn't be difficult to use once he'd built up enough force to put it into play, but the heaviness of it, the weight of it, was what he assumed detracted most from trying to use it. And once in use, it was unstoppable—there was no reversing this bit of magic. It would consume everything it was aimed at, absorbing them into itself.

He didn't realize until he looked down that his hand was in a fist, an invisible force holding the darkness in place. Looking back up at it, he released, and the cloud slowly drifted out of his grasp, until it was hovering far overhead once again.

It was in this moment he heard Amelia's voice calling his name, softly at first, then louder, until he was pulled out of the Between, away from its dazzling lights and dark spaces.

He opened his eyes, finding he was face to face with the smiling woman, who had taken a seat directly in front of him on the floor.

"How's Mrs. Patterson?" he asked, smiling back at her.

"She's fine," Amelia answered. "Or as fine as a crazy lady can be. Were you there?"

He nodded. "Yes."

"You got there all on your own?"

Again, he nodded.

Her small smile turned into a wide grin. "That's fantastic, Jack! You're getting the hang of it. What did you do?"

"Not much—just sort of felt around."

"That's a start. That's what you need to do." She glanced him over. "You look tired."

In that moment, Jack noticed he did feel drained. He hadn't noticed before, being filled with adrenaline. "Yeah, I am, I guess. I'm hungry."

"Well, let's get some dinner into you. Do you need to stay the night? Or can you make the drive back into the city?"

"Maybe. I don't know. We'll see how I feel after dinner. And after I check out that punching bag you got."

The two stood, Jack shakily. Grappling with the dark energy took it out of him. He and Amelia walked out of the room, past the overstuffed chair and the end table with the plant on it. He stopped short when his gaze fell on the plant, Amelia a few steps in front of him. From his angle, it was off-center, mere inches from where he thought he'd seen it before, as if it had been moved.

He shifted his weight, repositioned his stance, and once again, it looked to be centered. Yes, that was it. From different angles, he could clearly see it looked centered on the table, but from others, it was slightly off. A trick of depth perception.

"Jack?" Amelia looked over her shoulder at him. "What are you doing?"

He snapped out of it and looked up at her, breaking his gaze from the plant. "Nothing," he said hastily. "I thought…it's nothing. I just thought I saw something. Must've been a trick of the light or something."

✳

The next day, Jack awoke in the bed and breakfast—he had decided after all he was too tired to make the drive all the way back to his apartment in the city. Fortunately, there was an open room for the night, as the Blue Barn wasn't at full capacity.

He hadn't slept well, still thinking on the conversation with Will Foster—the subject of the plant and what he'd seen in the Between had drifted from his mind altogether. Even the time he'd spent with Amelia teaching her self-defense hadn't helped much, but he wouldn't tell her that. He was discouraged—how could a man who was supposed to be looking out for the good of this small town take advantage of his fellow citizens like that?

Money, of course.

He looked over at his overnight bag—he had in there the contract to finally acquire the land from the Kowalskis, some other neighbors of Amelia's. He had meant to go get Ruth Kowalski's final signatures yesterday, but after the conversation with Foster and feeling drained from the meditation session, he never got around to it.

He hated this part—taking someone's home from them, and for what? For some cookie cutter, overpriced, shoddily built condos and townhouses? And now he knew Foster had been bribed, he felt even slimier doing his job—this never would've happened if Foster hadn't been paid off.

He had to fix this.

261

He rose, quickly showering and dressing, grabbing his briefcase and heading downstairs. He overhead Amelia and Emily chatting in the dining room with Mrs. Patterson and the other bed and breakfast guests, and poked his head in. Amelia saw him and smiled, waving him over to join them. He shook his head, grabbing a muffin to go from the buffet near the door, pointing to his briefcase. Her face fell.

He hated that too—knowing he was disappointing her every time he went out to do "Dunstan Enterprises work." She knew he was trying to help, that he was working behind the scenes, he'd told her that, but he still couldn't help but feel she didn't entirely trust him.

He'd have to continue to prove himself, it seemed. He turned his back on the group and walked out to his car, driving the short distance to the Kowalski residence.

When he pulled up a few moments later, he smiled. The Kowalski property was similar to the Davidson property. Mrs. Kowalski, though a widow, took excellent care of the land—and her multiple children would roam free through it. He'd seen them playing outside during the previous times he'd stopped by, all blond-haired, blue-eyed, and ruddy-faced, covered in dirt and sand from their adventures, with giant smiles on their faces.

He envied their childhood, and mourned the one he never had. What it must have been like to grow up here, wild and free, with a family who loved you—not like he did, bounced from home to home, with no real stability or sense of self.

He approached the front porch—the children weren't here this time, most likely at school, seeing as it was a weekday. He wasn't sure if Ruth Kowalski would be here at her home, or at the bakery she owned in town—he had never been able to keep track of her schedule. He had a feeling she did that to him on purpose. She'd been making multiple revisions on the contract, procrastinating, and doing everything she could to make his life harder and put off the inevitable.

He knocked, patiently waiting to see if anyone would answer. If no one did, he knew he'd have to drive all the way the opposite direction back to town to see her at her bakery—and he didn't want to do that. He wanted to do this privately, not in public for others to see or hear.

Fortunately for him, Ruth was home that day. A few moments after he knocked, he heard her shuffling across the floor inside, the click of the lock, and those striking blue eyes peek out through the crack in the door.

"Mrs. Kowalski."

Ruth Kowalski's eyes turned to slits when she saw Jack at her door, opening it a hair wider, enough for him to see the look of disdain on her face. "What do you want, Mr. Garridan?"

"I just wanted to let you know the most recent set of changes has been made on your contract," Jack said, clutching his briefcase. "It's ready for you to sign, unless you have any further revisions."

Ruth sighed, resigned, now opening the door all the way. She'd known he'd be coming to do this. "I don't. I've thrown everything in the book at you, and you've been more than accommodating. I guess it's time for me to stop procrastinating, isn't it?"

"Mrs. Kowalski…you love your home, don't you?"

Ruth nodded. "More than anything. My husband built it. Lots of happy memories here."

"Then don't sign."

Ruth blinked, taken aback. "Come again?"

"Don't sign."

"I don't understand, Mr. Garridan. You've spent the past several months pestering me, insisting it was in my best interests, in my *children's* best interests."

"I know I did. And I was wrong."

"You all but *threatened* me for my land," she continued. "And then you gave me no choice when you told me if I didn't sell, you'd eventually be able to take my land with or without my permission."

Jack turned red in the face, remembering that conversation from a few months prior, before he'd become a regular at the Davidson place, and the fear and panic that had crossed Ruth's face in that moment. He'd made the same threat against the Davidson sisters, but Amelia had seen right through it. Ruth hadn't been as intuitive, unfortunately. "That was a lie, Mrs. Kowalski. A fear tactic. We're not doing that—legally, we can't do that. We don't have those powers."

Ruth took a step back, dumbfounded. "Are you kidding me right now?"

Jack shook his head. "I'm afraid not. And I'm so sorry for all I put you through."

"Do you have *any* idea the kind of strain you put me under?"

"Ma'am, you need to know, I was acting under my boss's orders."

"So you don't have a mind of your own?" she snapped.

Jack flinched. He deserved that. "I do now. And the way you've been treated by us is wrong."

Ruth eyed him suspiciously. "Why the change?"

Thoughts of Amelia, of fairies, of the corruption of William Foster and Adrien Dunstan, of Donn, of Emily, and of Charles raced through his head. But explaining that to Ruth would take too long.

264

"That's...a long story," he settled on. "But please believe me. I want to help now. I'm trying to undo what I've done."

"What's your angle?"

"No angle this time."

"What about the others?"

"I can't do anything about the Benedict land—it is what it is," Jack said heavily. "The Ericksons haven't signed yet either, and I plan to talk to them too. As for the Davidsons...well, they've been stubborn from the start."

"Good for them," Ruth huffed.

"You're a strong woman, Mrs. Kowalski. And I can't apologize enough for playing to your weaknesses. It wasn't fair of me. It was manipulative."

"How do I know you're not manipulating me right now?"

"You don't. But maybe this will help." Jack procured the contract from his briefcase, and a lighter from his pocket. Flicking the lighter a few times, he set fire to the corner of the document and threw it to the ground, where it went up in flames.

Ruth, however, remained skeptical as she watched the pages burn. "That's a very nice symbolic gesture of you, Mr. Garridan, but I'm sure that wasn't your only copy."

Jack smiled. "No, you're right, it wasn't. There were only two others. One on my computer, which I've already wiped. And one on a flash drive."

From his pocket, he pulled out the very drive and handed it to her. "Take it. Do what you want with it."

265

Ruth held the drive, marveling at it. "What if I *do* want to sign?" she asked, looking up at Jack. "The money you offered was pretty tempting, and could help us. And we've gotten this far anyway."

"Then it's in your hands. It's up to you, no more bullying or pressuring from me," Jack said gently. "You choose what you want to do, and I'll leave you alone, whatever your decision. Take a couple weeks to think about it. If you want to go through with it, print it up and call me, and I'll come over to collect the signed document. If you don't want to sign, call the office and tell them you're pulling the contract, that you don't want to sell after all. We can't do anything to you. We don't have your signature."

"I don't understand why you're doing this," Ruth said, bewildered.

"You don't have to. But let's just say I'm trying to do my part to help protect this little corner of the world."

Ruth smiled. "Amelia Davidson got to you, didn't she?"

Jack smiled as well. "Something like that."

"I always liked her. I'll think about it, Mr. Garridan." She paused, holding the flash drive tightly in her fist. "Thank you."

"Of course."

Jack walked away, leaving Ruth to her thoughts. At least he could say he'd tried.

✳ Chapter 24 ✳

Revelations

"Reading Grandpa's journal again?" Emily asked, walking into the room where Amelia was curled up in an overstuffed chair, pouring over the delicate, yellowed pages.

Jack had gone to work, a few of the guests were at the beach soaking up the sun, and Emily was getting ready to take a few of the other guests on the nature walk (fortunately, Mrs. Patterson had decided last minute she'd rather go to the beach than go on the walk, saving Emily from a headache). While Emily was doing that, Amelia was taking the time to pack for her next trip to Ireland, which was coming up shortly. She was currently taking a break, however, to once again look through her grandfather's journal.

"It's fascinating." Amelia looked up from his journal. This was probably her seventh time reading through the pages, and she was only just now starting to gain some insight into her grandfather. "He had this whole life he never mentioned to us. Sometimes he'd spend months planning an extravagant adventure. Sometimes he'd take the boat and just sail off. And it all just stopped when he went to war."

"Does he mention the stones anywhere in there?"

"No, not specifically, but he kind of leaves clues…he speaks in code, almost."

"Why was he looking for them though? He always told us not to."

"I think he was trying to make sure they were okay," Amelia said thoughtfully. "He always talked about how things with the magical creatures started to be slightly 'off' when he was young, remember? Migration patterns for some of them changed, a few exhibited new behaviors they'd never had before, that sort of thing. I think he was afraid someone had found a stone, and he wanted to rule that possibility out—or, confirm it, and go from there."

"Sounds like Grandpa—checking and double checking and triple checking and taking things on himself that he didn't need to. But what was he planning to do if he'd found out a stone *had* been taken from where it had been hidden?"

Amelia shook her head. "I don't know. He never says." She paused. "There's this other thing I found, and it doesn't make sense at all…"

"What is it?"

Amelia flipped to the back of the book and handed it to Emily. In a simple scribble, she read the words:

Those forgotten will be remembered
Those hidden shall be recovered
When the forgotten and hidden reunite
Darkness shall alight
Light shall dim
Where it all began
So it shall end
And when it ends
So it shall begin.

Emily looked up. "So what? What does that mean?"

Amelia shook her head. "I don't know. But look closer at the writing."

Emily looked again, studying the handwriting. It was sharp and neat, written with a black fountain pen.

"What am I looking for?" she asked, still not understanding.

"Em…that's Dad's handwriting."

Emily started. "What?"

"That's Dad's handwriting," Amelia repeated. "I pulled out one of my old Christmas cards from him to compare…it's definitely his. And it must've been written years after the rest of this. The ink isn't as faded as the rest of Grandpa's entries."

"I don't get it. Why did Dad have Grandpa's journal? And what does that mean?"

"I don't know," Amelia sighed, taking the journal back from her sister. "None of it makes sense. If Grandpa was here, he could probably tell us."

"Do you think he ever mentioned it to Grandma?"

"I'd be surprised if he didn't. They talked about *everything*."

"Do you think she might remember anything?"

Amelia hesitated, carefully choosing her words. "I think it depends on the kind of day she's having. And I think if we're going to visit her and ask her, we need to figure out some straightforward questions ahead of time, so we don't confuse or upset her. I don't know if I want to go to her first."

"Who else would we go to?"

"Mom, I guess."

Amelia had been keeping things shallow with Rosalie since those first weeks after moving into the cottage, and their relationship was still on tenuous terms. Rosalie would occasionally stop by the bed and breakfast to visit her daughters, or they had the occasional meal out in town with her, but the conversation was always light, with no real substance. It was exhausting, never really talking about anything.

Emily raised an eyebrow. "Mom? Really? What makes you think she'll know something?"

"I'm not saying she will. But Grandpa might've told Dad something, and Dad might've told Mom something."

"You know she hates talking about magic. I think you should call her and talk to her…but not about that." Emily was alluding to Amelia's current strained relationship with their mother.

"I know," Amelia sighed. "And I think there's something to that, something *she* experienced that she won't talk about…and I think it's time to figure out why. Our whole life, she's been anti-magic, and it impacted Dad. I'd like to find out what happened that made them that way. And I think it might be connected to Grandpa's journal. So yeah, I think we should try to ask Mom and Grandma."

"And if we don't get anything out of either of them?"

"Then we're no worse off than we are now. And we just keep doing what we're doing."

"What about calling Jude?"

Amelia glared at Emily. "I don't want to call him."

"Amelia, he was Grandpa's best friend for *decades*. He might know something."

"He also betrayed the fairies and creatures on his land and sold out."

"Okay, seriously? The man has *cancer*. You can't hold a grudge against him for trying to make the last few months of his life simpler."

270

"He could've left his land to his son. Hell, he could've left it to *us*. He could've had it turned into a park, something, *anything*. He had options. But he took the money and ran to Hawaii."

"He was trying to make sure Delia was taken care of after he was gone," Emily argued.

"She would've been *fine*. Elliott would've taken care of her. And I'm sure Jude had some kind of life insurance that would've helped her out."

Emily was shocked at how cold her sister was being about the whole situation. "You know, for someone who's so willing to trust a stranger in our home who was literally trying to *take* it from us, you're pretty unforgiving towards the couple who were like second grandparents to us."

Amelia sat in silence, unable to respond.

"Just think about it." Emily rose from her chair. "You're always talking about forgiveness—I think it's time to let go of this one."

"I'd still rather talk to Mom first."

"Fine. Ask the woman who's never seen magic a day in her life. After that, go to the woman who can't remember *anything*. Great plan. Or, call Jude, the one person who might actually be useful and save yourself the headache. It's your choice. Personally, I don't care. If you'll excuse me, I'll be trying to manage our business."

She turned to head out the door, when Amelia said, "I'll think about it, okay? While I'm in Ireland. I'll do some serious thinking about it."

Emily rolled her eyes. "Yeah, okay, sure."

"Listen, it's just that—well, you know."

"Yeah, I know. You feel betrayed. But they didn't betray *you*," Emily emphasized. "They were just doing what they had to do."

Amelia sighed. "Yeah, I know."

"Listen, you forgave Jack…why can't you forgive them?"

"You're right. I know you're right. I just need time, okay?"

"Well, don't take too long thinking about it. If I were you, I'd call *before* Ireland. Jude has cancer, remember. He doesn't have all the time in the world."

Amelia sighed. "Yeah…I know."

"Then call them."

"I will call them if you promise to do something for me."

"What's that?"

"Be nice to Jack while I'm gone."

"I'm nice."

"*Nicer.*"

Emily waved her hand. "Fine, fine. Nicer. Is that all?"

"I need you to take him out and see if he can spot magical creatures on his own. He's been reading about them long enough, and his intuition is great—and he's been able to get in touch with magic really quickly. It's time for him to go out there and actually see what we have around here, aside from fairies."

Emily groaned. "Do I have to?"

272

"I will call Jude if you do."

"*Fine.*"

"Don't have him work on summoning them yet…I'll work on that with him when I get back. Just see what he can find, yeah?"

"Yeah, yeah, okay."

✳

After Emily left for the nature walk, Amelia paced the floor of her room, her cell phone in hand, trying to work up the courage to call Jude. What would she say? The last time she'd spoken with him, she had been less than cordial. Would he even be willing to talk to her?

But she'd made a promise to Emily. Besides, she had seen a call come in from the Benedict household a couple weeks ago, and hadn't called back—she had still been too angry at the time. It was time to call back. She needed to put things in the past.

She dialed, sitting on her bed and tapping her foot anxiously as the phone rang.

Is it too early to call Hawaii?

She had forgotten to take the time difference into consideration. She looked at the clock on her nightstand—it was early afternoon here, which meant it was early morning there.

Crap.

She was about to hang up, embarrassed about calling too early, set on calling back again later, when she heard someone pick up on the other end.

"Hello?"

273

It was Delia, Jude's wife.

"Hi, Delia, it's Amelia." She waited for Delia's reply with bated breath.

After a moment of silence, Delia replied curtly, "Amelia. I wasn't expecting a phone call from you."

"I know. I'm sorry for calling so early. I forgot about the time difference."

"Clearly."

"I'm…Delia, I'm sorry for how I acted the last time I saw you two."

Delia's tone softened. "I appreciate that. How have you been?"

"Good. The bed and breakfast is up and running. We're settling into the cottage. We've been keeping busy."

"I'm glad to hear it."

"How are you?"

"Oh, you know, about as good as can be expected."

"Delia, can I talk to Jude? I have a couple questions about Grandpa I need answered."

Silence.

"Delia?"

"Amelia…Jude died."

Amelia's heart sank. "What? When?"

"A couple weeks ago."

The missed call. The deleted message. Amelia winced.

"Oh, Delia…I'm so sorry. I didn't know."

"I called you. I tried Emily too, but her voicemail box was full, I couldn't leave a message. I'm not sure she even knows I called."

Amelia winced again. That wouldn't surprise her about Emily—she had a tendency to forget to call people back if she saw a missed call, and if her box was full, she wouldn't have that as a reminder. But this was a call that shouldn't have been missed, and both of the sisters had blown it.

"Delia…I'm sorry. I'm so sorry."

"I know you are, dear."

"Is there anything I can do?"

"From all the way in Maine? No, I'm afraid not much. But I appreciate hearing from you."

"It's good to hear from you too."

"What did you want to know about your grandfather?" Delia asked, changing the subject. The elderly woman wasn't in the mood to dwell on her dead husband. "I might be able to help."

"Well—we found out he did a bunch of traveling before Dad was born. He had this old journal we found, and he talks about these crazy trips, and he mentions Jude in some of the entries. So, I wanted to see what they were all about and try to understand it."

"Yes, I remember some of those trips."

"So…what were they about? And why didn't they ever talk about them?"

"Amelia, I have a feeling you know what they were about, and you're just looking for confirmation."

"Yes. You're right," Amelia replied, seeing no sense in beating around the bush. "Delia, were they looking for stones?"

"They were."

"But why?"

"Your grandfather was worried about things he was seeing change with the creatures. He wanted to see if they'd been disturbed in some way, and if that was the cause. He talked Jude into going on some of those trips with him."

Amelia's suspicions were confirmed. "Delia, what did they find? Grandpa never really said outright in his journal, and the entries stopped when he was drafted."

"Jude never said." She paused. "You know, he kept a journal from around that time of his life as well."

Amelia's ears perked at this statement. "Did he really?"

"He did."

"Delia...would it be too much of an inconvenience if you shipped it to me? I'd love to see it."

"I'll have to ask Elliott. I gave it to him so he'd have something of his father's. And I'll be honest, I don't know what you'll find in there, if there's even anything worth reading. There were some painful memories in the first few entries...and it'll be up to him if he wants to share it or not."

Amelia's hopes sank. Of course Delia would give the journal to Elliott. It only made sense.

"But I'll at least ask. Maybe he'd be willing to scan the pages and e-mail it to you."

Amelia brightened. "Yes, please! I'd appreciate that."

"I'll see what I can do."

"Thank you."

"Amelia…be careful. Whatever you're looking for in those pages, just be careful."

"I'm not planning to go searching for the stones, Delia. I'm just trying to piece together a few things about my family I don't understand."

"Still. Be careful."

"I will."

"I miss you, Amelia."

"I miss you too, Delia." And she meant it. With her own grandmother's mind mostly gone, and her other grandmother (her mother's mother) dead, Delia was the closest thing Amelia had to a grandmother figure. She didn't realize how much she'd missed that, or needed that in her life.

"You know I love you, right? And that Jude loved you too?"

"I know. I love you both."

"He felt so terrible about the way everything ended," Delia continued. "It ate at him, knowing he'd let you and your family down. He was just trying to do what he thought was best."

"I know. And I'm so sorry for the way I treated you both. It wasn't right."

"You're a protective woman, Amelia. You get that from your grandfather. We understood. You were just as hurt."

"I'm still sorry."

"So are we. Please keep in touch, won't you? I miss talking to you."

"I will. I miss talking to you too. This place isn't the same knowing you guys aren't right next door."

"Send my love to Emily, Rosalie, and Lizzie."

"I will."

"I'll talk to you soon, Amelia."

"Talk to you soon, Delia."

✳

Jack returned to the Blue Barn that afternoon for his things, knowing he couldn't stay another night there without drawing suspicion. He had to head back to his apartment and go into the office the next day, and after yesterday's conversation with Foster and today's conversation with Ruth, he knew he had some work to do—and he had to call Max, the Calvary development's former project manager. He needed to know more, and he needed to know if he was doing the right thing. Max had always been a good moral compass, even if he was a Dunstan Enterprises employee.

Amelia, however, caught him as he was walking out the door, about to go for a jog with Cosmo to clear her mind after the telephone conversation with Delia.

"Hey there!" she said cheerily. Cosmo expressed the same level of cheeriness—or perhaps more—when he jumped on Jack, demanding to be pet. Jack obliged, setting down his briefcase. The mutt rolled onto his back, tongue hanging out of his mouth, enjoying the belly rubs.

"Heading back to the city?" Amelia glanced over at Jack's overnight bag and briefcase.

Jack nodded. "I am."

"Well...then I guess I'll see you in two weeks?"

Jack blinked. "Two weeks?"

"Yeah, Ireland, remember? I'm a travel journalist," she reminded him with a playful poke in the arm.

Jack had forgotten. He'd gotten so used to Amelia being around, he forgot she had a whole second career. The amount of writing she did in his presence should've been enough to remind him, but apparently it wasn't. "That's right. Sorry."

"Anyway, I talked to Emily, and she'll work with you while I'm gone."

Jack snorted. "How much did you have to give her to get her to agree to that?"

"Just my dignity and self-respect, that's all."

Jack laughed, picking up his bags again. "Sounds about right."

The two continued walking towards Jack's car, Cosmo at their heels.

"I talked to Ruth Kowalski today," Jack said hesitantly.

Amelia stopped walking, turning to face Jack. "What about?"

"I did some thinking about that conversation we had a while back…the one where you asked me to stop going after your neighbors."

"What about it?"

"I told her she didn't have to sign the contract. I told her, actually, to *not* sign the contract."

"Jack, why'd you do that?" Amelia asked, shaking her head.

This was not the response Jack was expecting. "I thought you'd be happy about it."

"I mean, I am, but…Jack, that was risky of you. What if your boss finds out? He'll figure out you've been undermining him this whole time. I just worry you're trying to keep up appearances, and this might blow your cover."

"Ruth Kowalski was already a hard sell," Jack replied, trying to alleviate Amelia's concerns. "She had us revise the contract about a dozen times. It wouldn't be out of character for her to back out last minute. She didn't want to leave. She *never* wanted to leave." He paused. "She reminds me of you, in a way."

Amelia gave a small smile. "I like Ruth."

Jack smiled in return. "I do too. She hasn't made up her mind yet, anyway…but I needed to try."

They continued walking, silence falling between them for a moment. Amelia broke it by asking, "So are you going to do the same with the Ericksons?"

"I haven't decided yet."

"Don't."

Jack raised an eyebrow. "Amelia, I thought you wanted this land safe."

"I do. But I also want *you* to be safe. And losing two properties back to back…that's going to raise suspicions."

"So what do you want me to do?"

"Just…I don't know, procrastinate or something."

"Amelia…"

"I just don't want you to have to stop coming here sooner than planned. That's all."

Now it was Jack's turn to stop walking. "Excuse me?"

"I've gotten used to you coming around. And it's nice to have someone else to talk to about everything," Amelia said hurriedly.

"Amelia, you know we'll still be friends after everything."

"Yeah, but, if you have to leave the area after you leave Dunstan Enterprises, or worse, if your boss catches on and is able to twist something against you…"

"That's not going to happen."

"But how do you *know*?"

"I don't, I guess. But I have faith." He grinned. "You can't get rid of me that easily, Davidson."

Amelia snorted. "Funny how a few months ago all I wanted was for you to leave my life forever."

"Life is good at playing jokes like that, isn't it?" Jack grinned. "Listen, let's take it one day at a time…and trust me, okay?"

"Okay. I trust you."

"Good." He leaned in and gave her a hug, which she returned. "Be safe in Ireland, yeah?"

"I will. You be safe at work, yeah?"

He smirked. "I will."

The two held each other for a moment longer before letting go. Jack climbed into his car, wondering why he was so disappointed about the fact he wouldn't see Amelia again for two weeks. As he rolled down the driveway and out of sight, Amelia wondered the same about him.

✸ Chapter 25 ✸

Threads

A few days later, Jack sat in May's Diner once again, anxiously tapping his fingers on the table as he waited for his lunch guest. He glanced at his watch—12:03. He was late.

The bell dinged, and he looked up. Charles walked in, and though Jack liked Charles, he felt his face fall. He wasn't who he was waiting for.

Charles strode over to the booth where Jack was sitting, a smile on his face. "You still hanging around these parts, Jack?" he asked with a hint of bemusement.

Jack offered a weak smile. "You know it."

"Waiting for anyone in particular, or can I join you?"

"Actually…I am waiting for someone." Jack glanced nervously at the door. "But you can join me until he arrives."

"He?" Charles said, eyebrow raised, sitting in the booth.

"An old colleague. Max. The guy I was telling you about."

"The guy who was taken off the project?"

"Yeah."

Charles looked Jack up and down, his intuition kicking in. "Jack, I know I've asked you this before, but what are you up to?"

Jack shook his head. "Charles, if I could tell you, I would. But I can't."

"Does it have anything to do with the Davidson sisters?"

"Sort of."

"Are you trying to take advantage of Amelia Davidson's good nature?"

"What? No. Why would you ask that?"

"It's a small town. People know you've been spending a lot of time there—and they also know you haven't acquired her land yet. So, the only thing we can think is either you're there making social calls...or you've got something a little less than honest in mind."

"Believe me, Charles, it's neither. I'm not making 'social calls,' and I'm not taking advantage of her."

"Then what are you doing, son?"

"I can't tell you."

Charles sat back in his seat. "I see. Okay, Jack, I'll believe you for now. You haven't given me a reason otherwise yet. Just you take care and don't do anything stupid, all right?"

Jack chuckled. "Trying not to."

The bell at the entrance dinged, and both men turned to the door. Max had walked in. He glanced around the diner before his eyes fell on Jack and Charles.

As Max approached, Charles stood. "I'll leave you to it."

Max and Charles nodded at each other as they passed before Max took Charles' place in the booth.

"Coffee, please. Black," Max said to the waitress passing by. As she obliged and walked away, he turned to Jack. "Okay, Jack. I drove two hours to meet you. Why am I here?"

"What I'm trying to figure out is why you're *not* here," Jack replied. "You and I have a conversation about some subpar building materials, and suddenly you and your entire team are on a different build?"

Max shrugged, sipping his coffee. "Adrien does what Adrien wants. You know that."

"Yes, but Adrien doesn't normally remove his project manager and completely flip a crew right in the middle of a build."

Max remained silent, staring down into his mug.

"Max, what happened?" Jack asked in a hushed tone. "Why were you taken off the Calvary project?"

Max shook his head. "I don't know, Jack. But I get the feeling I was just slowing Adrien down."

"What do you mean?"

"He didn't just take me off—he took *all* my guys off, and moved us onto something else in the city. We were all concerned about the build, we were working slower because of it, and we were holding it up. It got to a point where we said we wouldn't continue until things were straightened out."

"But that's what I don't get—if materials were an issue, why didn't he just replace them?"

"Replacing them would've taken weeks. For whatever reason, that wasn't acceptable."

"So, he took you off and assembled a new team that would keep pushing through instead."

"Seems like it."

"So, Jeff Black, the new guy—does he know about the materials?"

Max shook his head. "I don't know much about Jeff. He's a kid, fresh out of school, that's all I know. I think he's so naïve and so eager to prove himself he'll do whatever Adrien says. Which is probably exactly what Adrien wants."

"Max, this is weird—Adrien's not usually like this about builds."

"No, not with the urban ones, he's not…you're right," Max said slowly. "But I've noticed since he started acquiring this coastal land and trying to build these little residential communities, his standards have changed."

"What do you mean?"

"I mean I don't think it's about the build, Jack. I think it's about the location—like he's trying to gobble up property for the sake of owning it and doesn't really care what happens to it. Like the build itself is an afterthought."

Jack pursed his lips, thoughtful. "Max, he lied to me about you calling the office when I talked to him—both he and Stephanie said you never called."

Max snorted. "I talked to Stephanie myself."

"I believe you. But why would they lie like that?"

"Probably because if they admitted I'd called, they'd have to say they were doing something about it, and that would hold up the build. By saying I didn't call, they could keep pushing on."

Jack sat back in his seat, bewildered. "It's all so stupid. What could possibly be so important that Adrien can't wait a few weeks to get the right materials?"

"Beats me. But whatever it is, it's changed his whole demeanor. He's not like he was before—he's almost acting desperate."

Jack leaned in. "I've been finding out some things about him, Max...he's been bribing people too. The project probably never would've been approved in the first place if he hadn't."

Max raised an eyebrow. "You sure about that, Jack?"

"Pretty sure."

"Pretty sure isn't enough. You need to be *really* sure."

"I know he paid off at least one person."

"One's not enough." Max took another sip of his coffee.

"One's enough if it's the planning director for the town Calvary."

"Jesus...really?"

"Yeah."

Max gave a low whistle. "So, what are you going to do about it?"

"I've got a recording, and an account statement that has his name on it for a payment...but I don't know if that's enough to turn over to the authorities. I think I need to keep digging. If this is as widespread as you say it is, if it's been impacting all the coastal properties he's been

287

acquiring, that means hundreds, maybe even thousands of people could be affected…I think I need to find that paper trail."

"Good luck with that, Jack. But I don't know how you'll get that, or if it even exists."

"If it doesn't, I'll just go with what I've got and see what happens."

"So, what's your goal with all this? Shut down the company?"

Jack shook his head. "No…no, I don't want to shut it down. But things need to be changed. They're impacting people's lives—and not for the better—and don't even care."

"You know if things are going to change, it means a *lot* of people will lose their jobs, right?"

"I know," Jack said stiffly.

"You ready to take on that kind of guilt?"

"I…don't know." Jack now felt foolish.

"Before you keep going, you're going to need to figure that out," Max advised. "Sounds like to me, either way, a lot of people are going to get hurt. You just need to figure out which ones you're okay with hurting."

"I don't want to hurt anybody."

"You don't have a choice. You stay quiet, and the people who own that land or who live in those homes get hurt. You speak up, and the innocent people in the company who have nothing to do with this get hurt when they get caught in the crossfire."

"So what do I do?"

"I don't know, Jack. But now you've got me wanting to abandon ship before this all goes down."

"You won't tell anyone I'm working on this?"

"No, Jack, that's not my place." He paused. "I think you know what you need to do. But I'm not going to tell you what that is. You need to figure that out for yourself."

Jack sighed. "You're right."

"I'm sorry I couldn't be more helpful."

"No…no, you were plenty helpful. More than you think. I'm sorry I dragged you all the way out here on your day off. I just needed to meet you somewhere far away from him."

"It's no problem. I always kind of liked this place. Hell, when we were building, I was thinking about getting one of those houses myself—you know, until I found out what we were working with." He smiled grimly. "Sometimes it's good to be on the inside."

"Sometimes it's not," Jack said solemnly.

"Adrien riding you hard, huh?"

"Like you wouldn't believe."

"You're too young to let people push you around, Jack. You need to get out. Do something you enjoy, not something you'll regret."

Jack's mind flashed to his regular meetings with Amelia, the things she was teaching him, and he smiled.

"I am, Max. Don't worry about me."

Max raised an eyebrow. "I mean it, Jack. Be careful with Adrien. Something's not right with him, and I don't want to see you hurt."

His sentiments were eerily similar to the warnings Amelia had given him a few days previous.

"I'll be careful, Max. Promise." He looked at his watch. "Listen, I only have a few more minutes to eat, then I need to head out."

"You meeting up with someone else to plot the downfall of Dunstan Enterprises?" Max teased.

"No, not exactly."

*

Emily was struggling—not that this was news, but she was. The Blue Barn was doing well, which was great, and she was pleased about that, but the charter fishing portion with Stuart's old boat, not so much. In a town that was composed mostly of fishermen, not many of the locals were interested in that part of the business. And as for out-of-towners...well, she'd had a few customers come through who were guests of the bed and breakfast, but not many who wanted to pay what it cost. Quite simply, they'd rather pay a reasonable price for a good seafood dinner prepared by a restaurant than an outlandish cost to rent a boat and catch their own. The adventure of it apparently wasn't as appealing as she'd hoped it would be. If she were closer to one of the larger cities, had access to a larger population, perhaps she would do better, but then she'd have more competition to deal with. She knew it would be a struggle getting this portion of the business up and running, but she didn't realize how much of a struggle. And now that summer had come to a close, and autumn was beginning, business was even slower—i.e. there *was* no business. Not even an inquiry in weeks. In the moment, she didn't feel like she deserved that business degree she'd spent all that time on.

Amelia had been nothing but graceful about the whole situation over the course of the summer season, even *encouraging*, reminding her they were a new business, these things took time, next summer would be better, offering to help with the marketing, etc. But honestly, her positive attitude about it all made it that much more annoying—she almost wished her sister would snap at her, so she could snap back. She had a few bones to pick, regarding the amount of time Jack was spending at the place, how he was staying overnight without being charged, how much food he was eating, and how she was expected to help him out when Amelia was off traveling for her job with the magazine…but she couldn't express any of this while Amelia was being so *nice*. That was one thing that had always irked her about her sister—when Emily wanted to be mean, Amelia generally took the high road, forcing Emily to feel like she had to be a better person when all she wanted to do was kick and scream. It was exhausting keeping up with Amelia.

And there was the matter of her mother. Amelia had been avoiding her for months now, ever since that day when she'd been by to pick up Cosmo, keeping interactions brief and shallow. Rosalie had recently called Emily, aggravated by Amelia, asking for her help—Emily didn't like being placed in the middle like that, and told her mother the two of them needed to work it out for themselves. Rosalie reminded Emily the only reason they even owned a bed and breakfast was because of *her* generosity in giving up her share of the inheritance from Stuart. Emily hated her mother using that against her, and though she recognized it for the guilt tactic it was, it didn't make the situation any more pleasant.

Not to mention the second wave of fairies had left a few days prior, and along with it, Emily's hopes. She was afraid of what it would mean for the area, for the creatures, for her home—though her land seemed safe for the moment, she couldn't be sure how long that would last, and seeing her neighbors move and the magical creatures on their land migrate was becoming too much to bear.

It also didn't help she'd been stalking Dan's social media accounts again—she knew she needed to stop, that it was over, that it had happened *months* ago, but still, she couldn't help it. Amelia had almost caught her that one night—hell, she probably knew what she'd been doing, but being so nice and polite, chose not to say anything, making Emily feel even more guilty about it. But at the same time, she felt entitled, like she needed to check in on him. They'd been together a long time, they'd *lived* together, for Christ's sake. She had genuinely thought she was going to marry him. That was foolish, though. She knew they never would've been married—he didn't know about her being a Guardian. She'd never divulged that part of her life to him—in hindsight, that was for the best. He would've freaked out. They all did. Both she and Amelia had learned to keep quiet about that part of their lives when it came to dating. But still. She'd loved him. Secretly, she was scanning all his social media profiles to see if he was miserable, if he regretted his decision, but the smiling faces of him and Leslie together that popped up every time she logged on said otherwise, tearing her heart open in the process.

She knew she shouldn't have introduced him to Leslie—something in her gut told her their meeting would cause disaster. And when they all agreed to live together…ugh. She still couldn't get that image out of her head, of them making out when she'd walked in that night…it was awful. She should've listened to her gut. But then again, her gut had told her initially Leslie was a great friend, and Dan was a great guy…she questioned her own judgment about people now.

And it was this questioning that caused her to be in this current state of emotional turmoil. She was already low on herself, though she wouldn't admit that to Amelia. But she didn't know if her feelings and suspicions about Jack were right, or if she was once again wrong and Amelia was in the right. She didn't know what *was* wrong or right anymore, when it came down to it. She didn't know if her decision to move away from the city was a good one, or if it was making her life worse, being in Calvary with half of a failed business.

She sighed, walking down the main street of Calvary, hands stuffed into her pockets on this unusually warm autumn day. Right now, it didn't matter. She was to meet Jack while Amelia was in Ireland, and walk him through some of the things Amelia had wanted him to work on while she was gone. So, she put on her best fake smile, and would push through it.

God, this was annoying.

She arrived in front of May's Diner, where Jack was standing outside, waiting for her. He waved awkwardly as she approached, and she did the same. No hugs, just a nod acknowledging him—she wasn't Amelia, after all. She was teaching him, and was all business.

"You been waiting long?" she asked.

"No, not long. I got here early for lunch."

Emily raised an eyebrow. "The only good thing at May's is the pie. And maybe the soup sometimes."

"I know. That's what I had."

Emily snorted, trying to keep back a laugh. He was funny sometimes, but she wouldn't let him know she thought that. Jack smiled at her snort, but otherwise, didn't say anything about it. He didn't want to put her in a bad humor.

"So, what are we doing today?" He knew she'd appreciate cutting directly to the point, with no nonsense.

Emily *did* appreciate this gesture, but she wouldn't tell him that. "Amelia wanted me to take you here to play 'find the magical creature,'" she said as she walked down the street, motioning to Jack to follow. "She said she'll work with you on summoning them later, but right now, just wanted to see if you could spot them, after everything she's had you reading."

"I'm pretty sure I can find a fairy if it's flying in the middle of the street," Jack said wryly, thinking back on his run from a few months prior. He'd since changed his route, though he had a feeling that didn't matter— if Lila wanted to find him and harass him, she'd find him and harass him. She'd made that perfectly clear.

"You'd be surprised. Most people don't see what's right in front of them. That's what makes Guardians different: we're drawn to them, and them to us. We *notice* them. Other people can't...they might see something out of the corner of their eye, but when they go to get a better look, it will be gone. They'll brush it off as a trick of the light or an insect or something. We can actually look at them and understand what we're seeing and interact with them."

"So, magical creatures are living all around us, but people just don't notice them? How is that even possible? I thought they were like...hidden away in forests or the ocean or something."

"Some of them are. But others aren't. But they have deflecting spells. It's part of their protection. Some creatures can't help living near humans. But for their own safety, they can't have humans actually see them. So, with the deflecting spell, you can't ever look directly at one unless you're a Guardian."

"Trippy."

"Very. Especially when you're the lone Guardian in a crowd and you see an Elf walking down the street and nobody else notices."

"That happened?" Jack gaped at Emily.

"Once. In his defense, we were in New York City, and that place is full of...*unique*...people. If anyone had actually gotten a good look at him, they probably would've assumed he was on his way to a comic book convention or something."

"I thought Elves were hiding in the mountains," Jack said, remembering his reading.

"Most are...but some kind of like to push their boundaries every once in a while. Besides, skyscrapers are like manmade mountains."

Jack's head was reeling at this. "So, what are you having me look for?"

Emily smiled coyly. "I'm not telling. That's for *you* to figure out. I want to see if you know them when you see them. If you've been doing the reading Amelia gave you, you should be able to recognize them by now. The only hint I'll give you is there are two different kinds of creatures, aside from fairies, that hang out around this town regularly in broad daylight."

"So...what, I'm just aimlessly wandering around looking for them?" This seemed like an odd task.

"Yup," Emily nodded. "But not aimlessly. Amelia said you've been doing a good job at feeling for magic. Use that."

"Use that? Meditate, right here in the middle of the street?"

"If that's what you need to do, yes. You need to feel for other magical energy. That's what those lessons she's been having you do can help with. Remember, we're homing beacons for magical creatures—they're drawn to us, and we're drawn to them. So reach out for their magic."

Jack took a deep breath, and standing right there in the middle of the sidewalk, closed his eyes. He shut out all the other sounds around him—the blowing of the wind, the rustling of leaves, the clicking of shoes from other passersby, the honking of car horns.

He was in that cavernous place again. This time though, it was like a ghostly version of the town—silent and still, with just him and Emily standing there. He looked around, feeling for magic—non-human magic, specifically. Not the glowing bits of energy he was able to manipulate before...something different.

He turned his head and saw a silvery strand glowing down the empty street. He felt it touch his heart, softly, gently. He looked down, following its trail—the strand weaved behind the old market once owned by the Davidson family—something coming from the waters on the docks.

He opened his eyes, and he and Emily were once again in the waking world.

"There's something behind the market."

Emily smiled. "Show me."

Briskly, he walked that direction—funny, how in the waking world, he could still feel the gentle tug of that silvery strand, guiding him towards the docks.

As he made his way behind the building, he looked down—the rocks in the harbor below were filled with seals sunning themselves in mid-day.

Then it struck Jack.

"Those aren't really seals, are they?" The creatures looked like seals, but something about them was off. He could feel that silvery energy coming from them. In that moment, Jack realized what it was: their eyes. Instead of having the big, dark blank expression of a normal seal, their eyes looked *human*, full of expression and life and intelligence. Some had blue eyes, some brown, some green, like actual people.

"Good catch. No, they aren't really seals. They're selkies."

"What's a selkie?"

"They're kind of like mermaids...but seals. They take on the form of a seal when they're out in the water, but they also have the ability to transform into humans."

"So, they're shape shifters," Jack concluded.

"Yes. But the only shapes they can take are human or seal. A little boring, if you ask me."

"Are there mermaids around here?"

"No. Amelia swears she saw one when we were kids, but even Grandpa said that was unlikely."

"Why's that?"

"Mermaids prefer warmer waters. If you want to see a mermaid, go to Florida or Hawaii." She paused, staring at the selkies. "They should be migrating by now. I wasn't originally going to have you look for them, but when I saw them still hanging out earlier, I figured I'd see if you could figure it out."

"Selkies migrate?"

"Yeah. Like other sea creatures, they migrate during mating season. But they usually start their migration at the end of August—it's September now."

"We're not that far into September," Jack pointed out. "They're not that off. Besides, it's been an unusually warm month so far."

"Yeah…that must be it," Emily said, accepting this conclusion. "Global warming."

Carrying on, they continued to stroll down the sidewalk. As they walked, the clouds overhead darkened, as if a storm was rolling in. Droplets of water fell from the sky to the ground below.

Jack furrowed his brow, examining the approaching storm, feeling the energy in the air shift. The change wasn't due to the barometric pressure. There was something different about this—something magical. He didn't need to reach into the Between to feel this one—it was powerful, magnetic, electrical in its approach.

"Was it forecast to rain today?"

Emily smiled coyly. "No."

As he watched the sky, he saw a shape emerge from the clouds—it was the largest bird he'd ever seen in his whole life, probably twice as tall as a grown man, with a wingspan twice as long as the creature was tall. Its feathers were vibrant shades of crimson, orange, and yellow. Most notable was with each flap of its wings, lightning crackled around it, encasing the bird in its own personal electrical storm. When it cawed, the lighting would burst forth, striking the earth below. The closer it flew in their direction, the harder it rained, to the point where it was pouring, and Jack could barely make out shapes clearly, as he couldn't wipe the water from his eyes fast enough.

Jack stood frozen in place, both petrified and awe-struck by the beast circling overhead. He looked around, and noticed no one else walking down the street seemed to even see the bird above them. Instead, they were simply calmly taking cover from the rain, either pulling out umbrellas, covering their heads with newspapers, or standing under awnings, waiting for the storm to pass.

And it did pass. As soon as the bird flew out of their sight, the skies cleared, the sun peeked out amongst the clouds, and a rainbow formed in the wake of the bird.

"What the *hell* was that?" Jack turned to Emily, who was unfazed by the bird's passing.

"Thunderbird. It lives in the mountains, but flies down here to the ocean sometimes to hunt for food. No, it doesn't eat humans," she said quickly, seeing the look of terror on Jack's face. "Mostly deer and seals and large fish."

"NOBODY ELSE SAW IT."

"Exactly."

"How the *hell* do you miss something like that?!"

"Part of the protections placed on it. People around here seem to think we just randomly get the occasional quick mid-afternoon thunderstorm."

"But that NOISE!" Jack insisted. "How can they miss the noise it makes?!"

"Jet plane going overhead."

"But why doesn't anyone just LOOK UP?!"

"If they do, they'll see nothing. They'll be looking in the direction of the clouds, or the lightning, or the rainbow…their sight is directed away from the bird itself."

"But…I…but…how…" Jack stammered, distraught by this point, his eyes widened into an almost maniacal expression.

"I think you've had enough for today." Emily was trying hard not to laugh at Jack's distressed, incoherent jabbering. "Let's go back to the cottage. I'll make you some tea."

Jack nodded, his eyes still wide, darting in the direction the bird flew.

As they walked down the street towards Emily's car, Jim McCarthy emerged from his law office.

"Hi, Emily!" he said cheerily as Emily and Jack walked by.

"Hi, Jim!" Emily greeted him in return.

"Boy, that was one doozy of a storm, wasn't it?" he commented, looking toward the skies and the clouds, now in the distance.

"Sure was!" Emily agreed, nearly at her breaking point for containing herself.

"I swear, we were forecast to have sunny skies all day. These weathermen don't really have a clue what they're doing."

"Nope, they sure don't," Emily agreed quickly, now in front of her car with Jack. "See you later, Jim!"

"Yup, see you, Emily!"

And with this, Emily pushed a babbling, wild-eyed Jack into her car, slamming the door shut behind him.

As much as she disliked Jack, she certainly enjoyed *this*.

✳ Chapter 26 ✳

The party

After recovering from the shock of the thunderbird with a few glasses of wine and a somewhat restless night's sleep at the Blue Barn, Jack once again had to flip the switch from Guardian to acquisitions director the next day. That weekend was the annual party celebrating Dunstan Enterprises' anniversary—it was also the only time each year Adrien Dunstan opened his private home to his employees and colleagues.

Adrien's home was based on a small island off the coast, allowing for maximum privacy, and required a ferry to get there—at least, a ferry for the guests and staff of the household. Adrien himself preferred to travel via helicopter to and from the private island.

Though Jack had been to this party every year since starting with Dunstan Enterprises, the island never failed to impress. As the ferry approached land, he could make out the outline of the boathouse, which housed Adrien's private yacht, as well as an assortment of other smaller vessels. Beyond the boat house and down the path to the left were the stables, which Adrien kept full of horses he rode for personal use, as well as a few he kept on hand for racing. If one went to the fork on the right and continued for about a quarter mile past the main house, one would find the helipad. All along the island there were also small stretches of sandy private beaches, broken up by bits of the rocky, jutted cliffs the coastline in the particular portion of the world was so well known for.

At the center of it all was the main house, spectacular even when not hosting glittering galas or sensational soirees. The four-story brick mansion was fortress-like, surrounded by impeccably-kept gardens and groves of miniature forests, and amongst its most notable details included a large inner courtyard complete with fountains, carved to resemble those of the Renaissance masters'; a giant garage that housed twelve antique automobiles; a grand ballroom adorned with crystal chandeliers and marble pillars and floors, with its towering windows overlooking the ocean; a wine cellar that stretched almost the entire length of the basement; an Olympic-sized pool outside, and a small lap pool inside; and a two-story mahogany-paneled library that boasted amongst its collection a first edition, signed copy of Mark Twain's "The Adventures of Tom Sawyer." The rest of the house included several bedrooms, bathrooms, living rooms, parlors, studies, and even a kitchen and a dining room on every single floor, all tastefully decorated and well-kept.

Currently, the entire place was lit up, and live music could be heard coming from the courtyard. As Jack entered into the throng of people, his senses were bombarded with all the usual sights and scents of luxury: perfumed women wearing their finest evening gowns and dripping with diamonds and pearls; men in tuxes with silk ties and spotless shoes; caterers milling about in their black and white uniforms with platters of top shelf drinks and expensive hors d'oeuvres; and lavish floral arrangements dotting any spare surface not already overflowing with trays of elegantly arranged food, towers of champagne, or a seven-tiered chocolate fountain that a majority of the women were currently gathered around.

Jack looked at all the extravagantly-dressed people and felt a bit out of place all of a sudden—the invitation had said "black tie optional," but given the number of tuxedos and gowns, it seemed as though more people opted for black tie than the "optional" this time around. Even though he was sharply dressed in his three-piece charcoal-gray suit and silk cobalt blue tie, he didn't feel like he belonged—not that he felt like he belonged anyway, given his current situation, but he certainly didn't enjoy feeling like he stood out with his attire.

Jack grabbed an appetizer from a passing caterer and stuffed it into his mouth as he made his way toward the bar, the gravity of his situation coming down on him like a hammer. He usually enjoyed this celebration, basking in the laughter, the conversation, the music, the food, and the alcohol, but things had changed drastically in the past few months, and he felt like an outsider sitting in the fringe, looking in. The people surrounding him were mostly fellow employees, many of whom he knew, and some he was only vaguely familiar with, but tonight he preferred to keep his own company, attending largely to keep face amongst his colleagues and make the obligatory social appearance. A few people he didn't know at all, and he assumed they were some of Adrien's friends, family, or other professional contacts. Not that it mattered: this time next year, he wouldn't be attending this party. If all went according to plan, there wouldn't even *be* a party for these people to attend. The brightly-lit house echoing with music and merriment would be dark, still, and silent.

He ordered a Jack and coke at the bar, smiling wryly as he looked around, marveling at the ignorance or sheer lack of concern of the people surrounding him. Not a single one of them gave any indication they, like him, knew something was amiss within the company, that it was built on a series of bribes and lies. By this time next year, they'd know. He felt a small twinge of guilt as he came to terms with the fact many of these people would be innocent bystanders and probably lose their jobs in the process; but he also knew it was a necessary evil, that several of them were not as innocent, playing their own roles in aiding Adrien's rise in status and fortune for their personal gain. In his mind, those were the ones who deserved to lose everything. For now though, they were blissfully unaware.

As he sipped on his drink, he saw Adrien weaving his way through the crowd with a glass of champagne in his hand, making his rounds as host. Jack's initial instinct was to avoid him at all costs, but he knew this effort would be futile: eventually, Adrien would catch up with him. He always made an effort to personally say hello to every single guest at his home. He decided to bite the bullet, pretend all was normal, and approach Adrien first. Taking a final swig of his drink, he stood and made his way towards his boss.

Adrien immediately noticed Jack, and a look crossed his face that Jack could only describe as disapproval masked by feigned politeness. Clearly,

Adrien was still displeased with Jack's backwards progress with the Calvary project, but for his party's sake, he would be putting on a show and pretend all was well tonight.

"Good to see you, Jack," Adrien said with a stiff smile.

"You too, sir."

There was an awkward pause. It was usually around this time Adrien would ask about the Davidson property and chastise Jack for his lack of progress, but both knew this was neither the time nor the place. To Jack, it was a welcome relief, but to Adrien, an annoying elephant in the room.

"Some weather we've been having, huh?" Adrien remarked about the unusually warm autumn. He hated small talk. But he also hated making a scene.

Jack nodded, swiping a full glass of champagne off the tray of a passing caterer and taking a large gulp of it. "Unusually warm."

"You still running?"

"I am."

"Any races coming up for you?"

"None at the moment."

"You enjoying the party?"

"It's very nice. Always is."

Adrien decided now was his time to exit the conversation with this particular aggravating employee. "Well, thanks for coming, Jack. Always a pleasure."

Jack sighed, relieved Adrien was about to move on from him, and would thus probably leave him alone for the remainder of the evening.

His relief, however, did not last long.

Before Adrien could even step away, out of the corner of his eye, Jack saw William Foster amongst the party-goers, making his way towards Jack and Adrien. Jack quickly turned around, hoping Foster wouldn't see him, trying to blend with the other partygoers. He glanced about, trying to figure out an exit route, but found himself encumbered by the bar, a table of food, and a small group of drunk dancers. He was cornered in until one of the dancers moved, and given the fact two of them had just begun a voracious make-out session, that wouldn't be happening anytime soon.

Adrien also saw Foster, and his face lit up with delight. "Will! Great to see you!" he exclaimed.

"Great party, Adrien!" Will said heartily, raising a glass of champagne to his host.

"This is nothing compared to last year's—we had a full troupe of acrobats swinging in the trees around the property," Adrien said, almost humbly, as if this year's party was meager.

"Acrobats, huh? That would've been something to see."

"It was."

"The girls you hired as mermaids for the pool though are really something. And that poolside bar is pretty fantastic. I can't wait to see what you come up with next year."

"Well, with any luck, you will be attending parties for many years to come."

As this exchange was happening, Jack was doing his best to remain unnoticed, his back turned to the pair, hoping to escape. The dancers still hadn't moved, despite trying to push through them.

His luck, it seemed, was not with him tonight, as Foster did in fact notice him.

"Good to see you again, Jack," Foster said heartily, taking a sip of his champagne.

Jack's heart stopped as Adrien glanced back and forth between the two men. Whatever he was thinking was a mystery, as his facial expression remained blank.

"I see you two have become acquainted since you've been spending time in Calvary, Jack," Adrien said casually, taking a sip of his own champagne.

"Indeed we have," Foster replied before Jack could say anything, looking between Adrien and Jack, as if trying to determine if he should bring up the conversation about money or not.

"Yes, we have," Jack croaked, taking a swig of his own alcohol.

"And Jack knows he has friends in Calvary if he needs them," Foster commented, patting Jack on the back. Adrien didn't even blink at this gesture.

Jack's stomach churned as Foster grinned what could only be described as the slimiest, most despicable smile he'd ever seen cross the face of a man in his entire life. Adrien remained expressionless.

"Well, I'm going to check out this chocolate fountain everyone seems to be so keen on," Foster said after a moment of awkward silence. "Thanks for the invite, Adrien, you've got a great place here, and this is a fantastic party."

"Of course, Will. Anytime," Adrien replied, allowing himself to smile.

As Foster walked off from the bar, Jack froze in place. He glanced about frantically, trying to find a way out of Adrien's sight and the inevitable conversation about to take place.

"So, Jack—how was it you met Will?"

Too late.

Quickly, Jack opened the recorder on his cell phone and pressed play before shoving it in his pocket, saying a quick prayer it would pick up the conversation they were about to have above the din of the party. He'd been able to manipulate Foster, and though Adrien was a tougher nut to crack, he figured a mixture of honesty with a little lie might work.

"Too busy texting to have a conversation with me, Jack?" Adrien asked, clearly annoyed.

"Sorry, sir. That was Amelia Davidson texting me," Jack lied, keeping his cool.

Adrien started, not expecting that response. "Amelia Davidson?"

"Yes. I told you, I've been trying to get her to see me as a friend, to trust me."

"And it's working?"

"It is."

Adrien smiled, a clear shift in his countenance. "Excellent." He paused. "But again, how did you meet Will Foster?"

"I approached him," Jack answered, taking a sip of his drink. "Seeing as he's the planning director for the town, I figured it might be useful to get to know him."

STONES ✳ RJG McManus

Adrien raised an eyebrow. "You approached him?"

"I did."

"And what, may I ask, did you talk about?"

"This and that. The development. The issues I'd been having with the Davidson sisters. I asked if he had any insight, if he could provide any assistance in any way. This was before Amelia warmed up to me, of course. I'll admit, I was a bit desperate when I went to him."

"What did he say?"

Jack knew he was going to take a risk with this reply, and more questions would come up. He'd have to be quick with his answers. "He'd be happy to help…if we doubled."

Jack visibly saw in Adrien a momentary betrayal of his emotions, seeing confusion and anger flash in his eyes. But in an instant, he was composed again.

"If we doubled?" Adrien repeated.

"Yes."

"Do you know what he's asking to double?" Adrien hissed.

"Yes."

"Garridan, I'm going to ask this once—how did you find out about Foster?"

"It's a small town. I told you, I've been trying to integrate with them, get their trust. Rumors have been flying around him. People in the town have been talking, wondering if he had anything to do with the project being approved, if something happened behind the scenes—there was so much public opposition to it. So, I decided to test it and approach him, see if there was some truth to what they were saying, if he was a friend to us and might be able to help me…or if it was just small-town talk. Like I said, I was desperate."

"That was a bold move, Garridan. But what would you have done if he *wasn't* friendly with us? He could've used that on *us*; didn't you think about it?"

"I had an exit strategy," Jack lied, remembering the brief moment of panic he had in Foster's office, wondering if he'd made the wrong move. It was only luck his hunch had turned out to be correct.

"I see." Adrien looked Jack up and down warily. "That was very astute of you. But when exactly were you going to tell me about it?"

"To be honest, Adrien, I wasn't going to tell you." Jack was truthful in at least that statement. "I wasn't going to burden you with that. When Foster wanted double, I saw who he was, and I took the liberty of deciding he was asking too much. He was unreasonable. I decided to figure out another way to get the Davidson property. A man like that isn't a man we want to associate with too regularly, unless as an absolute last resort. He could be damaging."

"You're right there." Adrien glared across the garden at Foster, who was mingling with a few of the other guests and guzzling alcohol. "But what would you have done if he had approached me about your little chat?"

"I would've been honest with you and told you exactly what I thought about him—he's a last resort kind of friend."

"Mmm," Adrien grunted, still glaring at Foster.

"If it means anything, he's being a bit flashy about everything, and that's stirring up some of the talk in town. Buying new suits, a new car…he's not helping us."

309

"Flashy, you say?" Adrien said distantly.

"Yes. And think about it—he's clearly not a *real* friend to us. The Davidson sisters were still able to start their bed and breakfast, even though he knew we were after their land—that's something he should've been able to help prevent. He's playing both sides, sir. Seems to me like he's only out for himself. I don't trust him."

Adrien turned to Jack, and very seriously said, "Keep your distance from that man, Jack. We don't need him involving himself any more than he already is."

"Yes, sir."

"But keep him on the backburner as well, just in case."

"What would you like me to say to him exactly?"

"Tell him we won't need his further assistance at the moment—but when we do, we'll be in touch."

"I will."

Adrien started to walk away, but before doing so, said, "Jack?"

"Yes, sir?"

"Let's keep this between us, shall we?"

"Of course."

Adrien paused. "And keep up the good work. I sincerely hope I don't have to fire you in November."

"I hope you don't either," Jack said, truthful in that regard. His hope was he'd already have enough evidence turned into the authorities about bribery and other misdeeds within the company, and he himself would already be long gone from Dunstan Enterprises by that time of his own volition.

Adrien grunted, then went over to a group of party guests, returning to playing host.

Jack smiled and clicked the button in his pocket to stop recording. He hoped he had picked all that up.

✳

Jack stumbled into the mansion later that evening, somewhat inebriated. He'd been drinking since the conversation with Adrien, and anxious to see if his phone had picked up the conversation, desperately wanted to find a private place to listen to the recording. The bathrooms wouldn't do.

In his drunken logic, he decided wandering away from the party and into the inner sanctum of Adrien's home would be the best place for the privacy he desired. Adrien would be busy with his guests, there would be no one there to overhear him. His impatience was overwhelming—he had to know if the phone recorded everything.

As he roamed the halls, loosening the tie around his neck, he made his way to the third floor, standing in the frame of the staircase. The halls and chambers of this floor were silent, the sounds of the party happening below muffled. He was alone.

Except he wasn't. As he pulled his phone out of his back pocket to open it and play it, a tiny light seemed to whizz out of one of the wall fixtures, smacking his hand. He started, stumbling back into the wall. As he focused his vision, he was once again face to face with a fairy—Lila.

"Hey!" he cried out.

The fairy waved her little finger at him, shaking her head.

311

"What, this?" he asked, raising his phone up.

She nodded. He shouldn't be listening to that here.

He suddenly felt very sober.

"Do you know what I'm trying to do?"

Again, she nodded.

"Are you going to help me?"

She smiled, waving for him to follow her.

Jack trailed after the fairy, looking over his shoulder the entire time. They were deep in the house now, in Adrien's private living quarters, an area he'd never been before.

"Where are you taking me?" Adrenaline was now taking the place of alcohol in his bloodstream, and he was becoming much more focused and aware of his surroundings—as well as aware of the stupidity of what he had almost done, listening to the recording where anyone could find him.

The fairy simply motioned, *Come.*

And so he followed. Moments later, Lila stopped in front of Adrien's private study, and pointed inside Jack pushed the slightly cracked door open all the way, stepping inside. It, like Adrien's office in the city, was minimally decorated with a few pieces of art hanging from the walls and a large desk upon which a laptop computer sat. The fairy directed Jack to open and turn on the computer. Hesitantly, he did, keeping an eye on the door as he did so, and praying under his breath no one had seen him go this way.

A screen popped up, prompting Jack to enter a password. He turned towards the fairy.

"What's the password?"

With this, the fairy flew about, spelling out in glittering gold dust in the air so Jack could read:

MILADA

Jack sat, puzzled by this for a moment. Milada? What did that mean?

He shook his head, knowing he didn't have the time at the moment to decipher Adrien's cryptic password, and went to work punching it in on the keyboard. He hit "enter," and Adrien's desktop appeared on the screen. Jack scanned it, looking for something, *anything*, that could lead him to the information he needed.

"Keep an eye out for me," he muttered to the fairy as he perused the files. The fairy, ever vigilant, flew to the study entrance, keeping watch for anyone who might approach. Not that Jack knew what he'd do if someone caught him—he couldn't hide, as he was on the third floor, and there were only two ways out—the door by which he'd entered, or jumping out the window. He'd have to talk his way out of it if someone came by.

And that was when he found it. It was an unlabeled file, not even named, with just the default "New folder" title. It was almost as if Adrien had left it nameless to escape detection. But inside that folder was a treasure trove of documents, information he hadn't before seen relating to many of the projects Dunstan Enterprises had spearheaded, organized alphabetically in folders by project name. Jack opened a few, his mind reeling as he read them.

The town of Calvary wasn't the only one that had officials paid off to approve projects—there were at least a half dozen others. He was relieved to see all of the urban builds looked like they were up to code, alleviating his fears about future disaster, but for the smaller ones—specifically, the ones along the coastline in areas similar to Calvary—they were riddled

313

with issues of poor workmanship, code violations, and sub-par building materials. He even found a few recall notices within some of the files, but noted nothing was ever done—the materials weren't replaced by Dunstan Enterprises, they were simply used as if nothing had happened. He also noticed on these particular projects, personnel turnover was high, reminiscent of what had happened to Max and his team—it was almost as if whenever someone spoke up about any issues they were seeing, Adrien replaced them with a new group of workers to keep the build going.

Jack was appalled and confused. On these particular projects, it was clear Adrien didn't even care about the workmanship—he was throwing up buildings haphazardly, like Max had said. It was a stark difference compared to the time and care he put into the city builds.

But why? What was the difference between the city builds and the urban builds, aside from the obvious factor of location?

It hit him—that was it. The location. This was proof of Max's theory. All the builds that had issues were along the coast, like Calvary. But what exactly was on the coast that caused him to change the project management and quality? Why didn't he care about those builds? Especially when, in Jack's experience, Adrien had been so persistent about acquiring the properties? What was it about those properties that made Adrien so determined to have them, but that he cared so little for the quality of buildings that went on them? What was he doing?

As Jack pondered these questions, he procured a flash drive from his pocket (having learned from his experience with Stephanie's computer) and plugged it into the laptop, knowing he had to copy these files over and study them—and after doing so, he had to turn them over to the authorities. This was the final nail in the coffin he needed to get Dunstan Enterprises out of Calvary for good, and hopefully, prevent future builds, thus protecting both the magical creatures and humans who called those spaces home.

As the large number of files copied over to the drive, Jack heard footsteps down the hall. Lila fluttered into the study, motioning frantically somebody was coming. Jack panicked, staring at the screen, the files still not completely copied.

"Come on, come on!" he muttered, urging the computer along. The fairy, meanwhile, hearing the approaching footsteps come ever closer, flew to the ceiling light to hide, her own glow blending in with the glow of the fixture.

And then, it was complete.

Just as Jack pulled the drive from the computer and powered it off, quickly slamming the laptop shut, Adrien emerged in the doorframe of the study, looking incredibly startled to find Jack standing in his private office.

"Jack? What are you doing here?"

"The bathrooms on the first two floors were all occupied. I came up here to find an empty one," Jack lied. Any drunkenness he had been feeling was now gone, and he was in survival mode.

Adrien raised an eyebrow, and wryly, said, "Does this look like a bathroom to you, Jack? Am I going to find something unpleasant under my desk?"

Jack laughed nervously at Adrien's dry joke. "No, sir, it doesn't—I'm sorry. I was on my way back downstairs when I passed by and saw the door cracked open, and couldn't resist getting a closer look at this painting on your wall. *The Scream* by Edvard Munch, correct?"

He motioned towards the first painting that caught his eye. It depicted a ghostly robed man standing on a dock in the foreground, with his hands on either side of his face, his mouth open as if screaming. In the background, the artist had swirled about the paint in an eerie, almost frantic fashion, with the sky ablaze in vibrant hues of reds and yellows and oranges, a stark contrast to the water in the painting, the only calm thing about the whole piece in its array of blues and greens.

"Good eye, Jack," Adrien said, only mildly impressed, given the notoriety of the painting. "Yes, it's one of my favorites. Munch painted it to symbolize the anxiety of modern man at the time, representing the feelings of helplessness and depression we're so prone to in our often meaningless lives. Here we are, well over a century after it's been painted, and I still find it to be quite apt. Don't you?"

Jack nodded his agreement. "Very. But why keep it in your study? Seems to me like it'd be a distraction when working, having it looking down at you."

"Motivation," Adrien said with a shrug. "Motivation to never become that sickly, sorrowful, hopeless thing, just a shadowy shell of a man."

Jack leaned in closer to get a better look at the painting. "It's a well-done replica, sir—or at least, I assume it is. I've never seen the original."

"No, many people haven't."

Jack recalled something he'd learned long ago in school from the recesses of his mind. "It was stolen once, wasn't it?"

"Yes, a couple versions were. Munch painted more than one copy of it."

"Smart. Did they ever recover the stolen copies?"

Adrien smiled wryly. "They think they did. But who really knows? You may not be looking at a replica after all."

Jack blinked, a bit taken aback, looking back and forth between the almost certainly stolen painting and his incredibly wealthy, now sinister-seeming boss.

"I'm kidding, Jack," Adrien said, seeing the concerned look on his employee's face.

"Of course." Jack forced a laugh.

"Why don't you get back down to the party, Jack? Enjoy the evening. After all," Adrien said, his tone now more serious, "it may be the last one you're able to attend. Savor it."

Jack's smile disappeared, taking the vague threat behind Adrien's words. What Adrien didn't realize, however, was Jack legitimately did hope it would be the last party, but for very different reasons.

"Yes, sir, you're right about that," Jack said shortly, playing the part Adrien expected him to play. "Thank you for talking to me about your painting. It was incredibly enlightening."

Adrien remained silent, simply giving Jack a stiff nod.

Jack turned and hastily retreated downstairs back to the party, a reason to celebrate contained in his pocket on the flash drive. He finally had all he needed.

Adrien, meanwhile, stayed for a moment longer in his office, staring at his painting, sipping on the glass of wine in his hand.

"I won't ever be you," he said softly to the frozen face on the canvas.

The face, in return, continued to scream in silence.

✳ Chapter 27 ✳

Jude's journal

Two weeks had passed since Amelia left, and as the days crawled closer to her return, Jack found himself growing increasingly anxious to see her again. On the day of her expected arrival, he had set his alarm to wake up extra early, hoping to be at the cottage by the time she got home. He knew there wouldn't be any lessons that day, but he didn't mind: he just wanted to see her again.

When he arrived at the cottage, he had the sudden realization he probably should have consulted with Emily. Though he was excited about Amelia's return, Emily was less than thrilled about seeing him on her front porch so early in the morning, while she was still dressed in pajamas.

"What are you doing here?" she yawned, mug of coffee in her hand.

"I…" Jack trailed off, not sure how to answer, suddenly feeling incredibly foolish.

"…you're here to welcome Amelia home," Emily finished for him, turning her back to top off her cup.

He stepped inside tentatively. "Yeah."

"She should be here soon. Her flight landed about an hour and a half ago. Get some coffee while you wait for her."

"Thank you."

After helping himself to a mug, he wandered back into the living room, where Emily was sitting in one of the armchairs, sipping on her cup, Cosmo at her feet. Jack sat in the armchair across from her, sipping on his own.

"So…can I help with anything for the bed and breakfast this morning?" Jack asked, not enjoying the awkward silence between the two of them.

Emily shook her head. "Breakfast is already done and waiting for the guests."

"Gotcha." He paused. "Anything you need help with for the charter fishing?"

"No," she said curtly, not making eye contact with him.

"Okay." He paused. "How about—"

"Jack, it's early," she cut him off. "We both know we don't know how to talk to each other well unless we're doing something involving magic. So let's just *not* talk, okay?"

Jack nodded, relieved at this suggestion. "Okay."

The minutes ticked by slowly, painfully, as they sat in that living room, each sipping on their coffee, waiting for Amelia's arrival.

Finally, after what felt like an eternity, Cosmo sat up and gave a low *woof,* trotting over to the front door, his tail wagging excitedly. Jack and Emily turned their heads toward the door, hearing the sound of a car door slamming shut outside. Amelia had finally arrived.

They stood when she entered, lugging a suitcase behind her, struggling as she tried to juggle that with her carry-on and her purse. Jack immediately rushed to her side to help.

"Thanks," she said breathlessly. "Wait, what are you doing here?"

319

"I'm..." he trailed off, once again not knowing how to answer.

"He's being weird, like usual," Emily replied, walking over to hug her sister. "Welcome home. There's coffee ready for you, and some bacon and eggs on a plate in the kitchen."

Amelia smiled, hugging her sister in return. "Thanks. I'll eat after I unpack."

"Here, let me help you." Jack grabbed her suitcase as she headed towards her bedroom.

"Thanks."

They walked upstairs, and entering Amelia's bedroom, Jack realized he'd never stepped foot in there before. He looked around, taking it in. The walls were painted white, and the curtains on the window looking out towards the ocean were a subtle shade of seafoam. The walls were decorated with an eclectic collection of colorful art, acquired from her travels, and built-in shelves showed off pottery and statuettes, as well as family photos and a substantial collection of books. The wooden floors were covered in plush, intricately pattered rugs, and the desk in the corner was neat and tidy, an organized retreat for the writer. The room as a whole could only be described as colorful and vivid and a bit eccentric, but at the same time, soothing and calming—much like the person who inhabited it.

"How was Ireland?" Jack asked as Amelia rifled through her suitcase.

"It was good," she replied, pulling her dirty laundry from her bag and sorting it into piles. "I punched a guy."

Jack started. "What?"

"I was at a pub. He was drunk and groped me. So, I used one of the moves you taught me and punched him. And he left me alone after that. It was awesome. So, thanks."

"Happy to help," Jack replied, amazed by the small woman in front of him.

"How were things here?"

"I saw a thunderbird."

Amelia smiled, stopping her sorting briefly to look up at him. "How'd that go?"

"Terrifying."

"That's normal. What else did you see?"

"Selkies."

Amelia raised an eyebrow. "Really? They're usually out of the area by now."

"Yeah, that's what Emily said. They don't usually migrate this late or something?"

"Right." She paused. "There was some strangeness while I was in Ireland too."

"Like what?"

"Well, the leprechauns were hiding their gold, like they were trying to protect it or something. Lots of rainbows."

"The leprechauns…wait, what?" Jack wasn't sure where to even begin with trying to piece together the information from that statement.

"Leprechauns. They're a thing."

"Right, got that part."

"They hide their pots of gold when they feel they need to protect it from something," Amelia explained. "The problem is, leprechauns are forgetful, so to help them find their gold where they left it, their pots are magical and shoot rainbows out of them as a way of helping them find their way back. I swear, I think I saw at least seven rainbows a day while I was there."

"You sure those weren't just normal rainbows?"

Amelia shook her head. "It was sunny and clear the whole time I was there. Not even misty. No chance for rainbows. It was weird. The last time leprechauns were this active was during the Potato Famine."

"Wait, what do leprechauns have to do with the Potato Famine?"

"Little known fact about the Irish: they believe their mythology and magical legends, even if they're not Guardians and can't actually see the creatures," Amelia said nonchalantly as she went about her unpacking. "During the Potato Famine, the rich were still able to eat because they could afford it. The poor, however, were destitute and starving, and resorted to hunting for leprechaun gold, thinking it could make them rich and they too could afford food—which is absurd, of course, because everyone knows leprechaun gold has no value in the real world. It disintegrates when a human touches it. But the leprechauns took to trying to hide their gold anyway, which, like I said, is a bit ridiculous, because whenever a leprechaun hides its gold, the pot shoots rainbows out of it to mark where it is." She paused. "Leprechauns aren't exactly the brightest creatures."

Jack's mind was reeling by this point, unsure of how to react. Amelia, seeing the confused expression on his face, chuckled. "You okay there?"

"Yeah. So, Potato Famine included a leprechaun gold hunt…"

"We call it the Irish Inquisition."

322

"The Irish Inquisition?"

"Yeah. People turned on each other pretty quickly. If anyone was suspicious of you possessing leprechaun gold, things got ugly. Loads of people were tried, tortured, and even killed over it."

"How is this not in history books?" Jack asked, his eyes wide.

Amelia raised an eyebrow. "Do you really think a whole country wants to admit they had a raid on leprechaun gold and killed each other over it? Think about how ridiculous that sounds."

"Fair enough. But anyway, so you're saying this is happening again?"

"Minus the famine and the people killing each other part, yes. The leprechauns are hiding their gold again all over the country, and I don't know why." She paused. "I met someone over there. Another Guardian."

Jack looked up. "Really? How'd you figure out they were a Guardian?"

"The pixie he was swatting at was a bit of a tip-off. They're like gnats over there."

"So…what happened?"

"We met up a few times. He said the leprechauns were just a small part of it. It's like all the creatures he's encountered were changing, or migrating, and their patterns and habits were off."

Jack, however, wasn't paying attention at this point, stuck on the part where she'd met up with some strange man a few times. His stomach sank as he imagined Amelia spending her time with a young, attractive Irishman with a lyrical accent and convivial personality.

"So anyway, he said his father noticed things start to go awry over seventy years ago, and it seemed like the activity had been increasing recently in the past couple decades—"

"Wait, seventy years?" Jack interrupted. "How old was this guy?"

"In his late fifties, maybe sixties. Why?"

Jack sighed with relief internally, the image of a younger man wooing Amelia disintegrating from his mind. "Just curious. So, you said it's been increasing in the past couple decades?"

"Yeah. Weirdly, along the same timeline as what my grandpa described, his family noticed things acting strangely, and in the past couple decades, even more of an increase." She paused, then quietly, said, "I know this sounds crazy, but I think someone found a stone and took it from its hiding place around that time."

"Okay." Jack tried to comprehend this. "But how does that explain what's been happening in the past couple of decades?"

"I think…and I don't know, but I think maybe the stone was recently relocated. And things got all wonky because of it."

"Is there a possibility a first stone was found over seventy years ago, and a second one was found a few decades after that?"

Amelia shook her head. "I mean—it's possible, but it seems unlikely they'd be found in such a short timeframe. And I imagine we'd see more happening if there were two found and they were put together, like the dark creatures waking up. We haven't seen that yet."

"I'm not saying put together. I'm just saying found. Separately."

"It's possible," Amelia said, ruminating on this.

"So, what happens if there are two stones floating out there, removed from their hiding places?"

Amelia shook her head. "I don't know. But if they find their way to each other, things are going to get interesting."

✳

Later that day, after Jack had left and she was able to finish her unpacking and settling in, Amelia was typing away at her computer and working on the article for this past trip, though she was having some trouble focusing. It was strange, the way Jack had been there waiting for her when she arrived home. She hadn't been expecting it, and wasn't sure how to react to it.

And there was the way he was listening to her—*genuinely* listening to her, like how he'd talked to Ruth Kowalski to try and get her to *not* sign the contract after Amelia had voiced her distaste for the whole matter. She hadn't heard about a follow-up to that, but the fact he had tried, for her…well, it was something.

She wouldn't admit this to anyone, but she had been happy to see him when she walked through the cottage door after a long trip. And she had missed him while she was gone. And she was smugly satisfied when she saw the brief look of jealousy on his face when he heard she had met with another Guardian—and the look of relief that followed when he found out it was someone much older than her.

She shook her head. Why did she even care?

Because I'm invested in him. Yes, that was it. She'd spent a great deal of time with him, teaching him, that she'd simply grown fond of him. He was the brother she never had.

But you don't imagine romantic encounters with your brother, the voice in her head pointed out.

That, she had to admit, she didn't have an answer for.

She was staring at her computer screen, absentmindedly playing with the pendant on the necklace as she pondered these things when she saw a new e-mail pop up in her inbox with the subject line "Dad's journal." Her heart leapt, and she let go of the necklace. All thoughts of Jack left her mind in an instant, her attention refocusing on Elliott Benedict's e-mail.

She opened it, reading a simple, one-line message:

Hope this helps.

--Elliott

She clicked on the attachment to download the file, anxious to find out what treasures Jude's journal may have contained as it loaded. After a moment, the copied pages of his journal appeared on her screen. She scanned them, searching for clues to see if Jude had been a bit more open in his chronicling of his travels with Stuart. Upon first glance, she was disappointed to see he seemed to be just as discrete. However, flipping through to the end, she found the last few entries didn't end when he went to war like Stuart's did—no, he had brought his journal *to* war and documented his experiences. She smiled, excited—it was like coming to the end of a good book, only to have the author say, "WAIT! I have more."

She poured over the pages, saddened by some of the entries. Some of them were similar to her own grandfather's journal, documenting their excursions together, though vague in their details. Another detailed the account of Delia miscarrying a child and the strain on their marriage following this event—something Amelia had never known about that family.

That must've been the painful memory she was talking about.

Amelia remembered her phone call with the elderly woman a few weeks prior, her heart breaking for Delia, a wave of guilt washing over her once again at how she'd treated the couple a few months back. They were only human, after all, like Emily had pointed out—and Amelia had treated them terribly. She made a note to herself to call Delia and thank her—the woman had shown her more grace than Amelia deserved.

She continued to peruse the pages, now with Jude and Stuart in Vietnam, reading about the horrors of war, the men the two friends saw killed, the injuries sustained, the exhaustion, the fear, the longing for home, until…

July 9, 1970

It was a strange day. I don't know if I'll get out of this war alive—I came too close to the end today—so I need to put this here in hopes that if anything happens to me, maybe this journal will make it back to Delia. Stu told me to be careful about what I put into writing, to write in code or in vague terms, but at this point, I don't care—I need to be clear, so if anyone finds this, there's no question if I die.

I think I found a source stone. The thing is, it didn't follow the poem Stu's dad had been given all those years ago—there was no ice, no mountain or flames, no giants, no coast, no fruit—we've been searching all those places that match those descriptions for years now.

I was in the jungle with my unit, patrolling the area. As I was walking, a little separated from my group, this man comes out of nowhere. He wasn't Vietnamese—he was white, kind of skinny, wearing ragged clothes, like he'd been on his own out there for a while. He was just wandering…like he wasn't in the middle of a war zone, like he didn't even know what was going on around him. He was looking at something in his hand, muttering to himself, laughing. *It was the weirdest laugh I'd ever heard, eerie, creepy.*

He stopped when he saw me, and gave me the strangest smile, like he was looking into my soul, like he knew what I was. I asked him who he was, how he got here, if he needed help. He didn't answer the first two questions, and sort of stared at me blankly, but when I asked if he needed help, he said, "No one can help me. I need to help myself." Then he said to me, "Do you know what I have here?" and holds up this stone. It looked

327

like a piece of cobalt sea glass, but you could tell it was more than that—I could feel its energy even from where I stood. He said to me, "This is the start. I just need to find the rest."

I couldn't help it, I asked him, "Are you the Creator Sorcerer?" He gave that weird laugh again and said no—like he knew exactly what that was, like the question didn't even bother him. I was going to ask him next if he was a Guardian, or worse, the Fallen Sorcerer, but before I could, we were under fire. When the smoke cleared and the guns stopped, he was gone. I searched though the dead and wounded, but he wasn't among them. It was like he'd vanished into thin air.

I told Stu what I saw when we made it back to camp. He asked me if I was sure, but honestly, in the midst of all the death we've seen, all the chaos, all the men we've seen lose their wits, I have my doubts. I don't know. It could've just been a crazy man who went MIA and resurfaced briefly—we've had a few of those. It could've been in my imagination, for Christ's sake—sometimes I feel like I barely have a grip on reality, like I'm slowly losing my mind to this war.

Or it could've been real. But if it is, Stu and I can't do a damn thing about it right now—we can't go looking for that man, they'd think we're deserting if we do. We could come back after the war, but would it even be worth it at that point? He'll be long gone by then. He already disappeared from us once without a trace. So we're stuck. And we just have to pray he comes around again. Or if he doesn't…that the stone is safe with him, that it's supposed to be with him. Because if it's not…well, we're going to be in trouble down the line.

Personally, I'm praying the war is getting to me, that I'm just losing my mind, that he was in my head, that he wasn't real, that I was hallucinating—I never thought I'd pray for insanity before, but something about the thought of a source stone being in the hands of that weird little man scares the shit out of me.

Amelia stared at the entry, breathless, her mind reeling. Somewhere in the jungle of Vietnam, there was an insane man wandering around with a source stone. She may have been right after all in her guess during her earlier conversation with Jack—the things they were seeing were a result of a stone being moved from its hiding place.

Maybe. Or maybe Jude was hallucinating. Or, maybe yet, he *wasn't* hallucinating, there was a weird man, but he didn't have a source stone…just a regular rock, and he was just insane.

But still—she'd known Jude for years. She knew he wouldn't write something like that unless he felt convicted to do so. She read the entry again—no, there was something there. She knew war did strange things to men, but this was not one of those things.

And there was mention of the poem—and that it went at least as far back as her great-grandfather? Her head was spinning. This entry left her with more questions than when she'd started. She knew her great-grandfather had been killed during World War II, when Stuart was a little boy, so he must've gotten the poem before he died—but how? Why? When? And who was that man in the jungle?

So many questions. No answers. This both annoyed and intrigued Amelia. Her family history, as interesting as it already was with magic woven into it, was becoming more complicated.

She gritted her teeth. She was going to have to talk to her grandmother, which she knew wouldn't garner much, given her current mental state…which meant she was going to have to talk to her mother, something she was hoping to avoid. They'd managed to keep things fairly shallow since Amelia had moved to town, aside from the day she'd gone to pick up Cosmo a few months back. She liked it that way, even if she knew it wasn't the healthiest way to deal with their relationship. But it seemed she didn't have any other options. She was going to have to bite the bullet and have an adult conversation.

She'd try talking to her grandmother first.

✳ Chapter 28 ✳

Ripples

That next day, after the bed and breakfast's guests were out doing their own thing and the sisters were done with their morning chores, Amelia talked Emily into going to see her grandmother to discuss the contents of the two journals. Emily argued with this idea initially, not wanting to press her grandmother, but after Amelia's insistence and assurance she would be gentle and stop if Lizzie became agitated, she agreed.

The two once again found themselves at the nursing home, checking in at the station at the entrance.

"You just missed your mother," the nurse commented as the girls signed in. "She just left about an hour ago."

Amelia felt a small twinge of guilt—she hadn't even called Rosalie yet to let her know she was back in the country. She knew she'd need to get around to that, but frankly, she'd been keeping her distance from her mother. She could see the disapproving look on her face every time she'd stopped by to visit and saw Jack in the house, and she suspected Emily had told them what they were doing. She knew she couldn't keep this up forever though, especially if she needed information regarding the journal.

She sincerely hoped Lizzie was lucid that day and would be able to help. She *really* didn't want to talk to her mother.

The sisters walked into their grandmother's room. Lizzie was once again in the armchair in the corner, reading a book, though she had stopped, gazing out the window, as though she had caught sight of something enthralling.

"Grandma?" Amelia said softly, clutching at her purse, which contained the copy of her grandfather's journal.

Lizzie turned, and for a moment, Amelia and Emily weren't sure they were speaking with the grandmother they knew—her eyes were glazed over, and for a brief moment, she looked disoriented and confused as she tried to recognize the young women who stood before her.

Then, her eyes cleared and brightened. "Amelia! Emily! What are you doing here?"

The sisters relaxed, relieved. They had their grandmother, at least for the moment.

"We just wanted to say hi to you." Emily stepped forward and took her grandmother's hand. "How are you?"

"Oh, I'm fine…same old, same old," Lizzie said. "How are you girls doing?"

"We're good," Amelia replied. "I just got back from Ireland."

"Oh, I always *loved* Ireland," Lizzie commented, a grin crossing her face.

"You've been?"

"I…well, isn't that funny? I don't remember." Lizzie furrowed her brow. "Still, I love it."

The sisters exchanged a look, and Emily nodded toward Amelia, an indication she needed to jump in with her questioning immediately if she was going to get any kind of coherent answers from Lizzie. Her mind was clearly going in and out that day, much more rapidly than it had before.

STONES ✳ RJG McManus

"Grandma, we found this journal in Grandpa's things as we were cleaning out the house…can you tell us about it?" Amelia pulled the worn book from her bag.

Lizzie reached for the journal, which Amelia handed over. As Lizzie delicately flipped through the journal, her eyes grew wide and bright, as if she was seeing an old friend for the first time in decades.

"Where did you find this?" Lizzie asked, looking up from the yellowed pages.

"In a box in the study," Amelia answered.

Lizzie blinked, a confused look on her face. "Why are you going through my things?"

Amelia and Emily glanced at each other. Their grandmother had clearly forgotten she no longer owned the home, that they were the owners now, and living on the premises. They might not find anything out today.

"We're just trying to make sure the house is clean for you, Grandma," Emily lied, stepping into the conversation. "Amelia stumbled across it in the process."

"Hmmph," Lizzie huffed, mildly satisfied with this answer, glancing back at the journal in her lap, caressing its cover gently, as though it was some kind of sacred artifact.

"Grandma, can you tell us about it?" Amelia prodded.

"Your grandpa used to travel a lot."

"Why?"

"Because things weren't right."

332

"What wasn't right, Grandma?"

"Magic. Magic wasn't right. He noticed it before your father was born. So did his grandfather. I didn't see it, but he did. He saw things changing."

Amelia nodded, understanding what her grandmother meant. Having not been born from a Guardian line, her grandmother had never actually been able to see the magical creatures in her entire life. But despite that, she believed her husband and had faith herself, understanding magic's impact on even those who were non-magical. Her faith and understanding had always been astonishing to her granddaughters.

"What was he seeing? What was changing?"

"Creatures were moving, disappearing, patterns weren't normal—like they were hiding from something. Some were becoming more powerful, doing magic they hadn't been able to do before—at least, not that we'd ever seen."

"So why was he traveling? What did that have to do with magic?"

"He wanted to find out what was happening—he and Jude, sometimes they'd go together, sometimes they would go separately."

"Grandma, what did he find?"

Lizzie simply stared at Amelia blankly, not answering. In that moment, Amelia and Emily knew they had lost her. Her attention had been drifting even more frequently as of late, and the fact they'd even gotten this far in the conversation was a miracle in and of itself.

"Grandma?" Amelia asked gently, hoping her grandmother was still cognizant on some level.

"Who are you?" Lizzie looked back and forth between her granddaughters, her eyes wide in disorientation.

"It's us, Grandma—Emily and Amelia," Emily replied, gently holding her hand.

Lizzie pulled her hand from Emily's grasp, a look of fear and disgust crossing her face. "Don't touch me! I don't know you! Why are you here? Where am I?"

"Grandma, please, we're your granddaughters," Amelia pleaded.

"I don't have granddaughters! Don't lie to me!"

The sisters' hearts simultaneously broke as their grandmother cried hysterically, throwing the journal as hard as she could at them. As Emily called out into the hallway for help from the nearest nurse, Amelia picked up the journal from where it had landed and slipped it back into her bag, grateful the precious book seemed to still be intact after being chucked across the room.

The nurse came in, and seeing Lizzie's state, administered a sedative to calm the elderly woman. As Lizzie slipped into a calm stupor, she turned to the sisters. "What happened?"

Amelia shook her head, fighting back her own tears. "We were just talking and asked her about our grandfather, and she forgot mid-conversation who we were and got upset."

"She thinks we're strangers," Emily said sadly.

The nurse nodded, a sympathetic look on her face. "This is going to become more and more frequent—it won't get any easier. You need to be prepared for that."

The sisters nodded stiffly, glancing at their grandmother, who was now staring blankly out the window.

The three left the room, the nurse returning to her station. When she was out of earshot, Emily turned to Amelia. "That was horrible."

Amelia nodded her agreement. "I hate this."

"So, what now?"

Amelia sighed heavily, knowing what she had to do next. "We're going to need to talk to Mom."

Amelia dreaded that conversation with their mother, but knew it was necessary at this point if they wanted any kind of coherent answers. Their grandmother was no longer reliable. If she still had her mind intact, they knew she'd be able to answer all these questions—but then again, if her mind was still intact, they wouldn't even be living in the cottage in Calvary. Their grandfather wouldn't have had a reason to leave his home to them. The bed and breakfast wouldn't be in existence. They'd still be off living their own separate lives, doing their own thing. They wouldn't even have these questions, as they wouldn't have even come across the journal.

It's funny how a small ripple can make huge waves.

✳ Chapter 29 ✳

Creature of delight

As Amelia settled back in to being home, she and Jack settled back into their routine together, with Amelia teaching, and Jack absorbing as much information as he could. Both, however, had their respective issues nagging at them in the back of their minds: Amelia with the issue of her grandfather's journal, and how to approach her mother; Jack with the issue of having proof of wrongdoing within Dunstan Enterprises. He'd been reviewing the files he'd swiped off of Adrien's computer that night of the party, and some of the documents shocked him, even sickened him. Despite this though, he was wracked with guilt, knowing if he handed the items over, hundreds of employees would suddenly find themselves jobless. It was a lose-lose situation either way: either homeowners and property owners would be taken advantage of, or innocent employees would be caught in the fray. He opted for the moment to throw himself into the learning of magic with Amelia, a distraction he hoped would give him clarity as he worked through his thoughts.

Amelia, meanwhile, was grateful Jack's interest in their lessons together had seemed to increase—she too was looking for a distraction, something to keep her mind off her grandfather's activities. However, she knew eventually, it would need to be addressed—specifically, by her mother, if that little note in the back of the journal with her father's handwriting had anything to do with it.

On this particular day, in the midst of the two of them avoiding these topics, they were once again making potions in Amelia's kitchen, while Emily was out with Rosalie. Jack had taken command of whipping up a sleeping draught, feeling for the magic as he did so, knowing which energies he'd be directing if he'd been able to use the magic. He'd been entering in and out of the Between frequently lately, and had familiarized himself with as much as he was able.

"You're getting better," Amelia remarked, looking into the pot Jack was stirring. "If you had magic, this would be a pretty perfect potion."

Jack smiled. "I've been practicing."

"It's obvious."

"Thanks."

"So, I know we've been moving pretty slowly on a lot of things," Amelia said as Jack stirred. "And I think we can move onto the next step."

"What's that?"

"I want to see you summon a creature. I know we've been caught up in just having you learn how to feel for magic, reading, and the occasional potion, but I had Emily take you out while I was gone for a reason—we've reached that point where we can get you to start summoning. What do you think? Are you ready?"

Jack shrugged, still stirring the contents of the pot. "I think so. I've been reading the different summoning spells in one of the journals you gave me. It's simple memorization, really. My only issue is there are a *lot* of creatures, and they each have a different way of being called."

"I get that," Amelia sympathized. "My general rule of thumb is to memorize the ones that don't require much by way of props first—ones that require a simple spoken word or gesture or something. That way in a pinch, you've at least got those down. The ones that require more time and effort and all sorts of objects, you're probably going to have a book in front of you anyway to help guide you. Eventually you'll get some of those down, but they don't need to be the priority, and they probably won't be the first ones you're trying to call on."

"What's the most difficult summoning spell you've ever encountered?" Jack asked curiously.

"Oh, a phoenix, for sure," Amelia answered without hesitation. "It's this whole thing. They can only be summoned during the summer or winter solstice, it involves a bonfire built to specific proportions, you have to use this certain incense made with some pretty rare ingredients that's almost *impossible* to find or make yourself, and you have to chant this super long twenty-line invocation in *just* the right way—a certain pentameter and rhythm and emphasis on all the right words—seven times over. And even then, there's no guarantee a phoenix will *actually show up*—that's all just to get their attention. If they're not in the mood, they won't come, even with all that. They're pretty finicky, high-maintenance birds."

"And you've tried it?"

"Once, when I was a teenager."

"How'd it go?"

At this question, Amelia turned a bright shade of red. "Well, I almost burned the barn down, so…not well."

Jack laughed. "How'd you manage that?"

"It was a windy day," Amelia explained hastily. "A few embers blew out of the bonfire and hit the side of the barn. It would've gotten out of hand if Grandpa hadn't been there." She paused. "I wasn't allowed to try to summon creatures that involved fire for a while after that."

"And the phoenix?"

She shook her head. "I didn't even get through the first repetition."

338

Jack laughed, imagining the scene. "It's hard to picture you *not* good at any of this."

She blushed. "There's plenty I still don't know how to do."

"I don't believe that."

"It's true. I feel like I'm so ill-equipped sometimes, like I'm faking my way through everything."

"Well, you don't show it."

"You're too kind. But I really am."

"Why do you say that?"

"Well…to be honest, I only learned about this stuff during the summers, when we stayed here with my grandparents. The rest of the year, we weren't taught much. My parents didn't like it."

"Wasn't your dad a Guardian though?" Jack asked, confused.

"He was."

"So why didn't he like it?"

"Because my mom didn't like it," she said shortly. "And he loved her more than anything. So, there's that. So basically, I had to cram during the summers, and sneak it in here and there the rest of the year."

"Why didn't she like it?"

"I'm not sure, to be honest." Amelia shifted her weight uncomfortably. "But anyway, that's beside the point. You're doing well, so keep it up."

Jack could tell Amelia desperately wanted to change the subject, so he obliged.

"I'm much better at making pasta now too," he commented cheerfully.

She perked up, a smile crossing her face. "Oh, yeah?"

He nodded, looking pleased with himself. "Yup. I can make it perfectly al dente now. I can even heat up the sauce from the jar without burning it."

She laughed. "Well then, you're in charge of lunch today. And after lunch, we'll head out."

✳

After they ate, Jack and Amelia headed out to the forest on the edge of the Davidson property. As they walked deeper and deeper into the woods, the whole setting felt like something out of a fairy tale—light from the sun was glinting through the branches, casting flickering shadows of the trees. The scent of pine and beech and earth permeated his senses, and the utter silence—with the exception of the occasional bird chirping or scuttering of a rabbit or squirrel—filled the space with a mysterious, natural energy. These grounds were ripe for magic—there were creatures here unseen, living in these woods. Their energies surrounded him, their magic drawn to him.

"Different creatures are summoned in different ways," Amelia explained as they walked through the trees. "But you already learned that with the brownie."

"Donn. His name is Donn."

"Donn, right. Anyway, there once was a time when you could just call on the creature by name—and there are a few that you still can, if you're friendly enough with them, like Lila. But most magical creatures can't be called on without their respective summoning spells."

"And only Guardians can summon them, right?"

340

"That's right."

"Okay," Jack said hesitantly. "So…what are we calling on here?"

"An imp," Amelia said with a smile.

Jack raised an eyebrow. "An imp?"

"Yes."

"What's an imp again, exactly?"

"Well…they're kind of the red-headed step-children of fairies or pixies. They're little kleptomaniacs. They love pranks. They also hate clothes and are sometimes a bit rotten." She paused, looking at his wrist, to which his watch was strapped. "I'd put that in my pocket, if I were you. Once they catch sight of something pretty and shiny, it's game over."

Jack quickly took off the watch and tucked it into his coat pocket, and Amelia made sure the chain around her neck that held the amber pendant from her father was tucked into her shirt, with her scarf covering that and her jacket buttoned up over it for good measure.

"All good?" Amelia asked, after they'd checked themselves over for jewelry and other valuables.

Jack nodded.

"Good. So, I'm going to have you cast the summoning spell. It's pretty straightforward—imps are pretty easy and like to come even if they're *not* called, which is why I figured they'd be a good one for you to start with."

Jack nodded again, determined.

341

"The thing about imps is, even though they're rotten sometimes, they crave human friendship and attention. And they don't care what kind of attention they get—good or bad. They're kind of like toddlers in that way. So, the way to summon an imp is to tell a joke—imps love jokes and pranks. When a Guardian tells a joke, specifically meant for an imp to hear, the imp will appear."

"Got it. So…what joke should I be telling to summon an imp?"

"Any. Just start it by saying: 'Here me, imp, creature of delight'—then go straight into the joke."

"Creature of delight? Really?" Jack asked, eyebrow raised.

"They like having their egos stroked. Go ahead. Try it."

Jack stood silent for a moment. He was having trouble conjuring up a good joke in his mind.

Amelia, noticed Jack's hesitation. "It can be any joke. Even a bad one."

Jack cleared his throat. Facing the dark, emptiness of the forest, he called out, "Here me, imp, creature of delight: What do you call an alligator in a vest?"

He stopped, observing his surroundings—total silence. No sign of an imp.

"You have to say the punch line," Amelia urged.

Jack nodded, and finished into the silence, "An in-vest-igator."

"That was terrible."

"*You* try thinking of a good joke under pressure."

Suddenly, out of the darkness of the forest, they heard a distinct, shrill, high-pitched giggle. Slowly, the laugh grew louder and louder, its echo bouncing off the trees around them, making it difficult to pinpoint where it was coming from.

"There!" Amelia whispered excitedly, pointing to a tree. Sitting on the lowest branch was a strange, bony, purple little creature, with leathery wings, dark eyes, and oversized pointy ears.

Realizing it had been spotted, the imp jumped off the branch, and opening its wings, made its way to where Amelia and Jack were standing. Its flight pattern was erratic and haphazard, as if it had been knocked silly and couldn't fly in a straight line. It reminded Jack vaguely of a young bird leaving the nest for the first time—though much uglier, and possibly intoxicated.

Perching on another tree branch, this one closer to the pair, the weird little creature faced Jack, and in a demanding tone, screeched, "ANOTHER!"

Jack blinked, and briefly met Amelia's gaze. She nodded encouragingly, and he turned back to the creature. "Okay, another." He bit his lip, thinking for a moment. Settling on another joke that came to mind, he said, "Knock knock."

"Who's there?" the imp asked, bouncing up and down with anticipation.

"Interrupting cow."

"Interrupti—"

"MOO!"

The little creature squealed and clapped with delight, laughing so hard he nearly fell off the branch upon which he was sitting.

Jack smiled. *This is kind of fun.*

Suddenly, Jack felt a vibration in his back pocket and heard his cell phone ring. Both Amelia and the imp turned to him—Amelia with a concerned look on her face, the imp with a curious expression.

"What's THAT?"

The imp whizzed around to Jack's backside. Before Jack could say or do anything, the imp had pulled the phone from his pocket, mesmerized as it stared at the glow of the phone's screen. Its eyes went big, in awe of the curious device and new plaything.

"Hey, give that back!" Jack said, attempting to grab it from the imp.

The imp, in reply, shouted, "NO! MINE!" and clutched the phone close to its body, flying to perch on a branch just out of Jack's reach, giggling hysterically. With the phone still ringing, the imp began shaking it, then, swinging it against the tree trunk.

"Stop that! You're going to break it!"

Jack's pleas only seemed to fuel the imp, who whacked the device against the tree even harder.

"Help me!" Jack said to Amelia, who was doubled over with laughter at this point.

Before she could even calm down enough to do anything, they suddenly heard a voice come out of the phone, saying, "Hello?"

The imp, startled, jumped back from the phone, which still rested on the tree branch.

"Hello?" the voice asked again.

344

Jack froze as he recognized the voice of Adrien Dunstan. He jumped at the branch, trying to knock the phone out of the tree and away from the imp. Even jumping, he still couldn't reach the phone or the branch.

The imp, however, now inched closer to the phone again, curious.

"HELLO?" Adrien called out, his tone now turning to irritation.

"HELLO!" the imp shouted at the phone, a look of delight on its face, as it thought it had now found a new friend in the phone.

"Who is this?" Adrien demanded.

At this point, Jack picked up a stick he found on the ground, continuing to jump in an effort to knock the phone off the branch. On his third jump, he succeeded, and the phone tumbled to the ground below. Jack picked it up, grateful for the small miracle of the extra tough phone case he had invested in when he purchased the phone.

"Adrien, hi!" he said quickly.

"Jack? Who was that?" Adrien asked, skepticism and confusion dripping from his voice.

"Oh, that—I'm at the diner in Calvary, one of the kids at the table next to me grabbed my phone and started playing with it. Sorry about that." Jack hoped his lie sounded credible.

The imp was whizzing about Jack's head now, throwing acorns at him, and shouting, "GIVE IT BACK! IT'S MY FRIEND! GIVE ME MY FRIEND BACK!"

"Adrien, I'm going to have to call you back in a minute, the kid is having a tantrum, and it's a little hard to hear you."

Before Adrien could even reply, Jack quickly hung up, and turned to Amelia, asking frantically as he dodged acorns, "How do we make it stop?!"

Amelia quickly picked up a stone from the ground, and throwing it at the imp, shouted, "Oh impious imp, be ye turned to stone!"

As the stone narrowly missed the imp, a light burst forth from the creature, and it froze in midair, unable to move except for darting its eyes this way and that. As it hovered, Jack inched closer to it, examining the petrified little creature.

"What did you do to it?"

"Nothing. It did it to itself."

"What do you mean?"

"It's a kind of a flawed defense mechanism. If you throw a stone—or any object, for that matter—at an imp, it suddenly emits this force field...but in doing so, it doesn't understand its own magic and scares itself so silly it won't move—it physically *can't* move—for a few minutes."

"So, could it *actually* move if it wanted?"

"Yeah, sure. It's totally mobile. It just doesn't know it is. So, it's going to hover there for a little bit until it comes around."

"What about that line you shouted? About the stone?"

"Legend has it when Guardians had magic, saying that line as you threw a rock legitimately *did* turn the imp into stone—which, personally, I think is pointless, since they freeze themselves, so I don't know how credible that story is. I think they *thought* it turned to stone because it couldn't move. But now it's tradition to shout it whenever you throw anything at an imp. It's kind of fun." She paused. "We should get out of

346

here before it comes to. It is *not* going to be happy when it realizes it can move."

"Right. Good idea. And I have a phone call to return."

As they made their way out of the woods and out of sight of the petrified imp, Jack pulled his phone out of his back pocket, quickly dialing Adrien back. He had no idea what Adrien was calling about, but it couldn't be good, whatever it was—Adrien rarely called his employees unless it was about a serious matter. He generally preferred to do his interrogations in person.

The phone rang, once, twice, three times.

"Nice of you to get back to me, Jack."

"Sorry about that, sir. It was a little noisy in there."

"Did you know the contract for the Kowalski property fell through?"

Jack smiled, a surge of victory coursing through his body, but he kept a serious tone. He hadn't heard anything from Ruth Kowalski since their conversation a couple weeks prior, and had been wondering when he might.

"It did?" he asked, feigning surprise.

"Yes. Ruth Kowalski called the office a few minutes ago and told Stephanie she'd changed her mind, that she wouldn't be selling to us after all. Did she happen to mention anything to you in any of your conversations with her?"

"No, she didn't," Jack lied. "Last I spoke with her, it seemed like everything was on track."

"I need you to find out what happened, Jack," Adrien barked. "This is unacceptable, and isn't looking good for you. We're down by two

347

properties now, and I'm holding you accountable for it. I can't complete the project without the land. It's *your* job to get the land."

"I understand, sir. I'll fix this," Jack said, lying again.

"See that you do. You only have a few weeks left with our deal, Garridan. And at the moment, I'm not seeing you having a future with us. Prove me wrong."

"I will."

Jack hung up the phone and turned to Amelia, a grin on his face.

"What was that about?" Amelia asked.

"The Kowalskis pulled," Jack said triumphantly.

Amelia's eyes went wide in delighted surprise. "Jack, that's fantastic!"

Jack nodded. "It's good. It's really good. But it's not over yet. We still have to keep stalling on the Erickson property too. And we still have to make sure Dunstan Enterprises doesn't come back around at the end of my time there."

"But we're getting there. It's *working*. And that's what's important," Amelia said, hugging him. Jack returned the hug, awkwardly. "I'm proud of you."

"Thanks."

"We need to tell Emily. She'll be thrilled!" Amelia exclaimed. She also hoped this would help bring Emily around in her finally approving of Jack, and by default, Rosalie would find out.

"Let's keep it to ourselves for now," Jack said quickly.

A concerned look crossed Amelia's face. "What? Why?"

"I just don't want to go around advertising what I'm doing. I need to keep a low profile. And like I said, things aren't done yet. Let's keep it quiet until everything is settled, okay?"

"Okay. If that's what you want, I can do that."

"Thank you."

"So, what'd you think of the imp?" Amelia asked, changing the topic.

"I think I could do without another encounter for a little while."

✳ Chapter 30 ✳

Adrien's impatience

Adrien sat in his office, mulling over the situation he currently found himself in. It had been five months since he had agreed to allow Jack to continue pursuing the Davidson property. He would wait down to the very hour, just a few weeks from now. Still, though, he was concerned, especially with the inexplicable loss of the Kowalski property. Unless Jack played a hail Mary, Adrien's gut was telling him his employee would not be acquiring any further land.

The encounters with Jack at the party also caused him some concern. He didn't trust Jack with the information he knew about Foster, and all the alarms in his head went off when he had caught Jack in his private office. Yes, Jack had clearly been inebriated at that point, and he was probably—hopefully—harmless, but he couldn't be sure. Something inside him said something was wrong with Jack Garridan. He had been acting out-of-character for months now, and he was becoming something of a liability.

He was irritated. He'd spent years building this company up from nothing into a multi-billion-dollar corporation, and *not* due to the incompetence of lackadaisical employees. He was surprised at Jack, frankly: Jack had shown promise from the beginning, and was a go-getter. He'd never failed Adrien before. But with his inability to acquire this property, even with all the resources at his disposal, Adrien determined one of two things must be happening: either he'd overestimated Jack and underestimated the Davidson sisters; or worse, Jack was simply not trying on purpose.

Adrien hated to think this about one of his star employees, but after months of trying to acquire one property with no fruits to show for his efforts, he had to wonder. Something was amiss. Yes, he was pleased by Jack's acquisition of the Benedict property, of course he was. He was happy the Ericksons seemed to be on the right track, though he wasn't putting all his eggs in that basket—their contract negotiation process seemed to be long and drawn out as well. And with the loss of the Kowalski property, he couldn't be sure. He'd thought Ruth Kowalski would be sensible: she was a widow raising six children—the Dunstan Enterprises offer should've been a miracle for them. Why back out now?

But the matter of the Davidsons...they were stubborn, despite their circumstances. When they were pitching to Stuart, Adrien thought he would be easy, given his elderly age and his wife's deteriorating mental condition. When Stuart died, again, Adrien thought the granddaughters would be easy, not wanting to uproot their lives to the middle of nowhere. He assumed they'd take the money, put some towards Lizzie's care, and run with the rest. Clearly, he'd miscalculated their characters and perseverance. Or he'd miscalculated Jack's character and was being led down a rabbit hole. At this moment, he couldn't be sure.

He was frustrated. Millions had already gone into the marketing of this new community he was developing. Ground was breaking on the other sites, buildings already going up. This was supposed to be one of the crown jewels in Dunstan Enterprises' portfolio, an area he hadn't ventured into previously. Other developers and investors were questioning his decisions: his portfolio consisted mainly of urban developments—luxury apartments, hotels, and the like. To stray from his usual repertoire was out of character, but this was a project Adrien had been dreaming about for a long time now. To only see it a portion of the way there and to stumble before reaching the finish line would be an embarrassment, a black eye on his face.

He would give Jack the remaining weeks he was entitled to. However, that didn't mean he couldn't check on his employee's progress. Of course, he couldn't step foot on the property himself to monitor the situation—that would be too obvious, and a distraction to Jack. No, he needed to know what Jack was doing, *how* he was doing it, without Jack suspecting Adrien was watching him.

"Stephanie?" he called out his door to his assistant, who was passing with a cup of coffee in hand on her way to her own desk.

"Yes, Mr. Dunstan?"

"Please have my driver pull the car around. I need to take a quick day trip."

"Of course. Where should I tell him you'll be going?"

"That's not information you need to know, Stephanie," Adrien replied in a patronizing tone of voice. "I'll tell him myself where to go when I see him. Just have him ready the car. Immediately."

"Yes, Mr. Dunstan." She briskly walked to her desk to place the call.

Adrien sat back in his chair, rotating it to stare out the window at the city below him.

He hated relying on others. But sometimes, it was necessary.

✳

Adrien stepped out of the backseat of his car, clutching a briefcase, telling his driver to wait for him. He stood before a small, dilapidated house on the outskirts of the city. Paint was peeling from the siding, and Adrien nearly tripped over a broken step leading to the front porch. The other houses up and down the street were in much the same condition, and Adrien remembered a time when this neighborhood had been thriving, well kept, and full of life—now it was run-down and falling apart. He smiled wryly, thinking how this was also an apt description of the person who lived within the home he was visiting.

Approaching the door, he knocked. He heard shuffling inside, and saw a shadow moving past the closed blinds. The door cracked open, revealing a large, gruff man. His face was covered with an unkempt beard, his dark hair disheveled. When he saw Adrien, his deep brown eyes turned to slits, suspicious at his visitor's intentions.

"Hello, Caleb," Adrien greeted the large man.

"What do you want?"

Friendly formalities had never been Caleb's strong suit, and Adrien's appearance on his doorstep was no exception.

"The same thing you want, old friend—*more*," Adrien replied coolly.

"You and your damn riddles," Caleb huffed, rolling his eyes at the pretentiousness of his old acquaintance. "Just be straight with me. What. Do. You. Want?"

"I need your help with something."

Caleb squinted at Adrien. "The last time I did anything for you, it cost me everything."

"Well, not *everything*," Adrien countered. "But I get your meaning."

"Leave me alone, Adrien," Caleb sighed wearily, bored by this exchange, and already irritated by Adrien's presence. "Just let me live my life in peace."

He moved to close the door, but Adrien caught it before it shut all the way.

"Caleb, listen to me," he hissed. "I just need a small favor. After that, I'll leave you alone. Forever."

Caleb's ears perked. "Forever, huh?"

"I promise."

With this, Caleb opened the door wide, and motioned for Adrien to enter. Adrien did so, examining his surroundings as he stepped inside. It was a small, dingy home, desperately in need of some painting—it looked almost as though it hadn't seen a fresh coat since the middle of the twentieth century. Knowing Caleb, it probably hadn't. The place was well kept and organized, dusted and swept, with the exception of a few stacks of books and newspapers on the end tables and floor. The dinginess, however, seemed to come from the style of décor—it was a hodgepodge of antiques and outdated furniture, collected over many years, faded from normal wear and tear. Re-staining the wooden objects and re-upholstering the chairs and couch would do wonders to bring the place into the modern age, but alas, those kinds of details were usually the furthest from Caleb's mind.

"What do you want?" Caleb asked for the third time since Adrien had arrived, watching Adrien as he looked around his home.

"I need you to pose as a guest at a bed and breakfast in Calvary," Adrien replied, sitting on a lumpy, dusty blue armchair. Caleb sat opposite him on the couch. "It's called The Blue Barn. One of my employees has been spending a bit too much time there, and his work has been subpar as of late. I need you to check on him."

"There's probably a woman," Caleb smirked.

"Possibly," Adrien agreed. "The point is, he's supposed to be working on acquiring this woman's land…but his efforts have been fruitless—first with her grandfather, and now with her after his death. I'm concerned, you see. He was one of my best men at one point, but he's been stuck on this same property for months now, with nothing to show for it. I'd like to know if he's actually working on convincing her to sell out…or if he's playing me for a fool."

"You, a fool? Nah. Never." Sarcasm dripped from Caleb's tongue.

Adrien ignored this jab. Instead, he proceeded to set the briefcase he'd brought with him on the coffee table between the two of them, opening it to reveal an inordinate amount of dollar bills, all wrapped and stacked in perfect little bundles.

"I'll pay you $100,000 for the job, up front, in cash," Adrien said matter-of-factly. "And I'll cover all boarding expenses for the week you stay there. And you'll get $200,000 more after you're done. I believe that should be sufficient."

Caleb raised an eyebrow, studying the contents of the case, giving a low whistle. He leaned over and gently caressed the stacks with his fingertips. He hadn't seen Adrien this desperate in a while. If he was willing to offer this much up front, whatever he was trying to do must be terribly important to him.

"$300,000 is quite a bit just to spy on a random employee." Caleb leaned back in his seat, crossing his arms. "What's so important about him?"

"Nothing, I hope." Adrien shut the case. He wouldn't let Caleb look at the small fortune again until he'd agreed to help him.

"I see." Caleb paused momentarily, contemplating Adrien's offer. "And you said you'd leave me alone forever if I do this?"

"Until the end of all time and beyond," Adrien promised, raising his hand in a show of sincerity. Caleb ignored the gesture, both used to and irked by Adrien's dramatic flairs.

"Fine," Caleb agreed, deciding these terms were more than acceptable. "I'll do it. Why do you want this girl's property so badly anyway? Does it have a gold mine or something?"

"In a sense."

"You're still working it after all these years," Caleb said wryly.

"I never stopped."

355

"Typical," Caleb snorted. "What are you hoping to find out? Anything I should be looking for specifically that can help me out here?"

"Nothing in particular," Adrien responded vaguely. "Just keep your eyes open."

Caleb sighed. "Fine. I'll set up a reservation. Now, if you'll excuse me, I'd like to get back to my book."

"Of course." Adrien stood and extended his hand toward Caleb, inviting him to shake it. "It's a pleasure working with you again."

Caleb ignored Adrien's gesture, and simply grunted. Adrien, understanding the meaning, nodded, then turned and walked out of the small house, leaving the briefcase on Caleb's coffee table. Caleb, without saying another word, closed the door behind Adrien and locked it. He did, however, peer out the window, watching Adrien get into his car and drive off. As soon as Adrien disappeared from sight, Caleb sighed with relief. If Adrien upheld his end of this deal, this would be the last time Caleb would have to work with him. *Ever.*

Forever without Adrien would be an awfully long time—and much more pleasant.

✳ Chapter 31 ✳

A mother's reasons

"Remember, be gentle."

"I know."

"Be *nice*."

"I know."

"And for Christ's sake, be the bigger person."

"Emily, I *know*," Amelia said exasperatedly as the sisters walked up the steps to their mother's front door. "She's my mother, I know how to talk to her."

"Well, clearly, you *don't*, seeing as you've been avoiding her for months, and you needed me to come along for the ride."

"Touché."

"I don't know why you're even trying to have this conversation with her—she hates magic. What makes you think she's going to give us anything this time?"

"I don't know that she is. But I'd regret it if I didn't at least *try*. And you can't tell me you're not the least bit curious about Grandpa's journal and Dad's note in the back of it," Amelia retorted, clutching the leather-bound book in her hands. "A piece of Dad is in here, and I want to know what it's all about."

"And what's your plan when she freaks out and guilt trips us and doesn't want to talk about it?"

"Go back to avoiding her until it blows over, of course."

"Roger."

The sisters took a deep breath to ready themselves, and Amelia pushed the doorbell. A moment later, Rosalie answered, a giant smile on her face.

"My girls!" she exclaimed, giving them each a hug. "It's so good to see you!"

"Good to see you too, Mom," Amelia replied, hugging her in return.

"Amelia, I feel like I've barely seen you the past few months," Rosalie commented as the girls entered the townhouse and took their coats off, settling in at the dining room table, where a tray of cookies was sitting. "Emily at least makes time to have the occasional meal with me, but I only see you in passing. You've been too busy?"

"Well, I'm still traveling for the magazine, Mom," Amelia reminded her mother through gritted teeth. "And I'm co-owner of a bed and breakfast, so yeah, life is a little busy."

"Too busy to spend time with your mother, the financial patron of the Blue Barn?"

Amelia sighed, and Emily sat in an awkward silence. There was no winning with their mother. "I'm sorry, Mom. I'll try to do better."

"Well, I guess you *are* a little busy with your side project too," Rosalie commented in a condescending tone of voice.

"Side project?" Amelia asked, eyebrow raised.

"Yes, with your pupil. Teaching that man to be a Guardian? Emily told me all about it."

Amelia restrained herself from rolling her eyes at her mother, and from glaring at her sister. "Yes, I am."

"Amelia, what are you thinking?" Rosalie asked as she turned her back to prepare coffee. "The man is trouble."

"I'm thinking I'm trying to pass on a legacy you never wanted me to have, and a legacy he never got a chance to have," Amelia snapped.

Emily kicked Amelia under the table, mouthing the words *BE NICE* to her. Amelia, in return, kicked her back and rolled her eyes.

"That's not fair," Rosalie countered, turning back to her daughter, her knuckles white as she clenched the tray holding the coffee mugs. "I *wanted* you to have that legacy. I just wanted you to be careful with it."

"Well, you being careful meant Dad didn't want to teach us," Amelia retorted. "So we had to have cram sessions at Grandma and Grandpa's place. I'm still not where I should be. You shorted us, Mom."

"Is that what you think happened?" Rosalie slammed the tray on the table, causing coffee to slosh out of the mugs and her daughters to wince.

"All I know is when Dad picked us up that summer when we first saw Lila, and told us we'd be learning about magic, he explicitly said 'your mom won't like it.' So, I don't know, Mom, but that kind of leads me to believe maybe you had a hand in keeping things from us."

"You need to stop blaming me," Rosalie said wearily. "Because things aren't what you think they are. We were trying to *protect* the two of you by limiting your exposure."

"But *why?*" Amelia demanded. "Mom, enough is enough."

Procuring her grandfather's journal from her bag, she slid it across the table towards her mother. When Rosalie saw the journal, all color drained from her face.

"Where did you get that?" she whispered.

"We found it as we were decluttering the cottage," Amelia replied. "You've seen it before, I assume?"

"Yes."

"Then you know what's in it?"

"Yes."

"And you know Dad wrote in it too?"

"I didn't know he wrote in it…but that doesn't surprise me."

"Mom, tell us about it. We've exhausted all other resources. Grandma can't answer much. We got some info from Delia. We know Grandpa and Jude were searching for stones. Was Dad looking too?"

Rosalie sighed. "Today's the day, isn't it?"

"It is."

Rosalie nodded, resolved. "Fine. When you were young—Emily, before you were even born—your father took a job in Greece one summer."

Amelia touched the necklace with the teardrop amber stone that hung around her neck, the gift that came out of this trip. "Yes, I remember."

"At the time, he had embraced the fact he came from a line of Guardians. He devoured every story and could recite them by heart. He knew the spells of his ancestors, even though he couldn't use them—they were a part of him.

"The whole reason he accepted the job in Greece was because he was convinced there was a source stone there. He was following in his father's footsteps—Stuart had seen the shifts happening in magical creatures, and had taught your father to see them too. He was doing the same damn thing your grandfather had been doing—trying to find the reason *why*. They always needed to know *why,* those Davidson men. They couldn't keep their nose in their own business."

"Magical creatures *are* our business," Amelia reminded her mother.

"Yes, well, I wish they weren't."

"Mom, what happened in Greece?"

Rosalie sat back in her seat. "Your father got close. We found where the stone was, but it was protected by spells. Even so, without magic, your father figured out how to get around the first few.

"It was the last spell where things went wrong. In order for the spell to be lifted and your father to be allowed to reach the stone, he would have had to hand over the thing he loved the most in the world."

"What was that?"

"Me," her mother replied softly. "I was there with him. I don't remember much, except one minute, we were standing in this massive cave, with this beautiful golden tree in the middle that had a single fruit on it—we knew the stone was in the fruit. As we walked toward the tree, this snake-like dragon creature appeared out of thin air. It gave your father the ultimatum: me or the fruit on the tree. After that, I blacked out. The next thing I remember, we were on the beach in the sunshine, and he was standing over me, shaking me awake. I asked him what happened, and he

361

told me I'd been paralyzed by a spell and held in a suspended state while the creature mocked him, demanding he choose. When he chose me—the dragon let us go, with the warning to never return until he was willing to give up the thing he loved the most."

Emily gaped. "But that's not possible—Mom, you're not a Guardian. You shouldn't have been able to see any of that, or be around it."

"I *know*," Rosalie snapped. "That's how terribly powerful the magic was—even I could see it, experience it, *feel* it. It was awful.

"As for your father, he said it haunted him, that he put me in a situation like that, that he could have lost me. He was troubled by the cruelty of that spell, that it would have required him to sacrifice me. He decided he didn't want anything to do with magic anymore, if someone could use it for such terrible reasons. He was totally disheartened that the Creator Sorcerer, this entity he had in his mind as being ultimately good, could use a spell like that, a creature like that, to protect one of the stones. So, he walked away from magic.

"That is, of course, until he realized his responsibility to you girls. He knew no matter how hard he fought it, he was ultimately a Guardian, and you two were as well.

"So that's why he was hesitant. He was obliged to hand down the knowledge, but he didn't want you hurt. That's why you only learned the actual spells at your grandparents' house, not in our house—he had encountered real, terrible magic, and didn't want his hand in it. He didn't want to endanger me again, and he didn't want to endanger you girls. He chose us over the stone."

"So, you know where one of the stones is," Amelia said, her eyes wide.

"Is that all you're getting from this?" her mother snapped. "Yes, I know. And that's something I will take with me to the grave. I won't put you two through that. The stones are meant to be hidden, kept out of reach from us."

"Mom, why didn't you tell us all of this earlier?"

"Because I'm your mother. I'm not obligated to tell you everything."

"But this could have at least helped us understand where you were coming from!"

"I doubt that would've changed your feelings," Rosalie snorted. "You still would've blamed me for your lack of magical education. Your grandparents would have still been your heroes." With this, she sighed. "I know what I married into. And when I married into it, I was fine with it. I really was. But things changed after that day. I wanted to protect you from it all. Because I know someday, magic will re-enter the world, and the thought of you encountering dark magic is terrifying. I thought if I protected you as much as I could, you'd lose interest, and by not being involved in magic, you'd be safe. I know it was a dumb thought. But that was my reasoning."

She looked up at her daughters. "I know now I can't control what you are. You're Guardians. And if magic returns in your lifetime, you'll have it, and you'll be using it. And you'll need to know how to control it. I just hate the idea of something bad happening to you. I know you need to be ready, if that happens in our time. But I hate the thought of you not only preparing yourself, but preparing others, especially a man we didn't even trust just a few months ago."

"You act like we're going to war, Mom," Amelia said. "We're not."

"But you are," Rosalie said. "Your father made that very clear when he was alive: there will be a war someday. And if it happens in your lifetime, you will be a part of it. Every time you practice a spell, it's like you're putting on another piece of armor. And that scares the hell out of me."

"Well…wouldn't you rather we have armor on than go in unprotected?"

"Of course I would!" Rosalie snapped. "The point is, I don't want you to have to be a part of it in the first place!"

"We can't help that, Mom," Emily said, finally jumping into the conversation. "We can't help Dad's side is a line of Guardians. I don't know that it'll happen in our lifetime, but I'd rather be safe than sorry. And I don't trust Jack much either, but I'll tell you this, I'd rather Amelia be the one teaching him the light side than someone else gets their hands on him and teaches him otherwise. I'll take all the allies we can get. Even if he is obnoxious and rude."

Amelia smiled at her sister's compliment of Jack, and Emily briefly returned the smile. Turning back to their mother, Amelia asked, "Mom, the poem in the beginning…"

"Yes, those are clues to where the stones are." Rosalie waved her hand. "That's what drove your father and grandfather insane, that's what they were following."

"But where did they even *get* that poem?"

"From your great-grandfather."

"But he died in World War II," Amelia pointed out.

"Yes, but not before sending a letter back to your great-grandmother about what he had seen over there. He apparently met something while he was out there and was given that prophecy."

"Something? What something?" Amelia wondered what creature could have known where all the stones were. She wracked her brain, trying to think of all the creatures known to have prophetic tendencies in the area of the world where her great-grandfather had served during the war, but too many came to mind, none seeming to stand out amongst the others.

Rosalie shook her head. "I don't know. I didn't get those specifics."

"Do you know where that letter might be?"

Rosalie shook her head. "No. Somewhere in Stuart's things, I assume. But both Stuart and your father had that poem memorized."

"And this bit in the back…" Amelia flipped the pages to where Brennan had scrawled.

Rosalie took the book and read, her eyes squinting as she did so. "I don't know. Your father never told me about this part. I have no idea what it would mean."

Amelia and Emily sat back in their seats, each a bit discouraged by this, but also relieved: they'd finally, for the first time in their lives, had a real, honest conversation with their mother. They were given actual answers. Their relationship with her was now altered, they hoped for the better. And if nothing else, for the moment, that was enough.

✳

The sisters returned to the cottage that evening, neither sure how to process the information they'd received from their mother. Amelia decided to cope by getting to the business of managing the bed and breakfast. Emily decided to process by having a couple glasses of wine.

While Amelia sat at her laptop, going over budgets and forms, Emily gazed out the window, glass of wine in her hand, lost in thought.

"Speaking of wine, have you sent in the stuff for us to get a liquor license so we can finally start serving our guests alcohol?" Amelia asked, observing her sister drinking. The sisters had recently agreed this would be a nice perk to add to the menu for their guests—especially after several previous guests, specifically Mrs. Patterson, had requested it.

Emily nodded. "Yes."

"Great, thank you. Hey, I'm working on the budget for the next month—you haven't told me yet how many people we booked this past month for the charter fishing," Amelia said, looking back at the laptop.

Emily muttered something incoherent as she poured herself another glass of wine and took a sip.

"Sorry, what was that?" Amelia looked up from the spreadsheet.

"Four," Emily said louder, taking another sip, her grip tight around the glass.

"Four trips? Emily, that's not too bad!" Amelia said, trying to be enthusiastic. It wasn't great, but it was better than nothing. It was at least one trip each weekend.

"No…no, four *people*. One trip," Emily corrected her, the blood rushing to her face as she set the glass down, not meeting her sister's gaze.

"Oh." Amelia looked back at her laptop and punched a few numbers in. "Well, that's okay. We're still profiting with the Blue Barn. And we're getting into our slower season, so it's expected. At least we had more than that over the summer."

Emily nodded stiffly. "Yeah, I guess. Not much more though."

Amelia looked up again. "Listen, Emily, these things take time. We're a new business. The fact that the Blue Barn is even doing well is a miracle and *you* have a lot to do with that. We knew the charter fishing part might have a rough start, we planned for it, and we're fine. We're more than fine. We're actually doing really, really well—to a point where we'll be able to hire on someone else to help out within the next couple months if we keep trending in this direction."

Emily looked up, surprised by this news. "Really?"

"Yeah, really. And that's because of the hard work you've done." She paused. "After the final wave of fairies leave would be a good time to bring someone on board. I know they shouldn't be seen as is, but I don't want to risk it."

"Makes sense."

"Or…" Amelia said slowly, hesitantly. "Or we hire on somebody who knows about them or who can already see them, so it wouldn't matter."

Emily raised an eyebrow, knowing exactly what her sister was getting at. "No. No, I don't want to hire Jack."

Amelia sighed, dismayed by her sister's knee-jerk reaction. "This? Still? Even after all the nice things you said about him to Mom today?"

"Yes, this, *still*. And I didn't say *that* many nice things. I just sort of agreed having another Guardian around could be a good thing."

"Yeah, okay, keep telling yourself that."

Emily rolled her eyes. "Listen, isn't it enough I have to tolerate him a couple times a week and be nice while you're teaching him about magic? Now you want to bring him on full time and *pay* him to be here? I'd rather pay to have him go somewhere else!"

"Listen, I'm just saying, he knows his way around the place now." Amelia tried to remain calm in her sister's defiance. "We know he's going to be jobless in the next few weeks, one way or the other. And he knows about us and the creatures on this land, so it'd be easier than having to hire someone else we'd have to keep secrets from. The only other people in the world who know we're Guardians are either dead, living in Hawaii, living in a nursing home, or Mom."

"I don't want to work with Mom either." Emily wasn't thrilled about their options—or rather, lack thereof.

STONES ✳ RJG McManus

"Yeah, neither do I," Amelia agreed. "I love her, but you know she'd come in and try to change everything we've been doing, and you know we'd feel guilty and bend to it because she gave us her portion of Grandpa's money to start this in the first place. And after everything today…I just…well, you know."

Emily did know. She didn't know how to feel after the conversation with her mother either—on the one hand, she was thrilled the truth behind why she was opposed to magic came out. But on the other hand, she hated this secret had impacted her entire life, and right now, she needed time to process and figure out how the relationship with her mother would go moving forward. She hoped for the better, and with less secrets and more honesty, as well as more tolerance, but she couldn't be sure. The only thing she *was* sure of was she wanted a relationship with her mother, but she didn't want it to be a business one.

"Yeah, I know," Emily sighed.

"But with Jack, we'd still be the bosses. There wouldn't be that guilt. You could *legitimately* boss him around."

Emily had to admit that did sound enticing.

"Just think about it, at least," Amelia continued. "We don't have to make a decision right now. Like I said, it's still a few weeks down the line. And if you're still set then that you don't want to, that's fine, I'll respect that—we're partners in this, after all, and we need to be on the same page with hiring decisions. But it's just a thought and a suggestion."

"I'll think about it."

"*Seriously*, Emily. Don't say you will but already have your mind made up that the answer is no."

"I will *seriously* think about it," Emily emphasized, slightly annoyed.

"Thank you. I appreciate it."

In that moment, Amelia's computer pinged. Opening up the reservation screen, she smiled. "Looks like we've got a guest coming tomorrow. And he'll be here a week."

"Nice," Emily said with a small smile.

She took another sip of wine and went back to gazing out the window.

✳ Chapter 32 ✳

A way with words

Caleb stepped out of his car—a beat-up, dusty blue sedan he'd purchased about twenty years prior—and took in his surroundings as he looked out over the Davidson property. To his right, at the end of the driveway was his destination—a brightly-painted blue building, still resembling in shape the barn it had once been. Opposite the Blue Barn was a small, white cottage with a large front porch. Beyond the buildings, a field, which Caleb imagined was full of wildflowers during warmer months. On the north edge of the property, he observed a grove of trees which eventually became part of a larger forest. To the south, the field continued on, and he could see in the distance the structures going up on the Benedict property. Standing tall and proud right on the property line of the Davidson and Benedict land was an old willow tree, its leaves slowly turning and falling. Beyond all this, the vast expanse of the ocean, from which a cool breeze was blowing that day. Caleb shivered and pulled his coat around him a bit tighter. It appeared the unseasonably warm weather they'd been having had come to an end.

Throwing a backpack over his shoulder and carrying a camera case, Caleb entered the Blue Barn. He glanced around—to the right was the dining room, with doors closed to the kitchen. To the left, a sitting area of sorts. Down the hall, a restroom and what looked to be a storage closet— it was slightly cracked open, and he could see some toiletry supplies on the shelf. At the end of the hall was an exit to the field behind the building.

Most importantly, however, was what was before him: a large staircase leading to the guest rooms upstairs, and next to that, sitting in front of him at the check-in desk of the foyer was a petite, strawberry blonde woman,

370

typing away at her laptop. She looked up upon hearing him enter, and smiled.

"You must be Caleb Ogden," the woman said, extending her hand. "I'm Amelia Davidson."

"Nice to meet you," Caleb said with a warm smile.

This must be the girl Jack's willing to lose his job over.

He looked her up and down, noting her cheerful disposition, bright, striking blue eyes, engaging smile, and curvy, fit features.

Well, if he's going to lose it over anyone, at least he's got good taste.

He looked at the check-in desk briefly, seeing her cell phone light up as a text came through. He'd need to access that at some point, and early, so he could start tracking her as quickly as possible—Adrien's orders in a follow-up message. Jack wasn't the only one to be tracked, but the Davidson sisters as well. Or at the very least, Amelia, as she seemed to be the one who was spending the most time with Jack.

She glanced over, seeing him gazing at the phone. Noticing a message had come in, she picked it up, quickly typing something in, then looking back up and smiling at him as she set it down.

"Sorry about that. My sister wanted to know if we needed more fish for tonight's dinner."

"Fish sounds lovely."

Amelia grinned, sending another text as she did so. "We have the best in the state. Anyway, I have here you've requested the king ocean view for a week," she said, typing into her system.

"That's right."

"Excellent. And we already have a credit card on file for you. Breakfast is obviously included in the price, but we do offer dinner at extra cost. Here's this week's menu." She pushed a piece of paper towards him to glance over. "Would you like to join us for dinner while you're here?"

"Absolutely." Caleb seized the opportunity to spend more time with his hostess—and hopefully, by default, Jack.

"Great! Which nights?"

"Every."

"Really?" Amelia asked, confounded, looking up from the screen. Normally her guests only did a couple nights of dinner with her, and for the rest, they would either order in, or explore the local area and the seafood joints this particular corner of the world offered.

"Yes, every night."

Amelia noted to herself she'd have to let Jack know they'd have to do their sessions earlier in the day or later in the evening, since she'd be busy cooking dinner for this guest every night for the next week. Maybe he could join her in the kitchen while she was cooking. They'd figure it out.

"Sounds good." She typed his dinner plan into the computer. Once finished, she procured a key from the desk drawer and stood. "Let me show you to your room."

"I'm wondering, before you do, do you perhaps keep any extra toiletries around?" Caleb asked, hoping to get her to step away from her post and leave him. "I believe I may have left my deodorant at home."

"We do—it's in the back. Let me grab some for you, and we'll head up."

As soon as Amelia stepped away from the desk to go to storage room around the corner, Caleb glanced over—she'd left her cell phone behind, unattended.

Perfect. He'd hoped she'd do as much.

He picked it up, silently praying she didn't have a passcode or lock set up to access the device. He didn't have much time, and a passcode would hold him up, or even prevent what he could do in the limited moments he had.

He swiped his thumb across the screen—it opened with ease. No passcode. No lock. How trusting of her. How naïve.

Quickly, he downloaded an app to her phone that would give him the ability to track her every move, to see where she was at all times, and even read her texts. Now he'd need to figure out how to access Jack's so he could be tracked as well.

How technology had changed in his lifetime.

He heard footsteps. She was returning. With a few taps, he set the app to hidden mode and put the phone back on the desk where she'd left it. She'd never know the app had been installed, that she was being watched. He texted the access to Adrien, so he could monitor her too, though he did so with some resignations.

He felt a bit dirty. Though he'd only known her for a few minutes, Amelia seemed to be a kind, competent hostess, an innocent bystander in the vendetta Adrien seemed to have against Jack. He didn't like doing Adrien's work, he never had, but Adrien had promised this was the last time, and so he did what he had to do to get him out of his life for good—and he'd do just about anything to ensure that. For now, he had to play the part of a pawn.

"Got it!" Amelia declared, handing the stick of deodorant to Caleb.

"You're too kind." Caleb smiled, taking the stick from her hand. "I appreciate it. And I'm sure you and your other guests will too."

Amelia laughed. "Shall I show you your room now? Or do you need anything else?"

"No, I'm fine. I'd love to get settled in."

Caleb followed Amelia up the stairs, where she led him to the same grand room with ocean views that inspired awe in Jack the first time he had seen it. Even Caleb was impressed by the room, with the king-sized bed, tasteful, clean décor, and the expansive windows showcasing jaw-dropping views of the ocean and rocky shores.

"The Wi-Fi password and TV channel guide are both in the folder on the desk." Amelia remained in the doorway as Caleb walked past her and dropped one of his bags on the bed, proceeding to open it. From her vantage, Amelia saw camera equipment. "You're a photographer?"

Caleb smiled. "Amateur, but yes."

"Is that what brings you to Calvary?"

"It is," he lied. "I read an article in a magazine, about the town's 'pristine, untouched coastline, beckoning all those who hear its call to explore the beauty and delights it has to offer.'"

Amelia was taken aback, hearing those words come out of his mouth. "You read that?"

"I did. Sorry, I don't usually quote articles. I was just so struck by that particular poetic line. It sounds silly saying it out loud now."

"No, no, it's okay—I wrote that piece," she said, delighted. She'd never heard one of her own articles quoted back to her by a reader before.

"Did you really?" he said, feigning surprise.

"I did. I wrote it hoping it would draw people in."

"Well, job well done." Caleb gave her a warm smile. "You got me here, and that's a good start."

"Thank you." Amelia blushed. "You came at the best time of year too. Between the ocean, the cliffs, and the leaves changing colors, I'm sure you'll get some excellent shots."

"I'm sure I will."

"Also, if you get back on the road and head north for about a mile, you'll run across the town's lighthouse—it's lovely, high up on the cliffs, with the white waters churning around the rocks below. That will be a great place to get some photos as well. You can even see it from our beach here, which might be nice if you have a telescopic lens."

"That sounds wonderful. I'll have to head that way to check it out."

"Is there anything else I can do you for?"

"No, I'm good. You've been more than kind. Thank you."

"Anytime!" she said cheerily. "Well, I'll leave you to it—see you at dinner!"

"I'm looking forward to it.

And in truth, he was.

✳

The next morning, Caleb sat in the dining room of the Blue Barn, anxious. He glanced about at the other guests—none of them were Jack. Adrien had sent him a picture, so he knew who he was looking for, but he hadn't come across the man yet. He didn't come to dinner last night, nor had he seen him around the grounds at all either. He wondered how often Jack came around the cottage—according to Adrien, it was probably several times a week, but still, there was no definitive answer on that. The visits could be sporadic. Caleb only planned to stay for a week, and he intended to stick to that schedule. He wanted Adrien out of his life as soon as possible. But if Jack didn't make an appearance, he would have to extend the visit—not something he wanted to do. He wanted to get in, get out, get his money, and move on with his life.

His luck, it seemed, was changing. He glanced up, seeing a tall man with sandy brown hair and striking blue eyes enter the dining room. He glanced over at Amelia, who, along with her sister was serving coffee to a few guests, and saw her light up when she saw the man enter. Glancing back at the man, he saw his expression change to that of joy as well when he locked eyes with Amelia. He watched them greet each other with a quick hug, and watched as the man sat to have coffee with Amelia and the guests.

This was Jack Garridan. Perfect. He hadn't had to wait too long.

He sat quietly for a bit, listening to the others talk—mostly blather about the weather, the lovely scenery, etc. All shallow, nothing of substance.

After a few minutes, Jack turned to Caleb, saying, "Sorry, I don't think we've been including you in on the conversation. What's your name?"

"Caleb," Caleb replied with a smile. "And no worries. I'm just lost in my own thoughts."

"Nice to meet you, Caleb. I'm Jack."

"Pleasure."

"So, what brings you out this way?"

"Just looking for a little serenity," Caleb answered, half truthfully. "And I'm an amateur photographer. It so happens I read one of Amelia's articles, and was inspired to make the trip to see this beautiful place for myself."

Amelia blushed, and Jack smiled.

"It is beautiful, isn't it?" Jack replied.

"What about you, Jack? Do you live here?"

"Practically," Jack laughed. "I'm here often enough."

"Business or pleasure?"

"Business. Work brings me here often, and Amelia is kind enough to let me stay here when I'm in town."

"What sort of business are you in?"

"It's…complicated." Jack shifted his weight in his seat uneasily. "I'd rather not talk about work, if you don't mind."

"Of course, no worries." Caleb leaned back in his seat. Turning to Amelia, he said, "By the way, I was wondering if you could show me where to get that view of the lighthouse you were talking about yesterday? I'd love to get some photos today."

"I can this afternoon," Amelia replied. "I have a few things I need to work on this morning."

"Oh, I see—I was hoping to get some morning sunlight."

"I'm free this morning. I can show you," Jack offered. "I know the exact view she's talking about."

"Really? It wouldn't keep you from your work?" Caleb asked.

377

"No, not at all."

"Thank you, Jack, that's awfully kind of you."

✳

After breakfast, the men made their way across the field, past the old willow tree, and toward the cliffs of the ocean, Caleb with his photography equipment in tow. He'd managed to get alone time with Jack, which was key, but at the moment, Jack wasn't answering any of his questions as they talked. He kept his answers short and vague when it came to his work and his relationship with Amelia. This in and of itself was irksome, but Caleb wasn't too worried yet. He just needed to access Jack's phone, and he'd be able to find out more information without asking Jack questions directly. And with as congenial as Jack seemed to be, that would be an easy task.

Caleb put his hand in his pocket, where his own phone was placed. Pulling out the phone, he feigned a look of distress, then shoved it back into his pocket.

Jack saw the look on Caleb's face. "Everything all right?"

"Fine, fine, I hope," Caleb said. "It looks like I missed a call from my mother's nursing home. Must've left the thing on silent."

"Well, feel free to give her a call back, if you need. I can wait."

"No, no, it's no worries. My battery's low anyway, I forgot to charge my phone overnight. I don't want to call right now only to be cut off in the middle of a conversation because my phone dies. I'll wait until later."

"You look pretty worried, Caleb. Here, use my phone." Without hesitation, Jack pulled his phone from his back pocket, typing in the passcode to access the dial screen, and handing it over to Caleb. "Check on your mom."

378

How trusting, Caleb mused. *That was almost too easy.*

Caleb smiled. "Thank you, I appreciate it. It's just—well, I worry about her so much these days."

Jack waved his hand. "No need to explain."

"Thank you."

He stepped a few yards away from Jack, his back turned so Jack couldn't see what he was doing, and out of earshot so he couldn't overhear. Jack politely stayed where he was, watching the waves crash into the cliffs below, allowing Caleb his privacy and the time he needed with the phone. As Jack waited, Caleb downloaded the same tracking app he'd placed on Amelia's phone. He'd text Adrien the access code to Jack's phone as well when he got back to his room.

Caleb then dialed the number of the local nursing home so when Jack saw his call logs later, there would be no suspicions aroused.

A chirpy nurse answered the phone. "Our Lady of Perpetual Faith, how may I help you?"

"I'm sorry, I must have the wrong number," Caleb said softly, so Jack couldn't hear.

"No worries!"

Caleb quickly hung up, but pretended to stay on for a moment longer in order to make Jack think he was having a conversation with someone on the other end. When he'd waited long enough, he walked back over to where Jack was standing, handing him the phone back.

"Everything okay?" Jack asked as he slipped the phone into his back pocket.

"Yes, she's fine. There was just a quick question about a medication, nothing too concerning."

"Good to hear."

"Thanks for letting me use your phone, I appreciate it…though I suppose I could've used my own, if I'd known the call was going to be that short."

"No worries." Jack waved it off dismissively. "I'd rather you had the battery you needed and not have to use it, than not have the battery and have the phone die on you halfway through the call."

"You're too kind, Jack."

The men continued their walk towards the view of the lighthouse.

✳ Chapter 33 ✳

An off day

While the men were outside, Emily and Amelia were in the kitchen, cleaning up after breakfast with their guests before Amelia would take a few of them out on a nature walk. For a while, they worked together in silence. It was Emily who finally spoke.

"Listen…I've been thinking. And okay," Emily said, picking up a bowl of half-eaten eggs.

"Okay what?" Amelia asked, looking up at her sister.

"About Jack. Okay, let's hire him on. If he wants to stay, that is."

Amelia raised an eyebrow. "Really?"

"Yeah, really."

"What made you change your mind?"

"Listen, I've seen how helpful he is around the place. I saw how he just went out there with Mr. Ogden without even expecting anything. We may as well pay the guy for what he does. And you were right, it might be nice to have someone else around who knows about magic. Besides, it seems to make you happy."

"It's not about making me happy, Em. Are you really okay with this?"

"I am."

"Really?"

"Really."

"Okay, then I'll offer him the job."

"Good." Emily paused. "There's just one thing that's bothering me though."

"What's that?"

"I still don't understand why he's just now seeing magical creatures as an adult. Doesn't that bother you?"

"Honestly, it doesn't. It used to, but not anymore."

"I just…okay, well, I've been reading Grandpa's journal too. And Jude's journal. And there's nothing in it about Guardians starting to see as an adult, which is what concerns me."

"Okay, so, what will help ease your concerns?"

"I want us to talk to Grandma again."

"Em, you saw how she was last time…it was bad."

"It was. But she's still remembering things here and there. Mom doesn't know anything about it. Neither does Delia. And I don't know who else to ask. And there's going to come a point when Grandma doesn't have *any* of her memory left. I want to ask again before that happens."

"And that will help ease your mind about Jack?"

"Yes, if there's a reasonable explanation for it, it will."

"And if we don't get an explanation? Because you know that's not a guarantee."

"Then we can still hire him. But I'll be extra bossy."

Amelia laughed. "I wouldn't expect anything less."

✳

When Jack returned back to the house, Amelia and Emily were sitting at the dining room table, waiting for him.

"What's this?" Jack asked, glancing back and forth between the sisters.

"Take a seat, Jack," Emily replied, motioning across the table.

Jack did so, hesitantly, as Amelia poured him a cup of coffee and placed it in front of him.

"Is this an inquisition or something?"

"Should it be?" Emily asked.

"No, it's not," Amelia said before Jack could respond to Emily. "We have an offer for you."

"An offer?"

"Listen, we wanted to get your thoughts. Your six-month time limit from Adrien is going to be up in a few weeks, right?"

Jack nodded, taking a sip of his coffee. "Yeah."

"Do you have any job leads yet?"

He shook his head, embarrassed by this admission. He'd been spending so much time focusing on collecting evidence of Adrien's shady business practices, studying magic with Amelia, and doing *actual* work to keep his job afloat for the time being that the job hunt had fallen off. He hadn't sent in an application for anything in weeks.

Amelia had a feeling this was the case, and was glad for it. "Listen, we were wondering if after everything, you'd want a job here. We've been doing well and could use the extra set of hands. You know this place just about as well as me and Emily. I mean, it won't pay as much as your current job does, I'm sure, but cost of living is less around here than in Boston anyway."

Jack blinked. "How can you even afford that? You're actually making a profit?"

Amelia smiled. "Yes, Jack. We've been making a profit since day one."

"But *how?*" he inquired, in disbelief.

"Don't look so surprised by it," Emily said with a wry smile.

"Jack, we were able to pay for the renovations of everything up front from what Grandpa left us, with plenty leftover," Amelia replied. "We're good. We're bringing in an income. And if we stay on track with our current trajectory, we'll be able to hire someone else on by the first of the year—Thanksgiving and Christmas will be huge for us and give us a bump. Emily and I talked about it today. We want you on. That way you can be around here, and maybe have a little bit of a slower, calmer pace of life. I know that's what you've been wanting. What do you think?"

Jack was over the moon. The fog of depression and stress lifted off him, and he could see clearly. He really did love Calvary, and was surprised by this—he hadn't expected to fall for this charming little place when he first arrived months ago, but here he was, now considering becoming a local.

"Yes. I'd love to."

Amelia grinned. "Good. I'm glad. And you can stay with us until you find a place of your own if you need to."

"I appreciate that."

"It'll be good to have you around more."

"I'm already around almost every day."

"Yeah…well, still. More will be nice." She averted her gaze, glancing at the table in front of her.

"Yeah. It will," he agreed.

They both sat in silence for a moment, neither realizing the other's heart was fluttering.

Emily cleared her throat, feeling a bit awkward in the moment with the other two. "Anyway, there's one more thing."

"What's that?" Jack asked, turning to the younger sister.

"You need to come with us to visit our grandma."

"Why's that?"

"Because that's part of my comfort level. You don't make sense."

"I don't understand."

"Jack, you just now as an adult started seeing magical creatures. That's weird. All Guardians can see them from the day they were born. You couldn't. And for me to be comfortable working with you, I want to find out *why*."

"What can she tell us?"

"Probably not much—but if she's having a lucid day, she might remember something Grandpa told her."

Jack was skeptical. They were relying on a woman whose mind was barely there to recount Guardian history?

Amelia saw the look on his face. "We know it's a long shot. But it's all we've got right now. Grandpa's old journals don't say anything. None of the books say anything. Frankly, Jack, you're an anomaly."

Perfect, Jack thought, somewhat cynically. "I don't get what the big deal is though. What does it matter that I just now started seeing magical creatures?"

"Jack, it goes against what's been going on for centuries," Amelia explained. "Guardians see them and interact with them at infanthood— we're born into it. We know what we are from the start. It's just not heard of. It's not supposed to be *possible*." She paused. "Jack, are you *sure* Lila was the first ever creature you'd interacted with?"

"I'm pretty sure I'd know if I'd seen another fairy earlier on in life. It was kind of memorable."

"But that's just it—maybe you *did* see something, but wrote it off? Is that possible?"

"Amelia, Lila was honestly the first magical thing I've ever come across," he emphasized.

"Then we'd like to find out how that's possible and what it means. And Grandma might know."

"And what happens if we don't find out anything from your grandma? Does my job depend on this or something?"

"No, we'll still hire you," Emily replied. "I just won't be as nice."

Jack smirked. That was a typical Emily response. He seriously doubted it would go anywhere, but agreed to making a trip with the sisters to visit Lizzie in the nursing home the next day.

✳

The next morning, after the guests at the Blue Barn had been fed breakfast and taken care of, Amelia, Emily, and Jack made the trek to the nursing home twenty miles down the road. They entered Lizzie's room, where they found her once again sitting in the armchair. Instead of reading a book though, this time, she was merely gazing out the window. Slowly, they approached her.

"Hi, Grandma," Emily said softly.

Lizzie looked over, glancing at the trio.

"Grandma, it's us, Emily and Amelia. And this is Jack." Amelia motioned for Jack, who was behind the sisters, to step forward.

Jack did so, sticking out his hand to shake Lizzie's. Instead of accepting the gesture, Lizzie warily looked Jack up and down. "I don't like him."

"I don't much either," Emily snorted. Both Amelia and Jack shot her a sharp look.

"He's okay, Grandma," Amelia reassured her grandmother. "He's very nice."

"He looks sloppy." Turning to Jack, she snapped, "I don't understand why it's so difficult for you young men to just pick up a razor and shave nowadays—why do you have to walk around looking like a lumberjack all the time? Back in my day, men actually cared about their appearance and looked respectable."

Jack didn't think his minimal scruff necessarily qualified under lumberjack status, but he wasn't about to argue with a demented old

387

woman. He decided remaining silent and nodding and smiling politely was his best course of action.

Amelia sighed, frustrated. Turning to Jack and Emily, she said softly, "It looks like we've caught her on an off day. She doesn't know who we are…we're not going to get much out of her today."

"I know *exactly* who you are and I am *perfectly* lucid today, thank you very much," Lizzie chimed in.

The three turned to face Lizzie, shocked.

"Then why are you being so mean to Jack?" Amelia questioned.

"Because I've spent *entirely* too much of my life being polite," Lizzie answered. "I figure dementia is a good excuse to finally be able to say what I want and get away with it."

"Grandma, you're my hero," Emily said with a grin.

"I know, child." Turning back to Amelia, Lizzie asked, "So, why did you bring the lumberjack?"

"Jack recently discovered he's a Guardian," Amelia explained.

"He's awfully old to be just now figuring that out, isn't he?"

"That's just it: Emily and I figured it out when we were kids. Same with Dad and Grandpa…same with everyone we've ever known who was a Guardian. We never heard of anyone figuring it out as an adult. Did Grandpa ever mention anything to you about it? We don't remember him telling us anything, and we can't find anything like it in any of the books or journals he passed down."

Lizzie turned to face Jack, eyebrow raised. "You're just a contradictory little anomaly, aren't you? Trying to buy my husband's land to develop it, only to find out you're supposed to guard the creatures who live on it."

Before Jack could open his mouth to respond, Lizzie continued, "Yes, I remember you. I remember that first time you came by the house, trying to talk my husband into selling, before I came here. I remember my sweet husband visiting me, looking more frazzled each time, telling me how you were *hounding* him, relentless. I remember how stressed he was, I remember his heart palpitations. Even on my darkest days, when I barely remember who I am, I remember the face of the man who drove my husband into the grave."

She looked Amelia, red in the face with anger. "And *you*, befriending him, teaching him, and bringing him here! What do you think you're doing?"

"He's a *Guardian*, Grandma," Amelia protested.

"So was the Fallen Sorcerer, and look what happened there," Lizzie snapped.

"Grandma, *please*," Amelia pleaded. "Help us. Jack doesn't know his family. He doesn't know anything about the stories. And we don't know why he's just now, as an adult, able to see magical creatures. It doesn't make sense."

"Yes, it does," Lizzie said. "It means he's not actually a Guardian. It means a stone has been found and magic is seeping back into the world. And it means for whatever reason, this idiot is one of the first non-Guardians to be able to see magical creatures again."

Amelia, Emily, and Jack stared at Lizzie, completely floored.

"Wait...wait a second," Jack said slowly after a moment of silence, remembering what Amelia and Emily had been teaching him, and what he'd been reading. "That can't be it. I can't just *see* magical creatures. I can summon them too. And I can feel magic. Non-Guardians can't do that, right? Only Guardians can."

"Well then, you're just a late bloomer," Lizzie scoffed. "I don't know what to tell you. I've never heard of anything like it." She paused, motioning for Jack to come closer to her. Hesitantly, he did, close enough that he could feel her breath on his face. She hissed, "If you're *really* a Guardian, you best live up to that title and actually *guard*."

"I am. I'm trying," Jack replied softly.

"Don't *try*. *Do*."

All of a sudden, the intent look on her face was gone, replaced by a blank expression. She looked at the three young people in her room, bewildered.

"Who are you?"

The three sat back in each of their chairs, exchanging a look amongst each other. It was Amelia who spoke first.

"It's me, Amelia. I'm here with Emily and our friend Jack. We're here to read to you today."

Lizzie glanced at Emily, but her gaze fell on Jack. Squinting at him, she simply commented, "I don't like him."

✳

Caleb had spent the day without much he could go on—he'd taken a few photos, but there was nothing remarkable. While they had left the premises, he'd rifled through their files and checked out the kitchen and other areas of the bed and breakfast. There were possibly a few minor code violations, but nothing major that he hadn't seen before at other establishments, all things that were easily rectifiable—though he was sure Adrien would use everything to his advantage and blow things out of proportion.

Adrien had access to the spy app Caleb had installed on both Jack and Amelia's phones, but what he didn't know was he didn't have *full* access. He knew where they were, yes, and he could access their texts, but he couldn't see them or hear them—that was a function Caleb didn't let Adrien know existed. Their conversations were still private—at least, when it came to Adrien. He hated the idea of Adrien listening in on the two whenever he pleased—it was intrusive, dirty, *wrong*.

They weren't, however, hidden from Caleb. He had that function on his own phone. With a press of a button, he could tap their phones and hear what they were saying. *He* would decide what he wanted to give or not give Adrien. If it was important, he'd record it and send it off—but only if it was *very* important, something along the lines of Jack plotting to overthrow Adrien from his position as head of Dunstan Enterprises. Everything else, well, Caleb didn't care.

He didn't like being in the business of destroying lives. He'd already destroyed his own unintentionally years ago, back when he and Adrien were legitimately friends. He'd been selfish, greedy, caught up in Adrien's ideas—and after it all, found himself stuck. His life was in shambles, and the only one who he could possibly relate to was Adrien. Adrien was the only one who still checked in on him from time to time, still cared—or at least, Adrien's version of caring.

For a while, Caleb still accepted Adrien when he would turn up. But the last few years, it had grown exhausting. The man who he had once considered to be his last friend in the world was using him, that much was obvious. He didn't treat him as his own person, but as the willing lackey he had once been. He hated it. He'd come to the conclusion he'd rather be alone in the world, left on his own in peace, than have to do Adrien's bidding again.

Adrien picked up on that. Well, maybe he didn't so much as pick up on it as Caleb shouted it at him the last time he saw him—the time before he turned up on his doorstep, asking to spy on Jack. That had been a huge blowout. Adrien had left him alone for a while after, to give him time to "cool down."

Caleb snorted, thinking back on it. Funny, how Adrien determined when Caleb was done "cooling down," and just showed back up again, asking for this last favor. He was always impertinent like that, narcissistic like that.

Well, maybe not *always*—but life had changed him. Caleb remembered when they were younger, it hadn't always been that way— they'd treated each other as equals, were on the same page, were genuinely friends—brothers, nearly. But things happened…and here they were.

Funny how people can change like that.

But this was the last time. This time he was certain. With the amount of money Adrien was offering, he'd had enough to disappear, to leave this life behind, to be out of Adrien's reach. He'd contemplated moving to Ireland. He'd visited there once before, loved the land, loved the people. He'd never told Adrien, so Adrien wouldn't know to go looking for him there. There he could live a simple life in peace, without the drama Adrien always brought with him.

But to get there, he had to do this job. He clicked on the app, activating the function that allowed him to listen in on Jack and Amelia's conversations. He'd clicked it on and off throughout his visit so far, but hadn't heard much—the one frustrating feature. If he wanted to hear something juicy, he'd have to click in at exactly the right moment, or keep it on all the time—which simply wasn't possible. So far, the texts hadn't revealed much, nor had the photos he'd taken.

He listened to the conversation—Amelia and Jack weren't alone, they were with Emily and…an elderly woman's voice. He sighed. They were visiting Amelia's grandmother. That wouldn't reveal much, the woman was demented. He felt slimy, listening in on a poor old woman's conversation with her granddaughters.

But then, he heard Amelia's voice crackle through, saying four simple words: "He's a *Guardian*, Grandma."

Caleb leaned in closer, his interest piqued. She was talking about Jack.

Lizzie retorted with the words, "So was the Fallen Sorcerer, and look what happened there."

Caleb was stunned, his heart racing as he listened to the rest of their conversation with Lizzie. The Fallen Sorcerer…Jack seeing magical creatures…a stone possibly found…magic seeping back into the world…

What did it mean? What did all of this mean? His mind was reeling.

He clicked the app off after Lizzie returned to her demented state, sitting alone in his room in silence, mulling over what he had just heard.

There was more here than he'd been seeing. He didn't know if he should turn this over to Adrien or not, but he had a feeling he'd have to. He'd have to be more proactive, follow them more carefully. He'd been reluctant, but now…now he had no choice to be more involved. He'd have to find out more, be sure before he turned anything over.

He hated being in the business of destroying lives. But this was the last time, and he'd be free of Adrien forever.

That in and of itself was worth a life or two.

✳ Chapter 34 ✳

The selkie

That evening, Jack, Amelia, Emily, and Caleb were gathered around the dining table at the Blue Barn, eating in complete silence. The sisters and Jack were mulling over what Lizzie had said about magic re-entering the world, but were unable to make sense of it, as it didn't line up with Jack's ability to summon creatures.

Caleb was also trying to make sense of this, but wasn't leading on he had overhead this strange conversation with his hosts. He'd nearly canceled having dinner at the Blue Barn that night, as he didn't even know what to make of it, and he couldn't outright ask. But he also knew he had to keep as close to Jack and the sisters as possible. And he desperately wanted Adrien off his case once and for all. So, he stuck with the original plan, having dinner with them, but the lack of conversation that evening did not reveal anything. He could see everyone was processing the conversation from earlier that day.

"Well, I'm going to do a bit of reading," Caleb said, breaking the silence at the end of the meal. "Emily, Amelia, thank you once again for a delightful dinner. Jack, good to see you again."

The three nodded, barely acknowledging Caleb. He turned and headed to his room, anticipating he'd have to turn on the app on his cell phone in order to listen in on their conversation.

When Caleb was out of earshot, Emily turned to Jack and Amelia. "Today was weird."

Jack and Amelia nodded their agreement.

"Do you think there's anything to what Grandma said?" Amelia asked.

"I mean…maybe?" Emily shrugged. "You even said things were weird with the leprechauns in Ireland, right?"

"Right," Amelia said, biting her lip.

"It could explain things," Jack said, chiming in.

"It could, but it doesn't explain *you*," Amelia pointed out. "You still don't make sense."

"I'm used to that," Jack joked, trying to lighten the mood. "Listen, you've told me magic doesn't always make sense, right?"

"Right."

"So, this is one of those cases. Maybe there isn't anything sinister going on with magic. Maybe it's just global warming or something."

"Your sudden magical capabilities are a result of global warming? Really? *That's* what you're going with?"

"I did say *or something*."

"But what's the 'or something?'"

"Amelia, you don't have to *always* be a journalist and find out all the answers. You can just leave things up to faith sometimes."

Amelia raised an eyebrow, but smiled. "Wonder where you learned that."

"I have a good teacher."

✳

Late that evening, after the dishes had been cleared, Emily meandered back to the cottage, needing alone time to collect her thoughts and process the conversation with Lizzie that day. While she did so, Jack and Amelia stayed behind in the sitting room of the Blue Barn, discussing that day's events in hushed tones. The sky outside was overcast as a storm formed in the distance, casting eerie shadows throughout the room. Jack would be staying the night again, upon Amelia's insistence.

"Do you think a stone has really been found?" Amelia asked, sipping on a cup of tea.

Jack shook his head. "I don't know. I mean, I know we'd discussed it before…but hearing your grandma say it makes it seem more plausible."

"But you still don't make sense," she insisted, repeating her thoughts from earlier.

"Amelia, I've *never* made sense," Jack laughed. "Not even to myself." He paused. "I'm looking forward to all of this being done."

"What, your job?"

"Yeah. I'm just…well, I'm tired of living two lives. I'm tired of pretending. It'll be good to have some simplicity in life, you know?"

"I know what you mean."

"What about the magazine? You staying with them or leaving? Your contract's coming to an end soon, right?"

"It is. I haven't decided yet."

"You said you guys are making a profit here, right?"

"We are."

396

"Then maybe…I don't know, stay. Settle down for a bit."

Amelia laughed. "Settling's never really been my thing."

"I'm just saying, if I'm going to be around—well, it'd be nice to have you around too. Your mom and Emily don't really like me."

"Emily's okay with you."

"Yeah, but just being okay with me still isn't great." He paused. "You're great."

Amelia blushed. "I'm not that special."

"Yes, you are."

As Amelia contemplated how to respond, she caught sight of a tiny light twinkling outside the window before she could even say anything—and it was glowing an ominous red, as if to signify an emergency.

It was Lila.

Jack, seeing Amelia looking over his shoulder toward the window, also turned his head. Seeing Lila's unusual color, he asked, "What's she doing?"

Amelia stood, slipping shoes onto her feet and heading towards the door. "She's trying to get our attention. Something's wrong."

When Amelia opened the front door, she saw Lila frantically whizzing about, gesturing wildly.

"Calm down! You're going too fast, I can't understand you."

The fairy returned to normal color, and catching her breath, made a simple motion.

Follow me.

"What's going on?"

Lila made a few motions again, and Amelia's eyes went wide.

"What's she saying?" Jack still wasn't fluent in the intricacies of conversing with a fairy.

"There's a selkie stranded on the beach. She's hurt. We need to help her before the storm rolls in," Amelia translated, throwing on her coat. Before she raced out the door, she had a thought, and grabbed a throw blanket from the sitting room as well—the selkie would probably need to shift into its human form in order for them to help her, meaning she would be nude and exposed to the elements and in need of something to keep her covered.

Jack grabbed his own jacket, and the two followed after the fairy, who led the way.

✳

Caleb wasn't able to pick up the entire conversation between Jack and Amelia, as he hadn't clicked the app on in time. He did, however, catch sight of them leaving the Blue Barn, rushing past the old willow tree, and heading towards the rocky beach when he glanced out his window overlooking the field and ocean. There was something urgent in the way they were moving, that Caleb knew he had to see what they were doing. Quickly, he grabbed his camera off his desk and clambered down the stairs of the bed and breakfast in his pursuit.

He followed Amelia and Jack to the beach, keeping himself a good distance back, concealed by the shadows of the cliffs and rocks. The light of the moon was his only guide, though even that was becoming unreliable, as clouds were rolling in, darkening the sky and warning of an impending storm. He could barely hear their conversation over the

398

crashing of the waves and the rumble of distant thunder, just making out garbled bits and pieces of Amelia talking:

"...migration pattern off...stranded...separated from pod...injured...back to house to recover..."

After several minutes, the pair stopped, and Caleb observed them hunching over what appeared to be a beached seal, though it was difficult to tell in the shadows. Using the night-vision telescopic lens on his camera, he snapped a few photos. He looked at his screen, reviewing the roll to make sure he had captured them.

Nothing interesting here. Jack's just forming his own little animal rescue squad.

He looked back up to continue watching the pair, and started. The seal was no longer there. Instead, Jack was carrying a girl, wet and shivering, and wrapped in the blanket Amelia had been carrying. Blood was dripping from one of the mysterious girl's legs.

His eyes had to be playing tricks on him. Perhaps there had never been a seal, but it had always been a girl? But who was she? And why was she on the beach so late at night, alone and bleeding? He snapped a few photos, his mind spinning.

As he reviewed the photos from where he was hidden behind his large rock, he noticed a strange little light in a few of them, hovering mainly over Amelia's shoulder. On his tiny screen, it looked a bit like a firefly. He glanced up, and sure enough, as Amelia and Jack walked, there was that same little light hovering around them.

Strange. Fireflies aren't typically out this time of year.

He went to snap another photo, not realizing that in the midst of reviewing his pictures, he had accidentally turned on his camera's flash. As soon as the photo snapped, light burst forth from the camera, and realizing what he had done, he dove behind the rock, holding his breath, waiting. Surely, they would discover him spying on them. There was no way they could have missed that.

Amelia and Jack had noticed the flash a little way down the beach, out of the corner of their eye, and stopped walking momentarily, turning in its direction—but, in that second, Caleb's saving grace appeared in the form of a lightning bolt, streaking through the sky, immediately followed by a crash of thunder. The storm was close now, almost upon them. They resumed their trek back to the house, quickening their pace, brushing off that first flash they saw as lightning as well.

When they were further up the beach, out of sight, Caleb sighed with relief. He emerged from his hiding place, and quickly worked his way through the shadows. He wasn't sure what to make of it all. Still, this was what he had been hired to do. It was a strange day indeed, between the conversation he'd overheard, the midnight rescue, the drenched girl, the disappearing seal, and the twinkling little light.

✳

"Set her here," Amelia ordered Jack, pointing at the couch as they burst in through the door.

Cosmo, who had been sleeping, stood upright. Upon seeing the girl in Jack's arms, he barked, both excited and confused by an unexpected guest this late in the evening.

"Cosmo, down!" Amelia commanded. The dog obeyed, laying back on his bed, but remaining watchful as the humans worked.

"What's going on?" Emily rubbed her eyes sleepily as she entered the living room, having been awoken by the clamor and Cosmo's barking.

Jack was setting the selkie gingerly on the couch, wrapped in the blanket, and Amelia was going about shutting all the blinds and curtains throughout the house to give them privacy, not wanting any guests to stroll by and see inside. Little did she know the good this would do, as Caleb had been planning to do just that. After making sure everything was shut, she went about rummaging through the cabinets for items to care for the selkie's wound.

Emily, seeing the commotion, suddenly noticed the naked, wet girl wrapped in a blanked on the couch, and started. "Who's she?"

"A selkie," Amelia answered, pulling out gauze, thread, and her healing potion. "Lila found her injured on the beach. Can you boil some water, please? And grab the first aid kit."

Emily nodded her compliance, and hurried into the kitchen. Turning to the damp, shivering creature, Amelia asked, "What's your name?"

The selkie remained silent, staring at her hostess suspiciously, still shivering.

"We won't hurt you," Amelia said gently. "We're all Guardians here. We're here to help."

"Aerwyna," the selkie quietly, finally. "My name is Aerwyna."

Amelia smiled. "It's nice to meet you, Aerwyna. I'm Amelia. The man who carried you is my friend, Jack, and the girl in the kitchen is my sister, Emily."

Jack nodded his greeting with a small smile, and turned his attention to the fireplace, working to build a fire to help warm the shivering girl.

"What happened to you, Aerwyna? Where's your pod?"

"I don't know," Aerwyna replied, tears streaming down her face. "I lost them in the storm. We were separated."

"I don't understand. Why were you even migrating this time of year? It's October. Selkies usually begin their migration in late August, in calmer, warmer waters."

"Global warming," Jack muttered.

Amelia shot him a glance, and Jack shut his mouth, turning back to the fire.

Aerwyna looked confused. "Is it really that late in the year?"

Amelia nodded, a look of concern crossing her face. "It is."

"It doesn't *feel* that late. It feels earlier," Aerwyna said, her voice almost trance-like.

"What do you mean?" Jack asked. It certainly felt much colder than August to him, if the frost on the ground that morning was any indication.

"There's this—I don't know what you call it—there's this *thing* inside selkies that tells us when it's time to migrate," Aerwyna tried to explain.

Amelia nodded her understanding. "Kind of like how birds know when it's time to migrate."

"Yes!" Aerwyna exclaimed.

"So why is your timing off?"

"I don't know." Aerwyna looked distressed. "I didn't know it was this late in the year until you told me. None in my pod did. We all felt the pull, as we always do, and went when we felt it."

"So, something is wrong with the source of the pull."

"I suppose it is," Aerwyna said, crestfallen.

At this point, Emily returned into the living room with the pot of boiled water, clean hand towels, and first aid kit, then headed to her bedroom to find some clothes for the young woman.

402

Amelia took one of the towels, and turning to Aerwyna, said, "This will probably hurt a bit."

Aerwyna nodded her consent, and Amelia began the business of cleaning the gash in the selkie's leg. The selkie winced, but remained otherwise composed. Once cleaned, Amelia applied the healing potion to it.

"This won't do as much as I'd like. It's not made with magic," Amelia said apologetically. "But it will at least keep the wound from becoming infected, and should heal it quicker. I'll have to stitch you up as well."

Again, the selkie nodded, and Amelia procured the suture tools from the first aid kit Emily had provided. The selkie bit her lip as Amelia worked, trying to keep her leg from moving, but having difficulty doing so because of the pain. Once done with the stitching, Amelia applied a bit more of the potion, then wrapped the girl's leg in gauze.

"I'd give it at least week before you transform and head back out," Amelia said, once finished. "You'll need time for the skin to regrow, and I'm not sure what transforming with stitches will do. But you should heal fairly quickly as long as you keep the wound clean."

"But I'm already behind!" Aerwyna said frantically.

"If your whole pod was late because you didn't feel the pull, chances are, most other pods didn't feel it and are late as well," Jack pointed out, attempting to reassure the selkie. "So technically, you'll be on time."

Aerwyna, not having thought about it this way before, seemed to relax.

"You can stay with us," Amelia said. "We have plenty of room, and are happy to have you."

"Thank you," Aerwyna replied, as Emily returned with some comfortable clothes for her to sleep in that evening.

403

And sleep they all did, once everyone was settled in. It had been a long, eventful day, full of unexpected surprises.

Back in his guest room in the Blue Barn though, Caleb could not sleep. He was flipping through the photos he had taken on the beach that evening, disturbed by what he saw as he zoomed in to try and decipher the details.

That little light by Amelia's shoulder looked strangely like it had a human form.

✳ Chapter 35 ✳

Truth

Caleb Ogden checked out earlier than anticipated, claiming he needed to be with his ill mother. In truth, it was a bit of a relief, as it was one less guest they had to hide Aerwyna from. Amelia and Emily had been passing her off as a cousin who came to visit to the guests at the Blue Barn, and so far, the story seemed to be believed by everyone.

Jack, meanwhile, was still leading his double life: when in the city, he played the part of the dutiful employee; in Calvary, he was Amelia and Emily's friend and pupil. More than that, he felt free.

But that same guilt still haunted him. He had finished going through all the files he'd retrieved from Adrien's computer, and it was a mess. The company was mismanaged and corrupt to the core. But yet, he knew there were still good people within it—people like Max and his team. He knew he had to act, and he knew he was days away from turning in the information—days away from his own freedom, his own chance at a new life. He would be doing more than existing like he had been doing under the watchful eye of Adrien Dunstan—he would be *living*.

Jack sat in May's Diner once again, contemplating this over a cup of coffee before heading to the Davidson place. Amelia had called the night before, letting him know the selkie would be ready to leave that day, and she wanted to say goodbye to all of them. He had gotten up early and driven to Calvary to say his farewells to the creature. But first, he'd needed coffee—and though May wasn't very good at sandwiches, and was mediocre at soups, she was great at coffee.

"You look like you've got the weight of the world on your shoulders," Jack heard a voice say from behind him as he sat sipping on the warm beverage.

Jack looked up and smiled. Charles had entered the diner for his own morning cup of coffee.

"Nothing May's coffee can't fix," Jack replied.

"Ain't that the truth?" Charles laughed, sitting in the booth across from Jack and motioning for his own cup. "What are you doing here so early?"

"Just getting a head start on some work," Jack answered vaguely.

"What work can you *possibly* still have in this town? The Benedicts sold their land. The Davidsons won't budge. And I heard the Kowalskis pulled, and the Ericksons are stalling."

Jack smiled. He'd given the Ericksons a call a few days prior, after the selkie event, feeling more strongly than ever he needed to do what he could to protect this place from Adrien's grasp. He hadn't even told Amelia or Emily he did so, but news, it seemed, traveled fast.

"That's the work," Jack said. "Can't lose all that land now, can we?"

Charles raised an eyebrow. "I don't believe for a *second* that's why you're here."

"You don't have to."

"There's something else going on with you, Garridan. I can't quite figure it out, but there is. I can feel it."

"Maybe." Jack shrugged.

"So why don't you tell me?"

406

Jack hesitated. Tell Charles about all he was torn over? About his feelings about Amelia? About magical creatures? About how he was considered to be an anomaly in the Guardian hierarchy? About his plan to hopefully drive Dunstan Enterprises out of the community? About his guilt over what that would do to the innocent workers within the company? About his guilt over what that would do to the innocent property owners if he *didn't* go through with it?

No. None of that would do. But he did need someone to talk to, someone unbiased, someone he trusted. And Charles was the closest thing he had to that.

"I sometimes feel like I don't know what's real and what's not anymore," Jack said, keeping it vague. "Since I started coming to Calvary, it's like I don't know what the truth is about my life and who I am."

"Well, were does your heart lie?" Charles prodded. "What drives you? What, to you, is unquestioningly right—even if *you* don't agree with it? And don't give me the answer you want me to hear."

Jack sat for a moment, pondering this. "I don't belong with Dunstan Enterprises. But for the moment, I do."

"Why?"

"Because I have business there I need to take care of that'll hopefully help people in the future."

"Good start. What else?"

"My whole life is what I want people to see, not what I really am."

"What are you?"

"Terrified."

"Of what?"

"Of being found out."

"What do you think people will find out?"

"That I'm a fraud."

"Why do you say you're a fraud?"

"I don't know. But I've always had this feeling I am. I've always been good at pretending."

"So, what are you really? Take away the pretending and all that, what's left? Who is Jack?"

"I don't know."

Charles smiled, sipping his cup of coffee. "Sometimes the truth is difficult. Truth isn't meant to be easy. But what's so beautiful about it is it's unabashedly real. It has no pretense. It has no ulterior motivations. It just is. It's beautiful in all its simplicity. The problem comes when people try to twist that truth for their own personal gain, and it's no longer truth, but becomes a lie—that's where most complications arise. But if everyone just stuck to the actual truth, the world would be a much simpler, and much better place."

"So, I need to find my truth?"

Charles shook his head. "No. That's the problem. Everyone has their own truth, but it's not necessarily the *real* truth. You need to figure out *the* truth, the hard facts, what actually is, not what you think it is. Perception clouds the truth."

"Do you know what the truth is?"

Charles smiled. "I'm working on it. Some people never find out, but my hope is to figure it out before my time on this planet comes to an end.

Here's what I can see: you're a good man, Jack. That much I can tell is true. You just don't know what that means for your life and what, as a good man, you need to do—because sometimes good doesn't always seem good in the moment, but when you look back on it, you know it was good and right. It's when you figure that part out you'll figure out what's true."

Jack sat in silence for a moment, contemplating this. "I think I know what I need to do, Charles."

"And what's that?"

"I can't tell you."

"Is it true and is it right?"

"Yes."

"Then do it."

✳

Jack, Amelia, and Emily saw the selkie off later that morning. It was a gray, hazy day, and the group walked to the beach together, Aerwyna stripping her clothes off as she dipped her toes into the surf. Jack, out of respect, turned away as she did so, but not before catching a glimpse of the scar that ran up her leg from the injury she'd sustained a few days prior. It had healed nicely, and Amelia was able to remove the stiches the day before.

A moment later, he felt Amelia's hand on his shoulder, as she murmured, "You can look again."

He turned, seeing Aerwyna now in her seal form. She turned back to the group to look at them one more time before diving out to sea. The group on shore stood in place until she disappeared from sight. In the distance, they heard an ancient melody carried over the wind and the waves—the voices of dozens of selkies, singing as they swam. Aerwyna was back with her people.

The group walked solemnly up the beach, feeling an emptiness. The selkie leaving was another reminder that soon, the last wave of fairies would also be leaving. It was a sobering moment. Magic seemed to be drifting from this place.

"Are you going to stay for lunch?" Amelia asked Jack as the three walked, breaking the silence that had fallen over them.

"Sure." He paused. "I might say here overnight, if you're okay with that. How full are you?"

Amelia smiled. "Your room isn't booked, if that's what you're asking."

Jack smiled in return. "That's what I'm asking."

✳

Jack returned to his usual guest room to unload the overnight bag he'd come to always have on hand nowadays, shutting the door behind him. As he looked around the room, he smiled—it had grown on him (especially since Amelia had listened to his request to replace the twin-size bed with at least a twin extra-long, arguing it would be more accommodating to a wider variety of guests). Having spent an average of at least three days each week in Calvary for the past several months, he was starting to regard the small town as a second home, feeling like he belonged here even more than he did in his apartment in the city—the people here were more genuine, the relationships deeper, the landscape more pristine, the way of life slower, simpler.

Still, even with all of this, even knowing this was a place he wanted to preserve, even after the conversation he'd had with Charles, he was having his doubts. Yes, he had the statement showing the payoff of William Foster, with the recorded conversation from Foster himself. He had the recorded conversation with Adrien at the party, which was at times,

410

admittedly, a bit difficult to hear given the surroundings at the time, but the important elements were there. Finally, most importantly, he had the documents on the flash drive he'd managed to acquire only with the help of Lila, proving Adrien was paying off not just Foster, but others like him up and down the coast, and he was aware of the issues with the builds, but was doing nothing to rectify the situations.

But even with all this, he knew once it was turned in, once he became a "whistle-blower," there was no going back. Yes, guilty people would lose their jobs, and rightfully so, but innocent people would also be caught in the cross-fire, their lives put into a state of upheaval.

He sighed, sitting on the bed, opening the phone again and playing the recording with Foster. Clear as a bell, he heard his own voice ring out through the room, with Foster's following after...

"Well, I'm having a bit of difficulty acquiring the Davidson land. You see, Amelia and Emily Davidson refuse to sell."

A chuckle from Foster. *"Doesn't surprise me. That whole damn family is stubborn."*

"Yes, well, I'm wondering if you might be able to offer me any...assistance."

"Assistance? How so?"

"Well, Will, you're respected and trusted in the community. A good word from you, or a push in the right direction might help steer things along."

"I don't think so, Jack. That's not exactly my area."

"That's not my understanding."

Jack clicked the recording off, frustrated, resolved. He knew what came next—he had it memorized by now, he'd listened to it so many times.

Next, Foster would hint he wanted more. Jack felt sick, nauseous even, that two people, William Foster and Adrien Dunstan, were manipulating the lives of the entire population of Calvary—and for what? A few extra bucks in each of their pockets?

It wasn't right. He had to press forward. He'd made Amelia a promise he'd help save her land, and this was how it had to be done. He hated others would get caught up in it, but there was nothing he could do about that. He had to follow through.

✳

Emily, meanwhile, had gone upstairs to Jack's guest room, as Amelia had asked her to let him know lunch was almost ready while she put the finishing touches on it. It would be just the three of them dining together that afternoon in the house—the guests that were staying at the Blue Barn had opted to try out one of the seafood restaurants in town.

She disliked Jack less, though she wouldn't admit that to Amelia. She wouldn't exactly say she *liked* him, but since he'd become something of a regular on the Davidson property, he wasn't as aggravating. It was good to have someone around to talk to about magic aside from her sister, and it was nice he was close in age to them, being slightly older than Amelia. She wouldn't say he was her friend—he was more of Amelia's friend—but he wasn't terrible company. Slowly, she was beginning to trust him, especially after the situation with the selkie—he was good, she could tell. Obnoxious sometimes, and occasionally pushy, but overall good.

She stood outside of Jack's door, ready to knock to let him know lunch was almost ready, when she heard his voice through the door…

"… I'm having a bit of difficulty acquiring the Davidson land. You see, Amelia and Emily Davidson refuse to sell."

She heard a man laugh. "Doesn't surprise me. That whole damn family is stubborn."

Jack was talking to the man on speakerphone, and she knew that voice. That was William Foster's voice. He'd been a regular at the fish market back when her grandfather owned it. Why was Jack on the phone with William Foster? She leaned in, pressing her ear against the door to listen to more of the conversation.

Jack continued, "Yes, well, I'm wondering if you might be able to offer me any…assistance."

"Assistance? How so?" Foster asked.

"Well, Will, you're respected and trusted in the community. A good word from you, or a push in the right direction might help steer things along."

"I don't think so, Jack. That's not exactly my area."

"That's not my understanding."

Emily had heard enough. She turned her back on the door, walking briskly back down the hallway, not even knocking to make him aware of her presence or let him know lunch would be ready soon. She didn't care. She'd overhead him trying to talk William Foster, a pillar in the community, into helping him acquire *her* land.

Her gut had been right the whole while. She knew they couldn't trust Jack. He'd been undermining them the entire time, leading them on, pretending to be friendly—but in reality, he'd been working their weaknesses, trying to figure out a way to get their land from under them.

She didn't care if he was a Guardian or not, if he could see magical creatures—*he wasn't good*. And they'd been teaching him all about magic. It made her sick.

She had to warn Amelia.

✳

"We need to talk," Emily hissed, entering the dining room of the cottage, where Amelia was setting the table.

"Sure, what's up?" Amelia replied, setting down plates.

"Can you stop for a second?" Emily asked urgently. "I need to talk to you before *he* comes down."

"Who, Jack?"

"*Yes.*"

Amelia looked her sister up and down, noticing the tenseness. "Em, what's going on?"

Emily took a deep breath. "I heard him on the phone with William Foster. When I went to get him for lunch, I heard him talking on the phone…Amelia, he tried to talk Will into helping acquire our land! He's been sneaking around behind our backs and lying to us this whole time!"

"Well, that's ridiculous," Amelia scoffed. "Just the other week he talked Ruth Kowalski *out* of signing her land over. Are you sure you heard him correctly?"

"I…I don't know." Emily was suddenly doubtful.

"Listen, don't go making accusations before you know the truth. Jack's on our side."

"Are *you* sure about that?"

"I am," Amelia said confidently. "And it's rude to eavesdrop on people's conversations, Emily. Especially if you don't have the whole story. I'm sure Jack was just doing what he needed to do to help us."

"Yeah, well, it sounded pretty sketchy to me," Emily retorted.

"*Everything* is sketchy to you." Amelia rolled her eyes. "Have a little faith in humanity for once, huh? Now, enough of this. Can you please finish setting the table while I check on the food?"

"Yeah, sure." Emily was sullen, defeated as Amelia retreated into the kitchen to finish the meal. Her sister didn't believe her. It was a lost cause—Amelia was clearly on Jack's side and would stand by him no matter what Emily had to say.

In that moment, Jack entered the dining room. "Something smells good," he commented, a smile crossing his face.

Emily grunted in reply, not looking up from the fork she was holding.

"Amelia in the kitchen?" he asked, ignoring her grunt.

"Yes."

"Can I help with anything?"

Emily snapped her head up sharply, glaring at him.

"I don't like you," Emily said sharply. "I don't know what your game is, but I don't like it, and I don't like *you*."

Jack faltered back a step, confused by the young woman's sudden change in demeanor. She'd been perfectly fine when they saw the selkie off together merely a half hour ago.

"Where is this coming from?"

"Doesn't matter. But I don't like *you*."

"That's fine," Jack replied, aggravated by this childish response and lack of explanation. "I don't much like you much either all the time."

"*Excuse me?*"

"You heard me. You're obnoxious and petty and immature and rude, and you need a serious attitude adjustment." Emily opened her mouth to protest, but before she could, Jack continued, "But there's no game, or whatever you think is happening here. You don't have to believe me. I wouldn't trust me either if I were in your shoes. But I hope someday you will. Because frankly, you and your sister are the closest thing I've ever had to family, as weird as that is. And I'm working every day to prove you wrong, and I don't know why you can't see that."

Emily stood silently, glowering at him, unable to come up with any kind of response.

Before either of them could say anything else, Amelia entered the room, carrying a bowl of fruit and a plate of hot sandwiches, each precariously balanced in her hands. Jack, seeing her full hands, crossed the room to help her, grabbing the fruit so she could put both hands on the sandwich platter.

"Thanks." She set the tray down, and looking up, and saw the dour looks on both Jack's and Emily's faces. "Everything okay here?"

"Just fine," Emily snapped. Without another word, she stomped past Amelia and Jack, making her way to the Blue Barn.

"Aren't you hungry?" Amelia called out as Emily went to exit, bewildered by this mood shift in her sister.

"NO!"

SLAM.

Both Amelia and Jack flinched as the door swung shut behind Emily. Amelia, confused, turned to Jack. "What was *that* about?"

"She doesn't like me."

416

"Well, I knew *that* already." Amelia rolled her eyes. "But did you say anything *specifically* to piss her off?"

Jack hesitated.

"Jack?"

"I…may have said she was obnoxious and petty and immature and rude, and that she needed an attitude adjustment."

"*Seriously*, Garridan? She's going to be in a mood for *days* now!" Amelia groaned, slumping into one of the dining table chairs.

Jack internally debated if he should tell her the next part of the conversation. But, seeing the look on Amelia's face, he decided he needed to, and sat next to her. "I also told her the two of you were the closest thing I've ever had to family, and that I hope she'd trust me someday."

Amelia blinked, taken aback. She hadn't even considered this possibility, but it made sense, now that she was confronted with it, and given the amount of time they'd been spending together. She knew Jack's background, and knew he longed to belong somewhere and to someone, but it didn't register with her until this moment he might have become attached to the sisters.

"That's…wow. That's sweet, Jack."

Jack shrugged. "It's true."

"And you told her that?"

"Yes."

"Right after insulting her?"

"Yes."

"Well, that explains the wild mood swing. You broke her."

"Yeah?"

"Yeah...Emily's kind of like an overgrown fairy: not very good at processing more than one emotion at a time."

Jack smiled. "That's the best description I've ever heard of your sister."

Amelia returned the smile, and placed her hand on top of his. "Give her time. She's a hard sell. But she always comes around eventually."

Jack nodded. "Hey, Amelia?"

"Yeah?"

"Thank you."

"For what?"

"For everything."

Amelia smiled, the blood rushing to her face as she did so. "You're welcome." She paused. "Jack...I need to ask you something."

"Anything."

"Emily said she overhead you on the phone with Will Foster just a few minutes ago...that it sounded like you were trying to talk him into helping us get our land. I know that's not the truth, but for my own peace of mind, what was that about?"

"She heard that?"

Amelia nodded.

"No wonder she was so upset," he said, running his fingers through his hair. "That wasn't a phone call. That was a recording."

"A recording?"

"Yeah. I did have a conversation with him…and I did make it sound like I was bribing him. But it's not what you think. I was trying to get him to admit he'd already been bribed by Dunstan Enterprises."

"Will Foster was bribed by your company?" She was astounded.

"Seems that way. Seems like Adrien's been doing a lot of shady deals like that. Amelia, if Foster was never bribed, this project never would've been pushed through—there was too much public opposition to it. He's basically the reason it happened."

"Will Foster…Jesus. I can't believe he'd sell out like that. He never seemed the type."

"Everyone has their price," Jack said cynically.

"So that recording…what are you going to do?"

Jack sighed. "I'm trying to figure it out. I know I need to turn this and the rest of the evidence I have into the authorities, because I know plenty of people like you are being impacted by Adrien's deals. But I also know a lot of innocent people in my company will be laid off when all this goes down."

"That's a tough call." She didn't envy Jack's position.

"What would you do?" Jack asked, looking up at her.

"I'm biased, Jack. You know what I'd do."

Jack nodded. He did know.

"You'll figure it out though. I think you already know."

"Yeah," Jack said distantly. "You're right."

Amelia felt fairly satisfied with this conversation and Jack's explanation, knowing Jack hadn't *really* been bribing William Foster.

Still, why did she feel that nagging doubt again?

✳

A little while later, after Amelia and Jack had eaten and Jack returned to his guest room, Emily came stomping back into the house, heading straight for her bedroom. Amelia took this opportunity to follow her, intending to tell her about the conversation she'd had with Jack about the recording, hoping to help clear up the misunderstanding.

"Hey, we need to talk about that conversation you had with Jack." Amelia leaned against the doorframe of Emily's room, arms crossed.

Emily rolled her eyes, slumping onto her bed. "What about it?"

"You snapping on him like that…that wasn't cool."

"Yeah, well, I don't trust him."

"Listen, you misunderstood what you heard. He was listening to a recording. He wasn't on the phone. That was him trying to collect evidence to use."

"And you believe that?"

"I do."

"Well, I *don't*."

"Yeah, well, you're going to need to get over that, kid. He's sticking around. We already offered him a job, remember?"

"And that's another thing—you need to *stop* calling me 'kid.' I'm not a kid anymore, Amelia. I've got a master's degree. I own a business with you. I pay bills. I'm an *adult*."

"And yet you still have temper tantrums and storm off into your bedroom like a teenager," Amelia commented dryly. "Start acting like an adult and I'll start treating you like one."

Emily glared at her sister, fuming. "This coming from the girl who doesn't have a grip on reality and needs to jet off around the world to escape her problems."

"I jet off around the world because it's my *job*, not to escape anything. It's part of what brings in money for *us*," Amelia snapped. "And I have a grip on reality, a little more than you do. At least I know what's going on outside this town! You can barely get beyond your own head!"

"Shut up," Emily said in a low growl.

"Does this have anything to do with Dan?" Amelia asked, referring to Emily's ex-boyfriend. "He broke your trust, so now you won't trust any man?"

"I said *shut up*," Emily said, louder.

"Listen, I know he broke your heart—but that doesn't mean every guy out there is bad," Amelia pressed, ignoring her sister's warnings. "Jack's good. I know it. Dan was a jerk who didn't deserve you, and I know it sucks, but what happened is for the best. It's been *months*. It's time to get over it and move on."

"SHUT UP!" Emily finally yelled, loud enough even Cosmo jumped from his position laying at her feet and dashed out of the room, not

421

wanting to be anywhere near the loud noises. "GET OUT OF MY ROOM! NOW!"

Amelia took a step back, not expecting her sister to explode like this. Before she could say anything, Emily stood and physically pushed Amelia out, slamming and locking the door behind her. Behind the closed door, Amelia could hear her sobbing. Amelia sighed heavily, leaning against the wall. Cosmo, meanwhile, had returned, and sat at Amelia's feet, a sympathetic look on his face. He nuzzled at her leg, demanding to be pet.

"You're lucky you're a dog," Amelia said, acquiescing to his demands. "You don't have to deal any drama. All you do is eat, sleep, play, and poop, and everyone still loves you. Must be nice."

Cosmo simply wagged his tail as he looked up at her.

"You don't have any idea what I'm saying, do you?"

He continued to wag his tail.

"You just want to play catch, don't you?"

At the word "catch," he sprung to his feet, his whole body waggling in excitement. Quickly, he skittered into the other room, returning a moment later with his favorite ball in his mouth, looking up at her in anticipation. Amelia smiled.

"Okay, buddy. Let's play. I could use a breather anyway."

✳ Chapter 36 ✳

A bad day

A drien sat at his desk in his office in the skyscraper, examining the images Caleb had e-mailed.

The first few pictures were a bit uninteresting: photos of Jack sitting at dinner with the sisters, drinking wine. Photos of the grounds, rooms, kitchen, and other work areas. Photos of the licenses and legal documents for the Blue Barn. Adrien made a mental note to himself that he didn't see an alcohol license among those documents, yet he did see Jack, supposedly a guest at the facility, drinking. He might be able to use that to his advantage.

He continued to click through. The next few photos were difficult to make out, due to it having been dark and stormy when they were taken, but he was able to see the outlines of Jack and Amelia, walking along the beach toward a dark, hunched over shape in the distance. The next photo was a bit clearer, as the moon had broken through the clouds, giving Caleb a bit more light to work with momentarily. Zooming in on the picture, Adrien could clearly see the dark shape was a seal—there was no question about it.

Really, Jack? Risking your career to save some stupid seal?

The next photo, however, gave Adrien a start. The seal was gone, nowhere to be seen—it was as if it had vanished into thin air. Instead, Jack and Amelia were facing the camera, walking back up the beach, and wrapped in a wool blanked in Jack's arms was a young girl. She was soaking wet, and looked as though she was maybe in her early twenties, with big, doe eyes, and a large, bloody gash on her leg. Not a whisker grew from her pale face, and far from blubbery, she was toned and slim.

Adrien flipped between the two photos, at a loss for words. There was no way he could have mistaken the seal in the former photo for the girl in the latter. Perhaps the seal dove back into the sea? Perhaps the girl was always there, just off-camera, hidden in the shadows until now?

Unless, of course, the girl was the seal.

At this thought, something stirred inside Adrien that had been dormant for a very long time.

He continued to look through the remaining images, beads of sweat now forming on his forehead. There, in the last few photos, a little glowing light, hovering between Jack and Amelia. His gut told him this spot was not a blemish on the lens or a trick of the light. He zoomed in to the point where the photo was pixilated, but even in its grainy state, Adrien could make out a human-like, feminine figure in the middle of the glow.

A fairy.

He was looking at photographic proof of the existence of magical creatures. As this realization dawned on him, a flood of emotions washed over him: joy, excitement, anger, sadness, and relief all at once. Half laughing, half crying, Adrien sat back in his chair, his head in his hands.

This changed everything. He picked up his phone, dialing Caleb's number. After what felt like an eternity on Adrien's end, Caleb finally picked up.

"So you saw the pictures," Caleb said gruffly, not even greeting Adrien with a simple "hello." He'd anticipated this call. He wanted to get it over with.

"I did. They were very interesting." Adrien sat back in his chair. "Tell me—what did *you* see? While you were there, that is? What was it like in

424

person? It's hard to tell by pictures alone, if I'm really seeing what I think I'm seeing."

Silence on the other end.

"Caleb?"

Finally, "I don't know what I saw."

Adrien expected as much. Caleb had spent his entire life trying to move on from the past. But Adrien wouldn't—he *couldn't*. Not after he'd come this far.

"Caleb," he urged. "Tell me what you saw."

"What do *you* see in the pictures?" Caleb asked, turning the tables.

"You know what I see."

"That's what I saw."

"I need you to say it out loud."

"I can't do that for you."

"Caleb."

"Listen, I'll tell you this much—the place *felt* like how it used to feel, you know? That warmth, like energy or electricity pulsing through you. It felt like that. It felt good. It felt comfortable."

"I remember. But what did you *see*?"

"Look at the damn pictures."

"Caleb, I need you to confirm it. *I need to know*."

"You promised this was it. After this, you'd leave me alone forever. I did my part. I did what you asked. Now it's time to uphold your end."

Adrien sighed. Caleb wasn't going to be cooperative anymore.

"Adrien?"

"Yes?"

"What are you going to do?"

The corner of Adrien's mouth curled up in wry, sadistic smile. "Like you said, Caleb: you did your part. I'll leave you alone now. What I do from here on out doesn't concern you."

With this, Adrien hung up the phone, cutting off the last tie to his past he had. It was a pity. He'd grown fond of Caleb over the years, even if Caleb didn't share the same sentiment for him.

He needed to make a trip out to Calvary. He needed to see the Blue Barn in person, see the land, and he needed to make sure Jack wouldn't be there, or anyone other guests, for that matter. The Davidson sisters might complicate his investigation, considering they lived there, but that's what his hired men were for. If needed, they'd be able to take care of that part.

He dialed his secretary's extension. "Stephanie?"

"Yes, Mr. Dunstan."

"Get the Department of Health and Human Services on the phone. I need to speak with them."

"Yes, Mr. Dunstan."

He hung up, pondering his next moves. He needed to confirm his suspicions. The Department of Health and Human Services would give him the opening he needed to step foot on the land without being noticed by other people. And if the Davidson sisters jumped to the conclusions Adrien was banking on them jumping to, it would clear Jack off the land as well.

His line rang. "This is Adrien Dunstan. Thank you for speaking with me. I need to tell you some concerns I have about a relatively new bed and breakfast that's been established in Calvary, the Blue Barn. I'm afraid they may be in violation of a few food and alcohol codes, and I wanted to bring it to your attention. I have photographic evidence, I can send it to you right now. Is it possible for this to remain anonymous? Good."

✳

A few days had passed since Amelia and Emily's argument. Emily's anger had died down, and girls were now in full swing of planning and preparation for the Thanksgiving rush. They were completely booked for the holiday weekend, and had planned a traditional New England Thanksgiving feast for their guests. Jack had offered to lend a hand, picking up groceries, decorations, and other items needed for the celebration, just a week and a half away now.

Emily felt foolish about her outburst that day, once again seeing how helpful Jack was around the bed and breakfast. She had to admit, he would be a good addition to the team. She felt silly for doubting him. *Of course* it was a recording. *Of course* he was trying to help them. What disturbed her though, was the thought someone she'd known for years, who was in a position of authority, would sell out the town like that. It was hard to believe William Foster, the kind, friendly patron of the fish market she remembered so well, would do something like that.

She was mulling over this prospect as she unloaded a case of wine into the refrigerator, anticipating their alcohol license would be in by the time Thanksgiving rolled around. She'd applied for it a few weeks ago, and hadn't heard anything yet. As she put the bottles into the fridge, she felt her cell phone ring in her back jean pocket. She pulled it out and answered, not even looking at the number on the screen as she did so, tied up in her work.

She would come to regret that action.

"This is Emily," she chirped into the phone.

"Hey, Emily, it's Dan."

Emily felt as though her heart had stopped. It had been months since she'd heard his voice, and all the emotions from that period of her life came flooding back—the anger, the sadness, the betrayal, the fear, the disappointment.

"What do you want?" she asked coolly.

"I wanted to let you know something before you heard it from anyone else or saw it online…Leslie and I are engaged. We're getting married in June."

This time, Emily was convinced her heart legitimately *did* stop. She knew they had been serious about each other, they shared some kind of love between each other, but she was *sure* they would eventually part ways…until this very moment.

"Emily? Are you there?"

"Why are you telling me this?"

"I just…I don't know. I figured it'd be better if you heard it from me directly instead of finding out secondhand. After everything, I guess I owed you that much."

"You don't owe me anything," she said stiffly. "I don't *want* anything else from you. *Ever.*"

"I know," he sighed into the phone. "Listen…I'm just…well, I'm sorry about the way things ended between us. I'm sorry we left it that way."

"No, you're not," Emily replied bluntly. "You've got what you want. You've got your perfect little life and soon you'll have your perfect little wife."

"*Jesus*, Emily, I'm trying to be civil here."

"I don't *need* your civility. I don't *want* your civility. I told you, I don't want anything from you *ever*. Have a nice life. Lose my number or something, okay?"

With this, she hung up. Momentarily, she wished he had called her on the house's landline, rather than on her cell phone. The click of the "end" button wasn't as satisfying as slamming down a receiver, but still, it would have to do. She'd made her point. Hopefully he'd take it.

Why wasn't she free from him? Why couldn't he leave her alone to live her life in peace? Why the *hell* did he get to be so happy in his life, after he'd *cheated* on her, and she, who hadn't done anything wrong, have to be so miserable, floundering in every area—socially, romantically, financially? It wasn't fair. She hated it. She hated *him*.

From the other room, she heard Jack and Amelia laughing. She rolled her eyes. There was the next bane of her existence in formation. She was convinced it was just a matter of time before something romantic happened between those two. It irked her, for two reasons: first, she still didn't trust Jack much, and thought Amelia could do much better than him; second, if something *did* form between the two of them, she would be the third wheel again, the outcast…she already felt that way. Not that she'd dare vocalize that to Amelia. She'd just say Emily was being silly, she was reading into things too much, she'd *never* be the third wheel, blah, blah, blah.

It sickened her sometimes how sweet her sister was. It also made her jealous. Maybe if she was more like Amelia…

429

No. Enough with this. I need to get some air.

Stepping outside, she saw the mail truck pulling up. A welcome distraction.

"Hey, John, how are you?" she called out, walking down the dusty driveway.

John was an older gentleman, and had been Calvary's mailman since before Emily was born. Emily always enjoyed it when she ran into him, as he was always in good spirits. Occasionally, he spewed some anti-establishment conspiracy nonsense, which Emily found amusing and ironic, considering he worked for the postal service, a government establishment. Once, she had pointed this out to him, and he simply replied, "Darling, I'm working it from the inside." She didn't know what he meant by that, and didn't ask him to elaborate, though she was pretty sure he was saying that just to mess with her.

"Hey, Emily!" John returned her greeting. "Pretty good, how are you doing?"

"Been worse, I guess."

He laughed. "I hear that."

"Anything interesting today?" She peeked over his shoulder at his mailbag.

John rifled through the bag, procuring a small stack of envelopes, which he quickly flipped through for her. "Junk mail...bills...oh, hey, here's something from the government for you." Emily couldn't help but notice the look of disdain on his face as he handed it over, the word "government" dripping from his tongue like it was a filthy word.

Emily took the stack from him, examining the envelope of interest. "Must be our liquor license. I've been waiting for that."

"I thought you already had one?"

"Not yet."

"You haven't been giving any guests alcohol or anything, have you?"

"No—well, sort of, but he's also kind of a friend of Amelia's, and we don't charge him for it…and we're hiring him as an employee by the end of the year, so it doesn't really count," Emily replied, remembering that night so many months ago when Jack's car had broken down—the night he found out about fairies, and the morning after, where he'd accused Amelia of slipping something into his food or drink.

"You should be more careful about that sort of thing, Em. Government finds out, you could be shut down. They're black and white like that."

She snorted. "Okay, John, thanks for today's conspiracy theory."

"I'm serious, girl—I'd hate to see you down on your luck, after all you girls have done to try and build this place up. Your grandparents would be proud of you—don't let them down by doing something so stupid and petty as serving alcohol without a license."

"I hear you, John. Thanks for the concern. I appreciate it."

"Anytime. You take care now."

"I will, thanks," Emily said, waving as she strolled back up the driveway toward the cottage.

Walking into the house, she set the stack of envelopes on the end table at the entryway, with the exception of one she assumed to be her liquor license. Opening it, the first thing she saw was the words _CEASE AND DESIST_ in big, bold, red letters.

431

This time, she felt her heart racing instead of stopping. Reading on, she felt blood rushing to her cheeks as every emotion she could possibly feel coursed through her body. Quickly, she picked up the landline next to the front door, and dialed the number at the bottom of the letter.

"Department of Health and Human Services, this is Gertrude," a woman with a dreary voice answered on the other end.

"Hi, Gertrude, my name is Emily Davidson, and I just received a cease and desist letter," Emily said, doing her best to remain calm. There had to be some kind of mistake.

"What's your property?"

"The Blue Barn Bed and Breakfast in Calvary. I'm a bit confused by the letter. I think there's been a mistake."

Emily heard typing on the other end of the line. "No, no mistake. We had an anonymous complaint. You're shut down until we can get a health inspector out there to check the place."

"Who complained?" Emily demanded, losing her patience.

"It's *anonymous*," Gertrude said snidely. Emily could almost feel the bureaucrat rolling her eyes through the phone. "I can't tell you that."

"Okay, well, when can the inspector come out so they can *see* a mistake has been made and we can open up again?" Emily asked through gritted teeth.

More clicking on the keyboard. "Next available slot I have is three weeks from today at four in the afternoon."

"*Three weeks?!* But we have a Thanksgiving feast planned for our guests!"

432

"Honey, that's not going to happen," Gertrude said, uncaring. "Either take it or leave it."

"Obviously I'll take it," Emily spat. "How long will it take for our license to be un-suspended after the inspection?"

"Could be up to thirty days."

Emily had an inkling it would be *exactly* thirty days, given Gertrude's attitude.

"That means we could miss our Christmas crowd too." Emily attempted to do the math in her head for the amount of money they'd be losing out on. It was too much.

"Could be," Gertrude said nonchalantly. "I've got you down for three weeks from today. Can I help with anything else?"

"No, that will be it."

She slammed the receiver, feeling a fleeting moment of pleasure that she had chosen the landline for this particular phone call. It *was* much more satisfying hanging up on someone that way.

Picking up the letter, she stormed into her grandfather's old study, where Jack and Amelia were pouring over old journals.

"WAS THIS YOU?!" Emily demanded furiously, slapping the piece of paper in front of Jack.

"What is it?" Jack picked up the document to examine it.

"It's a cease and desist," Emily grunted. "The Blue Barn is being shut down until further notice."

"What? Why?" Amelia snapped the paper from Jack's hands.

"Improper food storage and handling, apparently," Emily answered, fuming. "Unsanitary conditions. Along with serving alcohol without a license."

John's warning, it seemed, had been prophetic.

"What? That's ridiculous! We read the state code backwards and forwards and followed it to the letter," Amelia argued, in disbelief.

"Yes, well, *someone* sent in an anonymous complaint, it seems, and claims we're not doing things the right way."

"And you seriously think it's me?" Jack said, offended by the accusation.

"First of all, you are the *only* person we have ever served alcohol, so yeah, I kind of think it's you. Second, the offenses go pretty in depth, right down to describing the layout of the kitchen. And no one else, but the three of us, has spent enough time in our kitchen to know this kind of detail," Emily countered.

"What about your mom?"

"Seriously? Our *mom*?" Emily asked, hysterical now. "You think our *mom* reported us for food and alcohol violations? Don't be stupid! She helped us *build* this place! If she *did* notice anything, she would've told us so we could *fix* it, not report it and shut us down!"

"Okay, let's calm down." Amelia stepped between Jack and Emily. "We know there's nothing wrong with the Blue Barn. So, we just shut down for a few days until the health inspector comes around. He'll see there's been a mistake, and we'll be back up and running in no time. Simple."

"Three weeks," Emily said bitterly.

Amelia blinked. "What?"

"*Three. Weeks*. I already called. That's the earliest an inspector can come out to check the place. And it could take another thirty days after that for them to un-suspend our license, *if* we pass."

"But…but our Thanksgiving rush is in ten days," Amelia sputtered.

"I'm aware."

"And if it takes thirty days to get the all clear…we might not be back up in time for Christmas."

"I'm also aware of that. *Someone* is trying to sabotage us." With this, she turned to glare at Jack.

"I'm telling you, it's *not me*," he said defensively.

"You were after our property for *months*. I *knew* this was some kind of ploy of yours!"

"I promised I'd *stop* trying to buy your property! And I did! I haven't done a thing in *months*!"

"Yeah. You stopped trying to *buy* it. Now you're just trying to *take* it from us!"

"*I. Didn't. Do it*." Jack was seething by this point. He whirled around to face Amelia. "You believe me, don't you?"

"I…I don't know, Jack." Amelia didn't meet his gaze, still looking at the cease and desist letter, absently twirling her necklace in her fingers as she tried to process all of this. Memories of their early relationship swirled through her head, the anger, the spite, the distrust. She found herself looking back on Emily's outburst about the so-called recording from a few days previous, and was having her doubts. What if it wasn't a recording? What if it *had* been a call? What if he had been trying to acquire their land the whole time, right under their noses?

435

"This letter…it's detailed," she continued, her voice wavering. "It's got things in it someone wouldn't know unless they've spent a significant amount of time with us. And that alcohol thing…I just don't know."

"Amelia, come on. You don't really think I did this, do you? After everything?" he asked helplessly.

"I think…I think you shouldn't come around here for a while, Jack. Until things are straightened out," she answered, avoiding looking him in the eye.

Jack felt as though he'd been slapped in the face. "Fine. If that's what you want."

"It is," Emily snapped. Amelia remained silent, still staring at the letter.

Without another word, Jack grabbed his jacket and exited the cottage. He had an inkling he knew who was behind all of this.

It was time to confront Adrien. And it was time to follow through on his plan.

✷ Chapter 37 ✷

A friend

As Jack made the trek into the city, he made his calls and sent his files over his phone—the Federal Trade Commission, the Better Business Bureau, the state's attorney general…anyone who'd listen, anyone who could investigate, anyone who could hold Dunstan Enterprises accountable, he contacted. He'd had everything prepped for weeks now, waiting in his drafts, and he'd been sitting on the information for long enough. And he wouldn't be anonymous about it—he wanted Adrien to know who was bringing him down.

After what seemed like a never-ending drive from Calvary, Jack finally swerved to the front of the building, and put on his hazards. He wouldn't be here long. He entered, stormed through the lobby, and rode the elevator up to the floor that contained Adrien Dunstan's office.

Stephanie, Adrien's secretary was already there, waiting for him.

"Jack! What are you doing here?" she hissed.

Authorities had already been in touch. In the couple hours it took for Jack to get from Calvary to Boston, the company was already under investigation. Jack smiled wryly. Sometimes—rarely, but sometimes—it seemed bureaucrats could act quickly when they wanted to.

"I'm here to see Adrien," Jack replied shortly, moving towards his office, Stephanie walking briskly at his side.

"Jack, what's going on?" she asked pitifully. "Why did you do it?"

"Because it's what's right," Jack growled. He continued, "Get out of here. You're too smart. You can do better. Trust me. Get out while you still have some integrity intact."

Without even letting her reply, he entered Adrien's office, slamming the door behind him, a bewildered assistant left in his wake.

"So kind of you to grace us with your presence, Mr. Garridan," Adrien said coolly as he looked over some documents before him, not even flinching as the door slammed and he was faced by his estranged employee.

"What did you do?" Jack demanded, ignoring Adrien's comment. "And how did you do it?"

"Seems I should be asking you that question, Jack." Adrien looked up. "We've heard from a few agencies. Seems we're being accused of misconduct, and we're under investigation." He sighed, looking back at the documents in front of him. "And you had so much potential."

"Why do you want her land so badly?"

"Because, Jack, in order to move forward in this world and get what we want, sometimes, we need to give other people a bit of a push."

"What about just letting people live out their lives in peace?"

"Well, that doesn't exactly help us fill our wallets, does it? Jack, you knew this is all part of the job. You can't get caught up in the personal lives of these people. I'm so disappointed." He paused, then looking up at Jack, casually commented, "I heard the Davidson sisters are a bit down on their luck right now anyway. Closed for food and alcohol violations? How unfortunate. If they don't pass their inspection, well…maybe it will finally incentivize them to sell."

Jack was fuming at this point. "What did you do?"

438

Adrien simply smiled a knowing smile. "I don't know what you mean, Jack."

"You know *exactly* what I mean. Did you put in the anonymous tip to shut them down during their busiest season?"

"How could I do that? I've never even been to their establishment. I wouldn't know if they served alcohol to guests without a permit, or what the layout of their kitchen was, or how they stored their food. Though if it all comes out it was true, it's a good thing they're shut down. Could be a health hazard to their guests."

That was the final straw for Jack. "You know what? I'm done here." He moved towards the door.

Adrien laughed wryly. "Yes, I already knew that, given the reports you sent in."

"I'll see you in court, Adrien. You won't get away with ruining people's lives anymore."

"Perhaps."

"You know what? You're a terrible person. Truly. I've never met anyone so twisted, so manipulative in my life. You're a weak, petty little man. You deserve whatever happens to you."

"Jack, if I were you, I'd leave before security gets here," Adrien said through gritted teeth, not allowing Jack to see his words had stung. "Get out of my sight."

"With pleasure."

With this, Jack turned on his heel, feeling free for the first time in years.

439

"You made a mistake, Jack," Adrien called after him. "You made a mistake."

Jack paused. There was so much he could say in return, but he remained silent. Without turning to meet Adrien's glare, he walked out, slamming the office door behind him.

As he walked, he pulled out his cell phone, and dialed Amelia. It went straight to her voicemail. "Hi, Amelia, it's Jack. Listen, call me. I have something important to talk to you about."

Inside his office, Adrien was standing at one of the windows, looking out over the city, fuming, but at the same time, not surprised by what had happened.

He'd underestimated Jack. He wouldn't make that mistake again.

✴

A couple hours later, Jack was back on the steps of the Blue Barn, exhausted from having done the long drive twice that day. Amelia didn't answer her phone, and he'd left several messages, trying to explain things. Emily didn't answer either, but that was less surprising. His only other option was to try and see the sisters in person.

It was dark by the time he reached the cottage. The guests' cars, he noticed, were cleared out. His heart broke—he knew how much time they'd spent trying to build up clientele, and to see the drive empty, devoid of any indication of guests, saddened him.

He stomped up to the steps, knocking as hard as he could on the cottage door. Inside, he heard Cosmo barking like a madman, and he saw a light flick on—with it, a flicker of hope. If he could just tell Amelia about the encounter he'd had with Adrien, how Adrien had specifically mentioned the shutting down, had all but admitted he'd been behind it...

But Emily answered the door.

440

"You have some nerve," she snarled, glaring at him.

"Emily, you need to listen to me—Adrien's behind it. It wasn't me."

"You know, you have been nothing but a pain in the ass since the moment you set foot in this town," she snapped, ignoring his pleas. "First you basically kill my grandfather with stress, then you shut down our business—what's next, kidnapping Cosmo?"

Cosmo, meanwhile, whined in the background.

"Emily, will you get over yourself and listen to me for a second? I turned Dunstan Enterprises in earlier today. I talked to Adrien—he all but admitted he was behind it!" Jack snapped.

"I don't believe that. And you know why? Because I don't believe a word that comes out of your mouth. Never have."

"Then let me talk to Amelia," Jack retorted. "She'll believe me."

"*No*," Emily said firmly. "You stay away from my sister! She invested too much into you, and this is how you repay her? Do you have any idea what you've put her through?"

"But if I can just explain…"

"LEAVE. NOW."

And with this, Emily slammed the door in his face. The light inside went dark, and so did Jack's hopes of reconciliation.

✳

Jack sat in May's Diner, trying to regroup. It had been a long day. He didn't have a place to stay in town that night. He was far from his apartment in the city. He was jobless. And he'd lost the people he was closest to in a matter of hours.

Things were not going well.

It was then that Jack looked up. Charles was entering the diner, stopping in to pick up a late dinner. Seeing Jack, he moved towards the booth he was sitting in.

"Didn't expect to see you here this late, Jack," Charles commented as he sat across from Jack, motioning to the waitress for a glass of water.

Jack shrugged. "It's been a long day."

"Tell me about it. I made three deliveries today, clocked in about three hundred miles," Charles said wearily. "Was just picking up some food before heading home."

"Sounds better than my day," Jack said wryly.

"Oh yeah? What happened to you?"

Jack shook his head. "I can't tell you." He paused. "But you might find out eventually. In fact, I'm sure you will, if you read the news in a few days."

"What'd you do?"

Jack, however, remained silent.

Charles looked over the younger man. "Jack, I've gotta ask: are you even hanging around town for work anymore? Or are you here for other reasons now? Because I've gotta tell you, if you're here for work, you're really bad at your job. You've been around for about six months now, and as far as I know, the Davidson sisters haven't agreed to selling you anything."

Jack had to smile at Charles' bluntness. If only he knew what had happened that day. "I guess you could say I'm here for other reasons now, Charles."

Charles raised an eyebrow and sat back in his seat, motioning for him to continue. "Tell me."

Jack shook his head. "I can't."

"Does it have anything to do with Amelia?"

Jack hesitated. "Sort of." He took a sip of his drink.

"You dating her?"

Jack almost choked on his beverage. "No! No. No, we're not dating."

Charles smirked. "You're protesting an awful lot there, son. Nothing wrong with it if you *are* dating her. She's a good girl. Pretty little thing too. You'd be a lucky guy. And hell, she'd be a lucky girl."

Jack smiled. "I appreciate that, Charles, but I can promise you there's nothing romantic going on with me and Amelia."

"Why not?"

"Call it a conflict of interest."

Charles sat back in his seat. "Suit yourself. So, if you're not dating Amelia, and you're not here for work, what are you still doing in Calvary?

"Re-examining my life, I guess."

"You're a little young to be having a mid-life crisis. What could you have possibly done in your short time on this planet that's made you feel the need to re-examine it?"

443

"I think it's what I *haven't* done."

"Okay, so what *haven't* you done?"

"I haven't taken the time to slow down and enjoy life, you know? Ever since I was a kid, I've been on the go, pushing myself, trying to make my life better, always reaching for the next goal…and not that there's anything wrong with that, goals are good to have. But I've been so caught up in myself I haven't paid attention to the world around me. And there's a *lot* I've been missing. Seriously, Charles. You, Amelia, and Emily are the closest things I have to friends."

Had, his mind reminded him. *Amelia and Emily aren't talking to you anymore.*

"Anyway, what's that saying about me?" Jack continued with his train of thought.

"It says you're having your mid-life crisis a little early," Charles laughed.

"*Seriously.*"

"Okay, fine: it says to me you're a good man. That you're *not* so caught up in yourself you don't recognize the problem. That you've caught it in time to make the changes you need. Because son, life goes *fast*. Believe me, I know it all too well. You don't want to get to the end of it and have regrets. So, I don't know what it is you're doing, or what it is you're looking for, and you don't have to tell me—but if a man is trying to better himself and better his little corner of the world, there's honor in that. And that's all that matters in the end."

"I appreciate that, Charles. Really, I do."

Charles nodded, taking a sip from his own drink. "You're right about one thing, Jack: we are friends. And as your friend, if you ever need anything, you just let me know."

444

Jack sat silently for a moment, staring into his mug. "Hey, Charles?"

"Yeah?"

"I need a job. And a place to sleep tonight. And a place to live here in Calvary."

Charles smiled, taking a sip from his glass. "I can help you with all of that."

✳ Chapter 38 ✳

The Fallen Sorcerer

"**Y**ou sure you don't want to ride with me?" Emily asked Amelia.

It was Thanksgiving Day. The events of the past couple of weeks were still fresh, and the Blue Barn remained empty. Amelia and Emily had both been avoiding the fish market, as word had spread Charles had hired on Jack there. He'd tried to call, several times, but neither of the sisters wanted to talk to him. The emptiness of their business was still raw. That day, rather than hosting their guests as they had originally planned, they would be going to their mother's, spending a quiet meal with Rosalie and Lizzie, who they would be checking out of the nursing home. It wasn't a bad plan, but it wasn't the original plan, and they were disheartened. Every day meant another day closer to the inspection, but they were nervous. They'd put their hearts and souls into their business, and didn't want to see everything fall apart just as it was coming together.

"Yeah, I'm sure. I just want to tie up a few things around here. I'll meet you at Mom's in bit."

Emily looked at her sister skeptically. "It's all going to be okay, you know that, right?"

"Yeah, I know," Amelia said dismissively. "The inspector will come by, he'll see we're all up to code, see it's a misunderstanding, we'll be open by Christmas." The words were mechanical by now, as the sisters had been repeating that mantra to each other since everything had happened.

"No, I mean…well, you know."

Amelia winced, thinking about Jack and all that time she'd spent with him. And with the Blue Barn shut down…it was too much. He'd been calling her, but she just couldn't bring herself to respond—she had nothing to say to him. There were a few moments of weakness, where she wanted to hear his side, and considered reaching out to him, but Emily had talked her down, arguing, "He's not worth your time or the amount of energy you're putting into this emotionally. Let it go and move on."

Still, she felt like there was more to the story, like it was all a big misunderstanding. Despite it all, a part of her still trusted him. She'd seen too many movies and read too many books where the characters misunderstood each other and it caused a huge falling out that could've been avoided if they'd bothered to *listen* to each other. She hated feeling like this was that very situation. The journalist in her needed to know; the woman in her dreaded finding out the worst.

"Yeah, I know," Amelia repeated. "Don't worry about it."

"I'm not worried about *it*. I'm worried about *you*. You were really invested in him, and I know it's been hard on you."

"Don't worry. I'm fine," Amelia said curtly, with a quick smile. "Now get out of here. Grandma's waiting for you to pick her up, and Mom's waiting for the both of you. I just want to finish pulling together a few of these documents for the inspector and tidy up the place. I'll see you at Mom's in about an hour, okay?"

Emily nodded slowly. "Okay. I'll see you there. You bringing Cosmo with you? Or do you need me to drive him too?"

Amelia shook her head. "No, I've got him. Not sure how Grandma would do riding in the car with him. He's always a little crazy on car rides. Probably best they're driven separately."

"Good call. I'll see you there."

"See you there."

With that, Emily threw on her jacket and grabbed her keys, patting Cosmo on the head once more before walking out the door to her car.

When she had driven out of view, Amelia stepped out of the cottage and crossed the lawn to the Blue Barn. From her view of the outside, it looked cold and uninviting, a looming reminder of the disappointing events of the past few weeks. Its windows were dark, its normally bright blue paneling seemed bleak against the gray November sky. She pulled her coat around her tighter, and wrapped her scarf once more around her neck so even her necklace was hidden from view, shivering as if she could almost feel the cold emanating from the building.

Procuring a key from her pocket, she unlocked the front door, gazing about. Inside it was even more drab and gloomy, the normally bright white hallways seeming to be tinged gray—she couldn't tell if it was her mood biasing her perception of the color, or the dreariness of the cloudy day outside. Not that it mattered. The usually warm, welcoming space was empty and devoid of life. She hated it this way, filled with a bitter disappointment as she thought on all they had planned that wasn't coming to fruition, and fear they might see this great experiment come to an end quicker than anticipated. She hoped, desperately, things would go well in a few days.

She took off her coat and left it on the coat rack behind the front desk, and also took off her shoes as they were pinching a bit, though she left her scarf on, still slightly chilled. After doing so, she stepped into the back office, unlocking a file cabinet and gathering up any documents she might need for the upcoming inspection. After carefully assembling them in order and placing them in a binder for the inspector's review, she put the binder back in the cabinet and locked it. She went into the kitchen, where she pulled some rags and cleaners from under the sink, and set about dusting and wiping down the place. Though everything was in impeccable order, due to the lack of use over the past few days, a fine film of dust had settled on the surfaces throughout the building. She went about wiping the gray away, her spirits brightening some as she saw things come back to life. She smiled. Everything would be okay. It had to be.

As she passed by one of the front windows, she stopped, her attention drawn to the driveway. Memories of Jack driving up that same stretch overwhelmed her mind. She squeezed her eyes shut, trying desperately to push the thoughts out of her head, but to no avail. She sighed, opening her eyes, staring longingly down the empty dusty path.

Enough of this. Forget what Emily says. You need to know his side.

Pulling her phone from her back pocket, she clicked to her contacts, typing in "Jack Garridan." She hesitated for a moment when it popped up, her thumb hovering over his name. Should she?

Yes. She should.

Before she could change her mind, she hit his name and put the phone to her ear. It rang, once, twice, three times, four times…voicemail.

"Hey, this is Jack. I can't come to the phone right now. Leave a message and I'll call you back as soon as I can."

The message tone beeped. Amelia's heart raced, unsure of what she should say. She hadn't planned on voicemail. She'd planned on him answering. She fumbled, "Hey, it's me—Amelia. Listen, I'm going to Mom's for Thanksgiving, so if you call back tonight, I probably won't answer, but text me or something, let's figure out a time to meet up. I want to talk."

She paused, not sure how she should end the message, her mind reeling. Finally, she simply uttered the words, "I'm sorry I wouldn't listen before. Just…get back to me, okay?"

She hung up and put the phone back in her pocket. She sighed heavily, running her fingers through her hair anxiously. Whatever was going to be would be at this point—if he called her back, great. If not, so be it. Not that she'd blame him in the least, after she'd been dodging his calls and avoiding him the past few weeks. But at least she could say she'd tried.

She went back to dusting, her mind elsewhere, so deep in her own thoughts she didn't even hear Cosmo barking outside.

✳

As soon as Adrien stepped foot on the property, he felt a familiar, comforting glow, like that of sunbeams warming his body on a summer's day, or a fire gently heating him after coming indoors from the frigid cold. The air around him was electric, the land coursing with energy, bursting with secrets it so desperately wanted to tell. It was like Caleb had described. To those who didn't know what it was, what was here, this would simply be described as a "refreshing" place, a "happy" place, a "comforting" place.

But he knew better. There was magic here. The photos from Caleb proved that much. It was physical and tangible and real, not just a "warm fuzzy feeling" non-magical people so often described when they came here. If he was lucky—and he sincerely hoped he was, or this trip would be for nothing—this wasn't just any magic. No, any old magic wouldn't do. Fairies and mermaids and selkies and elves and brownies were everywhere. They were a dime a dozen, their magic useless to him. If that's all it was, he would leave them be. No, it had to be a very specific magic, a broken magic, a hidden magic—*human* magic that had been taken from him long ago.

He'd wandered the globe searching for this magic for centuries. He'd endured every feasible hardship a human could possibly endure in his quest, and he'd done so over the course of several lifetimes. It was enough to make a man mad. But he wasn't totally mad yet, contrary to popular belief and opinion—he had hope, which kept him going (along with a little bit of ambition and a lot of vengeance in mind). He had a small piece of this magic already, having acquired it by accident over seventy years previously, though in the decades since, he'd almost given up on finding more. Until now, that is. He was so close, he could feel it coursing through his veins.

He knew this land. He'd loved this land once. He'd lived on this land, worked this land, and had everything he ever needed or wanted on this land.

That is, until he was banished from this land. By the time he'd made his way back, finally found it again, it was too late. People had settled here and claimed it as theirs. Oh, if they only knew what had happened here, who it had once belonged to—who it *still* belonged to, in his mind. They had no real claim to it. He'd been forced to leave behind that which he loved most in the world here. Now, centuries later, it was still buried on this land somewhere—but he would uncover it, someday. It was a matter of time.

In the meantime, he had to bide his time, wait for his opportunity, and for the technology to advance to where he needed it. He didn't care about the development—well, he did, but the money earned from the selling of the buildings was only a side perk. In the process of upheaving the land, he'd desperately hoped the workers would stumble across what he was looking for. And if not, well, at least he'd have the money. He liked being rich. He'd been poor once, and hated it. Centuries of hard work though, well, that kind of money adds up over time.

The landscape had changed over the centuries. He had a vague idea of where to look, but to go about it manually, alone, would take too much time—of course, he had all the time in the world, but he'd always been an impatient man. He'd waited long enough. He remembered the excitement he'd felt on the advent of the modern bulldozers and excavators, and knew he had to get into a business where these wonderful pieces of machinery would be used. The risks of damage from these machines to what he was looking for was there, of course, but they were faster and more efficient and effective than a shovel.

So here he was again, after all this time. And even after all this time, magic was here. It was beautiful, in a way. He felt like the prodigal son

451

returning home. He would have his celebration, his fatted calf. He wouldn't have a father to welcome him home, but he didn't need one. He didn't need anyone.

As Adrien stood in the middle of the dusty driveway leading up to the Davidson property, he procured a small, smooth stone from his coat pocket and held it in the palm of his gloved hand. Normally a deep, cobalt blue, it was now radiating with a soft, golden glow.

He smiled. That's what he wanted to see. His suspicions were confirmed. If it hadn't glowed, if it had remained the cold, lifeless object it usually was, he would've turned around and left well enough alone. He might've even given up trying to acquire the Davidson land, and left the sisters be in their pathetic, sad, secluded little existence. But this was his lucky day, and now he had no choice but to move forward. It was here, somewhere, beckoning him—he just had to find it.

As he stepped forward towards the door, a dog came bounding around the corner, barking wildly.

Adrien stopped, glaring at the animal. "*Leave*," he commanded.

The dog suddenly stopped in his tracks, whimpered, and scampered in the opposite direction.

With this, the Fallen Sorcerer approached the front door of the Blue Barn Bed and Breakfast, and knocked.

He was here for a second source stone.

✳

Had Amelia not been wearing a scarf that day, she might have noticed the stone hanging from her own necklace glowing as Adrien approached. But as misfortune would have it, she was too wrapped up in her own thoughts, so much so she nearly jumped out of her skin when she heard a knocking on the door.

452

Cracking open the front door a bit, she looked out to see a pale, thin middle-aged man standing at the entrance of the Blue Barn. He had sharp facial features, and slicked-back, dark hair, with icy-blue eyes. He was just a couple inches taller than Amelia, a bit below the average height for a male. He was clothed in a dark suit, which was currently covered by a long, black wool dress coat. When she opened the door, he smiled a wide, toothy grin.

"Can I help you?" Amelia asked, looking warily at Adrien.

"I'm so sorry to bother you," Adrien said, turning on the charm. "But my car broke down just down the road from here, and my cell phone apparently doesn't get great reception around here. I was wondering if I could use your phone to call roadside assistance?"

Amelia's initial gut reaction was to close the door on the man. The last time a car had broken down and someone had asked to use her phone, it was Jack, and look where that landed her: months of wasted time, a closed business, and a broken heart.

Still, though. That clearly wasn't *this* man's fault. She shouldn't project Jack's faults onto a complete stranger, who seemed sincere enough.

She opened the door, motioning for him to come in. "Phone's at the desk in the foyer."

Adrien nodded, and making his way to the desk, said, "Thank you, I appreciate it. I'm on my way to have Thanksgiving dinner with my mother at the nursing home—she probably won't remember it, but still, I'm trying to take in every holiday I can before it's too late."

This piqued Amelia's interest. "Which nursing home is she at?"

"Our Lady of Perpetual Faith."

"My grandmother is there," Amelia said, eyes wide.

"What a coincidence! Perhaps they know each other. What's your grandmother's name?"

"Lizzie—Elizabeth—Davidson."

"So, you must be Amelia Davidson? Or is it Emily?"

"Amelia. How'd you know?" she asked suspiciously, eyeing the stranger.

"Oh, my mother talks to your grandmother, who talks about you all the time. She's very proud of you, you know."

Amelia blushed. "Thank you."

"Amelia, I have to ask, why aren't *you* with your grandmother this Thanksgiving?"

"I'm actually heading out in a bit. My sister's picking up my grandmother from the nursing home; we're doing dinner at my mom's. I'm just tying up a few things here before I meet up with them."

Adrien glanced around, taking in his surroundings. "It's a nice place. I'm surprised you're not taking advantage of the holiday and having it open for business."

His remark stung, and Amelia visibly winced. "Yes, well, you know—family comes first."

"Indeed. I should make this call and get out of your hair." Picking up the receiver, he dialed. Unbeknownst to Amelia, Adrien was calling his men, who were waiting for his signal. "Yes, this is Aaron Daniels," he said, using the agreed-upon alias.

"Hey, boss, how's it going?" a big, burly man named Bruce answered on the other end. He and another man were sitting in their car down the road from the Blue Barn, tucked away, but with the driveway leading up to the Davidson property in plain view.

"Well, I'm all right, thanks, but I'm having some car issues. Can you send someone out to help?"

"Greg and I are around the corner. Marcus is on the boat. Good to go?"

"Yes, please. I'm at 1307 Calvary Road."

"On our way."

"Thanks, I appreciate it."

Adrien hung up the phone, and smiled at Amelia. "Roadside assistance is on its way. Is it all right if I stay here until they arrive? It's awfully cold out."

"Yes, of course."

"Are you sure? If it's too much of an inconvenience, I can wait out in my car."

"No, don't worry about it," Amelia said, the hostess in her kicking in.

"Thank you. You're too kind." He paused. "Can I trouble you for a glass of water?"

"Sure!" Amelia said, heading towards the kitchen, Adrien close behind.

While Amelia poured the glass, her back to him, Adrien reached to his side, procuring a gun.

"Here you g—"

Amelia turned around to face Adrien, only to find she was face-to-face with the barrel of a gun. She froze, dropping the glass, which smashed to the floor, scattering water and shards of glass all over the kitchen. Her speech faltered as she stared at the man at the other end of the weapon.

"Wha—" she started to utter, confused by the turn of events.

He put his finger to her lips. "Shh. Don't ask questions, Miss Davidson, and don't make a fuss. I don't want to hurt you. And I won't, if you're cooperative. But I need to ask you some questions, and I need your absolute undivided attention. Let's sit and chat, shall we?"

Not knowing what else to do, and backed into a corner without any sort of defense, she walked stiffly into the dining room, hands where he could see them. Adrien trailed a step behind, gun pressed into her back. He motioned for her to sit in one of the chairs at the table, and she hesitantly obliged.

"Hands behind your back, please," he instructed, calmly, almost politely.

She obeyed, intertwining them between the spokes of the back of the chair. Procuring a zip tie from his coat pocket, he bound her wrists together. As he bent to do the same with her feet, she kicked, narrowly missing his face. He, in turn, stood, cocking his gun and pressing it against her temple. She closed her eyes tightly, the cold, smooth metal against her skin. Her heart was pounding so hard by now she could hear it throbbing in her ears.

"Please, Miss Davidson," he pled. "Let's not do this the hard way. I told you I don't want to hurt you. Please believe me. But I will if I have to. Now, are you going to be a good girl?"

Amelia sat, silent, unmoving, refusing to meet his gaze.

Adrien applied a bit more pressure so she could feel the gun pressing into her head even harder.

"I said, are you going to be a good girl?" he repeated, more forcefully this time.

She nodded, shaking.

"Good." He slowly lowered the gun. "Now, let's try this again."

Adrien bent down again, and pulling another zip tie from his pocket, bound Amelia's ankles together. She was now immobile. He sat across from her at the table, and placed the gun in between the two of them. "Now we can talk."

"What do you want?" she rasped.

"Nothing much, Miss Davidson. I'm just looking for something of mine."

"Who are you?" she asked, looking him up and down.

"Oh, I'm sorry, I haven't properly introduced myself: I'm Adrien Dunstan." He extended his hand as if to shake hers, seeming to momentarily forget she was bound up and couldn't return the gesture. He laughed at his error, and put his hand down. "Oh, that's right. Sorry about that."

He's insane.

Amelia was now even more terrified than she had been just moments prior, something she didn't think was possible.

"You're Jack's boss." Her eyes grew wide with realization.

He nodded, smiled a toothy grin, and pointed at her, indicating she was on point. "Bingo! Well, I was Jack's boss, until he abruptly left our company in chaos a few days ago. I have a feeling his feelings for you played a part in that."

Amelia tried to wrap her mind around this information, and she momentarily felt awful for blowing off Jack's calls and messages, and for allowing Emily to convince her Jack was the bad guy. But she quickly pushed it from her mind, focusing on trying to figure out how to get out of this alive. "Do you seriously want my land so badly you're going to kill me for it?"

He laughed again. "No, my dear. I don't want the land. I mean, I do miss it a bit, but it's yours."

"You miss it?" she repeated, dazed and confused.

"Well, yes, it was mine long ago, but that's beside the point."

Amelia was reeling. The land had been in her family for generations: who was this crazy man who thought he had once lived here? That was impossible. Davidsons had been here, on this exact plot, for over a century, at least. There was no way a man who looked barely older than forty could have once owned any part of it.

As she tried to process this, Adrien continued, "I'm just looking for something that's on the land. And the only way for me to have free reign to search was to acquire it. But I have a feeling you've already found what I'm looking for, so we can make this easy. You can hand it over, keep your home, and I'll leave you alone. How does that sound?"

"What are you looking for?" She tried to remain calm in spite of the precarious situation she found herself in.

"Well, that's where things get a bit more difficult. I'm not completely sure what it looks like. But I'll know it when I see it."

Yes, he's DEFINITELY insane.

"Maybe…maybe I can help if you release me?" Amelia suggested.

Adrien laughed. "An admirable try, Miss Davidson. But no."

In this moment, two large men entered through the door, dressed in black.

"Everything okay here, boss?" one of them asked.

"Oh, just fine. I'm just having a chat with Miss Davidson here," Adrien replied.

"Need our help?" the other inquired, a sadistic grin crossing his face as he glanced over at the bound up young woman. Amelia felt her stomach churn.

"No, no, that won't be necessary yet. Not if she tells us the location of the stone."

Amelia's head snapped up at the word "stone." Could it be…?

And it all came rushing to her. The entry in her grandfather's journal—what was that line? *One in the thick, close to the coast; give up that which you love the most.* Her mother's story, about the creature demanding her father give up that which he loved the most…and the necklace she received after they'd returned from that particular trip…

Her eyes went wide. The necklace from her father, with the amber stone…the one she was currently wearing on a chain around her neck, hidden under her shirt.

She was wearing a source stone. And this man in front of her…this was the Fallen Sorcerer.

Adrien, noticing Amelia's reaction, smiled a broad, toothy grin.

"Ah, see? You know something."

"I don't know anything."

"Come, child. Don't play these games with me. You know."

"I know…I know who you are."

Adrien smirked. "Yes. I thought you might." Slowly, he crossed the room toward her. She shuddered as he sat beside her, brushed a loose piece of her hair behind her ear, and leaning in, breathed, "Tell me who I am."

"You're the Fallen Sorcerer," she whispered in reply.

He grinned. "Very good, Amelia."

"What do you want from me?" Amelia demanded, her face turning hot.

"The source stone you possess, my dear. That's all."

Amelia looked up at him. "I don't have one," she lied.

He gave a low chuckle. "That, child, is where you are wrong. You do."

"Even if I *did* know, I wouldn't give it to you!" she cried as she struggled against her bonds.

"And *that*, dear one, would be your biggest mistake." He leaned in, and hissed, "*Think*, Amelia!"

"I don't *know*!" she exclaimed, hoping the tone of her voice didn't betray her. "Find it yourself!"

He stood, and sighed. "Yes. I'd guessed I'd have to resort to that." He snapped his fingers, and the two men standing behind him moved to his side. "Tear this place apart. Find the stone."

"What are you going to do with it?" She watched as the men split up into separate rooms and began ransacking the place.

460

He smiled. "Never you mind, Amelia. But you'll find out eventually. I'm currently just piecing things together."

Piecing things together...

Amelia started. He intended to put all the stones together again. He intended to release magic back into the world. And if he'd been led here...he must already have one.

"You already have a stone," Amelia concluded aloud, her eyes wide as this realization dawned on her, remembering the entry from Jude's journal. Adrien was the man in the jungle in Vietnam. "That's why things are off with the magical creatures—you already have a stone."

"A very astute observation, Miss Davidson." A toothy grin crossed his face. "You're correct. I acquired one a few decades ago."

"In Vietnam," Amelia said quietly.

Adrien started. "No, not in Vietnam. Before Vietnam. But yes, I did spend some time there...how did you know that?"

"You made yourself known," Amelia replied sharply.

Adrien ignored this reply. He wouldn't let her throw him off. "The Creator Sorcerer hid the stones well, as it took several centuries for me to come across just the one," Adrien continued. "I'd almost given up hope of ever finding the stones. But finding that one renewed my resolve. After all, unlike you, I have all of eternity to search for them. It's just a matter of time."

"What are you going to do with them?" Amelia asked, trying to hide the quivering in her voice. The thought of the Fallen Sorcerer having all seven stones in his possession, with the ability to bend magic to his will, was terrifying.

461

"In due time, Amelia. Don't you worry your pretty little head about that right now." He paused, his eyes trailing to the glint of the chain that hung around her neck, from which the pendant was tucked into her shirt. "Now, how about we end this nonsense, my men stop tearing up your place, and you hand over the stone you have in *your* possession?"

Amelia glared at him, remaining silent. At this point, tied as she was, she knew there was nothing stopping Adrien from taking the stone. She'd never felt so helpless in her life.

In this moment, out of the corner of her eye, she caught sight of a golden little light dancing past the window.

Lila!

Sure enough, as she glanced quickly at the window to get a better look, she saw Lila had momentarily paused, her little mouth agape as she saw what was transpiring within. She gave the fairy a knowing look, and the creature disappeared from sight, before Adrien could turn around.

"What were you looking at?" he demanded, seeing her quickly look away from the window.

"Nothing," she lied. "The sun just got in my eyes."

"Hmmph." He turned to his men, and snapped, "Search the grounds. If there's anyone else here, tie them up too." Turning back to Amelia, he said, "Now, where were we?"

He pulled the stone he currently possessed from his pocket. It glowed brilliantly, so bright Amelia had to look away. As Adrien moved it closer to her, its glow became even brighter. Adrien smiled, and shoved the stone back into his pocket.

"I don't much care for liars, Miss Davidson."

Gently, he reached for the chain on her neck. She shuddered as his fingertips brushed against her collarbone, white hot rage rising in her. He pulled the necklace from her shirt so the pendant that hung on it sat in the palm of his hand, the teardrop shaped stone seeming to glow in the sunlight.

"Yes," Adrien said, his voice almost giddy. "There you are."

With a swift, solid pull, the delicate necklace snapped from Amelia's neck, and Adrien stood with it in his hand, admiring the pendant as it dangled on the broken chain.

"Where did you find this?"

"I…I didn't," she stammered. "It was a gift."

"I told you, Miss Davidson, I don't much care for liars," he hissed, leaning in.

"I'm not lying! It was a gift from my dad." She paused. "And he can't tell you anything, because he's dead."

"Pity." Adrien gazed longingly at the amber stone, not an ounce of sympathy in his voice. "It would have been nice to know where this came from."

Amelia, appalled and fearful as she watched Adrien examine the stone as if he was in some sort of mesmerized trance, was suddenly struck with an idea.

"*Hear me, imp, creature of delight,*" she whispered to herself. She looked up, checking to see if Adrien had heard her speak. He had not, being too entranced by the glittering jewel he held. "*Why did the chicken cross the road? To get to the other side.*"

"I'VE HEARD THAT ONE BEFORE!" a wild little shriek came from across the room. "IT'S NOT FUNNY!"

Adrien whirled around to see an imp perched on the windowsill, looking at Amelia very crossly.

"I know, I'm sorry, I'll tell you a better one later," Amelia said frantically. "But look what the nice man has for you!"

The imp suddenly took notice of the shiny object Adrien held, and squealed with glee. Jumping from the windowsill, it whizzed at top speed toward the jewel, arms outstretched.

Adrien, seeing the imp approach, picked up the nearest object at hand, which happened to be a heavy platter sitting on the table. His swing was true, and all Amelia could hear was a loud *SMACK!* as the imp went flying across the room, hitting the wall and falling to the ground.

"Really, Miss Davidson?" he taunted, turning back to Amelia. "An imp? You summoned an *imp* to help you?"

"You really shouldn't have done that," she commented.

Behind Adrien, the imp was standing, shaking off the shock it had just taken. Its eyes glowing red, it flew full force at Adrien in a fiery rage.

"GIVE ME MY PRETTY THING!" it screeched, picking up plates and other objects around the room and throwing them as hard as it could at Adrien, leaving disarray and destruction in its wake.

Adrien and his lackeys weaved about the room, ducking and diving to avoid being hit. The imp, infuriated and determined to not lose the shiny piece of jewelry it had claimed as its own, continued with its pursuit, and in a sudden explosion of magic, lifted the couch in the sitting area from the ground and let it crash down in front of the door, blocking Adrien's exit.

While this sudden fit might startle some people, Adrien kept his composure. Spotting a paperweight on an end table, he picked it up and chucked it at the imp, shouting, "Oh impious imp, be ye turned to stone!"

Instantly, as the paperweight came within an inch of the creature, the imp froze midair, unable to move. Adrien smirked, brushed a bit of dust off his jacket, and turned back to Amelia. "Good effort, Miss Davidson. Really, a great show. I admire your attempt. But don't forget: I may not have my magic anymore, but I still remember a few things."

"You won't get away with this," Amelia spat, struggling to free herself.

"But that's where you're wrong, Miss Davidson: I will, eventually. Like I said, I have all the time in the world. You, on the other hand, do not. We can do this dance for your entire life, but eventually, *you will die.* And when you do, I'll still be here. Even if you send your children and your children's children after me, even if you make it a generational family quest through the centuries to stop me, *none of you will succeed, because you will all die.* Time is on my side, not yours. That's the only benefit of my curse. So, don't waste your precious time, Miss Davidson, fighting something you can't possibly win. Enjoy your life. Don't worry about me. Go get married and have babies or something, whatever it is you good mortal women need to do to have a fulfilling life—and such a short one it is." He looked at the stone in his hand, and marveled at it, a smile crossing his lips. "Thank you though for your help. It's incredibly appreciated."

He turned to his lackeys, motioning for them to move the couch. They complied, and the three made their exit, Adrien leading the way. Amelia continued to struggle in the chair to which she was bound, trying to free herself. The imp was still frozen, utterly useless. Even when it came to, she doubted it would have the intellectual capacity to know how to unbind her. Knowing her luck, it would probably try to bind her even more, thinking it was some great game or joke. She tried to propel herself forward in the chair towards the kitchen window, which was always cracked ever so slightly in the event Lila wanted to visit.

Where is Lila and why hasn't she returned with help yet?

Impatient, Amelia edged as close to the open window as she could. In doing so, she saw Adrien and his men making their way to the boat dock on her property. Her eyes went wide as she came to the realization they were making their escape by *boat*, not by car. Where they were off to and how they would be found again was anyone's guess. Amelia was determined to not let them get too far ahead of her. If she could manage to get free, and get to the Blue Mermaid, she could plausibly catch up.

She inched the chair toward the kitchen counter, where the knife block sat. Struggling in her bonds, she managed to finagle it so she was able to bump the block closer to her in an effort to grab a knife. If she could get a knife in her hands, she reasoned, she could unbind her wrists and then her feet.

No such luck though. The knife block clattered to the ground as she tried to grab at it, out of her reach. Precariously, she tried to pick one up with her feet, but cut herself in the process. She yelped, now smearing blood about the tile floor as she tried to free herself.

"HELP!" she shouted frantically out the cracked window, tears streaming down her face, wondering if her screams could even be heard or if her effort was futile. "SOMEBODY! HELP!"

She struggled harder against her bonds, to the point where the chair tipped over on its side, Amelia still strapped to it. She hit the cold, unforgiving tile floor with a hard *thwack*, still bound, groaning in pain. By now, she was crying, losing all composure she had once possessed. She was angry, frustrated, and in pain, but worse than anything, she felt utterly useless and defenseless, a feeling she hadn't felt since her father had died and there was nothing she could do about it. The situation she currently found herself in was embarrassing and painful. She hated feeling like a damsel in distress, and had always prided herself on being the exact opposite of one—yet here she was, bound, bruised, and bleeding, unable to help herself. It was awful.

466

By this time, the imp had regained motion, and was bouncing around the house, screeching, angered at losing its shiny prize. It bounced into the kitchen, where it paused when it encountered Amelia on the floor.

"Please, help me," Amelia wept softly, looking at the imp. "*Please.*"

The imp, not saying a word in reply, simply whizzed out the cracked window. Amelia sighed, not knowing if it understood her and was going to find help, or if it was simply going home. It hadn't untied her though, so she had doubts it knew what "help" was.

She was all alone now, and afraid. All she could do was pray for a miracle.

✳ Chapter 39 ✳

Reuniting

It was Thanksgiving Day. Rather than enjoying the much-anticipated Thanksgiving feast at the Blue Barn, Jack sat in May's Diner, wrinkling his nose at the slightly overdone turkey melt before him.

It had been an interesting year, to say the least. A few weeks ago, he would have said he had much to be thankful for: he'd found close friends, he was on track to working a new job and starting a quieter, simpler life, and he'd discovered there is magic in the world. His life had been turned upside down, and for the better. Yet since the cease and desist letter, Amelia wouldn't even speak to him. He had a feeling that was Emily's doing, that she was the one planting in her sister's head it had been him who'd framed them, who'd tried to destroy the Blue Barn.

He'd quit working for Dunstan Enterprises, and had tried to call Amelia to tell her so—several times, in fact, but to no avail. She wouldn't see him. She needed "time to figure things out," she said, and recently, stopped even picking up her phone when he called, letting it go straight to voicemail.

So, he was giving her the time and space she requested—in the meantime, Dunstan Enterprises was under investigation for allegedly participating in illegitimate business practices, ranging from bribing officials to underpaying workers to purposely using inferior building materials to even blackmailing contractors. William Foster was also under investigation, and would likely be removed from his position—as were several others who turned up in the process. Though the build on the Benedict property was already completed, a strange mini-suburb in the

468

middle of nowhere, progress was halted on any other acquisitions—perhaps it would give the land a chance to heal, to stay wild and free. Possibly, even, fairies could return.

Things were coming out about previous builds—it seemed the Calvary project was only the tip of the iceberg. Jack was glad he was able to uphold his promise to Amelia that he would make sure Dunstan Enterprises was tied up in litigation—he hoped, desperately, this would be enough to keep them away from the Davidson sisters, and anyone else, for that matter. Only time would tell. He knew the next few months of his life would be in and out of courtrooms, giving testimonies and making statements.

It made Jack sick to think he was once a part of it all—he knew Adrien had a tendency to strong arm people, but to actually participate in illegal and unethical practices mortified Jack. It went against everything he had stood for, everything he valued. He was one who believed in building a better world—that's what initially drew him to Dunstan Enterprises, the thought of building something beautiful for people to live in and enjoy for generations. How naïve he'd been.

That same value was what had drawn him to Amelia in the first place—her belief in magic, in a better world, and even in *him*, that he was so much more than he thought he was, that he could do so much more and be so much more. But now, without her support, he felt lost. If the one person who had once believed in him more than anyone else in the world now doubted him, what was even the point?

So here he sat on Thanksgiving Day, in a dingy diner eating a dry turkey melt (something he didn't even think was possible, as the words "dry" and "melt" typically don't belong in the same sentence). He'd stay close, and whenever Amelia was ready to talk, to listen, he'd be there.

He was thankful for Charles, who agreed to have him on temporarily at the fish market until he landed on his feet—Charles even set it up so Jack could stay in the small guest room above his garage until Jack sold his place in Boston and was able to buy a place here in Calvary. The job at the fish market wasn't easy work, and more often than not, it smelled, but at least it was honest, and it wasn't under Adrien's thumb. Of all the things he'd found out about Dunstan Enterprises' dealings, Jack still didn't have physical proof it was Adrien who'd set up the Blue Barn. Still though, he knew it was him—Adrien all but told him so the last time they'd met. And when Amelia was ready to listen, she could find Jack at the fish market to hear his side of things. He'd called her to let her know that as well—she still hadn't responded.

The market was closed for the holiday, and Charles had invited Jack to join his family for dinner that night. Jack was debating on if he should attend—he appreciated the gesture, but he also knew his heart wasn't in it. Still, it beat where he was right now. May was great at pies and coffee, but turkey melts were not her strong suit.

As Jack picked at his French fries in the midst of this internal struggle, he pulled his phone out of his back pocket, wavering back and forth on if he should try to call Amelia again. He wanted to respect her space, but at the same time, he missed her—he didn't realize he'd miss her this much. And he so badly wanted to tell his side of the story. It was Thanksgiving, after all. She might be more receptive on a holiday, with all the warm feelings that came with the day. Or perhaps a text would be more appropriate? But a message would show he was sincere, she'd be able to hear it in his voice. Or should he continue to leave her alone, be respectful, give her the space she'd requested? He didn't want to be pushy or come off as manipulative either...

As he weighed his options, he looked at his phone: one missed call, and a voicemail, left about a half hour ago. Funny, he hadn't heard his phone go off...until he looked in the corner of the screen, where the mute icon indicated the phone was on silent. He must've accidentally turned off the sound.

Putting the phone to his ear to listen to the message, his heart leapt as he heard Amelia's voice ring through the speaker:

"Hey, it's me—Amelia. Listen, I'm going to Mom's for Thanksgiving, so if you call back tonight, I probably won't answer, but text me or something, let's figure out a time to meet up. I want to talk."

A pause, and for a moment he thought the message was over, until:

"I'm sorry I wouldn't listen before. Just…get back to me, okay?"

He stared at the phone in the palm of his hand, internally rejoicing, unaware of the large grin that had crossed his face.

She wanted to talk to him again. And not only that, but she was sorry for avoiding him.

Perhaps this could be a fresh start.

Per her instructions in her voicemail, he typed a text to her to let her know he'd received the message and yes, he wanted to meet with her to talk as well, when something in the corner of his eye caught his attention. Jack glanced out the window, only to see the sparkly little light that was Lila looking inward, staring directly at him. The look on her face suggested urgency, and she waved her arms at him frantically, beckoning him outside. Calmly, he took a final swig of the coffee, set a few bills on the table, and exited the diner.

"What's going on?" he asked under his breath as he walked briskly back towards Charles' house, trying not to draw attention to himself or to the fairy hovering around his head. He needn't have worried about this though—the streets were fairly empty, as most people were inside celebrating the holiday with loved ones.

Lila made a series of frenetic motions Jack couldn't decipher.

"Slow down! I don't understand you!"

471

Clearly agitated, Lila seemed to explode with twinkling fairy dust, and flying about, spelled out in large, glittering letters hanging in the air in front of him:

AMELIA IS IN TROUBLE

His eyes went wide, and he waved his hands through the letters to make them disappear, glancing around nervously to see if anyone had seen their apparition. He knew the fairy wouldn't risk being seen like that if it wasn't incredibly important.

"Where is she?"

This time, Lila simply glowed a shade of blue—the same shade, in fact, the Blue Barn was painted.

With this, Jack broke into a run towards Charles' house a couple blocks down, where his car was parked, Lila flying at full speed with him. Upon reaching the car, he jumped in, and went screeching out of the driveway to the outskirts of town. Thanksgiving dinner with Charles and his family would have to wait. Right now, he needed to get to Amelia.

✷

While Jack was racing across town to get to the Blue Barn, Emily was at that very moment pulling into her mother's driveway with Lizzie in the passenger side.

As she shifted the car into park, a purple blur hit the windshield. Lizzie seemed to not notice the *thunk*, but Emily jumped, slamming the brake, causing them both to jolt forward.

Lizzie, confused by her granddaughter's sudden lead foot, commented as she opened the passenger door to step out, "Hitting the brakes a little hard, aren't we, dear?"

"Sorry, Grandma," Emily muttered quickly, jumping out of the car.

As she walked around to see what had happened, she saw sitting on the ground a purple, leathery imp, clearly out of breath from having flown as fast as it could to her.

"Are you okay?" she hissed, crouching to see if it was hurt. "What did you do that for?"

The little creature, however, remained frozen from the impact. Emily sighed and rolled her eyes. She hated that defect in imps.

"You know you can move, right? You're not actually frozen."

The creature blinked, looking at her quizzically.

"Yeah, that's right. You just think you're frozen. You're not. Move your fingers. Try it."

The little purple creature wiggled its fingers and toes, a delighted smile crossing its face. It sat up, giggling.

"I can move!" the imp squealed.

"Yeah, see? Isn't that better?" A smile crossed her face. "You just need to get out of your own head."

"Emily, who are you talking to?" her grandmother asked, still standing on her side of the car.

"Just myself, Grandma," Emily replied hastily. "Go in the house, I'll be inside in a second."

Lizzie shrugged, shuffling towards the front stoop of Rosalie's townhouse.

Emily turned back to the imp. "Now, do you want to tell me why you nearly killed yourself on my windshield?"

473

"Amelia said she needed help."

Emily was confused. "Needed help? What for?"

The imp shrugged. "I don't know. But the mean man took my shiny necklace."

"Your shiny necklace…? Wait, what? What mean man?"

The imp, however, had lost its attention span, and proceeded to fly off, leaving a dazed and confused Emily standing in her mother's driveway.

At this point, Rosalie had opened the front door. "Emily? Are you coming in?"

Emily, however, was climbing back into her car.

"Emily? What are you doing?" her mother called after her.

"I just…I left something back at the house, Mom, I'll be back," she said quickly as she scrambled to buckle her seat belt.

Screeching out of the driveway, she headed back towards the cottage and the Blue Barn.

Something was wrong. Something was *very* wrong.

✳

Both Emily and Jack pulled into the cottage's driveway around the same time. As they saw each other, they stopped, unsure of what was happening.

"What are you doing here?" Emily snapped.

"Lila came for me, she said Amelia's in trouble," Jack responded.

474

"An imp came for me, he said the same thing," Emily said, casting aside any displeasure she had at Jack's being there.

In that moment, they heard Cosmo barking furiously at the front door of the Blue Barn. They glanced at each other, and ran towards the sound. He was scratching at the entrance, but no one was letting him in—that was not like Amelia at all.

Entering the building, they found drawers and shelves in disarray, the couch from the front room relocated to the foyer from the imp's tantrum, and general upheaval.

"What happened here?" Jack murmured.

Emily shook her head, in disbelief at what she was seeing.

That was when they heard the cries from the kitchen.

"Help…somebody…please…"

It was Amelia.

They raced down the hall towards the kitchen, where they found Amelia collapsed over in a chair on her side, bleeding and bruised, tears streaming down her face.

"Amelia, what happened?" Jack cried, scrambling to her side. "Are you okay?"

"It's Adrien!" she gasped as he untied her. "Adrien is the Fallen Sorcerer!"

"What?" he asked, working to remove her ties. "What do you mean?"

STONES ✳ RJG McManus

"He's after the source stones!" she explained, standing as the last of the ties were undone. Jack helped her to her feet as Emily dabbed a wet towel to her sister's wounds. "He already got two."

"But, how?" Jack sputtered. "What does that mean? What's he going to do with them?"

"I don't know!" she snapped, sitting in a stool, while Emily put ice to the bruise on the side of her face from her fall. "All I know is he needs to have all seven stones to do whatever it is he's planning on doing."

"How did he already get two? Where were they?" Emily asked gently.

She looked up at the two of them at this point, tears welling in her eyes. "I don't know where he got the first, or how. But the other one was from me. He got it from *me*. I was so stupid, I didn't even know I had one all these years! It was Dad's necklace."

Emily stopped what she was doing, bewildered, and Jack glanced briefly at Amelia's collarbone—the chain she usually wore around her neck that held the amber pendant was gone.

"Where did he go?" he asked her gently.

She shook her head. "I don't know. But when they left me, I saw them heading toward the dock when I looked out the window. They had a boat."

"When was this?"

"About a half hour ago."

"So, we're not too far behind. Listen, I think I know where he's going. He owns an island up the coast, about an hour's ride from here. I've been there."

"How do you know that's where he's going?" Emily inquired.

476

"Where else would he be going with a boat?" he countered. "And if he's not going there, at this point, we have nothing left to lose."

"Every villain needs his fortress," Amelia stated wryly.

Jack nodded his agreement. "We need to get to the island. We need to get the stones back."

✳

Adrien sat on the boat with Greg, Marcus, and Bruce as it sped away from land, mulling over his thoughts. He had a second source stone, which he'd placed in a case for protection once he'd reached the boat. That was a start, and something to celebrate. But Amelia hadn't told him *where* on the property it had been found. If he knew where the stone was found, he'd know where to look, where to dig…

But perhaps she really *didn't* know. Perhaps she had been telling the truth during his interrogation. Perhaps it had been found decades ago, a family heirloom passed down through the generations, a mere trinket to the living members of the Davidson family.

But *somebody* had found it at some point. Which meant *somebody* at some point had disturbed its place, had seen what else was there. This irritated him—no, not just irritated him, it *infuriated* him. Was nothing sacred?

Unless…unless this wasn't the stone he was looking for. Unless this was a different stone altogether, acquired from a different place. But how? If this wasn't the one he was looking for, where did it come from? How did they find it? Why did they have it? Which one did he hold?

He shook his head. No. Enough for now. He'd find out eventually which one he held. It was just a matter of time. He'd have to go back someday, further investigate, keep searching…not now though. No, they knew who he was now. They knew to look out for him. It would probably be decades before he could return again. But that was fine—he had all the time in the world. All he had to do was outlive them, an easy thing to do when one is immortal. In the meantime, he'd stay on course, search for the others.

He was a bit frustrated with himself. He hadn't been cautious enough. He'd let himself get worked up, get excited. He should've been more careful, stuck to the same routine, kept the same caliber of work when it came to the build—it wouldn't have aroused suspicions, wouldn't have ended with tying up Amelia. Jack had noticed the change in him, he was sure others had as well. Now there was the investigation into the company—his own fault, he admitted. Not that they'd find anything about what he was doing—all they'd know was he had used some subpar materials and bribed a few people. But they'd never know why. That much he was certain he had kept hidden well enough. The company wouldn't go under—there would be turnover, leadership changes, and he himself was resigned to being ousted, but it wouldn't go under. Not that he really cared at his point—he would disappear again. He was good at that. It wasn't the first time this century he'd had to do it.

He should've been more patient—he had eternity, all the time he could possibly need, that should've been enough to make a patient man out of him. But patience never was one of his strong points—a carryover of his mortality. Impatience was what had gotten him into all of this in the first place. You'd think after all this time, he would've learned…but old habits die hard. Does anyone ever really change?

He sighed. He couldn't turn back time, couldn't take things back—he just had to keep pushing forward, like he always did.

But right now, he smiled: he had two stones. Only five more to go.

He opened the case, where he saw the stones sitting side-by-side, each in their own separate slots, not touching each other. Gingerly, he picked them up, examining them. He didn't know what would happen when they joined together, but he knew in order to do what he needed, they would have to. He hadn't planned on joining them together now, he'd planned to wait until all seven were collected—but he also knew Jack would be on his tail, and he'd need all the magic he could get, even if it was just the little bit from these two. Yes, he'd been foolish, impatient. It didn't matter. He owned that. He was good at changing course.

He placed the stones side-by-side, bracing himself for some kind of burst of magical energy. But what happened was much more subtle than that. The two stones—one the amber stone from Amelia, the other the cobalt stone he'd already had—fused together, a small glimmer of white light sparkling where the separation had once been, then quickly fading out. When the light disappeared, there was no crack, no crease—just one solid larger stone, formed from where the two smaller ones had melded together. Each part still remained the color they had once been, but faded into each other.

Adrien wasn't sure what he had been expecting, but it wasn't that. He'd thought it would be a bit more dramatic, a release of pent up magical energy into the world. But these were just the first two—he had a feeling more would be released as they were joined with the other missing pieces.

Hopefully, whatever little bit of magic escaped into the world with that light, would be enough. In his experience, even the tiniest bit of magic was enough to change the course of history.

"We're almost there, sir."

Adrien looked up, seeing his island in the distance, a dark rock in the middle of the swirling sea. He'd approached his home from many different directions over the years, spent hundreds of seasons watching it shift and change slowly over time, knew its landscape and its views from both onshore and offshore by heart.

Today, however, there was something different about their approach—something he hadn't seen in a very long time. As they drew closer, a grin spread across his face as he saw shadowy, foreboding figures lurking in the shallows offshore, their eyes glowing red.

"Sir?" Marcus also saw the ghostly shapes surfacing from the murky depths. He'd never seen anything like it, and though Adrien had warned the three of them ahead of time what might happen, he was still startled by the sight.

"Don't worry, Marcus, they'll let you pass," Adrien said calmly. "You're with me."

The lackey nodded stiffly, gripping the helm so his knuckles were white. Bruce and Greg exchanged a glance, but remained silent.

Adrien, meanwhile, grew complacent, content as they neared shore. For the first time in centuries, with the appearance of those figures, the island finally felt like *home*, something he hadn't felt since the curse. He was reinvigorated. It appeared that little light did make a difference, had stirred some of the slumbering to wake. Good. No, not good: fantastic. Better than he could have hoped for.

Five more to go.

Yes, he would find them. He had forever, after all.

As the boat slowed, the dark creatures with their red eyes approached their master, awaiting instruction.

"It's been a while," Adrien said to the leader of the pack.

The creature grinned, its razor-sharp teeth prominent.

"There may be others after us. If they arrive, keep them busy until we leave," Adrien instructed. "I have a few things I need to gather before our departure, and I'd rather not be delayed."

"And after?" the creature rasped in a guttural voice.

Adrien grinned. "Have fun."

480

✳ Chapter 40 ✳

Teardrops in the ocean

"I don't understand," Amelia said woefully as they set forth up the coast toward the island in their grandfather's boat. "How did Dad even get the stone? Mom said he had to give up that which he loved the most—if it wasn't her, what was it? And *why* did he give it to me? And why couldn't I feel the magic coming from it? Why couldn't *any* of us feel its magic? It doesn't make sense…none of it makes sense…"

"Amelia, those are all great questions, ones we'll try to figure out later, but I'm going to need you to focus right now," Emily said as she steered the Blue Mermaid. "We need *backup*. We're going up against the *Fallen Sorcerer*."

"Okay, but he doesn't have magic, right?" Jack interjected. "That was part of his curse. He can't do anything magical to us. I mean, he might be able to shoot us or something, but aside from that…"

"Jack, haven't you been listening to *anything* we've been teaching you?" Emily snapped, frustrated by Jack's ignorance. "As the stones are put back together, magic as it was *before* the spell the Creator Sorcerer cast will slowly seep back into the world. He has *two stones*. If they're put together, some of the corrupted creatures the Fallen Sorcerer had created could wake up from their hibernation, and even *he* might regain some of his magic. We don't know what we'll be walking into once we get to the island."

"I thought all that would only happen if they were *all* put together."

"*No*. It will happen incrementally as each stone is added, until they're all together and it's back in full force. And we don't want it to come back full force, because that could destroy the world as we know it." Emily whirled around to face her stunned sister. "*Amelia!* I need you to get it together and snap out of it. *We need to summon backup to meet us at the island*, and you've got the summoning spells memorized better than I do."

At this, Amelia seemed to come out of whatever stunned trance she had been in. Shaking her head and taking a deep breath, she asked, "What do we have on board that I can use?"

"Not a whole lot," Emily replied.

Amelia contemplated this for a moment. "So, we're limited to creatures that don't require much by way of props to summon them."

"Imps?" Jack suggested.

Emily rolled her eyes. "Sure, if we want spastic flying toddlers."

"Just trying to help," he said, perturbed by Emily's attitude.

"I'm going to need you two to get along right now. This is *not* the time for petty arguments," Amelia snapped.

Jack and Emily each muttered their apologies.

Turning to Jack, Amelia said, "Maybe on the imps. We'll see how things play out when we get there. If I know Lila, she's already rallying, so we should have a full fairy force on our tail shortly. The only other option that comes to mind is selkies."

"Okay, but, there's only one way to summon selkies," Emily commented offhandedly, focusing more on steering the boat at this point.

"I know." Amelia gazed intently at her sister.

Emily glanced over, and seeing the look on her sister's face, very resolutely said, "*No*. I'm not doing that."

"Em, right now, you're the only one on this boat who possibly can."

"Why can't you?"

"Because I'm fine," Amelia said. "*You're* the one who just found out your ex-boyfriend is marrying your ex-best friend."

"I'm not upset about that," Emily lied, refusing to make eye contact with her sister as she stared ahead at the horizon.

"Yes, you are."

"So, what, you're just going to take advantage of that?"

"It's not taking advantage," Amelia sighed. "It's just a coincidence that will *help* us."

"I don't understand what's happening," Jack spoke up, interrupting the exchange between the sisters. "What does Emily's breakup have to do with summoning selkies?"

"If a woman who's unhappy in her love life cries seven tears into the sea, she will summon a male selkie to her side," Amelia explained.

"That's a pretty messed up summoning spell," Jack commented.

"*EXACTLY!*" Emily exclaimed. "Thank you!"

"It was meant to bring companionship to the woman," Amelia explained. "But in our case, we can summon one and ask him to send for help from the rest of his pod. We just need Emily to cry seven tears into the ocean."

"That's actually a pretty good idea," Jack said, mulling this over.

"Yeah, well, I'm a little too busy steering the boat at the moment to go cry into the sea," Emily remarked.

"You know I'm perfectly capable of steering this thing," Amelia retorted.

"I was in the Navy. I steered a ship. I can handle it too," Jack offered.

"*No*. The answer is *no*," Emily said obstinately. "I *refuse* to cry over him just because you want me to. It's *demeaning*. Think of another creature you can summon that doesn't involve *that*."

"What other creature do you suggest I summon from the middle of the ocean that doesn't require any other props?"

None came to mind, and Emily remained silent.

"*Exactly*," Amelia said in response to her sister's silence. "Emily, you said it—this is the Fallen Sorcerer we're dealing with here. And right now, if you want more than just fairies on our side, *you* need to be the one to do this. I can't."

"*Fine*," Emily conceded. "But this is the *only* time you're allowed to use me like this, understood?"

"Yes."

"You owe me."

With this, Emily stepped away from the helm, and Amelia stepped into her place. Emily walked out of the cabin, and leaning over the handrail, took a deep breath, closed her eyes, and let all the memories and emotions she had been pushing back come springing forth, flooding her mind and overwhelming her thoughts.

The moment that started it all, of course—when she walked into her apartment and saw Dan and Leslie making out on the couch. She let the old rage, the anger, the betrayal wash over her, reliving that moment.

One teardrop into the ocean.

The moment she found out Dan and Leslie were more than a random fling, they were serious about each other, they *loved* each other.

A second teardrop into the ocean.

The look of relief on each of their faces when she told them she was moving, that she'd be leaving the apartment and the two of them for good. The sadness she felt at the realization neither of them wanted her around.

A third teardrop into the ocean.

The phone call from Dan letting her know he'd proposed, that he and Leslie would be getting married.

A fourth teardrop into the ocean.

The moment she realized Dan never really loved her.

A fifth teardrop into the ocean.

The fear there might not be someone for her, that she might never be loved.

The final two teardrops came from this thought.

With the seventh drop, Emily furiously wiped her eyes, gasping as she tried to keep the sobs from escaping her body, but to no avail. She crumpled on the deck, curling up into a ball with her head in her knees. She hated being vulnerable. From inside the cabin, Amelia continued to silently steer, and Jack stood, watching Emily, but respecting her space by keeping his distance.

A moment later, but what felt like an eternity for Emily, she heard something splashing alongside the ship. Brushing away the last few tears, she looked into the glassy sea, where she caught sight of a creature swimming beside the boat—a selkie.

"Stop the boat!" she shouted to her sister, who complied.

Once stopped, the boat bobbling listlessly as waves rolled underneath it, Emily leaned over the guardrail, and the selkie in its seal form surfaced, gazing at her intently.

"I don't need your companionship today," Emily said to the selkie. "But I do need your help."

The selkie didn't respond, but he didn't swim away either. He continued to float, looking at her as if he was urging her to continue, that he was listening.

"We're on our way to an island up the coast. It has only one large house. It's owned by a man named Adrien Dunstan. Do you know it?"

The selkie nodded.

"We need you and your pod to join us there—we don't know what's going to happen once we get there. But we do know two things: Adrien Dunstan is the Fallen Sorcerer, and he has two of the source stones."

The selkie's eyes went wide, and he emitted a low growl, which Emily took to be shock and disbelief.

"It's true," Emily said. "He said so himself. He's after the other stones. Go, tell your pod—tell them the Fallen Sorcerer has returned."

With this, the selkie dove into the depths of the ocean. Emily leaned against the guardrail and sighed, taking a moment to compose herself. Out of the corner of her eye, she caught sight of Jack and Amelia standing in the doorframe of the cabin, watching her. Standing upright, she marched in to join them, pushing her way past each of them, walking straight towards the helm. She fired the engine back up, and without saying a word to either of the other two, continued to steer the boat toward the island.

"Thank you," Amelia said softly, putting her hand on her sister's shoulder.

Emily flinched under her touch, shifting her weight away from Amelia. Amelia took her meaning, and stepped back a few paces, taking her hand away from Emily.

"Don't *ever* make me do something like that again," Emily said through clenched teeth. "Don't *ever* take advantage of my vulnerability again. *Do you understand me?*"

Amelia nodded, not saying a word in response.

The trio remained silent for a few minutes, none of them sure what to say after the selkie summoning—that is, until Amelia's cell phone rang. She looked down, and seeing her mother's picture pop up on her screen, bit her lip.

"It's Mom. What do I tell her?"

Emily looked up. "Tell her we're sorry, but we won't be having Thanksgiving dinner with her."

Amelia answered the phone. As soon as she did, she heard Rosalie's shrill cry on the other end, "*WHERE ARE YOU?! Your sister flew out of here like a bat out of hell, dinner is waiting—*"

Amelia winced, pulling the phone from her ear and her mother's screeching. "Mom—MOM! Calm down. We're okay. We won't be making it tonight. I'm sorry."

"*WHAT?!*"

"Something came up."

"*What could POSSIBLY be more important than Thanksgiving dinner with your family?!*"

"The Fallen Sorcerer returned. And he has a stone."

Rosalie fell silent.

"Mom?"

"*What are you doing?*"

Amelia looked at Emily, who nodded. "What we have to. I love you, Mom. Em does too. We'll see you soon." She paused. "And check in on Cosmo for us. He's alone at the cottage right now."

"*Amelia—*"

But Amelia had hung up, and turned the cell phone off. Emily, pulling her own phone from her pocket, followed suit, knowing she would be next to receive a call.

They needed to focus on the task before them.

✳

The island from the distance was dark, desolate—looming blackness in the middle of a gloomy sea and sky.

As they approached, Jack noticed a group of shadowy figures moving along the shore. He froze, bracing himself, his mind racing as he tried to remember every creature he'd learned about. What could possibly be waiting for them? The sun was nearly set, casting long shadows, so he couldn't tell what the creatures were.

As they drew closer, he could make out their shape, and sighed with relief—they were simply horses, wading in the water. The rest of the island was quiet and still. This might go smoothly.

He looked over at Amelia and Emily, expecting them to each look relieved as well. Instead, however, he was met with terrified gazes.

"What is it?" Jack asked, confused.

"Kelpies," Amelia whispered.

Jack wracked his brain, trying to remember what a kelpie was—and it dawned on him. Amelia had mentioned them long ago, when they'd first started meeting up, and he'd even read about them in one of the journals she'd given him, but forgot. They were creatures that appeared as horses along shorelines and riverbanks, sometimes shifting into human form. If touched by someone, that person would not be able to let go of them— and the kelpie would drag them into the water, drown them, and eat them.

Jack's stomach churned. "Are you sure? Because he keeps horses here. I've seen the stables."

Amelia nodded, her jaw set. "Their hooves are backwards. And their eyes. Look at their eyes."

So he did, while Emily stopped the boat's engine. The group sat in silence, drifting, watching the creatures closely. As they trotted along, he saw their hooves were indeed on backwards, a grotesque caricature of the horses they tried to emulate. Instead of the animalistic, brown iris found in a normal horse, these horses had eyes of a subtly glowing red, with a sharp intelligence in them. They were watching the approaching boat intently. Their wandering on shore was not random—they were getting into position, readying themselves to make their move.

"They're *awake*," Emily gawked. "They're *actually awake*."

489

"How?" Jack was becoming increasingly aware of the fact they were drifting closer to the demonic horses.

"He put the two stones together," Amelia said breathlessly. "The dark creatures are waking up."

"How many creatures are we talking?"

Amelia shook her head. "I don't know. But as more magic comes back into the world, the more powerful creatures will start to awaken."

"That's positive, right?" Jack asked, grasping for something hopeful. "That means kelpies aren't really that powerful?"

Emily turned to look at him, a stony expression on her face. "Just because they don't require as much magic doesn't mean they aren't dangerous. Don't underestimate them."

"How do we get past them?" Jack noticed they'd formed a barricade of sorts on shore, ready to pounce as soon as the boat touched the sand.

"Carefully," Amelia said. "Very, very carefully. And typically, with magic."

"Which we don't have."

"Yet."

Emily, meanwhile, was gazing back towards the water, a concerned look on her face, waiting for the selkies and fairies to arrive. "Where are they?

"They'll be here," Amelia assured her. "We just need to wait, they'll help clear our way."

"The longer we wait, the more likely it is Adrien will get away!" Jack argued. "We need to figure something out."

"He's on an island. How far could he get?"

"He has a helicopter!"

"Well, you didn't tell me *that* part!" Then, she declared into the evening air, "Hear me, imps, creatures of delight, why wouldn't the shrimp share his treasure?" A pause, then she continued, "Because he was a little shellfish."

Emily moaned, and Jack chuckled a bit, despite the precarious situation. A moment later, a flock of imps swirled around the boat, also laughing.

"Another!" one demanded, clearly the leader. The rest of the group chimed in, also crying out, "Another! Another!"

"I'll tell you another later," Amelia said. "But first, I need your help."

"ANOTHER!" the leader still demanded, now frowning.

"But I have something better for you—a game!"

"A game?" the leader repeated, its ears perked. The others, following suit, also chirped, "A game? A game?"

"Yes, a game. I need you to find something. Like a scavenger hunt."

"We like scavenger hunts!" the leader declared, clapping its hands cheerily. The other imps also clapped and laughed, excited about the prospect of this new game.

"I need you to find a helicopter. Do you know what that is?"

The imps furrowed their brows, shaking their heads.

"It looks like a great big shiny metal bird, with its wings spinning on its back," Amelia explained. "People can climb in and out of the bird and fly away in it. When you find it, you need to make sure it *doesn't* fly away."

"How?" the lead imp asked.

"However you want. Be creative. Have fun."

The flock cheered, and whizzed off towards the island, above the kelpies and out of their reach, excited about the game and being given free rein to wreak havoc as they wanted. Before they were out of earshot, Amelia cried out after them, "And *be careful!* There are things on the island that will want to hurt you!"

She turned back toward Emily and Jack, a worried look on her face. "I hope that works. And I hope they'll be okay."

"Imps are pretty durable," Emily reassured her. "They'll be fine."

Jack, meanwhile, was grinning and looking proud of himself.

"What's that look for?" Emily asked, noticing his bemused expression.

"You said we wouldn't need imps. I was right. You were *wrong*."

"Don't get used to it."

They continued to float, sitting ducks as they waited for reinforcements—they dared not attempt landfall until the kelpies were cleared from their path. The kelpies, meanwhile, looked as though they were growing impatient, stamping their hooves and whinnying, waiting for their prey to approach so they could drag them into the dark depths of the murky water.

"What if they don't come?" Jack asked of the fairies and selkies, anxious by this point.

492

"They'll come," Amelia reassured him.

"How do you know?"

"I just know."

"But what if—"

"*They will come.*"

They continued to watch the kelpies, who were watching them. As they looked on, the lead kelpie, a muscular creature with the blackest coat any of them had ever seen, stepped out further into the water. Soon, the other kelpies were falling into formation behind him, their eyes now glowing. The three watched in horror as the herd slowly treaded water, heading straight toward their suddenly insufficient boat.

"What are they doing?" Jack asked, his eyes wide as he watched this unfold.

"They're done waiting for us," Amelia replied, her own eyes wide with fear.

Jack's eyes darted about, desperately hoping he would catch sight of a selkie or a fairy—*something*. But they were on their own.

"What do we do?" he asked, seeing there was no help in sight.

"Emily, we need to move. *Quickly*," Amelia ordered. Emily nodded, turning the engine back on. It sputtered to life, a low hum beneath their feet.

Before Emily shifted into high gear, Amelia looked at her companions. "Remember—if a kelpie catches you, do whatever you can to get hold of its bridle. Control the bridle, control the kelpie. That's your only chance."

Jack looked out at the approaching kelpies, catching a glimpse of a glint of silver around their necks before they disappeared beneath the black water. They were now out of sight, surely swimming straight for the boat.

While Jack observed this scene, Amelia turned to Emily and said, "Do it."

Emily nodded, clenching her teeth. "Hang on."

Jack and Amelia sat, bracing themselves as Emily kicked the boat to the highest speed it could go, all three praying they would arrive onshore before the kelpies resurfaced.

Luck, however, was not with them. As they raced as fast as the small fishing boat would allow them over the dark, smooth water, they suddenly felt a *thump!* from underneath the vessel.

"What was that?" Jack asked, trying to keep panic from entering his voice.

"Kelpie," Amelia replied through gritted teeth. "Emily, keep moving. Don't stop for *anything*."

Emily nodded, pressing forward. They were coming closer to shore now. She shifted the boat to a lower speed to prepare for landing.

"What are you doing?" Amelia demanded, noticing the slowdown.

"Slowing down!" Emily yelled. "We can't go that fast in shallow waters! And we can't run ashore! It'll destroy the boat!"

"But if we slow down, *they'll catch us!*"

"Doesn't matter anymore," Jack said gravely, looking out into the water.

The sisters stopped arguing and looked out at the water themselves. Just below the surface, they saw the movement of dark shadows and bubbling, and the dim glow of those red eyes, imparting a general sense of doom upon the group. The kelpies were resurfacing. They had surrounded the boat, treading water alongside it, determined to guide it into shore, where they would capture their prey in the shallows, dragging them down to drown and consume them.

"Remember the bridle," Amelia whispered.

The group waited with bated breath, wondering if their time on this planet would be shortly coming to an abrupt end.

"Emily, *speed up the boat*," Amelia hissed.

"But we'll run aground!" Emily countered, knuckles white as she clutched the helm, eyes wide as she stared fearfully over the side of the boat.

"That's a chance I'm willing to take."

Emily looked at Jack, who nodded his agreement with Amelia.

"Do it," he said, entranced by the glowing red eyes of the kelpies that had surrounded them.

Emily, outnumbered, went to kick the boat to a higher speed. A sputtering, then nothing.

"What happened?" Amelia demanded.

"I don't know!" Emily cried out. "It's not moving!"

She toggled a number of switches, and tried again. Still nothing.

The kelpies now had complete control over the boat, slowly guiding it along towards shallow water and certain death.

495

"This wouldn't have happened if you'd just kept full speed in the first place!" Amelia snapped.

"If I'd kept that speed, we would've crashed!" Emily said furiously.

"Hey, guys…guys?" Jack said warily, interjecting himself into the argument.

The sisters turned to look at Jack, noticing he was looking out over the water. The kelpies had stopped treading water alongside the boat—the boat itself had stopped moving altogether. The glowing red eyes of the kelpies had disappeared…they had submerged once again, the only clue to where they had gone being the bubbling of air pockets from below the water's surface.

"Where'd they go?" Amelia whispered.

Jack shook his head. "I don't know."

Emily tried to start the engine again. Still nothing.

It was then that they felt the boat rocking. The water, which had been placid and smooth, started churning—mere bubbles at first, then violently in a swirl of frothy whitewater, beating the side of the boat and ever increasing in size and strength. The small boat was bobbing about, no match for the waves that were soon overcoming it.

Amelia grasped the railing of the boat as she realized what was happening. "They're trying to capsize us!"

"What do we do?" Jack asked over the deafening noise of crashing waves.

"Swim."

And with this, Amelia dove headfirst into the icy water in a last-ditch effort to reach shore. Jack, momentarily shocked by her action, composed himself and followed suit.

Emily, however, remained on the boat for a few seconds longer than her companions, distraught over the idea of abandoning her boat—no, not her boat, her *grandfather's* boat, the boat that held so many memories, that had been a safe haven for her in her teenage years. It was one of the few tangible pieces of Stuart she had left, and leaving it behind, to be ravaged by kelpies, was too cruel, too painful, too unfair.

But as the waves increased in size and strength, themselves looking eerily like the shape of those demonic steeds, she knew it had to be done.

And so, she dove. The freezing cold hit her first, like a thousand tiny knives stabbing every part of her body, numbing her senses and consuming her thoughts. She flailed beneath the water's violent, churning surface, gasping for breath at the shock of it, only for her mouth to be filled with the salty, bitter seawater.

Still, she swam as hard as she could, not even sure which way she was going—up or down, out to sea or towards the island. It didn't matter, so long as she *just kept moving*.

Something brushed against her and grasped her. In the darkness of the water, she couldn't see what it was, and alarms went off in her head. She struggled, fighting for her life, frantically feeling for the kelpie's bridle in order to control it, becoming sorrowful and hopeless when she couldn't find it, couldn't see it, couldn't feel it.

But that was when she noticed something—the creature holding her didn't have the feel of a muscular stallion. In fact, it felt blubbery and *squishy*. Warmth radiated from it, protecting her from the penetrating cold of the icy waters surrounding them. She also noticed with much surprise she could *breathe*, though she was well below the water's surface.

But perhaps, not as far below as she thought, as she turned her head to look up—she was able to catch a glimpse of the stars above, the sun now set over the horizon, as they were swimming towards the surface.

She looked over, and smiled—the creature holding her was none other but the same selkie she'd called upon earlier. She wrapped her arms around his soft neck as he hastened her to shore and out of the realm of the kelpies.

✳ Chapter 41 ✳

Kelpies

When the selkie and Emily came ashore, Emily coughing and choking, she looked about, searching for some sign of Jack and Amelia. Jack, she saw, was wading into shore behind her alongside another selkie, waterlogged and shivering, but looking very much relieved to be alive.

Amelia, however, was nowhere in sight.

"Where's Amelia?" Emily cried out frantically, sloshing towards Jack.

He stopped, frozen, staring at her. "She's not here with you?"

Emily shook her head, fear rising in her chest. "No, I thought she would've been here first, she was the first off the boat..."

Before she could continue, Jack had already turned back around, marching back towards the sea.

"What are you doing?" Emily gasped.

"Going to find her." Jack nodded towards the selkie at his side, who gave him a questioning look at first, but acquiesced and followed suit, also turning back towards the sea.

"But you might die!" Emily argued, now agitated by the thought of losing not only her sister, but her only other companion in this whole crazy series of events, and the idea of being left alone on this wretched island with the Fallen Sorcerer, who was up to God only knew what.

"We're all going to die sometime anyway."

He looked at his own selkie, and for the first time, noticed a small scar on her side. He smiled, realizing in that moment it was Aerwyna, the same selkie he and Amelia had rescued earlier in the month, when everything ahead of him seemed so bright and clear and hopeful. He still had hope—even in the midst of the swirling, cold, treacherous ocean, he had hope.

"Stay with me," he whispered to Aerwyna, grateful to have a familiar friend have his back. The selkie nodded, plodding alongside him, until they reached a point in the depths where he could dive and she could gracefully swim at his side.

And so he swam towards deeper water, warmed by the magical bubble that radiated off the selkie, towards the wreckage of the Blue Mermaid, the last place he saw Amelia before she dove overboard. The small vessel rested on its side, bobbing listlessly, half submerged and slowly taking on more water—he knew within a few minutes, the boat would be underwater, eventually coming to its final resting place on the ocean's floor.

Amelia was here somewhere, she had to be—he hadn't seen her surface when she dove, and in the moment, he hadn't thought much of it, he was so focused on swimming and staying alive himself. When Aerwyna appeared by his side, heating him through and helping him breathe in the icy depths, he assumed another selkie had found its way to Amelia and come to her aid as well. It was only when he reached shore and saw Emily alone panic set in. He couldn't lose her—he *refused* to lose her.

He treaded water near the overturned boat, looking for some sign of her—nothing. No flash of her strawberry hair, no glimpse of the blue blouse she had been wearing—nothing on the surface indicated she was there. He glanced down, momentarily seeing a faint, red glow—the glow of a kelpie's eyes deep below them. Dread filled him, but he knew what he had to do.

He looked at Aerwyna, who gave him a knowing look that said, "I'm still with you." He nodded, and the two dove together, Aerwyna staying as close to Jack as possible so as to keep him within the warm bubble full of breathable air.

As he swam, he was able to make out the dark, murky undersea world that lay before him. Thick fields of seaweed dotted vast stretches of sandy plains. Litter and trash, and even boat parts, lay strewn about. He and Aerwyna weaved their way through large, jagged rocks, keeping an eye out for any sign of kelpies and Amelia.

And there she was. Unconscious and wrapped and bound in seaweed, swaying gently with the tide. Jack swam harder and faster, fear filling every fiber of his being. She was pale, her lips a shade of purple. To him, she looked drowned, completely lifeless.

He was too late.

But even still…he had hope. Perhaps she was alive? Perhaps magic had prevailed, and he could save her?

And even if not…even if he was too late, if she was already gone, he wouldn't give the kelpies the satisfaction of desecrating her body. No, she deserved better than that, more dignity than that. He'd take her body ashore, and figure out how to get it back to her family for a proper funeral. He owed her that much. She'd given him a life worth living—the least he could do was give her a death befitting of the kind, beautiful woman she was.

So, he swam, not looking about for kelpies anymore, not even caring. He just had to reach her.

He motioned for Aerwyna to stay close, to envelope Amelia in her warmth and air as well. Once she did so, he felt for a pulse, trying to confirm if she was still alive. Putting his fingers to her neck, then her wrists, he couldn't feel anything—if she did indeed still have a pulse, it was too weak for him to pick up on it.

Then, as a last check, he put his head to her chest, to listen.

Thump thump.

Soft, weak…but alive.

Jack grabbed at the seaweed Amelia was entwined in, trying to unwind it from her body, but struggling to do so—there were so many pieces, so many strands, he didn't know where to start. It was an arduous process, and he was becoming frantic. He didn't know how long she'd been here, and though she was receiving air and warmth from Aerwyna's bubble for the moment, he didn't know how long she'd last. She needed to get to the surface.

As he worked at the seaweed, he caught a glimpse of something moving out of the corner of his eye. He looked, and saw a creature, humanlike in form, broad, dark, and muscular, with glowing red eyes, and backwards hooves instead of feet. As it drew closer, marching slowly across the ocean floor, it grinned the most malicious, terrifying smile Jack had ever seen, revealing mangled, razor-sharp teeth. Around its neck was a small, delicate, silver chain. Behind it, much to his dismay, he saw other murky figures appear out of the shadows, similar in appearance.

Jack was seeing the kelpies transformed into their humanoid iteration—and it was much more terrifying than their horse form.

Aerwyna also saw the approaching kelpies, and looked back and forth between them and Jack, not sure what to do: to transform into her own humanoid form and approach the kelpies and fight them would keep them away from Jack and Amelia, but it would also mean they'd lose her warmth and the ability to breathe underwater—something they desperately needed in the dark, icy depths. But to stay put would mean they'd be sitting ducks, and it would draw the kelpies close to them, give them the chance to reach them. She needed help.

She cried out, a high-pitched, melodic cry that seemed to make the ocean itself wave, and penetrated to the very core of the humans and creatures surrounding her.

All the kelpies, and even Jack, turned to look at Aerwyna, stunned and confused at first. It was only when a pod of at least fifty selkies were upon them the kelpies understood what was happening, what Aerwyna had done.

The selkies, one by one, transformed into their own humanoid shapes, armed with spears and swords. They charged upon the kelpies, who took the defense, fighting back with jagged daggers and their sickly teeth. Jack watched with pride as he saw a pair of selkies take down a kelpie, but that pride instantly turned to horror as a pair of kelpies jumped on a selkie, tearing at its flesh with their teeth and consuming it alive. They were bloody and ruthless.

As the selkies and kelpies fought and thrashed against each other, Jack moved quicker to release Amelia from her bonds, as Aerwyna stayed put, becoming restless as she couldn't join the fight to defend her pod.

Finally, Jack was able to untie the final strand, and Amelia, released from the seaweed, floated upwards. Jack grabbed hold of her by the waist, and kicked toward the surface, motioning for Aerwyna to stay with him.

And she did, for a time—until suddenly, Jack felt as though he had been dropped into a pool of ice. His limbs went rigid and numb as he flailed about. He gasped for air as he struggled to keep hold of Amelia, no longer able to breathe. He looked about wildly for Aerwyna, not knowing what had just happened or why she'd left his side. It was only when he saw a glint of glowing red below him he realized she'd been dragged down, engaged in a struggle with a kelpie. He watched, helpless, as she transformed into her own human form, fighting as hard as she could.

But he quickly realized this was merely a distraction. Out of the shadows Jack saw a different kelpie, the *lead* kelpie, surface and swim towards them, his eyes like embers, his teeth like jagged razors. He was now coming after them as Aerwyna was being kept busy in her own fight with his minion.

Jack kicked harder, every movement painful, a struggle, his lungs filling with seawater, and suddenly incredibly aware of the dead weight that was Amelia. Still, he couldn't let her go, not when there was a chance.

The kelpie was mere yards behind him now, and quickly closing the gap. A moment later, Jack felt its sharp claws for hands grasp his ankle. He kicked, trying to release himself from it, but it was dragging him down, down, down…no matter what he did, how he fought, it wouldn't let go.

He made the split-second decision to release Amelia—perhaps she would float to the top, perhaps she would regain consciousness, perhaps she could have a chance to live…but there was no hope, no chance if he kept hold of her.

So he did, and as he was dragged downwards by the kelpie, he watched her slowly float up, still, motionless, her hair waving with the movements of the water around her, resembling a much softer, gentler version of the seaweed below. He looked at her, memorized her, lovely even in this moment, sure this was the last sight he would ever see on this planet.

But then, he remembered her words, from not so long ago: "*Remember the bridle.*"

And so, Jack turned to the kelpie, and catching sight of the strand of silver around its neck, grabbed hold. In an instant, the monstrous, human-like distortion transformed into its horse form, kicking about under the water. He jerked on its bridle, forcing it to turn, to go back towards Amelia. Try as it might, the kelpie had no control over itself at all—every movement was under Jack's instruction.

The kelpie swam upwards, and as it did, Jack was able to grab onto Amelia, who was still slowly floating towards the top. A moment later, they surfaced, Jack gasping for air, Amelia slumped over the kelpie's back in front of him. He directed the kelpie toward land, where he saw Emily, sitting alone on shore.

Emily jumped to her feet as the kelpie, loaded with Jack and Amelia, galloped towards the edge of damp and dry sand. When it hit that line, it whinnied, unable to step foot onto the dry side.

Jack jerked at its bridle, causing the creature to kneel. Turning to Emily, he barked, "Get Amelia onto dry land! I've got it!"

Emily, still shaken by the sight of the kelpie, did as he instructed, dragging her sister off the kelpie's back and onto the dry sand. As soon as Jack saw Amelia was safe over the line, he jumped off the kelpie's back, and raced to dry land too. The kelpie, agitated, paced the border for a moment, irked it couldn't reach them. With another angry whinny, it turned its back, disappearing back into the ocean.

Jack, breathless and freezing, collapsed on his hands and knees, exhausted from the ordeal. He looked up to see Emily kneeling over Amelia, shaking her, crying and pleading, "Amelia...wake up! Please, *wake up*!" She looked over at Jack, and wailed, "She's not breathing!"

Jack crawled over, and pushed Emily to the side, grunting, "Move over." Before she could protest, he'd already switched gears, performing CPR on Amelia, remembering the training he'd received during his time in the Navy. Emily sat by helplessly, praying her sister would be saved.

He alternated between compressions and breaths, himself praying as he did so. Every second she didn't breathe, didn't awake was agony, and he felt himself grow increasingly distraught. Still, he had to stay calm, he had to keep trying.

It was when he was in the midst of giving her another breath that suddenly, she coughed, water sputtering out of her mouth. Her eyes fluttered open and she looked about wildly, startled, as the last thing she had seen before this moment was the kelpie dragging her down.

"It's okay, it's okay!" Jack reassured her as she flailed and gasped. "It's me! You're safe!"

She locked eyes with him, and realizing she was out of the realm of the kelpies, that she was on shore and safe for the moment, wrapped her arms around him, burying her head in his chest as she began to cry. He embraced her back, tightly, not sure if he'd ever let her go.

"I thought I was going to die," she said between sobs.

"I know," he whispered, running his hands through her hair, incredibly aware of how close he'd come to losing her. "But you didn't. You're okay."

"What happened?" she asked, looking up to meet his gaze. "How did I get here? How did I get away? Why didn't they kill me?"

He shook his head. "Doesn't matter. All that matters is you're safe now."

And in that moment, he meant it. Nothing else mattered.

But that feeling would be fleeting.

✳ Chapter 42 ✳

The island

As they stood on shore, plotting their next move, Jack caught sight of something out of the corner of his eye. In the distance, fast approaching, was what looked like a giant cloud—but it was shimmering and golden, and hung low in the sky.

"What's that?" he asked. Was this some other creature of Adrien's?

Amelia and Emily turned, and grinned.

"That's our backup," Amelia replied.

"Fairies," Emily agreed. "And it looks like they brought a friend."

The fairies had finally arrived, coming down upon the island in a swirling mass of light, vaguely resembling a sparkling tornado. And the crash of lightning revealed the crimson feathers of the thunderbird, circling the island.

Lila whizzed toward Amelia, who smiled upon seeing her friend. The fairy, seeing the group drenched and shivering, made a series of gestures to the rest of the cloud. The fairies clustered around the three, and began swirling—Jack was entranced by the glittering gold light spinning around him. As they slowed, he looked down at his clothes—they were now warm and dry, making it easier for the group to complete their task. He smiled.

"Thank you," Amelia said, grateful to no longer be cold and wet.

Lila smiled, then made a few gestures asking what they needed to do now.

"Scout the island," Amelia instructed. "We don't know what other creatures are hidden here. If you see a creature of the Fallen Sorcerer's, stun it." She looked at the thunderbird circling above her. "Have him take care of the waters—clear out the kelpies."

She turned to Aerwyna, who had escaped her ordeal with the kelpie, and instructed her, "But tell the selkies first, so they don't get caught in the crossfire."

The selkie nodded, and gave a cry out towards the sea—suddenly, dozens of selkies came plodding ashore, taking shelter on the island's rocks and stretches of beach, bracing themselves for what was to come.

Turning back to Lila, Amelia continued, "The imps are working on making sure Adrien can't leave on his helicopter—but if for some reason they don't succeed and he *does* take off, have him take care of that too." She glanced up, pointing at the giant bird overhead.

Lila darted up to relay this information to the thunderbird. As soon as she did so, the bird swooped low, nearly touching the water, circling the island—it was churning the waters and the kelpies lurking within, pummeling them against rocks in the depths below, driving them to the deeper waters they weren't meant to inhabit. As the bird went about this business, the fairies descended on the island in their massive cloud of light, darting through trees, setting the whole island aglow as they searched for anything malicious that might obstruct the trio from completing what they'd set out to do.

"Now what do we do?" Emily asked, watching this scene unfold.

"Now we find Adrien," Amelia said wryly.

"We need to split up, then."

Jack shook his head. "No. We don't know what we're in for. We should stick together."

"Jack, Emily's right—we'll cover more ground," Amelia said, agreeing with her sister. "We'll be okay. We have the fairies and imps and selkies to help us if we come across anything."

Jack pursed his lips. "Fine. But you two at least need to stay together. I can go alone."

"Fine. Em?"

"Yeah, that's fine," Emily said.

"You two head for the helipad," Jack instructed, pointing in the general direction. "I'll take the house. Those are the two places he's most likely to be."

"What do we do if we find him?" Emily asked.

"Stop him. It doesn't matter how."

So the group went their separate ways. Every tree, every rock, every nook, every cranny was alight with the twinkling of fairies. There was nothing dark about the island anymore, and to Jack, it reminded him of the glittering lights of the parties Adrien had held in this very spot. The beaches were crowded with selkies. In the distance, they could hear the giggling of imps. And circling the island slowly with bolts of lightning and crashes of thunder was the looming figure of the thunderbird, churning out the kelpies from their hiding places.

Magic was very much alive.

✳

"This place is creepy," Emily commented as she and Amelia trudged towards the helipad.

509

Amelia remained silent, simply nodding her agreement.

"What else do you think we're going to run into here?" Emily continued. "I mean, the kelpies woke up…what else does he have here?"

"Goblins."

"Okay, don't even joke about that," Emily shuddered.

"No. *Goblins.*"

Amelia had halted, staring out onto the helipad. Surrounding the helicopter were some of the most repulsive creatures she'd ever seen. They were about the size of brownies, but much less friendly looking, with gray, sickly skin, bulging eyes, yellowed, crooked teeth and sharp nails.

"Well, damn," Emily muttered.

At that moment, they heard a high-pitched giggle, and looked up—the imps had found the helicopter, and were descending upon it. The goblins, seeing the imps, picked up anything that could be tossed, and threw the items at the imps, freezing them mid-air. Emily and Amelia remained still from their position in the dark underbrush, watching the miniature battle unfold.

"Enjoying the show?"

The girls jumped as they heard the voice behind them, each feeling a hand on their shoulder. Turning, they found themselves face to face with Bruce, one of Adrien's lackeys, who had an amused, sinister twinkle in his eye.

It was in that moment Amelia was very glad Jack had insisted on teaching her self-defense.

✳

As the sisters left for the helipad, Jack approached the mansion, foreboding and ominous now. He burst through the doors, running through the maze of halls, up and down stairs, checking every room for Adrien. So far, he was nowhere to be found.

Until he reached the courtyard—the very one Jack had been in a couple months prior at Dunstan Enterprises' anniversary celebration. The courtyard was a stark contrast to what it had been—the lights were out, and it was dark, save for the twinkling of the fairies that occasionally zoomed overhead. The fountains were off, and the place was still, silent, and empty.

Except for one lone, dark figure, racing across the courtyard, carrying a briefcase.

It was Adrien.

"Give me the stones, Adrien," Jack demanded, stepping out of the doorway of the house.

Adrien stopped, his back to Jack, not moving.

"Jack, Jack, Jack…you don't understand, do you?"

"I understand that you manipulated me for *months*." Jack gritted his teeth, approaching his former employer cautiously.

"I wasn't alone in my manipulation." Adrien turned to face Jack. "You did a bit of your own."

"What I did was to *protect* others. You were just out for yourself!"

"Toh-may-toh, toh-mah-toh. We're more alike than you think, Jack."

Jack wasn't listening. "The development had nothing to do with the build—you were just digging for stones! All the bribes you made were just to get the land to get the stones. Even taking Max off the project—it was because he was just slowing you down. And the materials…you never cared how things were built. You were just trying to find what was in the ground as quickly as possible. The whole company…it's just a front, an excuse for you to dig."

"Well, of course," Adrien confirmed. "But I'm not trying to steal the *whole* world's magic, if that's what you think. I just need a *little*."

"Adrien, people could get hurt," Jack tried to reason. "Magical creatures could get hurt. It'll be chaotic. It's not what you think."

Adrien curled his lips into a thin smile. "Jack, I've been at this for centuries. I understand the ramifications. And it's a risk I'm willing to take."

"But why do you need the stones? What are you trying to do?"

Adrien laughed. "Oh, Jack…really? You're trying to get a villain monologue out of me, want me to reveal my whole master plan to you? This isn't a movie, Jack. Life doesn't work that way. It's nobody's business but my own."

Jack took a step forward. "Give me the stones, Adrien. Nobody has to get hurt."

Adrien raised an eyebrow. "You really think I'd trust *you*, of all people, with them?"

"What's that supposed to mean?" Jack asked, perplexed.

"It means let me go, Jack. This round is mine."

"No."

And Jack did the only thing he could think of—he punched Adrien square in the jaw. Adrien, however, didn't even flinch when Jack's fist made contact with his face. Jack faltered back a step, bewildered, as Adrien stood there, unmoving, a dark grin spreading across his face.

"You can't hurt me, Jack. I'm still immortal," Adrien mocked. "Let me reunite the stones, then take a swing at me."

"*No.*" Jack swung again, hitting Adrien again. Still, Adrien didn't even blink.

"I can do this all day, Jack, but I have other business I'd rather attend to," Adrien commented, almost as if he was bored.

Jack, in an act of desperation, tackled Adrien, knocking him to the ground. The two men tussled, Jack trying to reach for the case the stones were in, Adrien trying to block him. At one point, Adrien was able to stand, and he proceeded to kick Jack, who was still on the ground, as hard as he could in the gut. Jack doubled over at the force of impact, clutching at his abdomen. Adrien took this opportunity to snatch the case off the ground and run as fast as he could in the direction of the helipad, where his helicopter was waiting to carry him off the island.

When Jack was able to regain his breath, he staggered to his feet, beginning his pursuit after his former boss. Eventually, he caught up, astonished by the sight he was met with: the perimeter of the helipad was circled by a line of goblins, all standing guard against the onslaught of imps who were attempting to sabotage the helicopter.

Apparently, kelpies weren't the only creatures that had been awakened on the island.

The goblins were taking stones and thrusting them full-force at the imps, who were freezing mid-air, unable to move as they were being attacked. The fairies, meanwhile, were doing their best to attack and stun the goblins to keep them from freezing the imps.

Most worrisome, however, was the sight of Amelia and Emily, who had teamed up against Adrien's lackeys in an attempt to keep them from firing up the helicopter. Jack watched anxiously as Amelia ducked under a dark, tall man's punch, then with pride as she proceeded to kick him in the groin and he collapsed to the ground. Another man was already unconscious on the ground, knocked out by something an imp had thrown. Emily, meanwhile, was in the helicopter with a third man, trying to push him out, and he trying to do the same with her—Jack winced as the man shoved the girl as hard as he could, and she tumbled out, landing on the concrete ground. Amelia ran to her sister's aid, momentarily forgetting about her own foe, who, fortunately for Amelia, was still unable to stand.

In the midst of all the chaos, Jack saw Adrien approaching the helicopter. Jack picked up his speed and ran full-force at him, knocking him down again so hard that when he hit the ground, the case flew open, and the joint stone came flying out, clattering across the cement.

Adrien rolled over, grasping for the stone just beyond his reach. Jack was already running after it, and it was Adrien's turn to tackle Jack to the ground in an attempt to keep him from taking it.

Adrien and Jack each reached for the stone, and in the scrambled tussle, simultaneously put their fingertips on it.

In that instant, everything around them disappeared. Jack was no longer on the island. The fairies and selkies and imps and thunderbird and goblins and kelpies were gone, as were Emily and Amelia. Instead, he was in a small clearing in a forest, one he did not recognize, but at the same time, one that felt familiar. Moonlight was glinting through the trees, casting an eerie glow over the landscape. Strange bulging shapes dotted the clearing, like large boulders, though in the darkness, he had difficulty making out what they were.

He moved closer, or floated—he couldn't tell, as he was not voluntarily moving himself. It was almost like some kind of outside force was moving him closer to the center of the clearing. As he did so, he observed his surroundings, horrified as he came to terms with what he was seeing.

In the middle of the clearing, hunched over, was a dark figure, shrouded in tattered robes. Those shapes he had seen from a distance were not boulders. Everywhere in the clearing, surrounding the robed figure, were the maimed and bloodied bodies of dead unicorns. Their silver blood seeped into the earth, their dead eyes clouded over. Some did not have horns; some did not have limbs. As Jack examined the scene, he grew sick to his stomach.

Suddenly, out of nowhere, he heard a voice. Its tone a mixture of sadness and horror, the voice asked, "Oh, my child...what have you done?"

The figure in the center rose, and pulled back its hood—revealing the face of Adrien Dunstan. His hands and robes were covered in that silver blood, and his face splattered with it. His eyes were wide and wild, and all of it combined gave him the look of a madman.

"YOU BROUGHT ME TO THIS!" Adrien screeched, pointing directly at Jack. "IT'S YOUR FAULT!"

Jack, unable to move, realized this was a memory he was seeing—Adrien's memory of the killing of the unicorns. The voice spoke again, close to Jack, seemingly all around him—whoever was talking, that person must be right behind him, but he was unable to turn around to see. He was stuck in place.

"Oh, Adrien...didn't you trust me? Didn't you think I had the best planned for you?"

"LIAR!" Adrien wailed.

A burst of light came forth from around Jack—Jack, in this moment, realized the voice around him must have been the Creator Sorcerer, and this must be the spell that stripped Adrien of his magic and cursed him with immortality. Jack heard Adrien scream, perhaps the most sorrowful, pained scream he had ever heard, or would ever hear again.

That was it. When the light dissipated and the screaming faded, Jack found himself lying on the cold, hard ground, breathless. He turned his head, where he saw Adrien, also flat on his back. The two exchanged a glance, and in his eyes, Jack saw Adrien recognized what had happened as well. Momentarily they were stunned, each forgetting the stone that sat between them.

It was Adrien who recovered his wits first. Seizing the opportunity and Jack's momentary confusion, he grabbed the stone, and rising from the ground, ran to his helicopter. Jack ran after him, but it was too late. Before Jack could reach the helicopter, it was already taking off, Adrien safely aboard.

Jack watched anxiously, waiting for some magical creature to take down the helicopter—the fairies, the imps, the thunderbird, something, *anything*. But as each of those creatures attempted to approach the helicopter, which was now fading into the distance, whenever they got close, it was almost as though they were blocked from touching it, like a force field was encircling the helicopter. Jack, Emily, and Amelia each watched from their own vantage, horrified, as the helicopter that carried Adrien and his men flew further and further out of sight and out of reach, undeterred by the creatures' attempts at taking it down.

And that was when Jack realized the full force of the magic of the stones. If even a thunderbird couldn't take down a helicopter that carried only two stones on board, what would happen if all seven were reunited?

He didn't want to find out.

Adrien had two source stones. And Jack had unwittingly let him slip through his fingers.

Amelia and Emily ran towards Jack, Amelia reaching him first.

"Are you okay?" she asked.

He nodded, rubbing his head, bewildered by the vision he had just experienced.

"What happened?"

"I don't know." He shook his head. He really didn't, nor did he know how to put into words what he had seen. He looked up, watching Adrien's helicopter fly ever further from the island, angry at himself for letting him get away.

The three stood, watching as the helicopter disappeared from view, the thunderbird no longer in pursuit as it realized its efforts were futile, instead turning and heading back towards the island.

"So what now?" Emily asked, breaking the silence, her eyes still on the thunderbird.

"Now we go home and regroup," Amelia replied.

"How?" Jack asked, nodding offshore towards the wreckage of the Blue Mermaid, whose remains had just now finally slipped completely below the surface of the swirling sea. Their one mode of transport was now gone.

Amelia simply smiled, her gaze on the returning thunderbird.

✳ Chapter 43 ✳

A new day

Jack kept his eyes squeezed shut for the duration of the journey from the island back to the cottage. He'd flown many times over the course of his life, but this was one for the books: straddling the back of the thunderbird, clutching its feathers for dear life as he, Amelia, and Emily soared over the open sea. Amelia had her arms wrapped around his waist, something he would normally be paying much more attention to and be much more pleased about, but not in this instance—he was concentrating on just trying to hang on and not fall into the icy waters below. Emily, meanwhile, brought up the rear with her arms wrapped around Amelia. Each gust of wind, every turn the bird made, every tiny bounce of turbulence had him holding his breath, praying to every deity known to mankind to keep the three of them safe and allow them to return to the cottage in one piece, and most importantly, *alive*.

For as efficient as it was to fly by way of thunderbird, and convenient given the *Blue Mermaid* was now somewhere in the depths of the Atlantic and they had no other real alternative to get back to the mainland, it was still not an experience Jack wished to repeat. He much preferred airplanes, though after this, he was starting to question the concept of flying in general.

Maybe a train would be better for his next trip.

Jack was also still frustrated with himself for letting Adrien get away— he had been *so close* to getting the stones from him, and he'd failed. The rage he felt bubbled in the depths of his being, but it wasn't even directed towards Adrien—it was towards himself, for his own incompetency.

518

It was Amelia who broke through his thoughts by saying softly into his ear, "You can open your eyes now. We're home."

With her reassurance, he tentatively opened one eye, then the other, to see the land hurdling towards them. He felt a pit in his stomach similar to how it would feel on a roller coaster as the thunderbird dove, gliding with its great wingspan, then landed.

Relieved to be back on solid ground, Jack was the first to jump off the great bird, with Amelia and Emily shortly behind him. Amelia turned to the creature, and putting her hand to its beak, smiled and breathed, "Thank you."

The bird simply took flight again, and the three watched as it flew into the distance, thunder rumbling behind it.

When the thunderbird had disappeared from view, Jack said softly, "Now what?"

"Now we go inside and have a nice hot meal," Amelia said.

"Really? That's all you can think about right now? Food?" Emily snapped, turning to her sister.

"Well, we can't come up with a plan very well on an empty stomach, can we?" Amelia retorted. "It's been a long night. We all need food and sleep before we regroup."

Emily shut her mouth, realizing her sister was right. She was so exhausted she couldn't think clearly, much less try to come up with a whole plan on how to stop an immortal being from taking all the world's magic for himself. Food and sleep sounded good.

"This is all my fault," Jack muttered.

Amelia turned to face him, and sternly, said, "No, it's not. It's no one's fault but Adrien's. He has the advantage of having a few hundred years of planning on us. So we need to figure out how to keep up with him now."

"But I let him get away!"

Amelia put her hand on his shoulder. "You tried. You did what you could. We all did."

"It wasn't enough," he grunted. "We need to go after him. Get the stones back."

"You're not wrong about that. And we will, eventually. But we also know now that he's after *all* of the stones. And we know he only has two in his possession. Two won't hurt us much for now. It's if he gets a hold of more that we'll be in trouble. So we need to prioritize those."

"So, what? We go after the other stones and hide them from him or something?"

"Yes."

"We can use Grandpa's and Jude's old journals," Emily suggested, now much more subdued. Since Amelia had mentioned food, all she could think about was Thanksgiving leftovers potentially waiting for them. She was anxious to eat and sleep.

"What's that got to do with anything?" Jack asked.

"They went looking for them," Amelia replied.

"For the stones?"

She nodded.

Jack ran his hands through his hair, not believing what he was hearing. "So what, you're saying we follow some cryptic clues in a couple of old journals that may or may not lead us to the sources of all magic in the world?"

"Do you have a better idea?" Emily retorted, her stomach now rumbling. Hanger was setting in. And she was cold. She wanted to get inside and put this conversation on hiatus for the moment.

Jack did not. But still, he said, "We're eventually going to have to figure out how to actually stop him. We can relocate the stones all we want, but he has time on his side—we don't. He'll find them all eventually, even if it's after our lifetime."

"You're not wrong," Amelia agreed. "And that's something we can discuss after food and sleep. We'll figure out a plan when we're in a better mindset."

"We should talk to the Elves," Emily commented, moving towards the cottage, no longer caring if the other two followed, impatient to get said food and sleep. "We can start with the journals, but we need to see the Elves if we want to know what we're in for. They might be able to tell us how to break him. And they might be able to tell us how to protect the stones from him...and how to get to the other stones in the first place. I'm sure they're protected by all sorts of spells. Ours was until Dad broke it."

Amelia nodded her agreement, a twinge of guilt as she again realized the pendant was no longer hanging around her neck—her father's work all in vain. "Good idea."

"Wait, Elves?" Jack asked as he glanced back and forth between the sisters.

"The first magical creatures ever created," Amelia said. "If anyone can help us, it's the Elves."

She looked out over the horizon at the view she'd known for her entire life. She had a feeling this next chapter of life, which seemed to be suddenly thrust upon her, would take her far away from this place, and she wasn't certain for how long.

In the distance, she could hear Cosmo faintly barking, the noise he made coming ever closer as he bounded across the field towards the trio. Behind him, she could hear Rosalie's voice cry out, "AMELIA! EMILY!" Amelia noted there was relief in her tone, that her daughters were alive and well, but dread, as though she sensed something terrible had happened, and something would take her daughters far from her because of it.

She wasn't wrong.

But still, Amelia wouldn't turn to acknowledge them—not yet. She needed a moment longer, lost in her own thoughts, before returning to the realities at hand.

The sun was just rising over ocean, the sky lighting up with the most vibrant shades of orange, pink, yellow, and red, with the rocky cliffs casting long shadows over the beaches and water crashing below. Soon, the colors would shift to that beautiful blue.

A new day was dawning. It would be filled with activity, explanations, planning, arguments, and heartache, of that she was sure.

But first, rest.

✳ Acknowledgements ✳

I want to take the time to thank a few people who helped me through this process. *Stones* started as an image in my head of a young girl sitting in a field full of flowers, with a fairy flying about her head. My husband, Kevin, encouraged me to develop that image into something, and that little girl turned into Amelia, the fairy into Lila…and from there, a story began. I can't thank Kevin enough for his support, encouragement, brainstorming, and love throughout the entire process.

I also want to thank my first readers, who provided helpful suggestions, edits, and feedback when I nervously sent them my first draft: my parents, Tom and Donna Gosciej; my sister, Clarissa Legg; Susan Timm; and Amy Schleeper. Your thoughtfulness and encouragement helped bring this story to life.

Here's to the next installation.

✴ About the Author ✴

RJG McManus grew up in northwest Indiana, just outside of Chicago, where she spent the majority of her childhood reading, writing, exploring the city, or enjoying days by the lake. She currently resides in coastal Virginia, though that is subject to change regularly, as she is a Navy wife. She and her husband, Kevin, are the proud parents of a human baby named Leo and a fur baby named Moony. When not writing, she enjoys reading a good book, drinking a good cup of coffee or glass of wine, yoga, and surfing.

Made in USA - North Chelmsford, MA
1179646_9798633756982
10.13.2020 0919